DREAMSHIPS

"This is classic, oldstyle science fiction, with lots of sense-of-wonder and good storytelling."

—*Locus*

"Such noteworthy novels as *When Harlie Was One*, *The Moon is a Harsh Mistress*, and *Colossus* come to mind . . . a very different take on the same theme, and seems destined to become just as memorable an addition to the field."

—*Science Fiction Chronicle*

"The characters are thoroughly human and disarming—and hard to forget. . . . Scott blends science and humanity and comes up with a fascinating read."

—Frank M. Robinson

"Her intelligent consideration of the issues surrounding AI is rare and refreshing. . . . A solid, thoughtful novel."

Kirkus

Tor Books by Melissa Scott

Burning Bright
Dreamships

DREAMSHIPS

MELISSA SCOTT

A TOM DOHERTY ASSOCIATES BOOK
NEW YORK

NOTE: If you purchased this book without a cover you should be aware that this book is stolen property. It was reported as "unsold and destroyed" to the publisher, and neither the author nor the publisher has received any payment for this "stripped book."

This is a work of fiction. All the characters and events portrayed in this book are fictitious, and any resemblance to real people or events is purely coincidental.

DREAMSHIPS

Copyright © 1992 by Melissa Scott

All rights reserved, including the right to reproduce this book, or portions thereof, in any form.

Halleluiah Man by James Grant © 1989 EMI Ltd. All rights controlled and administered by EMI Blackwood Music Inc. All rights reserved. International copyright secured. Used by permission.

Edited by David G. Hartwell

Cover art by Tony Roberts

A Tor Book
Published by Tom Doherty Associates, Inc.
175 Fifth Avenue
New York, N.Y. 10010

Tor® is a registered trademark of Tom Doherty Associates, Inc.

ISBN: 0-812-51302-9
Library of Congress Catalog Card Number: 92-4034

First edition: June 1992
First mass market printing: July 1993

Printed in the United States of America

0 9 8 7 6 5 4 3 2 1

For Dave Ramirez,
who thinks strange and wonderful thoughts—thanks!

PERSEPHONE (Persephonean, Persephoneans): only inhabited planet of Hades, Midsector III Catalogue listing 1390161.f. CPC#A3B/G6171/884G(3). Surface gravity = 1.01 Earth. Astronomical year = 1.38 standard years; local year = (Conglomerate) standard year. Astronomical day = 80 standard hours; local day = 24 local hours/24 standard hours. Chronometric correction (standard): ATS 0.0. Climate: Persephone is officially classified as a warm planet, with average temperatures of 32°C; seasonal variation is minor, but travelers are advised that high/low extremes are common, and should consult local met. offices before traveling on the surface.

Discovered 998 PoDr. by CMS *Pentateuch* (Freya registry) while on extended materials survey. The Freyan government proving unable to exploit the planetary resources, Persephone was leased to the multiplanetary Shipyards Cartel, formed specifically to settle and exploit the planet. Opened for full settlement PoDr. 1079 as mixed Freyan/corporate colony. Provisional Conglomerate membership granted PoDr. 1277 as a result of the Fifth Freyan Revolution. No indigenous animal life. Primary city: Landage (dos 1079 PoDr., starport). Primary export products: starships; AI constructs; VWS software, limberware, bioware; IPU mecha, wireware, biofittings. Government: day-to-day government is handled by the Managing Board of the Shipyards Cartel, whose members employ 82% of the population; however, Freya maintains a competing Colonial Office on planet, which controls Persephone's noncommercial foreign relations and to which the population may appeal decisions of the Managing Board. Disputes between the two are settled in the Conglomerate courts. Language Group: Urban dialect of Freya (index of variation MS3/5.200935); Urban primary (index of variation MS3/0.002014).

Persephone is a barren planet, settled only because of the vast resources available both on planet and in the system's two asteroid belts. Because of the unpleasant climate, settlement has gone underground, or into natural and artificial caverns, and is largely confined to the Daymare Basin. 97% of Persephone's population is permanently resident in Landage or its suburbs; of that group, approximately 20% are periodically resident in the assembly complexes at Mirror-Bright (Whitesands) or the Rutland Seas. Travelers are advised to consult the local authorities and to employ local transport and/or guides if their business takes them outside the Daymare Basin. The Peacekeepers maintain a Class II Traffic Control base on Cerberus in the outer asteroid ring. The base is restricted; landing by permit *only*.

"When dreams don't become their people,
people become their dreams

When dreams don't become their people . . .
you bring the government down"

—James Grant, *Halleluiah Man*

1

It was dark under the eaves of Heaven, and she went carefully, more for the cracked tiles that shifted underfoot than for the chance of trouble in the unlit side ways. To either side of the empty street, houselights flickered wearily, barely the legal minimum of ten-lumen tubing outlining the main—the taxable—entrances. Most of the tubing had once been painted good-luck red when the door was cut, or at least when new people moved in, but that painting had nearly all faded, so that what light there was lay in sickly straw-and-amber puddles along the sides of the road. Overhead, the day lights were already dimmed: they went to bed early here in Heaven, to save the nighttime surcharge.

Light blossomed under the arch that marked the end of the street, the flash of the interchange's directional glyphs—themselves invisible as yet beyond the archway—reflecting at intervals across the gray-black tiles. Her steps did not alter, long legs outlined briefly as she came to the end of the road, striding contrary to the strobing lights. She blinked once, coming into the interchange and its glare, and that was all.

After the silence of the house rows, the plaza's murmurous

voices were quite loud, a rise and fall of tonal language, vowels drawn up and down the scale. Heaven's people— coolies all, by the sound of the voices, but lineworkers and construction operators mostly, not the lowest of the low— were out, savoring the sweaty, not-quite-cool spill of air from the great vents tucked up under the arch of the roof. Half a hundred men and women moved in that draft, filling the parklike space inside the four massive central columns—iron trees, carved and grotesque, false branches curving up with unnatural regularity to uphold the arch of the unreal sky, and the fans that brought in the wind. She smiled, seeing them, but kept to the perimeter walk.

Ahead, a construction gang, newly off shift, spilled out of the brightly outlined entrance to a beer shop, clustered loud-voiced around an outdoor server. She knew they were line-workers by their clothes and the heavy humpback packs, and her step did not alter. She swept through them, easy strides carrying her fast without having to hurry, and they made way for her, not grudging, and not afraid, but knowing her too, and her business. Someone called after her, just a greeting; she lifted a hand in answer, but did not slow her pace. The cooperative lay just beyond, its staircase picked out with bright blue-green tubing. The same lights outlined the window of the second-floor flat and formed the double-glyph above the door: *pilot*, and the clasped hands that meant *co-operative*.

As she reached the top of the stairs, the door slid open, spilling a different, yellow light onto the landing. She held out her hand to the sensors, seeing the wires beneath her skin darken suddenly, shadow-blue turned deeply green. In the same instant, she felt the pulse of the security system whipping hot along the tracery of the skinsuit's wires, and the inner door slid open.

The light inside was carefully natural, a sure sign the client had arrived. She made a face, and turned toward the desk where the imager stood, its screens displaying silent fractal patterns. The multicolored abstractions vanished as she crossed the sensor line and were replaced by a more familiar image: a dark woman in a flowered sari, her black hair rolled into a tidy bun.

"Good evening, Bi' Jian," the image said, and the woman answered, "Good evening, Daru." It annoyed her, as it always did, that she did not know the surname of the woman behind the image, that she could not address her with what the upperworld would see as proper respect—but Daru was keyast, proud of her secretarial status, jealous of the hierarchies. Jian put aside her irritation. "Peace said there was work?"

"Yes, bi'." Daru's image looked aside, at a point past Jian's shoulder, reading the messages that hung in the air, invisible except to her. "Ba' Malindy says you should go straight back. They're in the small conference room."

"Thanks," Jian answered. The image faded from the display column as she turned away. As she pushed through the door that led to the inner rooms, it occurred to her for the first time that the keyast Daru might not even exist, might only be a virtual person, the persona of some poor coolie slaving away for the secretarial service. If that was true, the personation was almost perfect: *more power to her—or him— the real "Daru," for fooling all of us*. The thought cheered her, and she was smiling when she keyed the conference room door.

The client was indeed waiting, and the others were there as well, so that she had to stop just inside the door to acknowledge their presence. Peace Malindy nodded to her from the head of the table, and Imre Vaughn wheeled in his pacing to give her a quick, crooked grin and the lift of an eyebrow. Jian nodded back, careful to include the third man—the redhead exactly as motionless and full of potential motion as a statue—but her eyes were on the client. The woman sat at Malindy's right hand, the ceremonial cup of tea acknowledged but untouched in front of her: a tall woman, dressed in rust-brown silk just darker than her skin, a woman with no marks of implants on her hands or face, just the wires wound through her heavy black hair to show she might—and only might—be herself on-line.

"This is the senior pilot of the team," Malindy was saying, and Jian hastened to obey the cue, easing herself into a chair at the redhead's left. "Reverdy Jian. Reverdy, this is Meredalia Mitexi, who's hiring."

For a job nobody's willing to describe, Jian thought, and Mitexi smiled as though she'd heard the unspoken words. Her face was rounded, unremarkable, a midworld face, but the smile changed, it redefined the broad cheekbones and the amber eyes. It was the smile of a woman who did not conceal or deny her own power, not complacent either, but dangerous and ambitious and amused in equal measures. Jian took a careful breath, keeping her own face polite and still. *I wonder what she thinks of me.*

"Hiring, yeh," Vaughn said, and stopped abruptly in his pacing. The flat yanqui accent—deliberately assumed, Jian knew—was harsh as a blow. "For what?"

Mitexi met his stare with the same smile turned bland, not—quite—contemptuous, and spoke to Malindy. "This is the full team?"

Malindy nodded. He was a smallish man, unimposing to look at, especially in the one-piece suits he habitually wore, but he seemed unaware of Mitexi's tone. "Yes. I understood you required pilots with experimental licenses?" His inflection made it just barely a question.

Mitexi sobered at once. "That's right." Having said that, however, she seemed disinclined to proceed, looked instead at the table in front of her. Checking her notes, Jian guessed: the invisible implants acceptable in the midworld were relatively limited, their internal projections only visible against a blank background. "I have some technical questions first, though."

"Go ahead." Malindy's voice was scrupulously neutral, as was the glance he directed at his pilots, but Jian understood the unspoken warning. She would behave, and see that Vaughn did the same.

"You're both licensed for experimental craft."

It was not a question, and had already been asked even if it had been, but Jian answered anyway. "That's right. Also for most starships built in the last thirty years, and for about half the mainline VWS-linked aircraft."

Mitexi nodded absently. 'What's your system?"

Jian heard a sharp intake of breath from Vaughn behind her, laid her right hand on the table, palm down, fingers curved in private still-sign: *shut up.* Vaughn shifted again, subsided. Jian turned her attention to the woman, deliberately placed her left hand on the table as well, and wound her fingers together to make the wires stand out. The shadowy lines darkened, became distinct beneath her skin, woven into the nerves of her hands. Those molecular wires covered her body, made up her skinsuit, the skinsuit that allowed her to interact with the overseer programs and constructs and control a starship in the chaos of hyperspace. They also made midworlders uneasy, and Jian waited for the other woman to look away.

"What's your system?" Mitexi asked again, and Jian felt herself flush.

"Mostly Connectrix biofittings, with some Kagami IPUs. It's modified Yannosti wireware—it would class out as a private-label operating system. It meets Standard Access Requirements, though, no problems."

"And you?" Mitexi looked at Vaughn. Jian tensed, but the other pilot answered coolly enough.

"Pretty much the same. I like Hot Blue bioware, though."

The redhead said nothing, as usual, even when Mitexi frowned in genuine annoyance. Vaughn answered for him, "Red's is a standard tech's setup, Staryards fittings and Datachain wireware. Also modified, but it passes SAR."

Mitexi stared at the redhead for a moment longer, her face unreadable, then glanced at the table again. "What about overseers? I understand you provide your own."

Jian's hands released each other, the right-hand fingers once again enjoining silence. Vaughn made a soft noise, breath hissing between his teeth, but said nothing. Jian said, "Unless the contractor wants otherwise. Yes, we each have an overseer—top of the line, a Spelvin construct." *How else would we fly the ship? Nobody can read hyperspace unassisted; you have to have an overseer—topline near-AI, with plenty of power and memory and a whole flock of virtual-world subroutines—if you're going to fly at all.*

Mitexi nodded again, almost to herself, still looking at the table. "Would you be willing to work with an experimental construct?"

Vaughn stirred again at that, and Malindy said, "That wasn't in the precis, Bi' Mitexi."

Mitexi slanted a smile toward him, unabashed. "No." She looked back at the pilots. "Would you be?"

"That would depend," Vaughn began, the yanqui accent forgotten in anger, and Jian cut in smoothly, "—on what the ship was like, how well tested your overseer has been, how easy it would be to dump and reload with our own constructs if yours turns out to have bugs. . . ." She matched Mitexi's smile. "So you see it's impossible to give you a solid answer."

Mitexi's whole attention was on her now, for the first time, and Jian found it an oddly disconcerting experience. The woman's eyes really were the color of amber, red-toned brown, and possessed of unexpected humor. There was something predatory in them as well, impatient and demanding, an urgency lurking in that glance, like muscles beneath the skin.

"If you had the appropriate assurances, then," Mitexi said, "you would be willing."

"I would consider it, yes," Jian answered, and saw the other woman's lips twitch into a fugitive smile at the changed verb.

"And Ba' Vaughn?" Mitexi seemed to have come to the realization that the redhead would not answer for himself if he could avoid it; her eyes flicked to the other pilot.

"We'd consider it," Vaughn answered. "But I want to know a lot more."

"Of course." The smile that seemed to be always close to the surface in Mitexi's expression broke free again. "As I'm sure Ba' Malindy will have told you, I have an unrated ship I need to have flown. It's old, but in good condition—an inheritance which has finally come fully into my control. It was built about fifty years ago, and at the time was considered highly advanced. I understand from the engineers that most of the systems developed for the *Byron*—the ship was commissioned *Young Lord Byron*—have since come into common use, so nothing should be too unfamiliar."

An inheritance, Jian thought. *A whole starship. I knew there were rich people in the underworld, but—* Even as the thought formed, it was rejected. Mitexi was not of the underworld, the richest classes who could afford to live in fully automated comfort far below Persephone's scorched surface. The clothes were wrong, for one thing, and the face—*and, more than that, she's hungry still. There's nothing to be that ambitious for, not the way she is, once you get down to the sub-Exchange districts.*

"Where would we be flying this ship of yours?" The yanqui notes were back in Vaughn's voice, a sure sign his annoyance was under control again.

Mitexi's lips twitched, but she did not succumb either to amusement or irritation. "Refuge."

Jian blinked at that, and then, when it became clear that Mitexi would not elaborate, could not help feeling a sneaking admiration for the woman. It took guts to say simply "Refuge" and not offer anything else, explanation, defense, anything at all to explain why anyone would willingly choose to go to Refuge, when there was anyplace else left to go.

Vaughn laughed harshly. "Not on your life."

The redhead stirred too, an infinitesimal movement of head and shoulders that shifted the coarse mane of his hair, but made no other comment. Jian glanced sideways at him, but his face betrayed nothing but his astonishing beauty.

Mitexi laughed back at them, the sound unforced music. It was the only thing pretty about her, and that prettiness was not intended. "I'm looking for someone," she said, "My brother. I have reason to think he's on Refuge."

Vaughn lifted an eyebrow at that, but said nothing. Jian waited, too, knowing that there would be more and willing to let the silence find it for her. Malindy glanced at his pilots, then at Mitexi, but made no comment.

Mitexi said, grudging the admission, "I'm not entirely my own master in this. I hope to franchise some of the standing systems and their limberware; my backers' investment was contingent on a lightspeed cruise, at least transsector. And I need to find my brother."

It was an odd choice of verb, Jian thought, but at least the rest of it made sense.

"Who's your backer?" Vaughn asked, and Malindy rolled his eyes in despair.

"Do you really expect an answer, Ba' Vaughn?" Mitexi answered, and the pilot shook his head, grinning. Mitexi nodded at him, almost with respect, and turned her attention back to Jian. "I have the technical specifications, if you want to look at them."

"Yes," Vaughn said rudely, and Jian said, "Did you really expect otherwise?"

Mitexi nodded again—not an answer, but acknowledgment of the deliberate parody. "Take your time with them," she said, and slid a package across the table. The datadisks gleamed inside their clear case, catching rainbow-colored lights from the fixtures overhead. "I'll give you some privacy." She pushed back her chair and stood, drawing the hood of her coat back up over her glittering hair. She used both hands, a movement practiced and graceful enough to draw Jian's attention away from the disks. Mitexi seemed unaware of the scrutiny, but then her eyes slid sideways, met Jian's look, and flicked away again.

Malindy was on his feet, too. "This way, bi'." He gestured politely to the door, and Mitexi lifted her hand to sign *open please.* The door slid back, its sensors recognizing the movement, and she preceded Malindy from the room. The coordinator paused for a moment in the doorway, glancing back at the pilots, then followed Mitexi, letting the door slide shut behind him.

"Why be polite to a damn door?" Vaughn muttered, and reached for the box.

Jian reached for the table controls instead, beating Vaughn to them by a hair, and touched the buttons that brought the player/projector up out of the central well. Vaughn gave her a glance that might have been oblique apology—she knew sign perfectly well, the stepfather whose name she bore had been coolie and deaf, and there was no call to insult either him or her—and fed the disks into the display slots. There was a faint whirring, and then red pinlights flared at the top of the projection ball: the machine was ready to display whatever was on the disks. She was out of line. She frowned, and shifted until she was looking directly into the nearest light.

"Wait," Vaughn said, though she had not yet touched the display controls, and glanced over his shoulder at the redhead. "You might want to see this, bach."

The redhead obeyed, moving to his left until he, too, was looking directly into one of the lights.

"All set?" Jian asked, and touched the start switch without waiting for the unneeded answer. Light flared in her eyes, her brain, drowning ordinary vision with the data that flooded along the carrier beam and into the processors implanted in her eyes. She felt the data streaming, a cascade of light and warmth and sheer sensation, along the molecular wires of her suit, and then she was looking inward, focused on the symbols bouncing back into the air before her face.

The ship's schematics flowered in her sight, rotating slowly as though the ship itself was showing off its virtues, the sleek lines of its hull, the invisible lines and points of its sensor net, made visible in the display. Then the hull exploded silently, revealing inner space: the lines of the decking, the interior systems and subsystems weaving a multicolored shell between the hull and the unfamiliar symbols of the cabin fittings. That too was stripped away, the power plant swelling so that they could see its familiar shapes and the labeling glyphs and numbers; the power plant faded back and the control links appeared—standing systems packages, mainstay subconstruct, overseer link, but no overseer—and then the image receded. The subsystems wove themselves back over the interior volume and the plates of the hull became solid again: the show was over.

Jian blinked hard, still dazzled, blinked again, trying to make some sense of the chaos of data she had seen. The overall systems, hull shape, overseer linkage, internal control train, were familiar enough—in outline, at least, all she'd seen, recognized—

She shook herself again, disciplining her thoughts, and tried again. The skinsuit's systems had not stored the data; mechanical memory was too precious to waste when training could bring natural memory within operating limits and external memory sources were so easily available. She closed her eyes, focused on retrieving the primary glyphs and matching them to the systems. The ship carried mostly standard fittings, there was no doubt about that, and the power plant—a Merlin IVa—was still being built, a good, reliable system with power to spare. There were nonstandard systems as well, but most of those seemed to be in crew support and living quarters; the environmental monitor itself was, reassuringly, a tried-and-true Ace/Kagami standing system. There were newer, flashier models, but this one could certainly be trusted to do the job. The overseer interfaces were SAR/normal, but there was no data on the overseer itself.

"Well, now," Vaughn said, and stopped abruptly.

Jian said, "Nothing on this experimental construct." The words were thick on her tongue, clumsy in realtime after the illusory speed of virtual space.

"Did you expect it?" Vaughn answered, but his tone was less sharp than the words.

"Not really." Jian closed her eyes, remembering. "I thought I might be able to get some hints from the interface structure, though."

Vaughn grunted agreement. "No luck?"

"None." Jian reached for the table controls. "Do you want me to run it again, or have you seen enough?"

"I say we take the job," Vaughn said. Jian raised an eyebrow at him, but he was looking at the redhead. "Well?"

Red looked down and away, long eyelashes veiling his dark eyes. "It looks all right," he said after a moment.

Vaughn nodded, satisfied. "Reverdy?"

"I'd like to know a hell of a lot more about the overseer."

"You're connected, you know enough constructors and shadows," Vaughn retorted. "The specs must be on file someplace."

That was true enough, Jian thought, and there were people she could contact to dig out the information—and she had hesitated only because Vaughn had assumed her consent. "It looks like a good ship, sure," she said aloud. "You're sure you want to go to Refuge, Imre?"

Vaughn grinned. "You can bet your sweet life I won't be going planetside."

"I say we do it, then." Jian reached for the table controls again, pressed the button that lit the signal in the second conference room. There was a polite interval—long enough and to spare to show that no one had been listening at the door, though eavesdroppers were hardly so crude anymore—before the door slid back again. Mitexi entered first, putting

back her wide hood with the same elegant two-handed gesture. Malindy, following, looking even less prepossessing
than usual in his crumpled one-piece suit. If he was aware of
the contrast, however, he gave no sign of it.

"You've come to a decision." It was only just a question,
and only for politeness.

"That's right," Vaughn said, and Jian cut in easily.

"We're willing to take the job, but with some provisos.
We're still not happy about this mysterious construct—excuse
my bluntness, Bi' Mitexi—and I'm not reassured by knowing
my construct will fit your standing systems. I want more details, and I think we're owed more pay. I'll leave that to you,
Peace. But I—we—want more tech detail."

"That is reasonable," Malindy said.

Mitexi frowned. "I think you also understand my position.
The construct is an extremely sophisticated program matrix;
obviously I can't take the chance of having it fall into . . .
my competitors' hands."

"I don't think we're talking about preflighting the full construct," Malindy said, with a glance at his pilots. Jian shook
her head. "Just some better idea of how well they'll be able
to interface with it and the ship."

Mitexi was still frowning. "I think I can provide some
information without compromising the construct. If I put together another disk, will that do?"

"We'll know when we get it, won't we?" Vaughn muttered, but nodded.

"I expect we can manage a compromise," Malindy said.
"And an appropriate hazard fee."

Mitexi nodded. "We can link in the morning, then." She
glanced sideways, positioning unseen projections against a
blank wall. "I will be available for contact after midday,
actually, if that's acceptable."

Malindy nodded his agreement, fingering the palmscriber
that hung at his waist.

"I'll expect to speak with you then," Mitexi said, and
drew her hood up over her coiled and wire-bound hair. "Ba'
Vaughn, Ba'—" Her eyes flicked over the redhead, dismiss-
ing him, settled on the other woman. "Bi' Jian. It was a

pleasure to meet you." She signed to the door and was gone
before the pilots could respond.

Malindy sighed. "Is that acceptable?"

Vaughn snorted. "Do you think she's going to tell us anything useful—or even true? It's a good thing you have friends,
Reverdy."

"I really don't want to hear this," Malindy said. Vaughn
grinned, and the co-op's manager shook his head in warning.
"I mean it, Imre."

"Fair enough," Jian said. "Your message said our standard rate, less co-op fees and sharetime, plus a quarter of the
balance?" It was the cooperative's usual agreement, and
Malindy nodded.

"Do you trust me to handle the tech negotiations, or do
you want to see the disks before I sign?"

"I trust you," Vaughn said easily.

Jian smiled. "So do I, but do you want her to know that?
Seriously, do you want to stall her?"

Malindy shook his head. "I'd rather not. I think she's in a
hurry, and right now she's willing to pay big."

"Then settle it however you want," Jian said, and Vaughn
nodded.

"I'll code you the details when I have them," Malindy
said.

"Thanks, Peace," Jian answered, and lifted her hand to
sign to the door. "I'll hear from you tomorrow, then."

Vaughn followed her into the corridor, darkened now that
the client had gone home. The redhead drifted silently at his
shoulder, only his eyes moving in his impassive face.

"Where are you bound, Reverdy?" Vaughn asked.

Jian allowed herself a crooked smile. "I was thinking of
going looking for somebody to do a little snooping for me—
Taavi, maybe, or Libra. Taavi for preference."

"Taavi's off," Red said.

Jian glanced at him, knowing better than to question his
accuracy, or ask how he knew. "Off-line, or off-world?"

Red looked away, as though the act of speaking pained
him. The light from the lobby—harsh white light now, cheap
light—leached all color from his already pale skin, drained

even the shadows from the hollow of his cheek. His hair
flamed even brighter by contrast. "Off-world."

"Libra, then," Jian said, and quirked another smile at
Vaughn. "So before you ask, Imre, no, you can't come with
me. He's not at all fond of you."

"Can't imagine why," Vaughn said with cheerful insin-
cerity. He put his hand on the redhead's shoulder, turned him
bodily toward the main door. "Come on, bach. If he needs
work space, Reverdy, you can bring him back to my place."

"I'll do that," Jian answered, but they were gone already.
She sighed to herself, and followed them past the security
scan out the main door.

Outside, the interchange was even more crowded than before, more figures in bright sand-silk milling about in the
shifting light of the directional glyphs. The rumble of voices
was stronger, too, punctuated now by the wordless cries of
the praline venders. The sharp, burned-sugar smell from their
carts filled the air. Jian paused at the top of the stairway,
pressed the access glyph tattooed on the inside of her forearm. Under the steady pressure, the control disk embedded
between the twin bones came slowly to life, the touchpad
hardening under her thumb. Below and beyond, the streets
came to life with it, a ghostly overlay of numbers and glyphs
and bright burst of symbols like fireworks. One point in the
crowd at the edge of the plaza flared bright, a double figure
shaped by a double glyph—she had learned long ago that it
wasn't wise to consider the redhead no more than an extension of Vaughn's personality, and had programmed her suit
accordingly—that vanished as Vaughn and his partner turned
out of her line of sight. Jian kept her thumb on the pad,
feeling it grow steadily warmer under her skin, and saw the
lights and symbols strengthen, a bright curtain between her
and the world. She turned her head toward the nearest store-
front, and prices blossomed above the hard goods, bright and
sharp enough to read even at this distance: her suit had picked
up the tightbeam transmission from the window's display
hardware and translated it into necessary information. She
smiled to herself, satisfied with the brightness of the projected glyphs, and took her thumb away.

"Input," she said aloud, to no one, to herself and her suit, and then, "Command." There was a response then, shadowy, a whisper of awareness, of receptivity, an inner shifting that promised that the ghost-self of the suit was listening, and she went on, "Function: find. Object: Robin Libra."

There was a pause, an odd emptiness, and then a fleeting sense of pleasure that she interpreted as confirmation: neurotransmitters only came in a limited array of flavors, carried a fixed range of emotional messages. She was no longer disconcerted by the sudden spikes of not-always-appropriate feelings when the suit was fully functional. In almost the same moment, a pinpoint of light flashed insistently at the edge of her vision, and she looked down and left to retrieve the message. The glyphs popped into existence, still blinking, then steadied: #Libra#—that was her own private glyph, not the space-consuming realprint—#not-found#.

"Command: continue last command," she said aloud. "Display yes-only."

Again the sense of pleasure, and Jian set her thumb on the access glyph. The colors that floated between her and the world brightened almost painfully, then dimmed. Now the symbols were no longer bright enough to distract, but still clear enough to be seen at need. The locator program would keep looking for Libra, scanning the networks each time the i/o devices mounted in her eyes came into line with an online transceiver. If it spotted Libra—or, more precisely, if any of his names or codes were linked to any activities on the networks—the suit would flash the message. The method wasn't foolproof, by any means: not only were the common transceivers less than perfect access into the nets where Libra worked, but she didn't know all, or even most, of the constructor's worknames. She smiled slightly then, and started down the stairs. She did, however, know where he did most of his work: a bar in the Shang-Ti Township, just a half-level above the flashy shops of the Zodiac that marked the midworld border. A lot of constructors—the failed ones, failure defined by their inability to win a place in the corporate structures—free-lanced from there, lured by the free-node room in the back and the secondhand hardware shops on the level above. It was Thirdday night, just before payday for most of the local construction lines, the time to beg loans, cadge favors: Libra would be working.

Shang-Ti was almost four levels below Heaven, far enough down to make the kilometer walk to the nearest Shaft One station worthwhile, rather than switching between the maze of local interlinks and one- or two-level elevator lines. At this end of Heaven, close to the Charretse Interchange that was the primary link to the Moorings, the streets were both busy and relatively safe, filled with day-shift workers from the port and the local assembly lines, even a few farm-line drivers from the fields at the edge of the Daymare Basin. Farther west, past Shaft Four, where the first settlement caverns had been opened out and then virtually abandoned as Landage grew, things changed. No one walked West-of-Four in safety, not even—maybe especially not—the uncounted, uncountable mob of coolies, Freyan contract laborers and illegal immigrants, who made up most of the district's inhabitants.

The plaza in front of the Shaft One station was less crowded than the Lochoi interchange had been, despite the expensive shops and the info-vendor's massive newswall. Jian glanced from side to side, sampling the projected glyphs. The police code, flaring hot red and brighter than all the other symbols, startled her into a second look, to see the floater grounded outside a Salli's, the two cops, Cartel Security rather than the Freyan Provisional Government's police, sitting companionably on the running board eating noodles out of self-heating cups. The floater's ID light was running, throwing red and blue lights across the plaza and broadcasting its glyph into the virtual world. There was still no word of Libra, nor had she really expected it.

The display board above the station's entrance flashed twice, drawing her eye, then spat a stream of glyphs and numbers. The suit supplemented that with further annotation, clusters of smaller symbols floating in virtual space between her and the sign. The next three cars would be running express to the Li Po Township Station—*shift change,* she thought, and was briefly annoyed at having forgotten—and regular service would resume in twenty minutes. Li Po was too far out of her way, would mean doubling back up through the local shafts before she could take the electrobus along the Zodiac. Better to wait, and go direct.

She crossed the plaza then, glancing almost idly at the info-vendor. Triggered by her suit's interrogative signal, the newswall blossomed to life, offering a montage of film and glyphs, accompanied by a smaller realprint crawl. She paused—like most of the city's population, she got her news from the walls' free teaser displays, rather than paying the fees either to subscribe to a service or even to view the more comprehensive reports the vendors sold—and the wall steadied into its summary. Glyphs highlighted the moving pictures, identifying the figures in their severe corporate silks, while the crawl updated the latest conference between the Staryards Cartel that managed the planet and the Freyan Provisional Government that actually owned the world: *Representatives of Kagami Ltd. and Anchor Corp. today proposed new terms for extension of the Cartel's lease. Their offer included concessions on citizenship and percentage-of-payment. However, the FPG negotiating team refused to take the offer under advisement, prompting complaints from other members of the Cartel that they had not been fully informed of the terms. Dreampeace spokesman—*

Jian turned away from the bearded technician scowling out of the film clip. *Damn Dreampeace anyway, it wasn't their business—* She checked the thought, smoothed the scowl that had appeared to match the speaker's. But Dreampeace was an aberrant movement, mostly yanquis, who didn't really fit anywhere in Persephone's layered classes—not upperworld, certainly, the upperworld was coolie or Freyan immigrant; not midworld, even though the yanqui townships lay mostly below Zodiac; and most certainly of all not part of the corporate underworld. Dreampeace was also mostly constructors, who by their vocation were a law unto themselves. They lived for and through machines and the constructs that ran them; they didn't care—Dreampeace didn't care—what might happen if Freya didn't extend the lease, didn't care at all what happened to the coolie labor force, so long as the constructs were given their due.

She made a face, recognizing coolie propaganda—*which isn't any truer than Dreampeace's; there are plenty of con-*

structors who've worked for coolie rights, and spoke out against the FPG—and shook the whole problem aside. It had been harder than she remembered to read the realprint crawl, harder still to resist the temptation to use the glyphs and SignText mobiles as a gloss on the commentary. She had worked hard to gain that fluency, a full literacy rare even in the upper levels of the midworld where she had grown up; she would have to work hard again to regain it. Frowning, she reached into her belt for a money chip—overhead, the wall shifted images again, the change triggered both by her inattention and the sudden rush of people leaving the Shaft One station—and fed it into the door monitor. The machine scanned it quickly, then spat back the square, its rich purple perceptibly faded. The lock clicked back, and she stepped inside.

The walls were covered with flatscreen displays and cheap disks racked behind locked plastic covers. She ignored the commentary droning in her ears—instructions on how to use the machines, how to reach the literacy codes stamped on each disk, how to obtain more information, and so on into infinity—instead studying the screens and the smaller realprint labels. Most of the main case was devoted to current news: the impending end of the Cartel's lease, the latest market reports and tonnage watch, one or two bright pink—propaganda/advertising medium—disks offering specs on a new Spelvin construct or a new family of starships. Jian's eyes lingered on the last of those, a gaudy promo for a new set of virtual-world interface soft- and wireware—*Technical breakthrough! Runs with most 5-SAR bioware! From the people who brought you Hot Blue skinsuits, the most vivid interface yet written. So real you'll know it's Mnemonex*—but she made herself look elsewhere. Technical promos never contained enough realprint to be good practice.

To the left of the main case were cases of instruction and commentary, most of them, up here, dealing with the possible consequences of the Cartel's failing to secure renewal of their lease. Jian's mouth twisted, looking at the titles: *Non-Freyan Citizenship and How to Obtain It, Your Rights as a Freyan Outworker, Fight the System and Live*. She allowed herself a brief smile at the last one, but shook her head. The

Freyan Provisional Government was no more competent to
govern Persephone than were the previous six governments,
or to govern Freya. Of course they had to make the appropriate noises now, demand more money, claim more and more
Persephone-born Freyans as their citizens, but in the end,
they'd grant the lease: they had no other choice. After all, the
last time Freya had tried to exert its authority, the rest of
the Conglomerate had protested, and the Peacekeepers had
stepped in, and stepped hard. No one was going to let Freya
get control of the Conglomerate's most important source of
starships and AI constructs.

She shook her head again, still smiling rather crookedly,
and began punching numbers into the order board. She would
rather read an analysis of the Dreampeace movement than
another panicked story of the horrors of the FPG. She fed
another money chip into the machine, and then, when it
beeped, fished a second from her belt and slid it into the slot.
The machine chuckled to itself for a moment, and returned
the second chip—faded almost pink now, perhaps ten work
units remaining—along with a bright pink disk. Jian stared
at the disk for a moment in utter disbelief, then, her eyes
narrowing, picked it up by the edges, holding it close to read
the realprint title. *AI, II, and the Turing Barrier: An Apology for Slavery.* A typical Dreampeace tract, she thought,
and not what I paid for. She glanced back at the order screen,
and then at the wall display, comparing numbers. No, she
had put her order in correctly; the fault was somewhere in
the software that delivered the finished disk. *And I know damn
well who planted that bug.* It was a typical Dreampeace ploy;
tie into the connections, then insinuate themselves into vendor's limberware that had no defense against that kind of
sophisticated tampering, and rearrange the system so that
anyone trying to get a standard newsnet analysis got this instead. *They probably arranged for the money to go to their
account, too.* The thought was irritating enough that she
turned back to the order board, initiating a refund request. It
was complicated and time-consuming—deliberately so—but
better than seeing Dreampeace get her money. She got the
accounts manager after a struggle, and persuaded it to credit
her public account; she would have preferred an immediate

refund, but the program seemed unprepared to deal with that demand. She swore at it, but accepted her printed receipt, and slammed out of the vendor's. The sign above the station entrance was flashing word of an approaching local car.

By the time she reached Lucy Li's, however, her annoyance had faded. The bar was filling quickly with the end of the first nightshift, and Jian paused just inside the doorway, scanning the well-lit room. Music was playing, unobtrusive, uninspired, mostly thumping bass, but enough to blur the sense of the conversations. News flickered across a wall screen, a talking head in the corner, commenting on the shifting images, but his voice did not carry beyond the closest tables. Most of the patrons were line supervisors and maintenance techs, who filed up the half-level interlink from the electrobus station on Zodiac Main to drop in for a quick drink before making their way back up toward Heaven, and the warrens and flats of home. Libra was nowhere in sight, as she had more than half expected. *He'll be working,* she thought, and walked past the bar into the narrow back room. There were constructors hooked up to most of the available nodes, blocks and input board balanced on the rickety tables, and most of them had clients sitting opposite them. The clients were mostly haul-jockeys whose faces bore a mask of lighter skin where the virtual-world mask had rested, or robot wranglers from the port, but there was at least one high-level tech in from the assembly lines south of The Moorings, made conspicuous by the portecasque slung across his shoulders. *Humpbacks*, the lineworkers called them, not without envy. Libra was working, a tall, sun-blasted woman sitting opposite him, her strong hands folded on the tabletop. Jian leaned against the wall to wait, shook her head at the inquiring barmaid.

There was a click from the back of the room where the lights were lowest, then a squeal of machine-speak and a soft giggle. Jian glanced toward them, recognized the glyphs on the helmet, and looked away. Dreampeace was working, and she had no time to confront some twitchy minder. Not that they were likely to notice, as deep in the virtual world as they seemed to be, but you could never tell for sure when a helmet was opaque. *And I've got better things to do than deal with fanatics.*

The woman at Libra's table had risen to her feet, was leaning over him now, both hands braced on the tabletop. The fragile structure shifted, made cracking noises; Libra looked up at her, half his face hidden by his monocular, the visible part of his expression nervous. Jian frowned and pushed herself away from the wall, crossed to them in time to hear the woman say, "—you'll forget this ever happened."

Libra took a deep breath, his eyes flicking from his customer to Jian and back again, and said, "Forget what?"

"Anything at all, sunshine," the woman said.

Jian said, "Problem, Libra?" She gave the name the midworld accent of their shared childhood, the *i* elided, stress on the second, long vowel, *lebray*, not *leebra*. The client turned mutely away.

Libra looked up at her, a smile on his bearded face, but the expression held more than a hint of worry, and Jian bit back a laugh. "Hello, Reverdy," he said, and she heard both the wariness and resignation in his voice.

She did laugh aloud now, and lowered herself into the client's chair. "I want to hire you," she said, and dismissed the menu flashing in the tabletop.

"Oh?" From Libra's expression, he was expecting to be asked to commit a significant felony, perhaps with firearms.

Jian smiled. "Do you still have accounts on any of the official connections?"

"Some, sort of." Libra looked at her with less apprehension. "I hire use of some codes, dummy accounts. What connections are you talking about?"

Jian lowered her voice, carefully did not glance over her shoulder. The tabletop creaked under her weight as she rested her elbows on it, and tilted slightly. "I need information, especially overseer specs, on a ship—starship—that's been in parking orbit or builder's cradle for the last fifty years or so. It was built fifty years ago, anyway. It's—or she says—a client's inheritance, so I don't know who would have jurisdiction over the files. It was disputed, she said."

Libra frowned, clearly drawn to the problem against his

better judgment. "The law courts, I would think, civil files—and they are hard to get into. But if it's settled . . ."

His voice trailed off, and Jian nodded. "It has been, I'm sure of that. I have names, both the client and the ship."

"I would hope so," Libra said. He was silent then, staring at his boards, and Jian watched curiously. He was slightly rumpled, as always, beard not quite trimmed, his thinning hair in disorder, but from the look of his clothes—plain midworld-style jacket, good cut, good fabric, not top-of-the-line expensive but not cheap, either—he was doing all right.

"Well?" she asked, and Libra sighed.

"I can do it."

From the sound of his voice, he was already regretting the decision, and Jian grinned.

"I don't want to try from here, though," Libra went on. "Too public, probably too well taped. It'd help if you knew of some place with a Finex node, or even Elelxa."

Jian paused, trying to remember which services Vaughn subscribed to. "What about Tricom?"

Libra nodded. "That would work, too."

"Imre's on that," Jian said, and waited. *I owe you fair warning.*

"Imre Vaughn?" Libra's voice flattened.

"Yeh." Jian let a warning creep into her tone. "He's my partner in this, Robin."

Libra looked briefly as though he would object, then shrugged. "Haya. Tricom will work."

He still sounded reluctant, but no more so than usual. "Get packed up," then, Jian said, "and we'll get going."

Libra nodded, touched keys on the input board, and then slipped off his headpiece, folding the monocular arm back into the protection of the main band. He unplugged the two halves of the system, board and the slim brainbox, and then touched the trigger that freed the power and data cables from the nodes beneath the table. He bent to tuck the pieces into his padded gripsack, and Jian allowed herself a quick smile. Libra could be nervous, sometimes overly cautious, but he was very, very good.

"Leaving so soon, Libra?"

The voice came from over Jian's shoulder. Libra shot upright, eyes briefly wide, and Jian turned slowly, to look up into the pretty, painted face of Lucy Li herself. She charged commission on all transactions managed through her nodes, Jian remembered: *no wonder she's worried.*

Libra nodded, said apologetically, "That's right, I have some outside work." He reached into the pocket of his jacket, fumbling for her share before she could hold out her hand.

"You're not coming back tonight."

It was not a question, was not particularly hostile, but Jian saw Libra flinch. "I will be tomorrow," he said, and added, like a schoolboy, "I promise."

Li's painted eyebrows twitched—*with amusement,* Jian thought—but the woman said only, "I can't always hold that table for you, Libra."

"This is an exception," Libra said, and held out two money chips.

Li accepted them. "I'll see you tomorrow," she said, and turned away.

"I'll be here," Libra said.

Jian heard the unhappiness in his voice, and wondered suddenly if this was more of a problem for him than she'd thought. "I'm sorry if I've caused you trouble," she said, and Libra shrugged, snapping shut the latches of his grip-sack.

"It's nothing."

"I'll take you at your word," Jian said. "Come on, we've got to go back Uptown."

Jian led them back through the bar and out into the narrow interlevel corridor, then along the sunken trafficway and down the first standing stair she found to the lights of Main Zodiac. She started for the electrobus platform, lifting a hand to cut the stop-beam at the edge of the stairs, overriding the fare-box—a pulse of pleasure knifed through her, confirming the contact, and the barrier snapped open—and had to stop and wait while Libra dodged a pair of secretaries and paid his way.

"I thought you said Uptown?" he said, when he'd caught up with her.

"Imre lives in the Larrikin Rooks," Jian answered. "We'll want Beta Shaft."

"I thought he was yanqui," Libra said. "Don't they like Crazy Imre any better than the rest of us do?"

"He's yanqui," Jian said mildly. *Like I'm yanqui, mostly the looks and very little of the culture. Though that's not fair, he's more connected than I am; I just have the genes, and he was raised there, probably in the Uptown community.* Glyphs flashed, signaling first an approaching bus, and then the news that it was running express. "We're in luck," she said aloud, raising her voice to carry over the noise of the bus. "It's express to Sanbonte, we can pick up Beta there."

"Haya," Libra said, and Jian saw him glance over his shoulder at the display board, which was just beginning to print the same message. He was not on-line, she knew, wore no implanted "suit": no constructor, at least not below the seventh-level corporate wizards, needed that expensive an interface when the routine of helmet and board and glove gave good enough access to the connections. Only pilots and engineer-technicians, the people who crewed the hyperships, really needed the closeness of that bond between the real and the virtual worlds. *And maybe it was nasty of me to remind him, but it can't be mended.* She climbed into the swaying body of the bus, and knew Libra would follow.

She caught at the nearest stanchion as the bus began to pick up speed, and steadied Libra when the motion and the weight of his gripsack threatened to unbalance him. The whine of the motors and the dull hiss of metal on metal drowned all conversation that was not signed, and the lurch and sway cut that short as well. The lights outlining the corridor shops blurred into a smeary bar of color, whipping past too fast for her suit to pick up their transmissions. They flashed through half a dozen stations—she caught a crazy glimpse of an old man shaking his fist at the bus—and slowed at last, brakes shrilling, to pull into the Sanbonte Interlink at an almost sedate pace.

Sanbonte Interlink was big even by the standards of Zodiac Main, second only to the Dzi-Gin Interlink itself, the gateway to the midworld. Clusters of columns reinforced the roof, and the storefronts—and the entrance to the Shaft Beta station—

were framed by the graceful arc of buttresses. Lights hung in multicolored wreaths from each of those beams, throwing multiple shapes and shadows across the ash-colored tiles to compete with the flashing lights and glyphs from the store displays. The Interlink was as busy as ever, day-shift workers crowding the shops and lined up outside the hatch of an all-night cookshop. A tidal rush of voices ebbed and flowed, but kept up a constant background rumble: a one-note sound, here close to the midworld, without the sharp tonal shifts. A bigger group, mostly midworlders in brilliant flowing drapes but a few coolies in paler, sun-faded work clothes, were milling about in the pool of smoky light outside a blue-note club. Music spilled out past them, bass and the stinging whine of muted strings. The board over the door alternately displayed the house glyph, and the symbol of the entertainer; Jian did not recognize it, but the quality of the crowd meant someone of importance, or at least of interest. Security—Corporate and private—watched from the entrance to the Dagon Arcade, and more Security had blocked off a side corridor, pushing heavy plastic barrels close together to keep out even the little piki-bikes. They had turned down the lights as well. Jian could just see, half obscured by the shadows, the hulking shape of a cargo hauler. A Security floater, glyphs muted, lights out, was grounded beside it, but she couldn't see if it was occupied.

There was more Security on duty at the station entrance—FPG Police this time, with the FPG sunburst splashed across his chest armor. Jian nodded to him, but the man looked back at her without expression, even his eyes unmoving in the broad, hill-coolie face. Jian shook her head, and went on into the station.

"Do you need a ride?" she said to Libra, and reached into her belt for the folder of transit passes. "It's my business expense." She showed him the cards, her body screening them from any other riders—a set of township passes, plus a surface worker's pass for the Charretse land ferry, a single multiride, multicombination pass that, used judiciously, could take her from Heaven all the way down past Exchange to the underworld. Libra shook his head.

"I've got it, thanks. How would you have justified calling in a constructor, anyway?"

"You don't want to know," Jian answered. *The paperclip fund, of course—and I'm showing off. Stop it.* She slid her card underneath the reader. The padded barrier slammed back, and she stepped through into the waiting room. Libra did the same, using his resident's pass, and Jian nodded to the nearest connection kiosk. "I want to give Imre a call, let him know we're coming."

"Fine," Libra said, and leaned against the nearest pillar, letting his gripsack slide to the floor between his legs. He kept the shoulder strap wound around his arm, Jian saw, and shook her head, heading for the kiosk. She fed a money chip to the cheapest terminal—Persephonet, a good basic communications connection—and punched in Vaughn's mail code. The screen flashed and went to a fractal holding pattern; a few seconds later, the screen lit, and Vaughn glared out at her.

"Yeh?"

"It's me," Jian said. "I found Libra. You offered work space, and I'm taking you up on it."

Vaughn grinned. "How's Libra taking that?"

"He doesn't like you," Jian said again. "Behave, will you? He says he can get the information."

"All right," Vaughn answered. "I'll be waiting."

"Haya," Jian said, and cut the connection. She glanced up at the display board, making contact with a hidden transponder. Glyphs sprang into existence in front of her eyes: a car was approaching from the levels below Zodiac, would reach Sanbonte in another four minutes. She nodded, breaking the connection, and went to join Libra.

It took the lift car—a local, stopping at almost every half-landing—half an hour to travel the five levels to the Comino Township Station. The Comino Interlink was one of the older district hubs, from before the Interior Beautification Acts; the once-pleasant buildings that ringed the central square had long ago been broken up into a warren of one- and two-room shops, and vendors' carts clustered around each of the street-level power nodes. The babble of voices had a sharper note to it, the singsong drone of a tonal language dominating the

sound: Comino was still largely a coolie district, Freyans
working out a labor contract; what spoken language there was
would be Freyan dialect. Jian saw Libra tuck his gripsack
even more closely against his side. Coolies weren't fond of
constructors, she knew—*how could they be, when they were
closed out of the good high-tech jobs by Freyan poverty?*—
but the concern seemed a little exaggerated. Then she saw
what he had seen, the red paint slashed across the painted
partiboard that closed a broken shop window. The glyph beneath the crude crossed circle was Dreampeace's anatomical
man, half the body abstracted to the lines of an antique computer chip.

"Silly gits," she said aloud, shaking her head. "Trying to
open an office up here."

"They've got some good points, Reverdy," Libra protested, and Jian sighed.

"Oh, I know. But it's still stupid to try and set up shop in
a coolie district."

Libra looked away. "How far is Vaughn's place, anyway?"

Jian accepted the change of subject. "It's not quite a kilometer—just across Decani Street."

"Wonderful," Libra said.

"Don't believe everything you hear," Jian said, and
lengthened her stride. On Comeaux Hale Street, Comino's
link with the Cavemouth Shaft, lights showed in most of the
flats' porthole windows, and little groups had gathered on
the short steps and in front of the crudely bricked-in porch-
ways. Outside one stack, a darkly pretty woman nursed an
infant and listened to an old man's gossip; her black eyes
followed the strangers along the street and out of sight. Jian
nodded to her, acknowledging her presence and her rightful
concern, but was aware of her gaze, a pinpoint laser between
her shoulder blades. This was a good neighborhood—*by
Comino's standards, a rich one*—and the locals would work
hard to keep it that way.

A little further, the neighborhood changed, stackflats giving way to storage barns and storefronts whose display windows were covered with shutters that looked as though they
had been salvaged from old military craft. Unlike the stores
in other parts of the upperworld, the advertising transponders

were switched off: *no use advertising what there is worth stealing behind those shutters*. The ceiling tubes were encased in wire-mesh sleeves, but despite the precaution one or two were broken, their glass swept carelessly onto the narrow drains. Jian glanced sideways, looking for the inevitable security displays, and the glyphs flickered orange and yellow. *Nothing to worry about, except the usual*. Still, she heard Libra give a sigh of relief when they came out into the brighter lights of the Decani Interlink, and walked up a standstill interchange to the next half-level.

Decani marked the border of the Rooks, and the district beyond was a real warren, doors and odd little half tunnels leading off the main passageways at all angles. Most of the buildings had once been normal stacks of flats, but the present owners had changed them beyond all recognition, subdividing the original three- and four-room flats into smaller—*and more profitable*—configurations. Crude bridges arched across the fire accessways, breaking half a dozen building codes in the process; others hung from the cavern ceiling, or leaned precariously against each other. Black-painted canvas screened off one-third of a garbage alley: *storage space, you'd think, until you saw the wall move and an elbow poke out under the heavy cloth*.

Farther up the street, the unmistakable greenish-black stain of fire suppressants was smeared around the doorway of the tallest stack of flats; the door itself was missing completely, the heavy-duty hinges drooping against the stained formestone, the shattered mail and security connection wires dripping across the cracked stair treads. Jian shook her head, but gestured to that gaping hole. "Here we are."

"Of course," Libra said.

Jian grinned and stepped over the last unsteady stair into a blue-lit corridor. Libra followed reluctantly. There was neither lift nor movingstair; instead, Jian led the way up a narrow side stair, and then out onto a half-floor landing. The security door was propped open with half a brick. Jian shook her head at that, but left it in place. Beyond the barrier, the area seemed better kept than the rest of the building, the walls and floor carpeted, the doors recently painted. She crossed to the nearest one, knocked gently. The door swung open at once, and Red looked out, only his eyes moving in the mask of his face. He slipped aside, and Vaughn took his place.

"Your door's gone again, Imre," Jian said placidly.

Vaughn ran one hand through his hair, pushing it back off his high forehead. "Yeh, I know. Somebody got the idea one of Dreampeace's stooges lives here. We convinced them otherwise." His eyes flicked to Libra, unreadable, and then he stepped back, gesturing with mock courtesy. "Come on in."

"Behave, Imre," Jian said under her breath, then added, more loudly. "You know Libra."

"We've met." The lines at the corners of Vaughn's eyes tightened, as though he might have smiled.

Jian nodded, aware of Libra's set face at her shoulder—*"It's not for nothing,"* the constructor had once said, *"it's not for nothing they call him Crazy Imre"*—and went on into the one-room flat. Vaughn closed the door gently behind them, and in the sudden silence they all heard the clicks as the triple locks went home. Inside, the air was warm and stale with the scent upperworlders used to mask the effects of sluggish ventilation; there were a couple of food packs on the floor by the trash burner, and a breadboarded computer link—input board and pilot's black and a data interlink—filled a stand below the connection board. Most of the space was taken up by a sturdy-looking loft, built just high enough for Red to stand upright under it, though Jian would have had to bend her head. Plain white workcloth curtains enclosed the space within the posts.

"Why don't you come up?" Vaughn said, and scrambled up the wide-runged ladder. Jian followed, and was careful not to look back at Libra clambering up behind her, awkward with the gripsack tucked tight against his ribs. The loft platform was reasonably furnished, but the chairs and couch were strangely truncated: foam pads maybe twenty centimeters thick backed by a thinner pad. There was not enough room for any of them to stand upright—*a suitable solution if you're Vaughn's height,* Jian thought, not for the first time, *but not for me*. She seated herself cross-legged on a cushion, then placed both hands against the ceiling and stretched luxuriously.

Vaughn moved, crouching, to a chair set against the back wall, just above the room's single window, and leaned over the edge. "Bring up some beers, Red." He settled himself in the chair, extending long legs across the faded rugs, and added, "So you decided to work from here after all?"

Jian nodded. "You said we could use your space—you offered, in fact. I also want your Tricom account."

Libra seated himself in the chair closest to the main wall, set the gripsack carefully between his feet. Vaughn made an odd noise, almost laughter, and then Red appeared at the top of the ladder, bottles tucked into the crook of his arm. He handed them out, unspeaking—Vaughn took his without even looking at it, his eyes fixed on Jian—then stretched out on a square of carpet in the far corner, propping himself up on his elbows. He had not brought a drink for himself, and Vaughn did not send him back for one.

"Anything else you want?" he asked, and Jian smiled.

"Not at the moment, thanks."

"Can you do it?" Vaughn said to Libra, and the constructor stiffened.

"I'll need a little more information—like a name."

"That's fair," Vaughn said.

Jian made a small noise of annoyance. "That's right, I didn't tell you. I told you about the ship, though."

"Haya," Libra answered.

"The client's name," Vaughn said, "Is Mitexi. Meredalia Mitexi."

"Mitexi Minor." Libra sat up as though he'd been shocked.

"You know her?" Jian asked, though the question had already been answered.

"Sort of—I know of her. I knew her brother better." Libra shook his head at the memory, and Jian frowned.

"Brother," Vaughn said, and Libra visibly jerked himself back to reality.

"Yeh. Yes. He was a constructor, Venya, his proper name was, about my vintage or a little younger. Top of the line, really, went independent before he was thirty." Libra stopped, shook himself again. "Sorry. But, yeh, he did have a younger sister, and she was a constructor, too."

Jian glanced at Vaughn, saw the same wariness she felt reflected in his tightened mouth. She said carefully, not knowing what Libra felt but recognizing strong feeling, "Her brother's involved, too, she says. But tell me what you know about the sister."

"I thought Mitexi Major was dead." Libra stopped, frowning, began again. "Sorry. I don't know that much about Mitexi Minor, really, just that she's his sister, and a constructor—top of the line, too, though not as good as him. She started with Aifers, but she's probably gone independent by now. I don't know, I don't move in her circles."

"Would you trust her?" Vaughn asked, and Libra shrugged.

"I told you, I don't know her. I just know the name." He looked at Jian. "How's Mitexi Major connected with this, can you tell me?"

Jian grimaced. "I don't exactly know," she said, after a moment. *Better to tell him what I do know, regardless of what he feels, and see what he makes of it.* "She—Mitexi Minor—said she needed to find her brother, and she wants us to fly this ship of hers to Refuge to find him."

"Refuge." Libra's voice was for once unguarded, openly indignant. "Venya Mitexi is not on Refuge—you shouldn't mention him in the same breath with that place. I knew him; he was good, the best I ever saw."

Jian spread her hands. "I'm sorry, I didn't mean to insult him. But that's what Mitexi Minor told us. And this is in serious confidence, Robin."

"Haya, I understand." Libra looked down, the momentary anger gone again, and Jian risked another question.

"Tell me about Mitexi Major. I mean more, besides what you told us."

Libra sighed. "He was one of the Dreampeace founders—"

Vaughn made a disgusted noise, and Jian said, "Shut up, Imre."

"He was one of the Dreampeace founders," Libra repeated, and anger sparked briefly in his eyes. "And whatever else you think about them, they're right about one thing. Once we achieve AI—true artificial intelligence—then we're going to have to treat the constructs like people."

Jian nodded, willing Vaughn to keep quiet.

Libra went on, his tone flattening again. "Sorry. Venya Mitexi also developed the first persona matrices, and designed the basic near-AI spaces for use in the new generation of overseers—your constructs probably use his matrix, you know."

"He was the guy who claimed the Aster overseer passed the Turing test," Vaughn said. "Oh, yeh, I remember."

"Shut up, Imre," Jian said again. She remembered the incident, too; it had been about the same time that Dreampeace had formed, when several constructors had announced that they had developed true AI. Kagami, Limited, who owned the Spelvin construct at issue, had denied it, and eventually proved their case in court. Dreampeace was still claiming there had been a cover-up.

"That's right," Libra said, in the detached voice of a man struggling to keep his temper. "And Kagami were no saints in how they handled that one, either." He took a deep breath. "Whether Venya was right or not, he stopped working for the Cartel after that, devoted himself to Dreampeace. And then, about a local-year later, he just vanished."

"How vanished?" Jian asked. "For real, or just virtually?"

"Off the connections *and* physically, as far as I know," Libra answered. "He never showed up on any of his old connections, and I haven't seen any of his work since." He stopped then, looked at Vaughn, then looked back at Jian. He said, more softly, as though he was talking to her alone, "He was good people, Reverdy. He—he cared about things. Talked like he was just angry, but you could hear him hurting. When he went off-line, we thought he was dead." He looked at Vaughn again, challenging him. "We thought Kagami had offed him."

Vaughn made a soft sound through clenched teeth, but Jian's glare silenced him.

Libra said, "He had a pretty distinctive style. I think I'd know if he was on-line anywhere."

"But in the real world, Robin?" Jian said.

Libra shrugged. "I didn't know him except virtually. But the people who did say they haven't seen him since, either."

"For what that's worth," Vaughn said. He snorted, slanted a conspiratorial smile in Jian's direction. "And they say only yanquis develop Frankenstein's complex."

"That's Frankenstein complex," Libra muttered, unfortunately just loud enough to be heard.

Vaughn lifted an eyebrow at him. "Whatever. Sounds like it's an occupational hazard to me."

"Obviously," Jian said. "Give it a rest, Imre." She waited until she was sure Vaughn would behave, then looked back at Libra. "Do you think you can find out about this ship of Mitexi Minor's? We're especially interested in anything you can find out about the overseer that was built with and for it. It's supposed to be something very special."

Libra shook his head, said doubtfully, "I don't know. It's not going to be easy, not with one of the Mitexis involved. I mean, she may not be as good as Venya was, but she's still supposed to be one of the best around. Not corporate, so she won't have their security, but she's good enough to set some pretty nasty traps if she wants to." He shook his head again. "I'll see what I can find in probate, but I can't guarantee more than that, and I doubt those records will be much use. But I'll try, if you want."

"Thanks," Jian said, and smiled. After a moment, Libra smiled back: *no hard feelings, then*.

"Haya," Vaughn said, and handed his beer to Red. "You can patch in to my setup if you want, or come in roundabout. I'll get onto Tricom."

"I'll patch in once you're on-line," Libra said, and Vaughn nodded.

"Suit yourself." He pushed himself up off the low chair and came forward, crouching, until he could swing himself onto the ladder. Libra followed, and knelt on the floor beside Vaughn's breadboarded machines to unpack his own equipment.

Jian watched in fascination, leaning over the edge of the loft. She had seen the preparations before, but they were still interesting, so utterly foreign to her own experience. To enter the virtual world, she had only to look, to lock eyes with a data node and let the eye-mounted processors read the transmission. Shipboard, it was even easier; she stepped into the pilot's cage and was surrounded, instantly enclosed, transported to the virtual world that was translated hyperspace. On the floor below, Libra was unpacking the tools of his trade, the VWS helmet and the wirebound gloves. She watched him check the drug reservoirs tucked under the left earpiece—one was a local anesthetic, the bright green stuff was neurelax, the thick tube was countermand, and the fourth, the one that was almost empty, was the hallucinogen that helped make the simulations real—and reach for a new vial to replace the emptied one. He tugged the used one free of the intake spike, wiped both the neck of the new vial and the spike with a sterile chemcloth, and forced the new vial onto the spike.

"I'm up and running," Vaughn said. "Let me know when you're ready to go to Tricom."

Libra nodded absently, digging into the gripsack again.

There was plenty of power available—Vaughn's machines took up only two of the five access nodes—but Jian grinned, watching Libra fit his machines into the most economical configuration: no input board, no symbolset and display screen, just the brainbox and the two-hundred-centimeter cubes of the VWS mediator. He was very careful seating the cables, and Jian shook her head again at something alien to her own experience. If the cables slipped, were pulled loose or somehow malfunctioned, Libra would be thrown back into the claustrophobic embrace of his helmet: *all I have to do is blink, and I'm back in reality*.

"Would you bring me a couple of pillows, something to sit on?" Libra asked, and Jian reached back for one of the cushion chairs. She lowered it over the edge. Vaughn caught it easily and set it on the floor at Libra's side.

"Thanks," Libra said absently, checking the fit of his gloves. Jian clenched her fist, watching the wires take on apparently solidity under her skin. They ran in the same patterns as the wires laced across Libra's glove; she shook her head again.

"Is there anything else you need, Robin?" she asked.

The constructor shook his head, arranging himself in the chair. "I think that's it, thanks. Watch my lines, would you?"

The request was unnecessary, here where the light was good and everyone would be careful to avoid jarring the machinery, somehow pulling a cable or wire loose, but Jian nodded anyway.

"You know I will."

"Thanks," Libra said again, and set the helmet into place. The flat faceplate was utterly featureless, disconcerting in its emptiness; he would be breathing through the gaps in an unstable lining, Jian knew, but the thought was still unpleasant. She saw him close his hands convulsively, triggering the gloves and catapulting himself into the virtual world.

#I'm leaving Tricom,# Libra's voice said—from the speakers in the interface, not his throat—and then he went limp against the cushions.

Vaughn shook his head, looked up at the loft. "This could be a long night."

2

   Jian woke from a restless sleep with the taste of stale coffee still clogging her tongue. She sat up, grimacing, jammed her fingers into her hair as though that might clear her head. Her suit tingled for a moment, waking with her, then faded to the low setting where she'd left it. Someone— Vaughn, probably, in one of his fits of perverse charity—had dimmed the lights, but they were still bright enough to make her blink. Red was frankly asleep at the other end of the loft, his head pillowed on his folded arms, snarled hair obscuring his face. Moving carefully to keep from waking him, Jian pushed herself to her hands and knees, and came forward to lean over the edge of the platform. Vaughn was standing in front of the little galley-box kitchen, fiddling with the stained beaker of coffee, oblivious to the presence behind him. Libra still half sat, half sprawled on the low chair, fade hidden behind the featureless helmet, his hands in the wire-bound gloves twitching spasmodically, fingers barely moving, touching something only he could see. It was an oddly disconcerting vision, for all that she had seen it a dozen times or more, and she turned her back to him to slide down the ladder to the ground.

"How's it going?" she asked softly, even though she knew she could not disturb Libra.

Vaughn shrugged, reaching for one of the thick-sided mugs that hung from hooks below the kitchen recess. He filled it almost to the brim with the burned-bitter coffee and held it out, saying, "Who can tell? I fell asleep watching him waggle his fingers at nothing, and he's still doing it. I guess it's going all right."

Jian waved away the coffee, the movement a slurred signed *thanks-no-thanks.* "What time is it?"

Vaughn nodded to the chronometer stand on the wall above his breadboarded system. "He's been on about five hours, I make it."

So he should be finished soon. Even as she thought it, Jian saw Libra's hands drop bonelessly into his lap, and his head lolled backward in the heavy helmet, his neck bent at a painful angle. She had seen it before, but Jian still winced and fought the temptation to move him into a more bearable position. His shoulders twitched twice and one leg straightened convulsively, knocking against the table that held Vaughn's computer blocks. In the same moment, the blockwriter whirred to life, and Vaughn pushed past to stand over it impatiently.

"I guess he's done, then," he said.

Jian ignored him, watching Libra. Self-awareness was leaching back into the constructor's body. His head lifted—a deliberate movement this time, desired though clumsy—and one hand, still gloved, rose wavering to fumble at the latch of the helmet. He snapped it free, then lifted the faceplate with a shaking hand, and slowly freed himself from the helmet. Saliva had run and dried in his beard, and the skin around his eyes was swollen. He set the helmet aside and began to peel the gloves off, finger by finger, his eyes focused on nothing at all.

"There's coffee in the hob," Jian said tentatively, more for the sake of saying something than in any real hope she would be heard. To her surprise, though, Libra turned his head toward her, blinking even in the dim light. There were red-centered welts on his neck below his left ear, already fading.

"Thanks," he said, and had to clear his throat twice before the sound became human. "I didn't get much."

Jian filled a mug and the constructor accepted it gratefully. Vaughn scowled. "I thought you were good."

"I told you, she was better." Libra sipped cautiously at the steaming mug, effectively ending the conversation.

"I guess we'll find out," Vaughn muttered. He glared at the blockwriter as though that stare could speed the data transfer.

Jian rolled her eyes, and Libra managed a ghostly smile. "Where's the toilet?"

Vaughn pointed to a half-closed sliding panel. Jian said, "You want a shower?"

"I need a shower," Libra answered, and Vaughn said, "Down the hall."

"You all right, Libra?" Jian said softly, and held out her hand to help him to his feet.

"I will be." Libra hauled himself upright—Jian braced herself, but his weight was less than she had expected—and stood for a moment leaning against the nearest of the loft pillars. "I'll get this stuff tidied away in a minute," he said, staring at the blocks and helmet still scattered at his feet.

And you don't want us to touch it, Jian thought, with an inward grin. *I can't say I blame you.* "We'll leave it for you," she said aloud, and Libra nodded his thanks.

"Down the hall and to the left," Vaughn said, still intent on the blockwriter. "The dryers don't work that well."

"Thanks," Libra said, without inflection, and pushed through the main door.

"Well?" Jian said after a moment.

Vaughn shrugged. "The copy's finished, anyway. Christ, I'm tired."

No more than Libra, Jian thought, and allowed herself a grin. Vaughn saw, and his mouth twisted in wry response.

"Do you want food?"

"A good yanqui custom," Jian said. "If you can't sleep, eat."

Vaughn snorted and stepped past her, over Libra's scattered system, to catch the foot that protruded over the edge of the loft. "Go get us some breakfast, bach."

Red woke slowly, pushing himself up joint by joint, head down so that the thick hair hid his face. He shook himself and stretched once, catlike; in the moment just before full waking, his face lost all delicacy, and Jian blinked, startled by the sudden strength of his jaw and chin.

"Breakfast," Vaughn said again, and Red's eyes fell, mask falling into place as well.

Vaughn looked back at the other pilot. "What do you want, Reverdy?"

"Where are you going?"

Red gave an odd little half shrug, and lowered himself easily out of the loft. Vaughn said, "There's a Salli's on the corner, we usually eat there."

"That's fine," Jian said, and meant it. Salli's was a decent chain, serving a mass-market adaptation of coolie food with some yanqui meat dishes thrown in. "Get me a sausage pie, would you, Red? And a sweet-pack for Libra." She reached into her belt for her card case, but Vaughn waved away the proffered money chips.

"My treat, this time. Since you found a shadow for us."

"Not difficult, considering," Jian answered, but did not press the issue. Red glanced from her to Vaughn, and took the chips the other pilot held out to him.

"Get my usual, Red, and some flavorings," Vaughn said, and pushed him lightly toward the door. To Jian, he added, "I don't think your friend likes my coffee."

"I don't blame him," Jian answered, and thought she saw the flicker of a smile cross Red's face. The locks clicked, and he was gone before she could be sure.

Vaughn turned back to the blockwriter, frowning again. "I suppose you'll want a copy of your own."

"Absolutely, sunshine," Jian agreed, and produced a clean block from her belt before the other could ask for it. Vaughn favored her with a quick, crooked smile, and fitted her block into the backup space.

"He said it isn't very good."

"I still want a copy," Jian said. They stood in silence then, the quiet broken only by the soft whistling of the machine and the louder, irregular sighing—like the breathing of a drunken man—that was the ventilation system.

At last Vaughn said, "It's done." Jian held out her hand, and Vaughn gave her the block, saying, "You don't want to look it over?"

"Of course I do," Jian answered, and could not quite keep the impatience out of her voice. "Why don't you put yours on your main screen?"

Vaughn made a face, but slipped the first into the reader that stood at the edge of the loft. "After you," he said, and Jian swung herself back up onto the platform.

The half-meter-wide display screen was set into the top of the low table. Jian grimaced and pulled it upright, propping it up against the wall.

"Make yourself at home," Vaughn growled, without conviction, and she ignored the protest.

The screen crackled, filled with the scrambled numbers and glyphs of a pirate copy, and then settled to a steady stream of data. Jian lowered herself onto the nearer cushion, and touched the screen controls to slow the flow of numbers. Vaughn seated himself beside her, but she ignored him, concentrating on the screen.

Libra had accessed the probate court's records, that much was immediately obvious, and that was all he had been able to do. Judging by the file tags at the top and bottom of each screen, he had pulled this information from the final countout of someone's property—Mincho Mitexi, the name was, died at the age of eighty-nine of stress-related heart disease.

"Must've been Mitexi's, what, grandfather?" Vaughn muttered.

Jian shrugged and did not answer, flipping from screen to screen, past the seemingly infinite lists of bearer bonds and stocks and buyer options and patent shares, until at last she found the list of real property. A house was listed first, with contents—an expensive house, by the look of it, with the kind of domed central courtyard found only in the better districts of the underworld, below Exchange—and she flipped past a dozen or more screens that alternated images of richly furnished rooms with screens that listed cash value for each item shown. There was jewelry as well, and clothes, and finally the household karakuri, the mecha that performed the menial chores—several different cleaning machines, a secretary pillar, and a robot food server with the boxy body and cartoon face that had been popular thirty years before—before at last they came to the ship itself.

There was far less detail, just the same schematics Mitexi had already shown them plus one or two still images. The first of those showed it on the assembly line, the much-enhanced image a little brighter than reality to compensate for the scorching sunlight and the reflected glare off the pale sand of the background. It was a reasonably familiar hull shape, and Vaughn stirred.

"Where the hell is Red?"

The question didn't really call for an answer. Jian said instead, "Nothing new."

"Yeah." Vaughn frowned at the screen.

Jian shook her head and flipped forward a few screens, looking for the overseer data.

Below them, the door clicked open, but it was only Libra, returning damp and shivering from the showers. Jian beckoned for him to come on up, but he shook his head and headed for the beaker of coffee. Before she could say anything more, the door clicked again, and Red appeared, a string bag full of hotboxes slung over his shoulder.

"Well, at least we get breakfast," Vaughn said. "Even if we don't get any new information."

Jian touched the controls again, finally found the listings for the standing systems that managed the ship's housekeeping, environmental controls, and the interface with the virtual world. There was nothing new at first glance, and she set the control block aside to reach for the container that held her breakfast. The sausage was hot and sweet, wrapped in a greasy pastry; she ate slowly, savoring the flavors, but her eyes remained fixed on the list of specifications. There was still nothing on the overseer itself.

"So the overseer was built after this," Vaughn said, around a mouthful of his own sandwich.

"Why—" Jian began, and then focused on the red-starred numbers dotting the screen. "Oh, I see." Those were theoretical numbers, parameters into which a later construct would be fitted and fine-tuned. "They had something pretty fancy in mind, didn't they?"

Vaughn grunted agreement, his attention still fixed on the screen. Jian, who had not expected any more of an answer, scanned the lists again. It was a fairly standard architecture, but the overseer's responsibilities seemed to extend further than usual—into environmental control, for one, something usually handled by an independent routine within the standing system. "I don't like that," she said, aloud, and Vaughn glanced at her.

"Don't like what?"

"That, there." Jian reached out, almost touching the screen, careful not to leave fingerprints.

"Yeh," Vaughn said, and looked at the technician.

Red said, "They used to do it like that—run everything through the overseer."

"I can see why they changed," Vaughn muttered.

"I hope we can rerig it," Jian said.

Red shrugged one shoulder in answer, and Vaughn said, with a one-sided smile, "I intend to try."

Jian gave him an equally crooked smile in response—that sort of thing was easier said than done—and went on staring at the screen. The overseer would have to be a good one, to handle the various functions assigned to it—*maybe,* Jian thought, *even as good as Mitexi Minor said it is. But I still want backups, all the same.* The limberware specific to the interface was highly complex, too, more so than even the best Hot Blue systems Jian had worked with, designed to give an almost instantaneous response to a pilot's decisions and movements. Not that that was really necessary anymore, now that the virtual world itself had been tailored to allow for the millisecond lag between virtual action and real-world execution—the constructs compensated so thoroughly that the lag in effect did not exist. But back then, back when the *Byron* had been commissioned, designers had tried to eliminate the lag in the real world, in transmission time, rather than in the pilot's perceptions. *And that will make this a brute to fly, now that we're used to the new system. Still, if the overseer's been updated—and Mitexi did say it matches most modern specs—there'll be power and to spare for a working personality. . . .*

She shook the thought away and reached again for the control block, flipped to the next-to-last screen. It was a closely packed page of signs and numbers and realprint words, the projected specifications for the then-unwritten overseer.

"Holy shit," Vaughn said, and Jian nodded. The overseer was not only required to handle all hyperspace guidance and essential ship functions, but to provide simultaneous near-realtime VWS translation. The data cells and sheer brute processing power was rated in excess of most of the standard programs.

"Is that what you'll be working with?" That was Libra, a blend of surprise and respect in his voice, and Jian glanced up to see him settling himself on the cushion-chair at her right.

"We hope," Vaughn said, and Jian grinned.

"That's what the ship originally required," she said. "I just hope that's what we'll get."

"If Mitexi Major wrote it," Libra said, "you'll get that and more." There was an odd note in his voice, more than respect, this time, a sort of uncertainty as well. *A warning, maybe?* Jian thought, but Vaughn spoke first, before she could pursue the question.

"Another goddamn superconstruct."

Libra's face closed down. "Not really." He pushed himself to his feet, setting aside his emptied container. "Thanks for breakfast, Reverdy, but I've got to be going."

Jian nodded, inwardly cursing Vaughn. "What do I owe you?"

Libra shook his head. "I'm too tired to figure it right now, Reverdy. I'll bill you—I know you're good for it."

Jian reached into her belt anyway, sorted through the squares until she found six of the twenty-five work-unit chips, and held them out. "Let me know the balance, then."

Libra hesitated, but only for a moment. "Thanks," he said again.

"Do you want me to call a taxi?" Jian asked. The constructor's face was still puffy, his eyes reddened, heavy-lidded.

Libra shook his head. "It's, what, a minute or two to Pan-Ku Upper Station? I can walk."

The Pan-Ku line—one of the five midworld interlink systems—ran through Shang-Ti Township. Jian nodded. "Let me know what I owe you," she said again.

Libra nodded. "I'll leave word. Are you with Chaandi still?"

"I'm back at my old number," Jian said.

"Right, then." Libra stood, bending almost double to fit under the loft ceiling, and let himself down the narrow ladder. His carryall, Jian saw, was already packed, his various component blocks neatly tucked back into their padded compartments. "I'll let you know," he said again, and let himself out the door. It slid shut behind him, the locks seating automatically, two sharp clicks and a single, deeper, thud.

"So much for that," Vaughn said, and Jian glared at him.

"He'd've said more if you hadn't shot your mouth off. Christ, Imre."

Vaughn frowned, then shrugged. "Hell, I'm sorry. But I don't know what more he could've told us about the construct, not without seeing it."

"He knew Mitexi Major," Jian said.

"So talk to him again," Vaughn answered. "But I wouldn't expect too much."

Jian sighed. "I probably will." *To him, or John Desembaa, or Taavi, if she's back yet. But later, not today.* She said aloud, "I'm beat, Imre. I'm going home."

Vaughn nodded. "Yeah, I could use some real sleep, too. Call me if you find out anything else."

The words were more a command than a request, but Jian nodded. "I'll do that."

It was early morning by the time she made her way back through the Rooks to the Comino Interlink. Overhead, the lights were toned with blue, the color of sunlight filtered through the clouds she had seen on other worlds, but the streets were already damp, the water standing here and there in puddles where the drains were blocked or badly placed: the street cleaning was already over. The Comino Interlink was quiet—it was still an hour or so to shift change—but the lights still blazed behind the display windows' heavy security mesh, and glyphs flamed in virtual space every time she passed another hidden transmitter. She winced, said, "Input: command. Cancel display. Display only emergency."

She felt the familiar confirming pleasure—tired as she was, it made her feel momentarily worse and better, as though she were truly asleep, but had dreamed something good—and the glyphs vanished. She made her way into the Comino Station, and settled herself on the nearest bench to wait for a downward car. The suit filtered out the traffic information—time to next car, system delays, and so on—but she did not miss the flashing glyphs. She drowsed on the downward car, tucked into a corner bench, woke by instinct at the station at Kukarin Beta to catch the transfer tunnel to the Dzi-Gin Interlink. Even Dzi-Gin was quiet, only a handful of vendors clustered at the plaza's power nodes, unfolding their carts into kitchen and serving counters combined. At least one of them, bright beneath a vivid blue-and-yellow awning, seemed to be open, the smell of sweet spices floating from the vents of the central oven, but when she approached, the vendor shook his head regretfully, hands coming up to sign, *Sorry, not ready.*

Jian lifted a hand in acknowledgment, and went on into the station. She did not have far to go, only three levels, but the cars ran slower at this time of day. Still, the station was crowded—all traffic between the upperworld and the midworld had to pass through Dzi-Gin—and she had to use her full height and weight to wedge herself in once the downward car finally arrived, caught between a night-working data manager who barely reached her armpit and a warehouse bondsman. Then at least the car stopped, the glyph on the boards above the door proclaiming Main Middle, and she let the crowd take her out into Dzi-Gin Plaza. The light here was blue-toned, too, and she quickened her step, hoping to get home before the street sprinklers cut in.

It did not take her long to reach the Hawkshole Township, with its pink-and-blue-and-white-painted house fronts. Her brother owned a two-unit flat on one of the nicer blocks, and she made her way through the empty streets almost by instinct. She had lived in the second unit—*a one-room unit, hard to rent to anyone but family*—off and on for most of the ten years since she moved out of their mother's house, and had only occasionally regretted the arrangement.

The entrance to the Little Paradis block was closed off by a heavy security grille, painted white and gold in an attempt to disguise the heavy steel, with the block name spelled out in realprint over the archway. The telltale in the heart of the central rosette, a clumsy-looking flower with two buttons on the edge of each petal, glowed green: the security system was armed, waiting for a resident's code. She hesitated, staring at the lock. This was the midworld; entrances and exits outside the communally defined "acceptable hours" were closely monitored, and too many would result in a fine charged to the household, or even a notice to vacate.

"Input: command," she said, her voice just above a whisper. "Cancel last command. Recall file code-list." Once again, the air around her brightened—not many transmitters here except those attached to security monitors, but each one of them added a bright dot to the walls and ceiling. Then symbols flared in the air below and to the right of her line of vision.

"Display," she said, and obediently the list of numbers rose into focus. Each of the eight-digit codes was labeled with an identifying glyph; she chose one marked "maintenance" and punched it in, her fingers gliding easily over the rosette's worn metal. The gate swung open silently, and she walked through into the central gardens, pausing only to make sure the gate locked again behind her.

Each of the eight flats had its own three-square-meter plot of land, each little plot outlined by white-painted knee-high fences and topped with a latticework of glowing growlight tubes. Block regulations said nothing about the uses to which that land could be put, and the residents had taken full advantage of that leniency. Most had chosen to grow food crops, but even so each space was different, a vivid contrast to the identical gold-trimmed doorways. Here someone had chosen to start a fruit tree; it stood in solitary pride at the center of a closely trimmed lawn, barely as tall as Jian herself, but already richly in flower. Someone else had chosen a lush wide-leafed vine as their primary crop, and the stalks had wound themselves up and around the poles of the overhead lattice. Next to that was a plot that was all tidy, well-weeded rows of vegetables, and next to that a riot of flowers; beyond that was her brother's plot, plain grass, deliberately kept simple because his job allowed no time for anything more. She allowed herself a wry smile, seeing that—her brother and his wife were school-daddy and school-mama to different underworld families, nanny, tutor, and bodyguard to one particular child—and went quietly down the stairs to the basement entrance.

Her one-room flat had once been the servant's room—Hawkshole had once been a richer district, and Little Paradis had once had pretensions. "Room on," she said, and shut the door as the lights and ventilation came on together. The screen at the center of the wall unit was blinking. She glanced toward it, and a series of glyphs blossomed: she had messages waiting, two from Wilu and one from Chaandi. *Nothing I can deal with now,* she thought, and began to undress, piling her clothes on the chair beside the input board. The time display in the corner of the screen read 0532.

"Input: command," she said again, her voice briefly muffled as she pulled her loose shirt over her head. "Wake me thirteenth hour." She felt a spur of pleasure, and stepped behind the screen that half concealed her bed. "Lights off," she said, and—finally—let herself sleep.

A jab of pure fear woke her, jolted her bolt upright in the low bed even as she realized it was only her suit alarm.

"Display," she said, feeling her heartbeat slow toward normal, and obediently glyphs appeared, very bright in the darkened room: a priority message, with Peace Malindy's codes attached. "Shit," she said, and then, to the suit, "Accept. Voice only."

Instead of an answer, a red glyph flashed in the corner of her eye: *not-possible.* The room was turned off.

"Well, shit," she said again, and, more loudly, "Room on."

The lights flicked on—too bright for her morning eyes, and she winced and grumbled—and with them came the brief test-tone that signaled an incoming message.

"Reverdy," Malindy's voice said. "Sorry to bother you so early." There was irony in his tone, and Jian glanced at the chronodisplay: half past noon already.

"That's all right," she answered, and managed to keep the

just-awakened fuzziness out of her voice. "Did you hear from Mitexi?"

Even over the cheap comline, Malindy's satisfaction was clear. "I did. She's offering another fifteen percent hazard bonus, and she sent another spool of specs. Shall I send them on?"

Jian nodded, then remembered the connection was sound only. "Yeah, do that, please. How do they look?"

There was a pause, and Jian could almost hear the shrug. "More detail than last time, not as much as I'd like. But I think it's good enough." There was another pause. "Shall I go ahead and send?"

Jian said, "Wait a second," and stepped forward to touch keys on the wall unit's tiny control board. "Haya, go ahead."

"Sending," Malindy said, and a moment later an orange light flashed and then held steady above the blockwriter. Jian could see, in the corner of her eye, a second set of glyphs and a spreading bar-graph to let her know how much of the message had been transmitted, but she did not bother to bring them up into full view.

"I'd like to close the contract today if I can," Malindy went on.

"I trust you, Peace," Jian answered.

"If you don't get back to me by, say, eighteenth hour, I want to go ahead and close."

"All right." The glyphs vanished even as she spoke, and the orange light flicked out again. "I'll take a good look at it, and call if there are any problems—I'll call by sixteenth hour, definitely."

"All right."

"Have you talked to Imre?"

"Not yet." Malindy's voice was grim, and Jian wondered just what her fellow pilot had done this time. "I've left a message, but if you see him, tell him I won't send the specs until he can receive in person."

"I'll tell him—if I see him."

"Thanks, Reverdy. Call if you have any questions."

"I will," Jian answered, but the connection ended before she was sure the words had reached him. She shrugged to herself, and turned to the storage cells set into the flat's wall, pulling out clothes not quite at random. She pulled on a pair of loose sand-cloth trousers, lighter and more comfortable than the work trousers she had worn the day before, and then a bandeau-style undervest of knitted fine-gauge silk. She tugged the shoulder straps tight, kicked her chair into line with the wall unit's transmitter, then reached across the board to snap the filled block out of its cradle. She slid it into the player, then spun the chair so that it faced away from the unit, and straddled it, crossing her arms on the back of the chair.

"Input: command," she said aloud. "Interface mode." She waited for the thrill, the bone-deep pulse of pleasure, and fixed her eyes on the faceted bead that was the projector's mouth. "Output: playback block, instrument one."

Again the pleasure, and the bead flared red, the color drowning the room around her, helping the illusion. A design tree floated in the air in front of her, sketching the overseer function; she lifted a hand to make the stylized sign *rotate,* the wires implanted in her hand reading the movement, and the image spun dizzyingly. She moved her hand from side to side, palm down, twice, three times, and the image slowed to a sedate, readable speed. She let it revolve twice, studying the interconnected function blocks, then stopped it, and lifted a hand to bring the image closer until it seemed to surround her, so that she was inspecting it from the inside. The projection did not seem to provide any more information than the probate records, but nonetheless the graphic presentation of the control hierarchy was interesting. As Libra's stolen data had suggested, the interlinkages were highly complex, each control node interacting with all the others to allow the fastest possible response time.

Still, it's potentially pretty fragile, Jian thought, and rotated the image again to study the fail-safe connections limned in bright blue. *Looks adequate—but I'd like to have a pro look them over.* She glanced beyond the image to the chrono-display on the wall, a ghost shape beneath the more vivid virtual image: almost the thirteenth hour, and probably still too early to try to contact Libra. *And besides,* she thought, gesturing again to shrink and then banish the enveloping design tree, *I think I'd like to talk to John Desembaa about this.*

Desembaa was a custom-systems engineer, specializing in hard/bioware interfaces; he was also a Dreampeace activist, which ruled out bringing Vaughn along. Jian allowed herself a grin at the thought, and said aloud, "Output: stop playback. Input: command, exit interface mode."

The images faded. She pushed herself up off the hard chair, and reached again into the still-open storage block, pulling out a lightweight, sleeveless jacket. She wound the ends deftly around her waist, creating a shirt that hid most of her undervest, then knotted a long scarf over her untidy hair: coolie styles, both of them, suitable for the upper levels where Desembaa had his workshop. She scooped money chips and travel passes hastily into a belt pouch, and clipped the hooks onto her trouser straps. She would buy something to eat on the way up to Heaven.

Desembaa had a workshop high up in Heaven, in the industrial districts where direct ventilation from the surface was cheap and easy. Jian rode Shaft Alpha almost all the way up, to Monark Station just below the surface, and then walked east along the Broad-hi-way that ran the length of Heaven. It was a workday, but midshift; the pedestrian ramp and the side tunnels were almost empty, only an occasional work-suited figure hurrying from one faceless building to the next. The trafficway was busier, the whine of piki-bikes mingling with the high-pitched snarl of overloaded flatback carryalls. Most of those would be shuttling between the warehouses along Broad-hi to the holding shells and loading docks at The Moorings, but a few, carrying crates splotched with bright address markers, were clearly heading for the vehicular interchange and the lower levels. The air was warm, a faint metallic tang drifting down from the surface, and there was a scattering of sand in the trafficway despite the sweepers' best efforts. The light was different, too, brighter and blue-tinged as it filtered down from the light traps in the rock meters overhead.

Desembaa's workshop was a rented space in a multiuser warehouse about halfway between Monark and Charretse West Change, the terminus of Shaft Beta. Jian paused just inside the massive arch of the main entrance, blinking a little to let her eyes adjust to the dimmer artificial lighting. The floor trembled under her feet, the hiss and clack of metal against metal rising over the steady thrum of the motors, and she looked up to see one of the warehouse's mobilator webs creeping toward her. Its operator was dwarfed in its center, almost invisible in the blue-black worksuit that merged almost imperceptibly with the control cylinders encasing his legs and arms. The lights struck occasional sparks from the dark fabric, gleamed fugitive from the mirror-blank faceplate of his enclosing helmet. The operator ignored them—did not see them, as he did not see anything except the schematic reality reflected in his helmet—and went on working, his movements measured and grotesque. Along the edges of the web, manipulators the size of shipping pods slid and clacked and dodged past each other, shifting packages along the warehouse shelves. At another gesture, servos hissed, and the entire web crept forward on its soft tires, a pair of manipulators dipping low to place a four-meter-long canister precisely on the bed of a waiting flatback. Jian smiled, enjoying the commanding voice of gesture, the easy dance of the claws along their tracks.

Abruptly, the smooth movements faltered: she had watched long enough for the web's external sensors to notice her and incorporate her into its virtual world. The operator, now motionless at the center of his web, was dealing with her.

"Can I help you, bi'?"

The voice came from a wall speaker behind and to her right, but she kept her eyes on the web. "I'm looking for John Desembaa," she said, pitching her voice to carry over the steady thrum of the machines.

"Oa." The wall speaker made a mush of the liquid bisyllable: it was a coolie word, too variable for mechanized precision. "Off to your left, past Delta walk, that's where shops are." That came out better, but still heavy with the coolie accent.

"Thanks," Jian said. She had not needed the instructions, but it was easier than explaining why she had been standing there.

"Do I tell him you're here, bi'?"

"Yeh, thanks. Tell him Reverdy Jian."

"Haya, Bi' Jian." A moment later, the web lurched into motion again.

Jian lifted a hand in a thanks gesture he would not see—the worksuit would already have eliminated her from his vision—and turned away, following the bright yellow line painted on the metal flooring. It led her well around the trafficway—even so, she looked carefully to either side before she stepped into the crosswalk—and then onto a protected catwalk that ran along the inside of the warehouse's outer wall. From there, she could see part of the way into the long storage aisles, each one with a number-two-yellow barrier stripe across its mouth to mark the farther reach of its web and the ancillary machinery. The farthest aisle was dark, without even the suppressed, almost subaudible rumble of the power grid, and she guessed its machinery was down for repairs.

Beyond that, the lights brightened again, ordinary midworld strip lights casting their diffuse glow over a row of glyphed and lettered doorways. Jian quickened her step, eager in spite of herself, and touched the annunciator just below Desembaa's realprint name. There was no answer at first, but then the locklight went green, and she pushed open the heavy door.

The heat and the stink of hot fiber was like a blow. She winced and looked away from the white-hot mass glowing behind the shaping chamber's five-centimeter-thick viewport. Desembaa sat in the control chair, hands encased in wirebound gloves, his face completely hidden behind the plate of his helmet. Heavy, wrist-thick cables snaked across the floor, connecting the machines and computer blocks and servos; finer wires clustered and blossomed from less identifiable pieces of equipment, forming snarled webs to tangle the unwary. The floor vibrated to the rumble of the machinery, and an unoiled servo screamed as it moved. Wincing, Jian stopped just inside the doorway, not daring to come closer, and Desembaa's voice spoke from a point just above his masked head.

#Reverdy, it's good to see you. I've got a project going; it'll only take me a minute to finish it. You're welcome to join me, if you'd like.#

Jian nodded—she was always curious to see other people's virtual worlds—and a servo arm reached across to her, offering a pair of goggles. She took them cautiously—they were attached to an interface block by a length of flat cable, but, more than that, she was used to the overlap of virtual and real, not to going blind in reality.

#It's a standard interface,# Desembaa went on. If he had guessed her momentary uneasiness, he gave no sign of it. #You know, standard sign to move you around.#

"I know," Jian said, and put the goggles on. There was a pulse of pure sensation—not pain, not pleasure, just the sudden momentary consciousness of the wires that wound through flesh and bone—and then the workshop was gone. Instead, she stood in a haze of cool gray light, pale unreal walls, pale unreal floor and ceiling, pale world beyond the false window, the colors there grayed and swirled with a haze like thin clouds. There were trees in that distance, short and twisted, with round leaves like worn copper coins; and beyond them a band of darker gray patched with lines of white. Very faint, there was a thin cry—*like a flashhawk,* Jian thought, *only high and longer, lonelier*—and beneath that, a slow rushing sound that rose, crescendoed, and began again, a steady, oddly soothing rhythm.

#This is beautiful, John,# she said aloud, and the figure at the center of the world turned to face her.

#Do you like it, then? I was born on Njord.# The icon that was Desembaa was as much remade as the workshop itself, the crooked shoulder and the limp erased, the metal finger redrawn as flesh and blood.

#It's beautiful,# Jian said again, acknowledging her surprise, and lifted a finger to levitate herself toward the bench where Desembaa was working. In spite of herself, she took a step forward, felt her real toe jam painfully against something in the real workshop; she swore silently, and forced herself to stand still while the world moved around her.

#I miss the ocean sometimes,# Desembaa said, turning his icon-head tactfully toward the window. #And I've always liked fog. There's something secure about it, somehow. . . .#

#I'm all right, John,# Jian said. #But thanks.# It had been a while since she had been in this kind of virtual world, but she was getting the knack of it again, the trick of moving only her hands and not her body, translating instinct into gesture. This was what constructors did; she would never be as good as their best, but she could manage. She brought herself to a stop almost an apparent meter from Desembaa—not quite as close as she had intended, but close enough. #What're you working on?#

She had meant the question only idly, but the words faded as she saw the shape lying on the illusory workbench, an array of icon-tools spread out beside it. It was a mask, a face stark white, stone white, against a steel-gray matrix, a face at once familiar and a stranger's, transmuted by Desembaa's dream. She remembered, with appalled clarity, sitting in Vaughn's flat—not this one, but the one before, on the edge of the Yanqui Downs, another one-room flat too small to hold much more than his bed and a single chair. His computer and the construct blocks patch-mated to it had filled the fold-down table; there were emptied dinner trays on the floor by the bed and a crumpled container on the tiles by the trash burner.

"I missed," Vaughn had said, shrugging, seeing her look, and Jian had looked back at him, still trying to see if she would work with him. She had not known him long, then, had worked well with him but did not really know him, and did not know Red at all. Vaughn was sitting upright on the rumpled coverlet, pillows wedged between him and the wall: he had offered her the chair in one of his moments of quixotic courtesy. Red sprawled across the foot of the bed, head down, hair falling forward to hide his face, looking at nothing.

"Who's John Desembaa?" Jian had asked. The name had come up in conversation, not a common name, and the look on Vaughn's face had been anything but common.

"A friend of Red's," Vaughn had answered, still with that odd, gloating look in his eyes. "Thinks he's in love with him."

Red had moved then, his thick hair shifting fractionally—had he lifted his head?—but the gesture was so small Jian had never been sure, even after she'd learned to read him, what he had meant by it.

"He's a custom-system man," Vaughn went on, "you

know, precision gloves and masks, things like that. And an artist, or so they say.'' He had smiled then, with lazy malice. ''You've probably seen him, Reverdy, he hangs out in the spacers' bars. He's a little man, black man, one shoulder higher than the other.'' He mimed the deformity, and Jian nodded.

''He's in love with me,'' Red said tonelessly, without audible emotion, and Vaughn's smile widened.

''And so he is, bach, so he is.''

And he is still, Jian thought. *I thought it was Imre talking, just his nasty tongue.* She had stared too long at the carved face—Red's face—stark against its dark matrix. Desembaa's icon-face could not change, but he reached out to the maquette and wiped his hand across it, smudging the perfect features.

#Ah, don't,# Jian said, in spite of herself, and winced at the ruined beauty.

Desembaa's voice had twisted out of true. #Oh, I've made a dozen of these, Reverdy. This one wasn't even particularly good.#

#If that's right,# Jian said, groping for the right words, knowing she was clumsy, #the others must be—wonderful.# That was not the right word, she knew, nor should she have spoken at all. There was anger now as well as pain in Desembaa's voice.

#I've melted them all. Fiber of this quality isn't cheap, and the work isn't worth keeping.# The icon turned again to look at the smeared maquette. #I might keep this one, though. Maybe it'll remind me.# He took a restless pace away, turned back. #I'm sorry, Reverdy. End session.#

There was a rush of light, sound vanishing, as the images momentarily swirled together like water going down a drain. Then the goggles were dark, light leaking in a little around the ill-fitting faceplate. ''I'm sorry, too,'' Jian said, and peeled off the goggles. It was a little odd to be standing back by the door again, after having been next to Desembaa a moment before, but she shook the thought away and walked back toward him, stepping carefully over the straying cables.

''What did you want, Reverdy?'' The words could not

sound anything but ungracious, and Desembaa knew it, gestured an apology.

Jian nodded acceptance, answered the question as though there had been nothing before. "I've got a job, which involves working with an experimental construct—the VWS overseer, it is—and the client's being secretive. The only solid information I have is the interface and some shadow-bought architecture—plus what the client gave us, of course. What I was hoping was that you'd be able to tell me something about the overseer itself."

"Is this for pay?" Desembaa asked sourly, and then grimaced again, pushing himself up out of the control chair. "Sorry."

"No, of course I'll pay. It's business." Jian reached for the belt pouch, but Desembaa waved away the offer.

"Let me look at what you got, and you can pay me if I can tell you anything. Fair?"

"Fair," Jian said, and pulled a thin disk case from the pouch. "This is the first tape from the client, and this one supplements it; this is from a shadow." She paused, debating with herself, but the source would be obvious once the disk was read. "It's out of probate records."

Desembaa took the disks with a new look of interest on his broad face. "This may take a while."

"I'm in no hurry."

"Make yourself at home, then," Desembaa said, and turned back to his chair. He fed the disk into an externally mounted reader, then leaned close to check the readouts before reseating himself. He fitted the helmet back over his head and face—he had never removed his wire-bound gloves—and his body went limp as he reentered his world. Jian watched for a moment, then, moved by an impulse she could not quite define, walked over to the shaping chamber and peered in through the thick viewport. The mass of carbon fiber had begun to cool, the white distorted oval that had been a face fading now to cherry red, glowing against the solid steel-black base plate. Only one eye and part of a cheekbone remained intact; the rest had been wiped into a blurred and melted shadow of what Desembaa had made before. It was, however, still a recognizable portrait, and a disturbing one.

Jian turned away again, wondering uneasily if Vaughn would not like it.

Desembaa was still unmoving in the control chair, lost in his world. Jian sighed and settled herself on the nearest motor housing, resigning herself to a long wait. After a few minutes, though, the servo arm whined into life, offering the goggles again; in the same instant, Desembaa's voice said, #Sorry about before, Reverdy. Do you want to come in?#

"I've seen these already," Jian answered, but picked up the goggles anyway, peered through to see Desembaa's icon at the center of his illusory workshop, staring up at a two-meter-tall projection of the interface's internal architecture. This was nothing new, and nothing she particularly needed to see, and she put the goggles aside again, sighing.

#When was this built?# Desembaa said sharply, and Jian frowned.

"I'm not sure. Some time ago, I think—"

#Must be,# Desembaa interrupted, and Jian was certain she heard relief in his voice. #The way this is set up, it has to be.#

"Why?" Jian asked.

There was a pause before Desembaa answered, and when he did speak, there was a note of constraint in his voice. #It reminds me of someone—Reverdy, did Venya Mitexi build this?#

"Yes."

#When?# Desembaa said again, and then interrupted himself, answering his own question. #No, it has to have been from before.#

"From before Mitexi disappeared?" Jian said.

#Yeh. Who's been telling you about Venya, Reverdy?#

"Almost nobody," Jian answered, with automatic caution, and then, because she knew Desembaa, "Robin Libra, mostly."

#Haya.#

Jian frowned, certain she had heard relief in the other's voice. "What would somebody else have told me?" she asked, and there was another silence.

#That Venya was crazy,# Desembaa said at last. #Which I guess he may have been.#

"Oh?" Jian paused, and when the other said nothing more, added, "Should I be worried?"

#Hah.# Even in the speaker's mechanical reproduction, it sounded as though Desembaa spat.

"I guess I shouldn't." Jian twisted her voice deliberately, making the words almost a question.

#No,# Desembaa said, and then his tone eased. #No, I'm sorry, I didn't mean to snap at you. It's just—Kagami went out of its way to ruin him, spread those stories, made it so they might as well have been true. Hell, if he was crazy, there at the last, they made him.#

"That's not real reassuring," Jian said. Even over the speaker, she heard the indignant catch of breath, rode over it and whatever else he would have said. "Damn it, I'm going to be working with this thing, this overseer of his, I've got to know if it's going to work. So give, John."

There was another little silence, and she thought for a moment that she had gone too far. Then Desembaa said reluctantly, #All right. It's just—Venya was before your time, wasn't he?#

Jian nodded. "I'd never heard of him before this."

#The thing is—# Desembaa stopped again, abruptly, obviously groping for words, and Jian wished she could see through the concealing helmet.

#The thing is,# Desembaa began again, #he was a lot like Willet Lyardin was ten years ago, everybody's hero. You do know Lyardin?#

"I've heard of her," Jian answered. *Mostly the name, and the tone of voice Libra uses when he talks about her—envy and respect about equal.* "She's supposed to be very good."

#She's the woman who tried most of Kagami's current construction teams. Did it in her twenties; she's still their top constructor.# Desembaa sighed. #She could've gone freelance any time she wanted, but she stuck it out with Kagami. She made them give her her own division, what she says goes with them—but still . . .#

"Still what?" Jian said, doing her best to keep the impatience out of her voice.

#She's still with them. It's not like she's anti-Dreampeace, or anything like that, but she's not for us. That's all.#

And you'd feel a lot better about the real radicals in the movement if she was, Jian realized. She said, "What's this got to do with Mitexi Major?"

#He was a lot like Lyardin, at the beginning,# Desembaa said. #You know, top of the line, had his choice of the Cartel companies, all that. But he got involved in the Aster mess, went independent in protest, and the companies came down on him, especially Kagami. And he was always . . . brittle, I guess; he cared a lot what people thought.# Jian could hear the shrug in his voice. #That's what really killed him, I think.#

"You're sure he's dead?" Jian asked, startled.

#Oh, yes.# Desembaa's voice was absolute in its certainty. #Otherwise he'd be on-line somewhere.#

Jian bit back her instinctive response. The rest of it was Mitexi Minor's business, not her own; she had no right to betray it to Desembaa. She hesitated, groping for the right words, some way of getting more information without betraying what she already knew, but nothing came to mind. She sighed then, and settled herself to wait. She could feel the motor housing warm against her legs, caught herself wishing suddenly that she had eaten more than the sausage roll she had bought in the Peppina Interchange. She would pick up a box of noodles, noodles in salt broth and onions, good coolie food, on her way back down to the midworld— *no, not back to the midworld, but back along Broad-hi and down a level to the co-op. I should stop in there, see Peace, before I say yes or no.*

#Reverdy.#

Jian looked up, toward the work station.

#Come on back in. I want to show you some things before you decide to pay me.# Even as Desembaa spoke, the servo arm offered the goggles again. Jian took them, a little reluctant still, and sensation cascaded along the suit's wires.

The workshop had not much changed, still gray walls and gray lights and the slow rhythm of waves on sand. Only the first workbench prop was missing, replaced by the three-dimensional display of the interface's design matrix. Desembaa's icon stood next to it, staring up into the blue-ringed branches. Jian lifted a finger and drifted across the gray space to join him.

#I don't know how much of this you already know,# Desembaa began, #or how much use it really is. From what you've given me, I can tell you what the overseer has to be capable of, and that it's possible to write that kind of overseer.# There was a pause, and Jian could almost hear the wry smile in Desembaa's voice. #I wouldn't pay money for that, Reverdy.#

#A couple of questions, then, and you tell me if you'll charge for them,# Jian said.

#Agreed.#

#First, technical question, this is old-style, a near-real-time overseer. Are we going to go crazy trying to adapt to the lag?#

#No.# Desembaa's interruption was absolute in its certainty. #And I'll tell you that for free. At least, as long as the constructor did his job.#

Jian nodded. #All right. Second, what difference does it make if Mitexi Major or Mitexi Minor is involved?#

There was a silence, and for a moment she thought Desembaa would not answer. Then, quite slowly, the icon shook its head. #No charge for that either. Mitexi Major is dead; if—since he wrote this, it's old, but good. Mitexi Minor—that's still Meredalia, isn't it?#

#Yeh.#

#She's very good. Anything she writes will be reliable, maybe close to brilliant. There's talk on the connections that she's got some kind of in with one of the Cartel companies—nobody's saying which one—but that's always the gossip about free-lances.#

Do you believe it? Jian wondered, but did not voice the question. Desembaa, scrupulously fair as always, wouldn't say. #All right, then,# she said aloud, and lifted her hand again, raising her own icon off the illusory floor. #Thanks for your help, John.#

#For nothing.# That was Desembaa's usual answer, but this time it had an unpleasant ambiguity. Jian looked away, signing her departure from the virtual world, and saw, felt, the images drain away around her. She slipped off the goggles and looked back at Desembaa, still slumped at the center of the work station.

"Your disks are in the block, Reverdy," Desembaa's voice said from the speaker on the left-hand wall.

"Thanks," Jian said again, and, when there was no answer, crossed the web of cables to retriever her property. She turned back at the door, meaning to say good-bye, but Desembaa had made no attempt to track her progress, withdrawn into his own world again. She shrugged inwardly, a little annoyed by her own hurt, and let herself out into the yellow light and thumping noise of the warehouse.

3

Jian made her way back across Broad-hi toward the Igolka Interchange, feeling sulky and a little annoyed at her own clumsiness. At a street restaurant snugged into the portico of an importer's office, she stopped and bought a box of hot, heavily salted noodles, and settled herself on a low courtyard barrier wall to eat them. She was aware, out of the corner of her eye, of the measured flash of a security transmitter scanning the courtyard, and turned her head idly to pick up the transmission. It was scrambled, of course, but her sight filled momentarily with pale unidentifiable glyphs. She could also see pale lines crisscrossing the courtyard, security icons, a barely visible warning to those fortunate enough to be on-line. *Fortunate enough,* she amended, with a wry smile, *but also those with enough implants, and therefore enough money, to be presumed worth warning. If I stumbled in there by mistake—drunk, say, or just looking for a place to sit—private cops would be out in a minute to move me on.* She glanced up, toward the building itself, and found, as she had expected, the red light of a security scanner turned in her direction. She smiled again, and turned her attention to fishing the last few noodles out of the steaming broth.

This was an odd part of Heaven, made a bastion of the midworld by its proximity to the Charretse Interchange and the starport beyond. Coolie activists, demanding better conditions for Freyan contract labor, had made the district their target more than once; Dreampeace, too, had staged demonstrations here. Security was much in evidence, not just the scanners and the sensor webs, but, walking the streets, private cops conspicuous, going two by two with tommy-sticks in their belts. A few of the polite, quick-moving salarymen would be covert security, of course—probably the dark man in an aggressively plain square-necked hanten jacket over plain sober trousers, trying to seem inconspicuous as he pretended to read the display of the news kiosk outside the Asendi-Lunik Bank terminal, possibly the caste-marked secretary and the tall woman whose traditional sari had been reduced to a wide drape of gold-shot silk.

Her suit woke, sent a brief alert, less fear than fleeting apprehension, pulsing through the body. Glyphs flowed into her vision: *Ident inquiry*, and then the glyph for Hanse-Bank Security. *Respond yes/no?*

Jian hesitated for a heartbeat, irrationally tempted to refuse—*don't I have a right to be here, as much as anyone?*—but knew that her yanqui height and bulk, and the informal clothes, made her, if not suspect, at least out of place here in this plaza. "Respond yes, ident package one," she said aloud. That was the preset response that gave a minimum of information, name and guild number—a little more than the legal minimum, so as not to seem hostile, but not much. There was a pause, and then the suit faded back out of her awareness: local security had decided that she wasn't an agitator, Dreampeace or coolie, or a thief, or any other threat to local peace. That was a relief, since private cops had a deservedly dubious reputation, but the inquiry had spoiled her improving mood. She drained the last of the broth and stood, crumpling the emptied box. For an instant, she considered tossing it into the center of the plaza, forcing a cleaner karakuri to go out and get the debris and annoying whoever was watching from behind the scanners, but good sense prevailed. She dropped the crushed paper into the nearest trash bin, and continued sedately toward Igolka.

The intersection was relatively quiet, a few food carts clustered around a power node at the base of a support pillar, a handful of people—mostly staff from the little shops that ringed the plaza—queued up at each one. The corner cookshop was closed. So was the beerhouse, but Jian could see a shape, a thin girl in a too-large, too-sheer wrap-dress, holding back one drooping sleeve as she set the tables: almost opening time. The bright tubing that outlined the storefronts was almost drowned by the harsh glare from the overhead lights.

Jian made her way up the stairs to the co-op, pushed her way through the door and the pulse of the security screen. The lobby was relatively busy. A handful of other free-lance pilots sat or sprawled in the armless chairs, three on one side of the room, bent over a projector block. The rest were on the other side, with the empty table in between them, passing a blockreader from hand to hand. One of those lifted a hand in greeting, said, "Hah, Reverdy."

Jian nodded an answer, her attention on the imager sitting on top of the desk unit, but at the other pilot's words the figure reclining at his side sat up quickly, brushing an unfolded fax sheet away from his face.

"Reverdy, I wanted to talk to you."

The secretary's image was already taking shape, displacing the fractal pattern. Jian frowned. "Can it wait, Ruyin?" Usually that was enough, a polite warning or an equally polite change of topic, but this time the other pilot persisted.

"It'll only take a minute."

Jian glanced again at the imager and the waiting secretary, but smoothed her expression. "I need to talk to Peace," she said, as much to warn Ruyin as to pass the word to the co-op's manager, but Daru, the virtual Daru in the column, nodded anyway.

"I will inform him, Bi' Jian."

"It won't take a minute," Ruyin said again. "It's about the petition to acknowledge Dreampeace as a community-of-interest."

Jian sighed. Dreampeace was already an official lobby, registered with the Cartel and the FPG; community status would place them on a level with the ethnic and religious

groups that made up Persephone's polymorphous population.
''I can't sign that, Ruyin.''

''Why not? Reverdy, we are a community, joined by common beliefs and concerns—you're yanqui, you ought to know that.''

''I'm not yanqui,'' Jian muttered, but knew the complaint fell on deaf ears. She looked yanqui, all right, had inherited her biological father's looks and size; but he had left long before she could remember, had left her nothing but a biological kinship to his relatives in the yanqui quarters. Her real father was her second stepfather, Ahira Jian; if he had lived, his parentage, patronage, and sponsorship would have overcome even her looks.

''That's all the law requires,'' Ruyin was saying. Jian sighed, looking across at him—he was yanqui, too, her height, but slender—made herself listen with at least the appearance of attention. ''And it's important—vital—that we be represented on the Communities' Board when the treaty comes up for approval.''

''If there is a treaty,'' one of the other pilots—Mair-Nani Celestyn, small and round and bronze-skinned—said from across the room, and Jian realized suddenly that they had all been listening, waiting to see what she would do. ''I don't think Freya's going to give us one, this time.''

Celestyn was coolie-born; her grandparents had been contract labor, if her parents hadn't been. It wasn't the treaty that was the issue, but Dreampeace's demands: if the agitators got their way, Spelvin constructs would have more rights in law than most of Celestyn's people. Jian glanced around the room again, saw that the group was mostly midworlders like herself, watching with varying degrees of anger and approval. *When did this get so serious?* she wondered, and said aloud, ''Sorry, Ruyin, Dreampeace is a political party, not a community. I can't sign.''

''Haya,'' Ruyin said. ''But I think you're wrong.''

Celestyn made a small sound that might have been contempt, then flashed Jian a blinding grin. There was an ambiguous murmur from the other pilots, sidelong glances and quick suppressed sign, and Jian's eyebrows rose.

"If you want to know my politics," she said, and made the words a deliberate challenge, "ask me."

"People are going to have to take a stand, Reverdy," Ruyin answered, and to her surprise there was a sort of sadness in his voice.

"Bi' Jian," the secretary said, and Jian held up her hand.

"Just a minute, Daru." She let her eyes sweep the other pilots. "Let's get this out in the open. I'm not part of Dreampeace, I don't want to be part of Dreampeace. I don't give a shit about Dreampeace, except that they're screwing up any chance to talk rationally about some important issues. Does that answer everybody's questions?"

There was a little silence, and into it Daru said again, "Bi' Jian." There was no emotion in her voice; if she felt anything at all, it was well hidden beneath her trained control. "Ba' Malindy is waiting in conference room two. And you have messages."

"Thanks, Daru," Jian said. "Would you put the messages in the room systems?"

"Of course, Bi' Jian," Daru answered, and Jian walked past Ruyin down the corridor that led to the conference rooms.

Vaughn and Red were there before her, and the big wallscreen was lit, displaying a pastel standby pattern. Malindy frowned at her from the workstation at the head of the big table.

"I've been trying to contact you, Reverdy. Why don't you ever check in?"

Jian bit back her first response, said instead, "I've been talking to some people, Peace, in their worlds. I came straight from there."

Malindy nodded, his attention already returning to the display laid flat in front of him.

"Did you pick up anything useful?" Vaughn asked. He was sitting cross-legged on one of the overstuffed armless chairs that stood against the walls—*well away from the table, and anything like work, but giving him a good clear view of the wallscreen,* Jian noted sourly.

"Nothing new," she said, and, because she was still an-

noyed with Ruyin, added deliberately, "I talked to John Desembaa, he pretty much confirmed what Libra said."

Something ugly and unclear flickered across Vaughn's face,
was gone in an instant. Red, staring at nothing on the far
wall, did not move, or even seem to hear. Vaughn said, "You
always check up on your shadows? Or just Libra?"

Malindy looked up from his board. "Hey, people."

Jian made a face, shook her head wearily. "Sorry. It's been
a bad day."

Vaughn grunted, but said nothing more: clearly the apology had been accepted.

"Ruyin said he was going to talk to you," Malindy said,
with as sigh. "Would you mind telling me what you said?"

Jian's eyebrows drew together in a scowl, and Malindy
lifted both hands in surrender. "I'm not being nosy, Reverdy,
I need to know. You've got a lot of influence, and this is
something that could split the co-op wide open."

Jian nodded, appeased, but Vaughn gave a crow of delight.
"Reverdy's idea of influence is to change the subject—and
would you keep talking with her leaning over you?"

"Shut up, Imre," Malindy and Jian said, almost in the
same breath, and Jian continued, "I told Ruyin no, Peace,
no, I wouldn't sign his petition." She allowed herself a
crooked smiled. "I also told them all that I didn't care about
Dreampeace, except that it was making it impossible to talk
rationally about AI. Haya?"

Malindy nodded. "Mairi's already talking about leaving
over this, says she can't work with Ruyin. If she goes, so will
everyone else with coolie blood."

"Or coolie politics," Vaughn said, and Malindy looked at
him.

"You're not making the situation any easier, Imre." He
looked down at his board again. "Mitexi's gotten in touch
again, wants to sign the contracts and get under way as soon
as possible. She said something about having already given
us more information than was wise, and needing to avoid a
poacher. How soon can you leave, Reverdy?"

Jian considered, shrugged. She had not retrieved her messages yet, either at home or here, but there should be nothing
vital in any of them. "Anytime, I guess."

"Which is what I agreed to, too," Vaughn muttered. "So when is it, Peace?"?

"Whenever the client says," Malindy answered, and touched his control board. "I'm putting a call in now."

Which explains the warmed-up wallscreen, Jian thought, and seated herself in one of the more comfortable chairs.

"If there's anything we need to discuss, you two," Malindy went on, "now's the time."

Jian shook her head. "It looks doable. If you're satisfied with the safeguards, Peace—"

"They look all right," Vaughn interrupted. "Wish to hell you'd gotten a better set of stats, though."

"If you're at all unhappy with the job," Malindy said again, "we can put it off, renegotiate. But you've got to tell me now."

Jian shook her head again. "I'm satisfied," she said, and Vaughn nodded.

"So are we."

"Good—" Malindy broke off as something appeared in his line of vision, and his voice took on a suddenly formal note. "Peace Malindy, for Meredalia Mitexi."

There was no answer that the others could hear, but a moment later Malindy passed his hand across a tabletop control, and the wallscreen lit. "Good afternoon, Bi' Mitexi," he said, and waited for the picture to clear.

"Good afternoon." For all that it was midafternoon, the middle of the working day, Mitexi was not in any office—*or if she is,* Jian amended, *she's more important than I thought.* Mitexi sat cross-legged on a thick pillow-chair; out of focus behind her could be seen the expensive, stark furniture of a lower-midworld multiflat. Her ruby-colored tunic, silk with gold bands and tiny figures, was so sheer that they could all see, quite clearly, the sleek plain lines of her bodysuit and the honey tone of her skin. Her hair was down, Jian noticed, pulled back in a single braid, but that braid was bound with more glittering wire, wires that vanished into a discreet minisocket at the side of the constructor's neck: Mitexi was definitely on-line.

"I've spoken to my pilots," Malindy said, "as you can see. We're prepared to accept the revised contract."

Mitexi smiled. "Excellent. Are you prepared to meet my departure deadline?"

"We're ready when you are," Vaughn muttered, and Mitexi's smile widened.

"Then you can leave tonight. I've a departure slot reserved for eighteen-fifty."

Jian shook her head, less in disagreement than in disbelief. Leaving this quickly wouldn't make any difference if someone was trying to poach the program—if the poacher was good enough, he/she already had the data; if he/she didn't have it yet, three hours wasn't going to give it away. Mitexi was looking at her, and Jian said aloud, "I will need to pick up some clean clothes, Bi' Mitexi. There was nothing said about a rush job." Out of the corner of her eye, she could see Malindy nodding grim agreement.

"Can you make the eighteen-fifty shuttle?" Mitexi asked.

Yes, probably—certainly, if I get lucky catching the express cars, or if I just grab the quick-pack I've got stashed here. But that's not the point. Jian shrugged and said, "I can try. But I hope they're refundable tickets."

Vaughn said, "I hope there aren't any more surprises like this."

Mitexi ignored him. "We'll assume that you'll meet me at the shuttle port, then. Have you drawn up the revised contract, Ba' Malindy?"

Malindy nodded, reached for a sheaf of the heavy contract-weight paper, and fed it into the verifying scanner that sat next to his controls. The law, conservative to the last, still required one paper copy—realprint, not mixed text or glyphs, signed only with a real name or an attested mark, not a name-sign or a private glyph—to make the agreement binding. At the same time, he touched his controls, and a disk reader whined sharply. "Ready to transmit."

Mitexi looked away, then bent sideways to touch something off-screen to her left. "Go ahead."

"Transmitting," Malindy answered, and touched another control. The disk reader squealed again, and then was silent. Mitexi, however, did not respond at once, her eyes fixed on nothing for a long moment. Reviewing the contract, Jian guessed, and waited, trying to decide what she would do.

There wasn't really time to go back to the flat; better to take the pack—it had enough clean clothes to get her to Refuge and back, and she could buy anything else she needed in any of the shopping plazas between Igolka and Charretse. *I still have to call Chaandi, though, and Wilu, and whoever left a message here—*

"I accept the contract," Mitexi said formally, and Jian jerked herself back to the business at hand.

"Imre, Reverdy?" Malindy said, and Vaughn pushed himself up out of his chair. Malindy held out a pen, and Vaughn took it, scrawled his name and ID code across the bottom of all five pages. Jian did the same, and Red signed after her, slow and painstaking, forming each letter separately and with care. She still couldn't read the name.

"Excellent," Mitexi said, and her own voice went abruptly formal. "I accept the contract." That statement, subject to verification, was as binding as a signature; Malindy stared at his boards for a moment, waiting, then nodded.

"Verified and accepted."

Mitexi looked off-screen again, saying, "My bankers will release the first payment to you now."

"Thank you," Malindy said, his attention already elsewhere.

"I will see you at the shuttle port by eighteen-thirty," Mitexi said to the pilots, and Jian nodded.

"We'll do our best to be there," she said, and reached across Malindy's board to cut the connection.

To her surprise, the co-op manager made no real protest, said only, mildly, "The pay's good, Reverdy."

"I know," Jian said.

Vaughn growled, "She needs manners, Peace."

"Which one of us?" Jian asked, and Vaughn's expression lightened abruptly, became an urchin's grin.

"Her, I meant, but yours aren't above reproach, sweetheart."

"Can you make that shuttle?" Malindy asked, and touched the last sequence of controls that closed down most of the table. Only the red-glowing eye-contact nodes remained alive.

"I have a message to pick up," Jian said, "but that

shouldn't be anything important. I'm going to take the quick-pack, buy anything I've forgotten on the way.''

Vaughn nodded agreement. "Same here." He looked at Red, seemed to receive some kind of silent signal, and added, "We'll need to hit a chandlery and a dry-goods store—what's the season on Refuge, anyway?''

"You don't have to go planetside," Malindy said sharply. "That was very specific in the contract; she's got no right to ask you to.''

"If we—" Jian shook her head, and Vaughn corrected himself. "All right, if I want to go on-planet, I want to be prepared, haya?''

"Input: inquiry," Jian said, looking directly into the nearest table node, and felt the suit's confirmation tingle along her veins. "General Data, main datastore." She waited for a moment while the suit's interpreter units tied into the basic connection, and then into General Data's library programs. Glyphs flashed in the corner of her eye, too quick to be read, and then a brighter glyph steadied in the center of her field of vision: General Data's prompt, an outstretched hand with a question mark floating above the palm. "Well?" she said to Vaughn, and the other pilot shrugged.

"The current weather on Refuge, I guess. And the local date?''

It's a good thing GD's librarians are Spelvin constructs, Jian thought sourly. *It would take more than a mere expert construct to make sense of that phrasing.* She said aloud, "I would like to know the most recent weather conditions on the planet Refuge as recorded at the main starport. I would also like to know the local date of that recording. I would also like to know the local season, and if this record is within the seasonal averages for the planet.''

In her eye, the question mark vanished, and the hand curled abruptly into the still sign, *wait please*. There was a pause, the little green hand immobile, and then it abruptly vanished, to be replaced by a half-screen of text, mixed glyphs and realprint. *I should've specified print only,* Jian thought, but put the brief regret aside. "Refuge Mainport, locally known as Prime, reports overcast skies with scattered showers,'' she read aloud, translating the cryptic symbols into something more coherent. "High temperature was 7.25 degrees, recorded at 1442 local standard time. The low temperature was negative 5.9 degrees, recorded at 0328 local standard time. The season is local winter, and these readings are within the local averages. End query," she added, for the benefit of the system, and the glyphs vanished. There was no point in paying for additional unnecessary connect time.

"Fucking cold," Vaughn muttered. He reached across to touch Red's shoulder. "Come on, bach, we've got some shopping to do. Are you coming, Reverdy?"

"I'll catch up with you," Jian answered. "Where are you going?"

Vaughn shrugged again. "Kelemen's, probably."

"I'll meet you there," Jian said. She looked back at the nearest node, reestablishing contact. "Input: inquiry. Messages?" That was a personal command, not part of the main system; she waited while the suit translated her single word into a series of searches, aware at the same time of Vaughn's departure, Red at his heels as always. Malindy touched her shoulder.

"I'll need the room again in an hour."

"Haya."

"I mean it, Reverdy. We have clients coming in."

"I'll be gone by then," Jian said, and did her best to sound sincere. Malindy nodded, and stepped out of her line of sight. A moment later, she heard the door close behind him. In the same instant, glyphs formed in her eye: there were two messages, both marked with Chaandi's name-sign, the second flagged "urgent" as well. Jian sighed, facing the near certainty that she had forgotten something important, and flipped on table and wallscreen.

"Input: command. Respond to message two. Patch to table."

The suit confirmed, leaving her dizzy for half a heartbeat, and the data node winked out. The table whirred softly at the same moment, coming back onto line, and the wallscreen filled with a soft and fuzzy light. It took an unusually long time to make the connection, though, and Jian frowned, wondered if the system had had to track Chaandi down somewhere on the connections, or, worse still, at her every-other-day job as a body artist. If that were the case, Chaandi would be furious at being interrupted, and her boss would be even more annoyed than usual.

The screen lit at last, displaying the familiar crowded workbench and the thick pillars that held up the storage loft above the bedroom alcove. Images flickered on the multiple screens of the connection board, each accompanied by its own babble of voices. Jian blinked at the cacophony, passed her hand across the table controls to mute the noise. Chaandi herself, small and dark-skinned, coolie-born, a sleeveless work smock wrapped over her stained and ancient trousers, frowned out of the screen, hands poised to reject whoever had chosen to interrupt her work. Seeing Jian, she hesitated, and slowly smiled.

I'm glad you called, I've been trying to get in touch with you since yesterday.

Sorry, Jian answered. *Things have been kind of frantic.* Although she should have known better, she caught herself looking for the implant, and found it—as she had expected, as she should have known—sitting discarded on the table by the door. The deafness was common on Freya, the result of a simple mutation in a small colonial population, and it had come to Persephone with the Freyan contract labor, in the coolie gangs. *What Freyans can afford to correct prenatal,* Chaandi had said once, not bothering to hide the bitterness, *coolies have to fix with machines.*

Chaandi had seen that quick glance, was shaking her head. *No, I won't put on my ears. Not at home. Can you still work for me tomorrow?*

Jian winced. That was what she had forgotten: Chaandi's videomanga, the one she herself had agreed to lug equipment for. Chaandi directed, edited, and occasionally wrote and filmed a quirky, fairly well received series of manga, the video "comic books" that were the staple entertainment of the mostly illiterate upperworld. It was not an easy way to make a living—no way to make a living at all, really—and even less so when you were scrupulous about paying your actors. *I have a job,* she began, and saw Chaandi's face darken. *No, truth, it's a rush job, I just found out the client wants us to leave tonight. I didn't think we'd be leaving for another day or two.*

Chaandi's anger was already fading. *A good job?*

It pays well, anyway, Jian answered, and Chaandi sighed deeply.

I was counting on you, damn it. I need somebody to carry my equipment.

Can't you get Nils?

I have to pay Nils, Chaandi answered, with a look that held a sort of dark humor. *Hell, I wish you'd let me know, that's all.*

I didn't know myself until today. I'm sorry, Jian said, but the other woman waved the apology aside.

It's all right. I'll manage. She saw the wariness in Jian's expression, added, "Truth."

Haya. It probably wasn't all right, Jian knew, or not entirely—after all, she was letting Chaandi down—but it was easier to take the other woman at her word.

Do you have any idea when you'll be back? Chaandi asked, the question carefully casual.

Jian shrugged. *I don't know for sure—*

I didn't ask "for sure," Chaandi said, and her gesture mimicked Jian's midworld gesture.

I think a week, maybe a ten-day, Jian said, and Chaandi gestured an apology.

I am sorry, I shouldn't've snapped. She hesitated. *Will I see you then?*

I hope so, Jian answered. *I'd like to. Do you want me to call?*

There was a fractional hesitation, and then Chaandi nodded.

Thanks, Jian said. *I have to go now. . . .*

Chaandi nodded again, mouth twisted in a rather crooked smile. *Be careful, then,* she signed, and cut the connection before Jian could respond.

Left to herself, Jian slowly began to shut down the table, a vague feeling of guilt nagging at her. It wasn't that she had taken Mitexi's job—Chaandi would not have expected her to turn it down, for a day of unpaid physical labor—but that she'd forgotten that Chaandi had asked. Worse still, she strongly suspected that Chaandi knew it. Even so, it was too late to do anything about it. She sighed, touched the final key that shut off power to the tabletop, and turned away.

She found Vaughn and Red at Kelemen's Most-Excellent Chandlery, as promised, staring at the racks of foul-weather gear. Red looked toward her at the first soft sound of padded boots on tile, and then Vaughn turned too, saying, "What did you say the temperature range was, Reverdy?"

"Around water-freezing," Jian answered. "A little above to a little below. What are you up to?"

"Nothing," Vaughn answered, with a less than reassuring smile. "Trying to decide what jacket to rent."

"I didn't think you wanted to go planetside," Jian said.

"Not particularly," Vaughn said, "but I hate getting caught out."

"In fact," Jian said, as though he hadn't spoken, "you were the one screaming you wouldn't go planetside."

There was a pause, and then Vaughn shrugged, capitulating. "She was just a little too eager to have us stay shipboard, that's all. Especially when Peace got it written in the contract. I got a feeling it suited her, better than it suited me."

"And you're so good about obliging people," Jian said.

"Hell, Reverdy, I don't trust her," Vaughn snapped, and stopped abruptly. When he spoke again, his voice was under perfect control, even slightly mocking. "Tell me true, do you?"

Jian looked instead at the rack of coats, but then, because she'd heard the truth beneath the momentary anger, she looked back at him. "No," she said, "not entirely," and Vaughn nodded back at her.

"Well, then."

Well, indeed, Jian thought, with a crooked smile, and turned her attention to the coats. Vaughn had told her as much as he was going to, which was as much as she needed, for now. Most of the hanging garments were medium-weight padded silk, ordinary work jackets blazoned with the glyphs and trademarks of the original owners' company—adequate for most foreign worlds, but not quite enough for a planet as cold as Refuge. *Of course, definitions of cold were always relative: there were plenty of foreigners who thought Land-*

age—the underground, heat-shielded cave city itself—was miserably hot at the best of times. Those were the same people who flatly refused to go out onto the planet's surface. She lifted the sleeve of the nearest plain jacket, twisting it to bring the tag into the light. Numbers and glyphs rippled obediently in the iridescent depths, listing purchase price and a rent schedule—like most chandlers, Kelemen's dealt in rental goods as well as straight sales—and then the climates for which it had been designed. The designated temperature range was a little high for Refuge, but the garment was warranted waterproof, and the size marker indicated that it was outsized. She eyed its dimensions, and then pulled it to the full length of its cable to judge the potential fit. Surprisingly, it looked as though it might be large enough, and she shrugged it on, awkward because of the antitheft cable. It fit, and she struggled out of it again, turning the sleeve to re-check the hanging tag. As usual, it would be cheaper to buy the jacket, but she would probably never use it again, and she knew how little Kelemen would give her for a resale price.

"Found something?" Vaughn asked.

"Yeh. I'll probably rent this one."

Vaughn scanned the tag expertly. "You'll be cold."

"I'd rather be cold than have Kagami Limited plastered all over my ass," Jian answered, and, out of the corner of her eye, saw Red's fugitive grin.

Vaughn scowled, and put that jacket back just a little too quickly. He pulled out another, a plain one, not quite at random, glanced from it to Red. "This one'll fit you," he said, and the redhead looked sideways at him, unspeaking, saying neither yes nor no. "You will need it," Vaughn said, with emphasis, and selected one for himself without waiting for an answer. Red took the first, reluctantly, holding it at the end of its cable.

Jian raised a hand to signal to a clerk. Her hand tingled as though she'd laid it against a working engine, the touch of the shop's sensor net on her palm, and she looked at Vaughn. "Someone's coming to cut those loose for you. I've got a couple other things to get. Will you tell them to start my bill?'' She held out the hip-length jacket. ''I want this one, for rent.''

''Haya,'' Vaughn answered, but it was Red who held out his hand for the garment.

Jian turned away, moving quickly along the familiar aisles. Past the mixed racks of rental goods, clothes and gear, were rows of product dispensers, dedicated systems topped with display screens and multichannel speakers. She made her way between brightly lit consoles, through snatches of music and voices that were almost palpable, glyphs, real and virtual, flashing in front of her eyes, until she had to touch the access plate in her arm to dim the virtual symbols. She did not want much, needed almost nothing—she had checked the pre-packed case before she left the co-op—but there were a few things that would make the journey more pleasant. She stopped in front of a console that advertised cheap single-knit day wear, ran her hands along the index line until the screen displayed familiar corrugated undershirts. The thickest were certified for cold weather, and she touched glyphs to order two in the largest size. The screen went blank for a moment, and then flashed a confirmation: the shirts would be waiting at checkout. She stopped briefly at another console, called up a set of refill packs for her midikit, then made her way back toward the front of the store. Glyphs flashed enticingly in the air to either side, but she ignored them.

Vaughn and Red were waiting just past the clerk's barrier, their purchases neatly folded into a compact bundle wrapped in a length of cheap tissue-cloth printed with Kelemen's triple glyph. Jian lifted a hand in acknowledgment, but stopped at the last of the consoles to order a trio of manga. The dispenser hissed to itself, then dropped the freshly written spools—they were standard data disks, actually, though not of the highest quality—into her hand. The plastic was still a little warm from the drive. Two were Chaandi's work—*a monetary apology, at least,* Jian admitted, *even if they are good*—and the clerk smiled as she passed them through the price gate.

''She's good—I like her serials.''

Jian nodded agreement, but said nothing else, too aware of the Dreampeace badge set in the clerk's tangled hair to want to make conversation. The goods, jacket and shirts and midipack and manga, slid down the slope of the counter and onto another sheet of tissue-cloth. A two-arm karakuri wrapped it into a neat package, a bravura display of machine dexterity. Jian wondered how the clerk reconciled its presence with Dreampeace sentiments—*I suppose low-intelligence machines don't count*—but then tore her eyes away from the show. She signed Kelemen's rental contract, and handed over the necessary money chips. The clerk fed them into her reader and returned only one, its color drained to pale lavender. Jian pocketed it and pushed through the security barrier to retrieve the package.

"Will you come on?" Vaughn growled. "We're going to be late."

4

They caught the land shuttle at Tunnelmouth, the western end of the Charretse Interchange, where the wind was hot and stank of broken rock and exhaust gases, and the sand it carried stung the skin. Many of the locals wore fitted masks of thin, tough fiberfelt, and those who did not wore veils wrapped around their heads and faces. It was just the end of the normal working day: the shuttle that arrived from the port was full of cargo handlers and port workers, cheap, brightly colored cotton coats thrown on over their identical worksuits, less to protect the suits than to achieve some individual identity. They spilled out of the round, sand-scoured vehicle, filing between soft tires taller than any of them, swirls of color and sound filling the arrivals bay, and then vanished into the inner station, to catch trams and downward cars back to their homes.

The shuttle lurched forward, the sand tires making a squashing noise against the hard floor of the bays, and the steps folded down again. Jian clambered up into the dim, sweaty-smelling interior, seeing how the bright corporate logos were almost entirely rubbed away, pale shadows of their original brilliance. Inside, the padding was almost as worn, the nubbly carpet faded despite the sun-cheating film covering the windows. There was no driver, just the chunky box-and-cables of a retrofitted remote control link. Someone, somewhere, sat in relative comfort, encased in a display helmet, controlling it—and probably the dozen others in the port fleet—with virtual movements. *It was probably less boring than actually driving the machine,* Jian thought, *but not by much.*

Vaughn, following her, held out his hand for her surface pass. Jian gave it to him, and he fed each of the three cards through the fare box. The confirmation light flicked from red to green, and Vaughn settled himself on the bench just ahead of Jian, twisting in his place to return the card. Jian accepted it, stretching her legs into the aisle. There was not much likelihood of other passengers, not going to the port, not at this hour, but she was still vaguely surprised when the shuttle's door closed without anyone else's getting aboard.

The engine whined, and the shuttle lurched forward a few meters, stopped again, and pivoted on its left-side tires. Vaughn muttered something, too low for either Jian or the internal pickups to hear, but his expression was less than pleased. Jian grinned, but braced herself against the side of the car. Ahead, dimmed by the heavy sun shielding, a line of white light slowly widened as the double doors that closed the tunnel mouth itself slid back. The shuttle rocked gently as a blast of wind hit it, and Jian could hear the hiss of sand along the metal sides. She glanced back, to see the shuttle bay crew take shelter behind the screens that channeled the incoming air, the single guide man, masked though he was, still shielding his eyes with one hand as he waved the shuttle on toward the open door. She was still looking back as the shuttle passed through the great wall of metal and machinery that sealed the cave mouth, closing Landage off from the rest of Persephone, found herself looking up at the white-painted face of the mountain, a pale surface bristling with sun traps and ventilators and less identifiable shapes of metal and molded carbon. The doors began to close even before the shuttle and cleared the exit.

She shifted in her seat, turning away from the sunlight that bore in even through the shielded windows. It was just past

noon by the planet's reckoning; the mountains that defined
the Daymare Basin shimmered in the distance, silver-gray
against the hot metallic sky. Just past noon—*and only a little
past planetary dawn when I first met Mitexi Minor, and heard
about this job. Not quite twenty-four hours. I wonder if she
always moves this fast?*

The road ahead shone with a false wetness that reflected
sky and mountains before evaporating at their approach. Jian
watched the familiar phenomenon without really seeing it,
was only vaguely aware of a pair of half-tracks turning onto
the cracked pavement of the Darksands Haul. Too few to
form a convoy on their own, they would be joining other
conveyors on the long road to the Winter River and the little
town of Terminus. The supplies and equipment hauled to
Terminus would go to stock the farms of the Pleasant Valley,
the only naturally arable land on the planet; it had always
seemed strange to her that a few hundred people could feed
all of Landage. *Or most of Landage, anyway; still, the few
handscrabble factory-farms tucked into the Daymare Range
could not contribute that much to the population.*

The road swung right in a shallow curve that avoided the
runoff ditch carved by long-past rainfall. In the distance, Jian
could see the towers of The Moorings, each one topped with
flashing warn-off lights, most with a round-bodied cargo
shuttle snuggled up to its base; beyond them stretched the
interlaced runways, molten in the harsh light. To the left, a
shuttle hung in its launcher, ready to be pointed to the sky.
Probably the one they were supposed to be on, Jian thought,
and shrugged the concern away. Mitexi Minor had been
warned—and besides, it might almost be interesting to see
what she did.

"We're going to make it," Vaughn said, and Jian felt a
slight sting of disappointment.

But already the ground was opening ahead of them, or
rather, a long, too-smooth hillock split in half to reveal the
beginning of the ramp that spiraled down to the main level
of Mooringsport Under. Jian blinked as the shuttle passed
into the artificial shadow, and the hill closed again behind
them, throwing them into near darkness until the sun film on
the windows faded to normal levels. The shuttle driver, wher-

ever he or she was, pulled the heavy vehicle neatly into its bay, and popped the main door.

"All out, please," a coolie voice said from the speakers above the door. "All out." Jian ignored the droned list of possible connections that followed, and stepped down onto the worn tiles. There was still sand underfoot, even this far underground.

Mitexi Minor was waiting at the head of the dock, waiting without evident impatience, her own scant baggage—a single well-worn carryall—at her feet. As they approached, she gave a nod of acknowledgment but said nothing until they were within easy earshot. She had changed her clothes yet again, Jian saw with diminishing surprise, thrown another hooded coat—plain outside, but with gold-and-black brocade lining showing at the hood and sleeves—over the same translucent red tunic, and she had pulled a tube-skirt on over the body-suit. Her hair was bound up again, wrapped with gold cable, and now that she knew where to look, Jian could see one end plugged discreetly into the neck socket.

"I'm glad you're here," Mitexi said. She pitched her voice to carry, but not too far. "I was about to ask them to hold the launch."

Bullshit, Jian thought but did not say, and at her side Vaughn made an odd, strangled noise—*strangled,* Jian thought, *by the same suspicion I have. She might just be able to ask, and have them do it for her.* And that was power indeed, to be able to alter a schedule that depended on ce-lestial mechanics for its efficiency.

Mitexi Minor smiled slightly, as though she'd read the thought, and turned on her heel to lead the way up the board-ing tube. None of this was new, and Jian went through the routine by rote, her thoughts elsewhere. Mitexi had the tick-ets, and dealt with the destination disks. Jian stood quietly through the required search of herself and her baggage, won-dering if Chaandi had been able to bully Nils into working for less than the usual rates, and was only peripherally aware of the ground crew's looks of sympathy.

Aboard the shuttle, it was the usual group of passengers: pilots, local-system and long-haul, most of the latter foreign-ers from the Urban Worlds; businessmen with corporate badges at their collars, probably returning from commissioning starships or Spelvin and lesser constructs; a single family group—old-style family, man, woman, a single child—almost certainly on their annual off-world vacation that enabled them to evade the Citizen Laws. Jian leaned forward a little to read the pin adorning the woman's neat jacket. As she had expected, it was a Kagami subgroup glyph—Lincoln Systems, maybe, but she could not be sure. Persephone officially belonged to Freya, paid individual as well as corporate taxes to the Freyan Provisional Government, and the FPG was as desperate to increase its revenues as the corporations were to keep money out of its tills. The Citizen Laws said that anyone residing for more than ten consecutive standard months became de facto a citizen of Freya-on-Persephone, taxable as such, and subject to Freyan law. Any foreigner—any off-worlder—of sufficient status got an annual off-planet vacation at company expense written into their contracts before they came to Persephone. Those evasions were a sore point between the coolies—all ethnic Freyans, never able to achieve exemption—and the midworld. The child looked at once unhappy and frightened, and, as the shuttle tilted back on the launch cradle, it began to cry in anticipation. The woman leaned over to whisper to it, her expression impatient, and the man touched first her hair and then the child's face. The child continued to wail, until the sound was drowned in the roar of the launch.

The child cried all the way into orbit, keening on a note that cut through the dull roar of the engines. It kept crying, on a forlorn, exhausted note, despite the parents' best attempt to comfort it, for the full hour that it took for the shuttle to overtake the transfer station in its orbit, and stopped only when they came into the station's artificial gravity.

"She hates zero-g," the woman said apologetically, to no one in particular, and hoisted the girl onto her hip. The man, an equally embarrassed expression on his face, followed, balancing their oversized carryall as though it weighed a ton. The child, worn out with weeping, burrowed into the woman's shoulder.

"Hell of a way to have to manage things," Jian muttered,

torn between irritation and sympathy, and to her surprise it was Vaughn who nodded agreement.

"The transfer pod is waiting," Mitexi said.

She had reserved a single six-man taxi rather than one of the cheaper multiuser pods. Jian glanced quickly at Vaughn, and saw the same careful lack of expression on his face, as though they traveled by taxi on every job. She allowed herself an inward smile as she ducked through the meter-wide transfer tube: *it's not likely we're fooling her, but I'll be damned if I won't make the effort.*

There was no pilot for the taxi, of course: even Mitexi's money didn't run to that extravagance. Vaughn—*as usual*—took the backup pilot's place, with its set of rudimentary emergency controls, as though by right. Jian smiled and settled herself more comfortably in the couch next to him. She pulled the safety netting over herself, securing both her body and the single carryall against zero-g, and glanced sideways to see Vaughn running his hands over the unactivated board.

Relax, Imre, she thought and did not say—would not say, not with Mitexi listening behind them—but Vaughn met her eye, and pulled his hands back as though he had been burned. Jian looked past and through him, all she could do without acknowledging his one peculiar fear. Not that it was all that peculiar, really—taxis had fallen out of the traffic control net before now, which was why the emergency controls were installed in each of the units, and long-range pilots had proved their occasional incompetence in some fairly spectacular ways—but she had never felt the need always to fly backup. It had always seemed odd that Vaughn could not relax and let someone else do the work, but, once she had made sure it was not a matter of trust, it had been a fairly cheap concession.

The taxi trembled, and then Jian heard the dull chunk as the release units fired. The taxi seemed for an instant to fall aimlessly, free of the station's artificial gravity, and then the steering engines cut in, giving a brief illusion of stability. The taxi rotated on its axis, turning toward the picket lines where the ships too large—or too well adapted to deep space—to land hung in carefully planned and monitored orbits. The scene in the viewscreen steadied, the onboard computers displaying the schematic map of the lines of ships. There were dozens, some marked with blue corporate glyphs that indicated half-finished ships undergoing final fittings, others marked with shipping flags as well as the white triangular cargo icons. One or two were flashing yellow, warning the taxi pilots that they were scheduled to leave the system within the next six hours. The taxi swung wide to avoid the nearest.

"There," Mitexi said abruptly. "There's the *Byron*." She leaned forward against her safety netting, reaching forward between the two pilots to point to one of the glyphs at the top of the screen.

"That one there?" Vaughn said, raising his voice over the sudden thump and rumble of a steering engine, and touched the screen.

"Yes."

Jian glanced over her shoulder, to see Mitexi still leaning forward a little against the netting, eyes fixed on the glowing dot. She was smiling slightly, eagerly, but the expression in her amber eyes was stronger, almost a hunger. Jian looked back at the screen, wondering what the other woman really saw in it, and leaned across the aisle, across Vaughn's lap, to adjust the screen controls. The image shifted crazily, settled on the square icon that was the *Byron*, then shifted again, displaying a single line of glyphs. *Persephone built and registry experimental craft provisional name* Young Lord Byron *classification undecided, no further information available at this time.*

"No further information available," Vaughn muttered.

Mitexi laughed. "Did you really expect anything else, Ba' Vaughn? But it's a good ship, I promise you that. A very good ship."

There was an excitement in her voice that Jian had not heard before. Vaughn scowled, and slapped the screen back to its standard function.

"Can we tap visuals?" Jian said.

Vaughn glanced at her, a fleeting annoyance in his face, then ran his hands across the board, feeling for the right controls. The image in the screen spun crazily until he found the buoy's codes. The screen cleared slowly, produced the familiar faintly blurred shapes. The docking buoys provided visible-light transmissions only as backup, not as a primary information source; that was provided by the main sensor net that filled the virtual sky with lines and specks of blinding color. The ship that filled the screen was drab by comparison, a rounded pyramid capped by the smaller flared funnel that was the Drive shielding; the harsh sunlight leached all color from a hull dulled by a simple antiglare coat. Dock lights flickered at the pyramid's broad base and from the sensor dome that protruded from the center of that circle. They flared as well along the edge of the Drive shielding, brighter there, warning of a limited-radiation zone, and toward the apex of the pyramid, a cross of light that marked the docking point. Jian stared at the image, mentally reversing it to line it up with what would become the ship's internal axis under gravity: not a pyramid at all, but a child's toy, a top balanced on the flaring point of the Drive shield.

#Can I have my net-link back, people?# a voice said from the speaker above the console, and the screen went blank. The long-distance pilot was reclaiming control of the sensors.

"Sorry," Jian said, without particular sincerity, and settled back to wait.

The taxi settled into the *Byron*'s docking cradle, and the heavily padded seals clamped home, tightening one by one until all the lights in the telltale ring went from orange to green.

"All set," Vaughn said, unnecessarily, and in almost the same instant the remote pilot announced, #Docking complete. You may disembark whenever you're ready.#

"Thank you," Mitexi said to the overhead monitor, and freed herself from the safety netting. There was no gravity as yet—the *Byron*'s power plant would be functioning at the minimum levels, Jian knew; there was no reason to charge the gravitic units until the human crew was aboard—and Mitexi moved with a cautious grace, one hand always on or close to a guide line. Jian floated out of her own couch, but hung back a little to let the others go first, having learned from experience that her size was a handicap in the taxis' tiny airlocks. Over Vaughn's shoulder, she could see Mitexi struggling with a rainbow-glittering lockbox, one arm wrapped around the nearest handhold while she fought to apply the box. Then, quite suddenly, the stubborn mecha slipped into alignment. The atmosphere sensors flashed, then steadied to green, and the airlock's inner door slid shut behind them. A moment later, the outer doors, the taxi's and *Byron*'s outer airlock, pulled back, the *Byron*'s lagging by a few centimeters. They drifted together into the *Byron*'s chamber, and the outer seal closed again behind them.

The airlock itself was unexpectedly luxurious. Jian, balancing herself with one hand against what by consensus was the ceiling, could feel the depth of the carpet pile under her palm. It was not the usual harsh industrial padding, good only for keeping heavy cargo crates from denting the inner walls or each other, but quality stuff, better even than the forty-credit-a-square-meter carpet her sister-in-law had sighed over when they had refurnished the flat. The air was comfortable, too, neither too warm nor too cold, and the recirculation was good enough even at low power to avoid the faint stale scent of an unoccupied starship.

The inner door cycled smoothly, drawing back into its well without even a whisper of machinery. Jian blinked, then grinned—the taxi had come in to the docking ring askew; they were all hanging upside down in relation to the *Byron*'s interior—and Vaughn gave a snort of laughter. Mitexi frowned, and pushed herself forward into the ship, righting herself as she did so. The others followed, Vaughn imperfectly hiding his smile.

"Everything's on standby," Mitexi said, and Vaughn's smile vanished. Jian sighed. Standby meant they would have to spend hours—at least two, maybe four or five—bringing systems up to standard before they could hope to take the ship out of orbit.

"Can we bring your overseer on-line to help out?" she asked, without much hope, and was not surprised when Mitexi shook her head.

"Sorry. I don't want to risk that until the self-test programs have all been run."

Jian nodded—it had been a forlorn hope at best—and looked at the others. "Gravitics first, I think, then control?"

"Yeh," Vaughn said, and glanced at Mitexi.

The constructor touched a small square plaque set into the

bulkhead at her back, smiling slightly. "This has the basic layout—you'll find one at each major junction. I'll start bringing the standing system on line."

"Thanks," Jian said briskly, overriding Vaughn, and pushed herself over to the map. Mitexi nodded and turned carefully away, pulling herself hand over hand along the corridor until she had vanished around the curve of the ship.

The *Young Lord Byron* followed the standard small-ship layout only in gross detail. The decks were laid out in concentric rings around a central control core that formed the spine of the ship, but there the resemblance to anything else Jian had flown ended. It was too big, for one thing; the service corridor where they floated was too wide for zero-g, and lined with the same expensive carpeting that had filled the airlock. Here, though, it was color-coded, dark gray-brown below and beige above, to match the eventual pull of the generators: a completely unnecessary expense—*not even good for show, here in a part of the ship where passengers would probably never venture*. Jian shook her head, less in confusion than in sheer disbelief, and turned to Vaughn.

"There's a spoke a few meters on that leads right to the core."

Vaughn nodded, the same amazement reflected in his eyes. "Let's get on with it, then."

The junction of the service corridor and the interior spoke was sealed by a pressure door, its inner face covered in something that looked like quilted leather. Each intersection of the diagonal lines that divided the warm brick-red surface into palm-sized diamonds was set off with a gilt stud—*no*, Jian realized abruptly, floating closer, *not a stud, but a tiny, perfect face, bearded and grinning*. Tiny lights glowed in each of the hundred eyes. One pair abruptly seemed to wink—Jian felt the pulse of a signal in her outstretched hand, too quick to be identified—and the door sighed open.

"What the hell—" Vaughn said, and broke off as quickly, frowning. "Damn, Reverdy, I didn't feel a thing."

"I think I did," Jian said slowly, aware of Vaughn's unease and not sure she didn't share it. Usually, their worksuits picked up all the workaday transmissions of a starship, not just the virtual controls and displays through which the ship was managed, but the ordinary door guards and elevator signals that were the ship's subconscious. "The standing system's not up yet, maybe this was just mechanical."

Vaughn looked dubious, but said nothing. Jian touched the control disk embedded in her arm, brought her suit up to its most sensitive levels. Glancing back, she saw Vaughn do the same.

Beyond the airlock, the interior volume was unexpectedly dim, lit only by the pale-blue strips of the emergency lights. Jian let herself drift forward, one hand brushing along the carpeted wall to guide and slow her progress, the two men following with equal caution. Their shadows bulked monstrous in the cone of light from the open pressure door. They had drifted perhaps four meters from the door when a bell sounded, high and ghostly sweet. An instant later, the door slid shut, cutting off the light. Jian froze, bracing herself against the bulkhead, and Vaughn collided with her, one foot slamming painfully into her shin.

"Sorry," Vaughn muttered, and looked over his shoulder. "See if you can get it to open again, bach."

The technician nodded, his hair drifting in a cloud, and let himself fall back down the corridor. He slowed as he came within a meter of the door—it was padded on this side, too, but the padding was cream-colored, and covered with a lattice of fine silver wires—but nothing happened. He examined the glittering surface for a moment, then came back toward the others.

"It's a one-way."

"Right," Vaughn said, with an angry smile. "Never let the paying passengers into anything important—"

"There's enough light," Jian said. "Come on."

There was enough light, but only barely. A dozen meters on, the smooth arch of the corridor opened out abruptly, became instead a mere suggestion of a path, outlined by the blue lights and shadowy shapes like thick columns and barrels and walls of cold, distorting glass. It could not be glass, of course, Jian knew, or at least not the true silicon glass formed cheaply on Persephone's surface. It had to be braced or specially cast, strengthened in some way to withstand disaster, but it was still bizarrely beautiful, an eerie, ostentatious display of sheer wealth. It was not easy to maneuver in the corridor's open space, not in the lack of gravity; Jian pushed herself to the ceiling, and guided herself that way, the carpet still improbably thick under her hands. To either side was open volume, glass and shadow beckoning. Jian shivered slightly, in awe and pleasure, and kept her eyes straight ahead, refusing to be drawn.

"Must've been hell to get the safety approval," Vaughn muttered. "No wonder there were so damn many safety codes all over the specs, all this open space—wonder what they planned in case of hull breach?"

Jian shrugged, not really listening—Vaughn did not expect her to listen, was talking to himself, for himself—and fixed her eyes on what she thought was the silver column that hid the entrance to the core. It was perhaps thirty meters away, but looked farther in the uncertain light, a clouded curve of metal that ran from floor to ceiling. A spark flared once in its cool depths, but whether it was real or virtual she could not be sure.

"Imre."

It was Red's voice, and both pilots turned, startled. The technician was balanced against one of the glasslike pillars—it was carved in a smooth double spiral, the blue light reflecting in patches on its surface and in the distorted depths—looking out into the compartment beyond the vaguely defined corridor. Jian frowned, curious, and then she saw it: a forest of fine white-metal filigree, leaves and vines and fine gilded fruit, springing from—surrounding and embellishing—a spiral staircase. In the center of that metal garden, growing organically up out of the thickest of the vines, hung a sexless shape, a body human between waist and neck, but with the face of an owl. *A statue?* Jian wondered. *A karakuri? It looks mobile enough to be one, though what a service mechanism is doing there, apparently in the middle of nothing . . .* It was uncanny, unreal, and oddly disconcerting.

"It looks like something out of a wet film," Vaughn said, without conviction, and added, "Why not use ladders? That stairway must be a bitch in zero-g."

It's sexier than that, Jian thought, and knew the others felt it, too. She said, "You can always go climb it, Imre. Are we going to get this ship working, or not?"

"Haya," Vaughn said, and turned away from the hanging figure. Red followed more slowly, looking back.

The core was reassuringly familiar. Jian could feel the familiar honeycomb pattern of armorsteel beneath the thin cosmetic layer of faceted silver, and kept her hand on the column as she made her way around the curve and into the light that spilled from the open access hatch. Light and more: glyphs and lines flared as she came into line with the status transmitters set into the hatch, and she flinched back, groping for the control disk to dim the intensity. Behind her Vaughn swore, hit by the same barrage, but Jian ignored him, fumbling now to stop her inadvertent drift. She caught herself an instant later against the nearest pillar—it formed the edge of a long wall of filigreed metal that seemed to screen the core from the passenger volume—and steadied herself against it, pressing the control disk.

Vaughn muttered something under his breath, balancing himself against Red's shoulder, and added, more loudly, "At least we know the ship's alive."

It was a common metaphor, but, thinking of the owl-faced karakuri, Jian felt a shiver run up her spine. She smiled, the expression rather crooked, acknowledging fear and excitement, and let herself float back toward the core, ducking easily through the hatch. The interior of the column was relatively bright except for the empty space at the center that would become the ship's gravity well, and the glyphs clustered around the walls, defining the on-line systems. There were fewer than she had expected, from the first pulse of light, and she made herself look twice, turning head and body through the full three hundred sixty degrees, to make sure she wasn't missing anything. Nothing sparked to life, just the environmental indicators, and the red slashed-circle covering the gravitics and main-power glyphs. Behind her, she heard Vaughn sigh.

"How far down do you think engineering is? And did they have the brains to put in a ladder?"

"Near enough," Jian said. She pushed off from the nearest bulkhead, caught herself on the slim guide bar that ran the length of the ship and would divide the field that ran in the well into two currents, one pulling toward the bow, the other toward the stern. "As for how far, let's find out." She inverted herself neatly, switching her perspective with equally practiced ease, and began to pull herself up toward the engineering section, the polarized metal cold under her hands.

Engineering control was a place of sober normality after the extravagances of the passenger volume. The banked displays were old, familiar systems that they had all handled a hundred times before. They were in better shape than usual, however, less worn than most because they had never been used: *a better, more useful luxury than all the trimmings on the decks above*. Jian worked her way down the grab bars that studded the interior walls, moving at a diagonal to make the reference shift easier, inverted herself at last onto the nearest of the black-bordered gripways that crisscrossed the open space. The material gave slightly as her feet pressed against it, and then held her securely, upright in relation to the walls of controls. Red did the same, somehow managing to be graceful despite the halting gait produced by the sticky tile of the gripways, and made his way slowly across to the gravitics control. Vaughn, scowling slightly, clung to the wall, and Jian glanced back, lifting eyebrows in question.

"I just don't see why she couldn't start the warm-up before we got here," Vaughn said. "What a waste of time."

"Our time, her money," Jian said, shrugging, and looked back at Red. "How's it look?"

"All right." He stood staring at the controls for another full minute, however, before he touched the first set of buttons. "Charging the gravitics now."

It took a little less than an hour to establish standard gravity—the system's rated time, for once, to Jian's mild surprise. Once they had weight again, the secondary field formed in the ship's central well, invisible until the interior lights caught and flooded it, so that they could see the current outlined in pulses of light, rising from the generators along the guide bar to the top of the ship, then passing through the polarity cap to run back down into the engine room itself. Jian left the others to finish bringing the cool-feed plant up to full power, and rode the well the length of the ship to the main crew level just below the control room. Even shielded as it was, the well could not reach the final level without affecting the delicate net of hyper- and realspace sensors on which the pilots depended; Jian climbed the ladder between levels instead, slowly, unable to stop herself craning from side to side to stare into the half-furnished spaces. Even here, in what would have been built to be the crew's quarters, no expense had been spared. The floors and bulkheads were sheathed in carpet or quilted padding that mirrored the pale, subtly mottled browns of Persephone's surface, spiked here and there with sharp slashes of gold and red and yellow-orange hot as turmeric. If she bent sideways off the ladder, she could just see through a half-open door into one of the cabins. It seemed to have two rooms, and the outer at least was hung with cool-blue draperies, a startling contrast to the warmth of the public space. It was quite a contrast to the pale metal and glass of the passenger volume, too, and Jian balanced there for a moment, wondering again why anyone had gone to this expense. *There had to be a purpose to it; it would be insanity, otherwise—*

"Bi' Jian?"

That was Mitexi's voice, calling from the control space above. Jian shook away the unprofitable curiosity, and climbed the rest of the ladder, to emerge into a protective stairhead that was shaped unexpectedly, and rather unpleasantly, like an ornate bird cage. Jian ducked through the opening—it was to her left, and a hand's-breadth too low—and glanced rapidly around the control space. It was brightly lit, without the decorative frills she had seen below, the pilot's couch at the apex of a fan of controls that arced up and over the working position: the pilot's cage. There were display screens and data nodes, and dozens—hundreds—of the bright red eyes of projector lights. The standing systems weren't on-line yet, but she could imagine the flare of data lines and glyphs filling the air, stabbing through the couch itself to form the network of virtual transmitters and receivers that bound ship and pilot together into a single virtual entity. She frowned at the couch—a pilot's work was done standing, not lying passive in front of the controls—and only then spotted the faint cracks in the floor tiles that betrayed the well where the couch would sink out of sight once the ship flipped into Drive.

"Well, what do you think?" Mitexi asked. She was sitting at the systems monitor complex, a file box crammed with data blocks open at her feet. Lights and glyphs spilled across the boards behind her, but she ignored them, eyes fixed on the other woman. She had discarded the brocade coat somewhere below, and her hair was fraying loose from its braid.

Jian said, "It's beautiful. I've never seen anything close to like it. But what the hell was it for?"

Mitexi smiled almost gently. "For pleasure, Bi' Jian. For my grandfather's whim."

A folly, Jian thought. She remembered the sign first, her stepfather's hands carving the air outside the old mayoral residence, down in Visant Vihar, and then the equivalent spoken word. *That's what it is, a folly. Or, like you said, a whim.* "It was meant for a bigger crew," she said aloud, at random, and Mitexi nodded.

"Five-man crews were the standard back then, and then there was an allowance for human service as well as karakuri. But you don't need more than three, especially not with Manfred on line."

"That's your overseer?" Jian asked.

Mitexi looked briefly as though she wished she hadn't mentioned the name, but nodded again. "That was how my brother coded it."

"Any chance of getting it on-line now?" Jian asked again.

"No." Mitexi had spoken sharply; with an effort, now, she moderated her tone. "I don't want to bring Manfred up until we're out of the local traffic net. There's too much risk of piracy."

That was true enough, and Jian nodded reluctantly. "All right. Can we plug in our own constructs, work that way?"

"You shouldn't need to," Mitexi answered. "The standing systems were designed to be sufficient for ordinary management. Manfred handled data interpretation from Drive, and the interior effects."

"All the fancy stuff down in the passenger spaces," Jian said. "Light, sound, environmentals—holograms and karakuri?'' She hadn't seen holoprojectors, was only guessing that a ship this elaborate would make full use of them, and was rather pleased when Mitexi answered.

"Yes, all of that."

"Red's got the plant up to rating," Vaughn announced, and the bird cage rattled as he swung himself out into the control space. "How're things up here?"

"I just got here," Jian said, and Mitexi answered, "I've blended in all the standing systems. As I told Bi' Jian, you shouldn't need the overseer until you're ready to flip to Drive."

Vaughn's eyebrows rose, and he looked quickly to Jian, who shrugged.

"I figure we can bring our own blocks up, plug them in and all, but wait to see if we need to install them until we've channeled control through us."

"That's leaving it pretty late to install if this doesn't work, Reverdy," Vaughn said.

"We can let a tug take the ship out of orbit if we have to," Jian answered. She looked at Mitexi. "If you're willing to pay, of course."

"You're the pilot," Mitexi said. "Can I put in for departure clearance, then?"

"Yeh." Jian glanced at Vaughn, allowed herself a quick sideways smile. "I'll take first shift."

For a moment, Vaughn looked as though he were going to object, but then he grimaced. "All right, go ahead. I'll bring up your construct blocks."

"And yours," Jian said. "We might as well get both of them ready, just in case."

"Haya." Vaughn stepped back into the bird cage. "Anything else you want, while I'm at it?"

"Don't sulk, Imre, you got to back up in the taxi." The fleeting anger in Vaughn's face reminded her of Mitexi's presence, and Jian acknowledged it with a lifted hand. Vaughn nodded ambiguous acknowledgment, and let himself slide back down the ladder.

"It's a good ship," Mitexi said softly, after a moment.

"It looks it," Jian agreed, politely enough, letting her eyes

rove across the banks of controls, the pilot's cage. *Maybe.
But I can't wait to find out.*

Vaughn reemerged from the ladder a few minutes later,
Red at his heels, two carryalls slung over his shoulder. Mitexi
pushed herself away from the monitor that controlled the
standing system, and Vaughn took her place, frowning
thoughtfully at the multiple indicators. Red crouched on the
deck beside him, pulled each set of storage blocks out of the
carryalls.

"How soon can you leave orbit?" Mitexi asked, and
crossed the control space to the backup communications
node.

"Imre?" Jian asked, and the other pilot answered without
looking up from the standing system.

"Twenty minutes. But that doesn't include installation
time."

"Which we're not taking," Jian answered placidly. "Half
an hour, Bi' Mitexi."

"Very well," Mitexi said, and turned back to the communications system.

Jian turned her attention to the pilot's cage, searching first
for the lever that controlled the couch's position. Once she
had found it, she depressed it and stood aside while the chair
sank into the deck and the tiles closed again over it. Then,
smiling a little in anticipation, she stepped into range of the
projector lights, fixing her eyes on the nearest pinpoint.

Data flared along the wires of her skinsuit, bathing her in
a flow of information like a warm rushing wind. Her vision
doubled, virtual shapes crowding her sight, ghosting out the
curve of the instrument wall and the bulk of the hull around
her. She could feel the ebb and flow of data, could imagine
the information coursing along the wires, bouncing back to
the instrument wall, to be reabsorbed and analyzed as the
skinsuit and the standing system matched each other's parameters. Already she could feel the ship closing in around her,
its systems finding analogies in her body's functions, so that
she breathed now for all the ship, and her every move, her
every gesture, would be mirrored somewhere in the steel and
conduit and flowing electron fields that were the ship itself.
It was not that she *was* the ship, not quite; she knew herself

still, could see real space around her, felt the pressure of her feet on the soft tiles and the whisper of her clothes against her skin. She could read the glyphs that filled the air in front of the instrument wall, and knew it was not her they defined and placed. But the sensation of the ship filled her body; she could feel its moods and changes in her very bones.

#Input,# she said, #inquiry. Status check?#

The glyphs shifted in the air above her, ran and flowed, but she barely needed their specifics. She could feel the ship's health and readiness coursing through her—could have laughed aloud with the sheer pleasure of it—and hastily changed her command before that pleasure carried her away completely.

#Cancel: last command. Input: command. Run self-test, power level point five.#

The heady strength ebbed away a little, leaving her aware, but in control. The display of glyphs and symbols changed again, focused, and began to pulse in predictable, familiar patterns; at the same time, she could feel, more distantly, a sensation almost of exertion, of stretching along her limbs and through her muscles. There was none of the conscious communication that an overseer would provide, no voice, no presence commenting on what she saw and felt—that would come later, when Manfred came on line. For now, it was all wordless sensation, a glorious physicality that made her want to leap, to dance, and bring the ship to dancing with her.

"Reverdy," Vaughn said, and reluctantly Jian turned away from the pinpoint. She had only an oblique connection now; the suit would hold the last command and maintain ship's equilibrium until she came back into full contact. Looking sideways to listen to the other pilot, she could see herself webbed in virtual lines, wound in a net of virtual light that linked her every move to the sensors that bounded the pilot's cage.

"How does it feel?" Vaughn went on. "Do you want a tug?"

Jian smiled, and saw a look of speculative awareness come into the other pilot's face. "No," she said, "no, I can fly it just on this."

"I bet you can," Vaughn said.

Jian laughed at him, and turned back into the ship's embrace.

"We have clearance to leave docking in thirty-five minutes." Mitexi's voice was oddly faint, as though the brilliance of the glyphs somehow dulled Jian's other senses.

#Give me a countdown, please,# Jian said to Mitexi, to the ship, and a moment later numbers blossomed in the air to her left. #Imre, load the suit interface data files.#

"Loading yours and mine," Vaughn answered promptly. His voice was clear, as the suit adjusted her hearing for her.

Jian waited, savoring the feel of the ship. A chime sounded at last, and glyphs flashed: the files, the basic set of definitions and instructions that allowed the standing systems to translate her movements into commands to the ship, were loaded and ready to run. She lifted her left hand experimentally—left-hand movements, in her system, controlled internal maneuverings; right-hand and both-hand gestures moved the ship itself—and signed for another status check, this time moving the sign to the right and down, across her body, into the space assigned to the sensor web. The virtual display formed around her, spreading a sheet of dark-blue haze like a table just below her waist. Symbols flashed and sparkled in its apparent depths, blue-white triangles and diamonds for the other ships along the docking lines, pale-yellow circles in varying sizes for the various buoys and satellites. Most of them clustered low and to her left, just outside Persephone's atmosphere that formed a gauzy haze of pink light at the very bottom of the display. She turned slowly, and saw the brighter quarter-sphere that was the planet itself floating behind her, its color dimmed by the lights of the control space. Beyond the display, she could see the others, Mitexi watching with unabashed curiosity, Red still concentrating on the input boxes, Vaughn looking sidelong, his attention divided between Red's work and her own revolving figure. None of them could see her displays, of course, though Vaughn at least would be able to make a fairly good guess at what she saw. She grinned at him—*damn, it is a good ship*—and kept turning, scanning the display, until she once again faced the instrument wall. The main traffic corridor lay uncomfortably to her right, out of easy sight. She gestured again, signing her adjustment to the standing system, and reached down and through the display, turning it so that she faced the traffic corridor.

#Bring the maneuver engines up to standard,# she said, and the confirming glyph flared overhead.

"XRS *Young Lord Byron*, it is fifteen standard minutes to your scheduled departure." That was Traffic Control, a bored female voice with the remains of a midworld accent. "Will you be ready to leave on schedule?"

Jian reached up right-handed into the space assigned to communications and signed for the system to respond, in the same moment scanning the displays around her. #Everything looks fine here. I don't anticipate any problems.#

"Let us know if there will be any delays," Traffic Control answered. "We're running a very tight pattern here, and we can't afford to have anyone miss their place."

#Right,# Jian said, and just managed to keep from sounding as bored as she felt. The departure pattern was always tight—given the number of starships in orbit at any given time, it was amazing anyone ever made it safely out of the parking areas.

"I mean it, *Byron*," Traffic Control said, without much hope.

#I'll let you know if there are any delays,# Jian answered, and pulled her hand out of communications, cutting the connection. She could feel the maneuver engines gathering power, the conflicting fields building in their depths, a tightness and a prickling along her legs. The countdown showed another ten minutes remaining. Even so, she reached for the engineering controls, turning the fields until she could feel their perfection running under her skin. As the timing glyphs clicked into the last three minutes, turning from yellow to vivid red, she reached again for communications, using the sign that would leave the channel open.

#Traffic Control, this is XRS *Young Lord Byron*. We're ready to leave parking orbit. All our systems are good.#

"Thank you, *Byron*." Traffic Control did not sound particularly pleased by the news. "Stand by."

The last glyph vanished, to be replaced by a blinking

"start" symbol. Jian sighed. #I show time now, Control. Is this a hold?#

"Yes—no, the hold is canceled. You may proceed on the broadcast course. Please use one-third power."

#I confirm start, at one-third power,# Jian answered. A broad gold path appeared in the display almost as she spoke, a road curving around and between other ships and buoys before leading out of the parking area. She lifted her hands, gathering the ship around her like a coat, the ship's strength warm and reassuring in her body. At her gesture, the ship drifted free of the mooring buoy, pivoting slowly on its axis. She closed her hands, and felt the maneuver engines build within her; she gestured again, and that power was released, directed through the baffles and the complex ring of steering jets. The *Young Lord Byron* swung daintily away from the buoy and out into the main channel.

The *Byron* was easier to handle than she had anticipated, with none of the control lag she had expected from reading the shadow-bought specs. The ship danced with her, a perfect partner; she moved for it, ringed by the glyph-strewn blue virtual table of the course display. The sway of her hips translated instantly into the patterned firing of jets that slipped *Byron* neatly past an intruding mass loader. A complex motion of hands and head brought the ship up and around the curve of the planet, another gesture steadied them both, then fired the jets that brought the ship into line with the entrance to the acceleration lane. She was aware of each action, each reaction, and felt it, too, the whisper-soft, feather-light caress of the suit's confirmation, minuscule tuggings at nerves and brain, so that she wore the ship's responses like a ghostly second skin.

"XRS *Young Lord Byron*, this is Traffic Control. You are cleared to enter acceleration. Please report your projected rate."

#Thank you, Control,# Jian said, and pulled the numbers out of the air around her. #Our rated standard acceleration is factor three point five.#

"*Byron*, there is traffic ahead of you. Please maintain factor three."

#Very good, Control. We'll keep it at three.#

"Thank you, *Byron*," Traffic Control said sourly. "Have a nice trip."

#Sarcasm doesn't become you, Control,# Jian answered, and shut off her communications link before the other woman could respond. The lower level of acceleration would slow their progress, make the trip to the system's edge last—she pulled numbers from the air, watched them squirm through the calculation—almost four hours longer than she had projected. She waved the result away. The acceleration lane was created by the positions of the other planets in Persephone's system; if she didn't want to run the risk of colliding with another outbound starship, her only other choice would be to accelerate perpendicular to the plane of the system, and that created problems of its own. *And no,* she thought, with an inward grin, *I don't want to try flipping to Drive against the grain. We'll just go a little slow, this time.* Not that the acceleration factor was all that low: most of the common commercial ships she and Vaughn had flown accelerated at around two-and-a-quarter.

Her grin widened, reached her lips as she felt for the main drive controls. The sensors in her fingertips responded as her hand passed through the icon, so that momentarily she felt a solid bar against her hand. Power collected around her, coalesced until she was wrapped in its glowing shell. Tension knotted briefly through her muscles, and then resolved itself into movement, the illusion of movement driving through her, so real that she could almost feel the wind of their passage in her hair. The *Byron* bucked slightly, twisting out of true; she corrected it easily, the correct alignment resonating in her bones. *It is a good ship,* she thought, *fast and flirty, quick-handling—a good ship to fly. A good ship to be.*

Vaughn appeared to take over the controls four hours later. Jian sensed him put a hand into the pilot's cage, and looked away from the nodes, disengaging slightly. She shifted to one side to let him fit himself into the sensor web, conscious of a startled regret. *Which is stupid,* she told herself. *You don't want to be on another six hours. This way you can fly the translation to Drive.* She could feel Vaughn's presence now, the immediate intensity of the *Byron*'s input diminished by the sensation of his system, his responses overlaid on the ship's. She stepped back and felt him step forward, their linked movements setting up a tingle of feedback along the suit wires, fuzzing the ship controls.

#All yours,# she said, and heard jealousy in her voice.

#Thank you,# Vaughn answered, and she heard an answering hunger, an eagerness, saw and felt it too in the way his hands moved, calling up his own suit interface files, stripping her of the ship's power. It was a necessary diminution, one she had felt a thousand times before, and knew for an illusion carried on the suit wires—*no one pilot can fly forever, you'd die, burned out, body ridden to exhaustion*—but it was stronger this time, stronger than it should be.

#I want translation to Drive,# she said anyway, and Vaughn glanced sideways at her, frowning.

#You sure? That only gives you six hours' sleep.#

#But I'll be fresh then,# Jian answered, and stepped out of the cage. "Agreed?"

#Haya.# Vaughn stood now with his back to her, wrapped in pale lines of virtual light, gesture and larger movement blending into a solemn ballet. *He still doesn't know sign,* Jian thought, *just pidgin handtalk.* Her own piloting was better, smoother; she signed to the ship, and the ship responded to those far more sophisticated commands— She recognized what she was doing, and made herself turn away.

#Reverdy.#

"Yeh?" Jian stopped at the head of the ladder, one foot already on the first rung.

#Mitexi said we could crash anywhere we wanted, we don't have to stay in the crew space.# For an instant, she could hear the ghost of a grin in Vaughn's voice. #I've got Red picking us out a good one.#

"Great, Imre. Just don't put our tech out of action."

#I've never done that.#

"Twice."

#That was planetside.#

"I mean it, Imre."

There was a pause, and when Vaughn spoke, his voice was conciliatory. #You don't have to worry, Reverdy.#

"Haya," Jian said, satisfied, and slid down the ladder to the crew deck.

She was more tired than she had realized. Her legs were trembling, numb, and she had to stand for a moment at the base of the ladder, bracing herself against its solidity. When she released it, her hand was trembling as well. The deck curved away to either side, a broad corridor wrapping around the silver sheathing of the central well. The lights were well up everywhere, in the open doors of the cabins as well as in the public spaces, but she could see no sign of the technician. Probably down in the passenger levels, she thought—who would pass up the chance to travel in this kind of luxury?—but she started around the curve of the ship anyway, taking the long way to the door into the well. *Maybe I'll see a cabin I like. I wish to hell the overseer was on-line—I could just ask it to find him.*

To her surprise, though, there were noises from a cabin marked with an unfamiliar linked-circles glyph. She glanced in through the open door, and Red straightened warily from a floor-mounted console.

"Do you have my carryall?" Jian asked. The technician reached for it, handed it to her unspeaking. "Thanks."

Red nodded, still silent, and Jian turned away. Whatever he had been doing, he would not continue until she was gone. She kept walking around the curve of the crew deck, past a pair of one-room cabins marked with steward's caps, and past a room defined not with bulkheads but shimmering netlike curtains. There were tables there, and an autobar with the Joway Food Services mark embossed on the cover of each of its closed cells. She eyed it dubiously, hoping Mitexi had remembered to restock all supplies.

The pilot's cabin was only a few meters farther along the curve, set almost equidistant between the entrance to the well and the gravity carrier and the ladder that led to the control space. Jian hesitated for a moment—*who wouldn't want to try the luxuries of the lower levels?*—but common sense prevailed. She had to be near the control space, in case of emergency certainly, but also to make the work easier. There would be plenty of time to explore the rest of the ship.

The cabin suite was, despite everything she had already seen, still a surprise. There were three rooms, an outer room where one wall was filled with an expensive monitor/display console—*not top of the line,* she thought, startled, and then realized that it had been the best there was when the ship was built. The opposite wall was covered with diamond-shaped tiles the color of baked brick. She stepped closer, curious, but instead of the faces she had seen before the junctions where the tiles met were covered by much smaller, square plaques painted with black-and-white designs. No two seemed to be alike, but she pulled herself away from that unprofitable scrutiny before she could become too involved in the search. The bedroom was small but comfortable, the bed itself double-width and set comfortably into the curve of the inner hull; the bathroom was unexpected luxury. All in all, the cabin was bigger than her flat on Persephone: *not something that's likely to happen again. Better enjoy it while I can.* She unpacked her meager carryall, folding clothes into the storage cells—she used only one, and there was room to spare—then spread her sleepsack onto the bunk's generous expanse. It looked ridiculous, a sack-for-one on a bed designed for two or more, and she couldn't help laughing. It reminded her of something, too, and the smile faded while she searched for the image. Pirates, barbarians, camping in the ruined ship that was all that was left of a great civilization, too small for the wonders they couldn't understand: that was it, something out of a manga she had viewed years ago. *Well, the pirates won in that one. Let's hope that's an omen.*

She was tired still, but now that the immediate strain of flying the ship had worn off, she was restless, too keyed up to sleep. The joy of piloting still echoed through her body, an active pleasure, too strong to be easily released. She left the carryall on the cabin floor and rode the carrier down into the passenger area, catching the grab bar after she'd dropped three levels. There was no particular reason for choosing that place, or none that she was consciously aware of, but when she stepped out of the central core, she realized she was back among the columns of glass where they'd first entered the ship.

It was very different with the lights on, though if she had understood Mitexi's explanation none of the holograms and special effects should be functioning yet. Still, the directed washes of light gave new definition to the glass forms. Cool blue shapes glowed in the center of each glass brick that formed one wall, a cold fire that shifted as she walked along it. Curious, she touched the nearest cube, and faint pink threads jumped to meet her hand. She kept going, the pleasure that had filled her in the pilot's cage sustaining her, heightening her awareness and her pleasure in the shifting shapes. She turned left at the first cross-corridor, hoping to find the owl-faced karakuri that had so fascinated Red. Instead, she found herself in a forest of glass-and-darkmetal trees, under a canopy of thin crystal leaves that chimed like a string of bells as she walked under them. She reached up, unable to resist tapping the nearest branch, and the music clashed suddenly out of tune. Looking more closely, she could see hundreds of tiny repulsors set along each roughcast branch, emitting the low-power pulses that channeled the melody and kept dissonant notes from sounding at the same time. She shook her head, awed by the sheer irrelevant expense, and walked on. The high clear music trailed behind her like a cloud.

She came out of the musical forest into a space almost without glass, bounded instead by curving screens of gilt filigree. In the center of the space was a single deck-to-ceiling panel covered with brick-colored tiles dotted with smaller black-and-white squares, exactly the same pattern and materials that covered one wall of her cabin. She frowned, curious, and ran her hands across the surface, but could find no indication of its function. The other side was identical, the tiles warm to her touch. *Significant?* she wondered, *or just the effect of the lights?* She made her way through the next compartments—one was full of glasslike furniture, which glowed pink and blue and gold in the shifting light; the next was a metal garden draped with vines made of light—without really seeing the decorations, still mulling over the significance of the tile-covered panels. She pushed through the last screen of false vines—they were warm to her touch, and softly pliable, the light glowing through her fingers—and came face to face with another of the tiled panels. It was identical to the first, almost identical to the wall of her cabin, just beyond the garden. It, too, was set in a space defined by filigree screens; it, too, gave no clue to its function.

''What the hell?'' she said aloud, and there was an almost fierce delight in her voice at the puzzle.

''Bi' Jian?''

At first she wasn't sure she'd heard the voice, if it wasn't a product of her own imagination. Even a ship as quiet as the *Byron* was still filled with the whisper of the ventilators and a faint hum of machinery. Still, she moved toward what she thought she'd heard: if it was Mitexi, and there was no one else aboard who'd call her by her surname, maybe she would be willing to explain the strange panels.

The panel room gave onto another cross-corridor running from the core to the outer hull, and from it an arched doorway led into a space that seemed filled with dramatic shapes of light and shadow. The arch itself was edged with arabesques of gold; as Jian came closer, she could see that the curves were made up, not of leaves and vegetable shapes, but of twining naked bodies no bigger than her hand.

''Bi' Jian?''

''Yes.'' Jian used the midworld word deliberately, drawing it out. Mitexi's voice had been oddly directionless, though Jian was certain it had come from beyond the arch. She waited, but there was no response.

Beyond the arch, narrow cones of light fell at irregular intervals, striking shadows and reflections from the screens of glass that filled the space. They were offset from each other, some tilted askew, some straight, turned at odd acute angles to create a sequence of paths and tiny half-lit rooms. Most of them were clear, or transluscent, with only the hint of a shadow-shape in their heart, but some were mirror bright, throwing back reflections of the lights and the other screens, and Jian's figure standing in the curve of the arch. It was a maze, Jian realized, or something between a maze and the House Of Mirrors in the Kidsarcade on Main Zodiac. She smiled, and walked forward into the light.

It was not a very complicated maze, or rather, it was less a labyrinth to be solved than a single path winding in and out of a series of tiny rooms. The glass walls revealed rather than concealed the correct path, and even the short dead-end sections seemed to have some purpose. Curious, Jian followed one of those to the end, frowning curiously at the odd, in-

distinct shapes floating in the panels of smoky glass that half
blocked the curved corridor. It ended in a round little room
whose walls were made of dozens, hundreds of clear glass
tubes. There was utterly nothing there. She turned to retrace
her steps, and an image blazed back at her, a naked woman
carved of smoke and shadow hanging ghostly in the air, her
face turned away in passion and surrender, and herself behind
the stranger, as though it was her touch, her presence, that
compelled that response. Jian caught her breath, realized in
the same instant how it was done—each of the panels that
filled the corridor contained some part of the woman-shape,
and there must be a mirror somewhere beyond the entrance
to catch her own image, all of them carefully calibrated to
focus their effect here and nowhere else—but that understand-
ing did nothing to moderate the surge of recognition and
desire. She reached out experimentally, and her reflection
reached for the other woman, but her arms seemed to pass
through the floating shape, an oddly disturbing parody-
embrace. She stepped forward, and the woman-shape dissolved into abstract curves of shadow, leaving only her own
reflection looking foolishly surprised at the end of the long
corridor. She stepped back, and the woman reappeared, less
surprising now that she was expected. Jian stared at it for a
moment longer, wondering who had made this place, and
why, then started back down the corridor toward the main
path. As she passed the first of the smoky panels, she ran a
hand across its surface, and felt incomplete curves beneath
her hand.

The next of the dead-end corridors was brightly lit but
partially opaque, the many panels rough-frosted with clear,
hard-edged curves. Jian threaded her way eagerly along the
narrow path—it was choked with multiple panels, some only
half-height, so crowded that it was almost a maze within a
maze—and turned at the end of the path to find nothing waiting for her. She frowned, surprised by the strength of her
own disappointment, and glanced to her left to see if she had
missed anything. The image was there, waiting. A slim an-
drogynous figure—posed so carefully that she could not tell
if it was man or woman, and the fine-boned face, fine as
Chaandi's, fine as Red's, gave nothing away—crouched at the

feet of a sleek and naked man who looked down past the upward curve of his phallus to smile into the other's eyes. Caught as she was, as the artist had intended, half turning, sideways, her own faint reflection was caught and held within the star-white image of the standing man.

It was startling, but not unpleasant; she stared for a moment longer, and stepped away, her eyes focusing instead on the sudden opening among the crowding walls, a window formed by the conjunction of a dozen fully transparent panels. Mitexi stood framed between the pillars and screens of glass, still in the sheer tunic over the unconcealing skinsuit, watching—as she had clearly been watching for some time— the expression on her broad face at once remote and avidly amused.

Jian froze, anger and desire hot as rage rushing through her, intensely aware both of the other woman's stare and of the multiple walls between them. Then the absurdity of their position struck her—herself dancing with shadows, feeding desire with images as contrived and unreal as any wet film, and Mitexi watched that self-absorption with an eagerness born of distance and the walls between them. Jian laughed, touched lips and forehead in a mocking midworld salute. Mitexi smiled too, rueful and aware, and Jian turned away to retrace her steps through the maze.

5

Jian woke, having dreamed of Chaandi, and hung for a moment halfway between sleep and waking, a voice that might have been a woman's echoing in her ears.

"Bi' Mitexi?" she said aloud, knowing even as she spoke that that was less than likely, and self-betrayal as well—*and the honorific was fairly ridiculous, too, after last night*—and a clear inhuman voice spoke from the outer room.

"No, Bi' Jian. This is Manfred." The voice was cultured, accentless, pitched on the cusp between man and woman, so that it was genderless, defined only by the listener's desire.

"Manfred." In spite of herself, Jian felt a surge of anger. *How dare you install that construct without me, Imre? I'll have your balls for that*— Rational thought followed almost instantly, but only moderated the anger. *Sure, if I'm going to be the one to flip us into Drive, he ought to install the overseer, save me the hassle of doing that, too—but I know damn well he only did it now because he wanted to keep it to himself*—

"Yes. Imre said that I should inform you that we are one hour away from the translation point."

"Son of a bitch," Jian said, and untangled herself from

the crumpled sleepsack. Unlike many programs, Manfred seemed capable of distinguishing a comment that required no response. At any rate, it said nothing more until Jian had showered and pulled on a pair of well-worn workcloth trousers. She was still wrestling the cups of her knitted bandeau down over her heavy breasts as she stepped into the outer room.

A face was looking out at her from the center of the quilted wall. Jian tugged the bandeau hastily into place, and was mildly annoyed at her own reaction. *So what if the face was a bearded, grinning devil-mask, with neat little horns spiraling back from its forehead? It was only a construct.* Still, the black shape was unexpectedly solid-looking, and she stepped forward, trailed her fingers through the curved shadows, before she could be completely certain.

"I have several other visual templates available," Manfred said. "Or I can create a custom image, if you would prefer."

Jian glanced at the chronodisplay on the opposite wall: still forty-five standard minutes before translation. "Show me the preprogrammed templates, please."

"Very good, Bi' Jian." Even as it spoke, the devil shape dissolved, became momentarily a cloud of jet-black static, then re-formed itself into a woman's face surrounded by a cloud of snakes that moved as though they were alive, as though they were tousled by a gentle wind. Color bled into the snakes, turning them red and green and gold, but none of that color touched the serene black face. "Medusa," the construct said, and then the image shifted again. The colors ran into the face, which stretched downward, becoming animal, lizard, alien. Red-tipped whiskers sprouted along a muzzle covered with gold scales; a ruff of blue and red feathers framed the snarling face.

"Dragon."

The image changed again, horns and whiskers receding, the colors darkening into rich red-browns. The face that emerged had a bird's hot, small-pupiled eyes and a bird's beak, a predator's beak, that curved down over sweetly human lips. Tiny, stylized wings cupped cheeks and chin, forming the face itself.

"Hawk-spirit."

The colors disappeared. The face that formed was neither male nor female, and divided down the center line into a half of black and a half of pure, stony white. It had a pointed chin and strong but rounded cheekbones, a genderless perfection that was pleasingly nonhuman.

"That'll do," Jian said.

"Very good, Bi' Jian."

"I'd prefer you to call me Reverdy."

"As you wish, Reverdy." There was a pause, as though the construct was consulting some internal counter. "It is now forty minutes to translation."

"Yeh, I know." Jian turned back into the bedroom, rummaged in the wall storage cell for a loose hip-length mesh tunic. "Tell me, do you offer everybody a choice of presentation?"

"Yes."

"What happens if we all pick different faces? If two of us who've picked differently are in the same place at the same time? Do we each see what we picked, or do you decide for yourself what you're going to be?" She slung the tunic over her head as she spoke, stepped back into the outer room.

"Yes, I offer each crew member a choice of image, also the owner," the construct answered. Its clear voice sounded for an instant almost approving. "As for questions of priority: I can project direct-to-suit, which means you could see this image regardless of what other people see; however, that does take memory and projection time. The one time I have done it, I found the response to be somewhat sluggish. Otherwise, I have a fairly complex formula for deciding which projection should take priority, but it can be stated roughly as using the image appropriate to the person most concerned with my presence at the time."

"I see," Jian said. *I also see you're a talkative thing.* "I'm going up to control," she said aloud, and pushed through the cabin door before Manfred could respond.

Another of Manfred's devil faces peered from the wall next to the pilot's cage. It shifted as she stepped off the ladder into the black-and-white mask, and Vaughn said, from the cage, #You took your time.#

"Give it a rest, Imre," Jian answered. "What do you mean, installing the overseer without me?"

#Mitexi wanted to get him on-line now,# Vaughn answered. #I figured if you were going to take translation, I'd handle this for you.#

"I wanted to pick up any major bugs now," Mitexi said, and pulled herself the rest of the way up the ladder. She was no longer wearing the expensive tunic, Jian saw with some surprise, just ordinary trousers and a plain pullover vest. She looked very tired, with dark smudges under her eyes. "How does the system feel?"

#It's all right,# Vaughn answered, but Jian could hear solid satisfaction in his tone. Almost smug, she thought, and moved to the backup computer console.

"I want to upload by VWS files," she said. "You ready to accept them, Manfred?"

"Go ahead," the construct answered.

Jian nodded and ran her hands over the controls, feeling for the right sequence. The membrane was warm and pliable under her hands, guiding her as much by the gradations of temperature as by the glyphs that flickered and dissolved just under the surface. A deep-blue bar formed across the top of the board, turned red at the tip, and began to retreat, the red glowing like the ember at the end of an incense stick: the programs and the data matrices were feeding into the main system.

"How're we doing on storage?" she asked, and to her surprise it was the construct who answered.

"There is more than adequate space remaining to manipulate the material."

"Imre?"

#I don't feel anything different with your stuff in mainspace,# Vaughn answered.

"Good," Jian said. The glowing bar had almost vanished; even as she watched, the last millimeters winked out.

"Your program is in working memory, your data matrices are in soft storage," Manfred announced. "I would suggest you begin familiarization at once."

#I agree,# Vaughn said.

"Haya." Jian glanced at the board a final time, then

stepped into the pilot's cage. Vaughn moved aside to make room for her, and she was instantly surrounded by the bright shapes and shadows of his virtual world.

But not entirely his: already, Manfred was feeding her own symbols into the system, overlaying her glyphs and shorthand signs on Vaughn's very different markers. Vaughn himself was both man and glyph, an indistinct physical form overlaid by the brighter realprint letters of his name. Jian could feel the *Byron*'s status, the direction and velocity of its travel, but she felt it through the mediation of Vaughn's suit, and Vaughn's perception, Vaughn's instincts and decisions tugging at her body.

#Very impressive,# Jian said, and saw Vaughn's nod an instant after she felt his agreement.

#Pretty fancy, anyway.# Vaughn's tone, and the whole emotional tenor carried on his suit, was far more approving than his words. #Do you want me to stay on-line for a while? That way you won't have to worry about flying it, too.#

Jian could hear the reluctance to leave the system behind the polite offer, the same jealousy that she herself had felt before. #That's all right, Imre,# she answered. #I can take it from here.#

#Haya.#

Out of the corner of her eye, Jian could see Vaughn turn away from the nodes, his figure almost obscured by the blazing realprint label. She could feel his reluctance, sharp along the wires, but then his perceptions faded from her suit. Manfred smoothed the transition, tapering sensation, graying out his floating glyphs, and then Vaughn was out of the cage. Her own symbols whirled around her, rearranging themselves into her preferred configuration at almost blinding speed. Virtual space was ordered as she liked it, and every move could be instinctive, the proper course, the right moves as clear and obvious as a dream.

The ship's strength folded itself around her, stinging hot, and she frowned and reached out to fine-tune the warming Drive to the rhythm of space around them. The heat faded, became a merely comforting warmth.

#We are on the midline, optimum position for translation,# Manfred said, and for an instant Jian thought she had imagined approval in its voice. She pulled numbers from the air; set a countdown flashing in the air in front of her, then made a last check of the realspace surrounding the ship. At her touch, the display table rotated slowly, a wheel of stars and pale-blue symbols balance at her hips. As it swung, she could see a single ship inbound to Persephone—a bright green wedge, freighter of some type, not local registry—and then the bright scattered shapes of the Styx, the outermost of the system's two asteroid belts, the beacon that was the Peace-keeper base flashing white-hot among the irregular blobs. A few pale-blue mining platforms swung with them, and there were more in-system ships moving along the pale lines that marked the traffic corridors and the limits of Persephone's traffic control net. Persephone itself was a faint pink haze at the very edge of the display. It was a severely distorted pro-jection, but she read the symbols and corrected the relative distances with automatic, practiced ease. Then the table swung back, past the tiny, pitted shape that represented Orpheus-2, the system's outermost planet, dropping through the plane of the system on its way around its erratic orbit, to show only clear space ahead. Here the projection was cor-rect, size and distance in their correct relationships: nothing ahead but deep space and the distant stars.

#Give me grain lines, Manfred,# Jian said. She felt rather than heard the word of confirmation, and a dense grid filled the air ahead of her, a schematic representation of the com-plex relationship of time and space, the mass and energy available in this particular part of space. The lines were thin but bright, and there were gaps in the pattern, neat, regular spaces between the lines. The countdown was still ticking, the numbers clicking away in front of her eyes. She reached for the engines' power, dimly aware, off somewhere in real-space, in the heart of the ship, of Red's hands on his controls, brought them humming toward the pitch that would fling the ship precisely through those openings in the warp and weft of the space between the stars.

#The capacitors are approaching peak,# Manfred said, but she could already feel that tension clutching at her body, knotting the muscles in her legs and belly, clawing along her ribs and spine. #The capacitors are at peak.#

Jian smiled, saw the countdown reach its final numbers and flash away into nothing. The *Byron* was perfectly on the line, sliding with the grain, smooth as silk; she brought her hands down and together, and the capacitors fired. The *Byron* surged forward, a rush of power she could feel through her entire being, and then she and it together were flung into dreamspace as the hyperdrive cut in to sustain what the surge from the capacitors had begun.

The world re-formed around her with deceptive speed, Persephone's sky and sand steadying between her eyes and the instrument wall, so that she saw their shapes and glyphs through the brassy haze of the metal-bright sky. The controls of a skyhopper formed in front of her, a familiar icon with the illusion of constant wear on the handgrips. She set her hands in place—Manfred confirmed the illusion through the suit, sending steady pressure against her touch—and sent the ship skidding through the hot air. Clouds rose around her, welling into existence, culled from tapes rather than anything she had ever seen herself. They tumbled over each other, the tops flattening out into sullen anvils, and fat sparks of lightning sprang and vanished in their blue-black hearts. Jian grinned, enjoying the familiar challenge of bringing the ship through the last shreds of reflected gravity and into full hyperdrive, touched controls to bring the illusory aircraft up and around the shoulder of the nearest of the massive clouds.

As she had expected, from having flown ships out of Persephone literally hundreds of times before, and from the shifting numbers displayed through the virtual clouds, the *Byron* fought her hands, struggling to turn back into realspace where it belonged. The pressure intensified, and the scene around her changed with the hallucinatory illogic of dreams. The clouds thickened, stiffened, grew into jagged peaks and cliffs, starkly limned in light and rich shadow. The skyhopper was suddenly a balloon-wheeled transport, bucking along a road that was a river of sand rushing them backward toward the edge of a cliff—*not unexpected, but still dangerous.* Jian steadied the controls, fiddled the wheels, distantly aware of Manfred as it translated her movements, her choices into the complex series of orders that made fractional adjustments to the envelope that carried the *Byron* under

Drive. The first wheel caught, but the others spun helplessly, threatening to spin the transport; she eased power, twisting her own point of view until she found a ledge of rock. She was almost on top of it already, and as the transport crossed it, she stepped hard on the control icons. The wheels shrieked, spun, and then drove strongly forward. The transport melted around her, became a balloon that surged up out of the rushing sand. The cliffs and clouds fell away behind and beneath her, dissolved and flattened into nothingness; the world steadied to soft blue sky, and the sight of a planet—a green planet, no place she had ever been—spread out like a wrinkled carpet before and below her, a gentle current of air carrying her, the *Byron*, easily through virtual space.

#Drive is established,# Manfred said.

The construct's voice came from a point somewhere over her right shoulder, the place usually assigned to her own construct. She could not resist glancing up at it, now that the ship was stable, and saw the bicolored mask hanging in the air between two of the cords that would lead up to the nonexistent balloon. Those cords were props, displayed only to enhance the illusion, unlike the steerage wheel and the incongruous rudder pedals that formed the main control icons in this mode of her interface. Usually, her own construct was represented by another prop, a figure copied from a long-dead underground manga—*Elisee the Pirate, gray-haired, stocky, always with a swagger even when she was standing still, hero of her own short-lived series*— and it was something of a shock not to see her standing there.

#I can duplicate that image, if you'd prefer,# Manfred said.

#No.# Jian was momentarily surprised by the intensity of her own reaction, then allowed herself a sideways smile. That image—Elisee herself—was her own familiar construct, and even if she could already feel its limitations compared to Manfred, she was not about to let its presence be usurped by the stranger construct. Which was foolishness, she admitted silently. But Elisee was her own dream, and she wasn't about to share it with Manfred.

#You're fine as you are,# she said aloud, and turned back to survey the dreamscape ahead of her. #Show me a forecast, please, say, for six subjective hours.# That would take it well into Vaughn's watch, but there was no reason not to examine his chances as well.

A river formed across the curve of the ground, dividing the image of the *Byron*'s immediate vicinity from Manfred's projection of space temporally and spatially ahead of them. Slowly at first, then faster, the ground beyond the river began to flow toward her, fading into the water at the misty join of the images. The unreal landscape stayed flat and green for what seemed a long time, broken into an enormous regular checkerboard like an array of farms: good space, true-to-grain, undistorted by the reflection of objects in realspace. As the color faded from green to the grayed blue of distance, though, the terrain changed, too, became nubbled with clumps of trees that rapidly spread until the entire scene was carpeted in the thickly knotted growth. Lakes appeared, blued-steel holes in the solid forest: rippled space, where the grain was twisted, and space itself ran thick and thin. A mountain—some realspace object massive enough to cause a solid effect—appeared, but it was a vague shape, what should have been hard edges dulled by the uncertainty of the prediction. The flowing landscape slowed with its appearance, stopped with the mountain barely over the apparent horizon, then reversed itself.

#The probability of this projection ranges from ninety-nine percent at the first quarter hour, ninety percent for the first hour, seventy percent for hours two and three, fifty percent for hours four and five, twenty percent or less for hour six,# Manfred announced, almost cheerfully.

#Thank you,# Jian said. #Any guesses on what comes after that shadow?#

The image shifted again, reversed itself until the mountain stood once again on the horizon. It began to move forward slowly, the landscape beyond it blue and indistinct, but flattening rapidly into more of the checkerboard farms. At the same moment, Manfred said, #This is only an approximation. The probability is twenty percent or less.#

#Right. Thanks,# Jian said, and the image vanished, river and all, was replaced by a smooth swath of farmland, patched only occasionally with a tiny clump of trees, or the short threadlike curve of a lake. She touched the control wheel gently, feet moving with equal care on the rudders, and the balloon image—the ship itself—swung slightly, correcting its course away from the weak spot marked by the lake. The trees were different, more common and less dangerous, area where hyperspace was thick, resistant to the ship's passage; space was thin over the lakes, with nothing for the Drive engines to grapple with, and it would be very easy for the ship to slip out of Drive inadvertently. Vaughn would have some rough space to deal with—but it would be at the beginning of his shift, when presumably he would best be able to deal with it. And after that, space looked smooth again, the sort of thing even a construct could fly unsupervised.

#What's your autoflight capability, Manfred?# she asked.

#I am capable of preprogrammed ship-handling, and of correcting for unanticipated distortion up to a factor of two,# the construct answered.

#Two?# Jian asked sharply. Most constructs—her own construct, which was advertised as top-of-the-line—could only handle a very limited set of deviations from the predicted course, to a factor of one or at best 1.25.

#That's correct.#

Right, Jian thought. *I'll believe it when I see it.* She said, #All right. Give me a pen.#

A streak of fire blossomed by her hand, shaped itself into a neat rod of light. The landscape ahead of her shifted even before she could verbalize the command, became a map hanging vertically in the air in front of her. She grasped the wand, used it to trace an arc on the map, defining both space and time in a single movement. #I'm going to step off-line. That's your course.# Deliberately, she had extended the line for an hour, virtually ensuring that the construct would encounter deviations of at least factor one. She more than half expected it to protest, but, if anything, Manfred's voice held only satisfaction.

#Very good, Bi' Jian.#

#Off-line,# Jian said, and stepped back even before the image had begun to fade.

Mitexi was still in the control room, seated at the computer console, staring at the ever shifting patterns of light as though she could follow Manfred's performance in that display. *Which is probably just what she's doing,* Jian thought, and in that moment Mitexi swung to face her, smiling.

"Well, what do you think of Manfred?"

Jian hesitated, briefly reluctant to share anything of the construct even with someone who was not a pilot. The control room seemed very bright, the light harsh after the softened colors of her virtual world. She glanced over her shoulder into the now empty pilot's cage, watching the lights of the instrument wall: Manfred was holding the ship steady, all functions showing green. "I'm impressed," she said at last, and knew she was being ungracious. "It's very, very good."

"I'm glad to hear it," Mitexi said. Her voice was calm enough, the soothing, easy voice common to all the mechadoctors Jian had ever dealt with in her time as a test pilot, but there was a heat, an eagerness, behind that facade. That eagerness vanished almost before Jian could be sure she had seen it, leaving her momentarily disoriented. Mitexi went on as though she had noticed nothing. "I'd like to get a more detailed analysis after you've come off watch—if that's convenient, of course." Those words were courtesy only; the tone made it an order. "I know you've handled test regimens before."

Jian nodded. "It'll be a fairly rough assessment, though— I'm going to be pretty tired. You might want to let me sleep on it." She was being contrary, but Mitexi's assumption of compliance annoyed her—unreasonably, too, she knew, but there was something about the other woman that set her teeth on edge. *Of course, the problem is, we're a lot alike,* she thought, and hid a grin of recognition. *She wants to run everything, and so do I—none of this nice delineation of spheres of control for either one of us.* She had a sudden vision of the same struggle played out in bed, hands, bodies moving in the familiar patterns of exploration and seduction, strategies only a little subtler than the game of words they had been playing. She blinked, bemused, and realized Mitexi was watching her, waiting for an answer to something she had said.

"Sorry," Jian said. "I was listening to the ship."

"Is everything all right?" In spite of herself, Mitexi's voice sharpened, and she cast a quick, betraying glance at the instrument wall.

"Everything's fine," Jian said. "False alarm."

Mitexi nodded. "I said that a rough assessment would be fine. I've taken the owner's suite. That's on the level just below crew deck. Why don't you come down after you hand over to Vaughn?"

Again, the polite words masked an order. Jian smiled, said, "Haya. But, like I said, don't expect anything too coherent."

"That's fine." Mitexi rose easily from her chair. "I'll look forward to it."

"So will I," Jian said, but the other woman was already on the ladder. She disappeared before Jian could decide if she had heard.

Left to herself, Jian turned back to the pilot's cage, but did not step into the web of pickups. Instead, she fixed her eyes on the nearest of the data nodes, and said, "Input: command. Read-only link."

A partial landscape filled one half of her vision, made imperfect by the incomplete projection channeled through that node. Still, the image was clear enough to judge Manfred's progress. The construct had taken the ship farther along the projected course than she had expected—there was a small time-slip at work, Jian saw, speeding their apparent progress: a nice bonus, like a good tail wind—but otherwise everything was exactly as predicted.

"Input: command. Cancel last command."

Jian looked away as she spoke, studying the instrument wall instead. To her right, the sensor scan ran with color and glyph, displaying the chaotic hard-data flow that Manfred translated into something manipulable. Without its aid, she could pick out only gross patterns, barely enough to keep the ship steady against the Drive field's pressure. It was no wonder, she thought, not for the first time, that the first attempts at achieving FTL travel had ended in such spectacular failures.

#Reverdy. I am experiencing an area of increased deviation from the predicted pattern. Please advise.# Manfred's voice was as calm as ever—as calm as it always would be except under the most extreme conditions, when the pilot's reactions needed to be sharpened by adrenaline and fear.

"On-line," Reverdy answered, and stepped back into the cage.

She was instantly surrounded by the familiar shapes of the balloon-icon, the control wheel coming into tangible existence even as she reached out for it. Ahead, the landscape was patched with trees and crossed by the ghost-shape of a narrow river.

#Oh, hell,# she said aloud, and the construct, mercifully, ignored her. Elisee, whose original structure had been corporate, would have objected to the language. Jian put that thought aside, and studied the ground rolling past beneath her feet.

#What's the deviation?#

#A factor of 2.01 and rising,# Manfred answered.

#What was it when you called me?#

#A factor of 1.95.#

All right, I'm impressed, Jian thought. It had been a nicely timed call, letting her take control smoothly, without the sudden thrashing to reestablish stability relative to the grain that sometimes happened when a construct interpreted its instructions too literally. She shook herself, and made herself concentrate on the landscape instead.

This was ragged space, true deep space, where the veil of matter that wove the universe was stretched very thin. The Drive fields would have little to drive against, crossing the gap that was the river; it was not all that dangerous—or at least not unusually dangerous—but it would require some precision.

#Time to crossing?# she asked, and Manfred answered promptly.

#Eighteen minutes, according to my estimate. The probability that the estimate is correct is ninety-six percent.#

#Scale?#

#The distorted area appears to fall between a class one and a class two, with a slight bias toward a class one anomaly,# Manfred answered.

#Drive check,# Jian said, and waited until the glyph that indicated an open channel blossomed in the air before her.

#Red? I've got a probable class one, maybe class two area coming up. Is the Drive tight?#

There was a moment's silence, and then the technician answered, his voice ghostly in her ears.

#Yes.#

#He'll be down below backing you,# Vaughn said.

#I wasn't talking to you, Imre,# Jian said. #I'd appreciate the backup, Red.#

#No problem.# Even mediated through the standing system, Red's voice was reluctant, as though he was always looking away.

Jian nodded, knowing that the suit and the standing system would interpret and pass along that confirmation, and turned her attention back to the illusory scene in front of her. The balloon was approaching a clump of trees; she touched rudders and control wheel, banked the ship easily around them. She could feel a continued presence in the air around her, as though if she turned she would see someone besides the construct-icon standing behind her—more than one person, she realized, and the second one was not familiar. Which meant Mitexi: Red's deliberate nonpresence was no more than a faint touch at the back of her neck, hardly a contact unless she looked for it; Vaughn's obtrusive self-shape was entirely familiar, and not there at all. She could show off a little, for Mitexi.

#Fade in the precision filter, Manfred.#

#Very well.#

All around her, the images of sky and sun and field began to turn gray, color draining away into nothing. To either side, the struts of the balloon-icon thickened, darkened, became iron-gray cylindrical shapes that duplicated themselves, spreading forward until they formed a corridor. The cylinders deformed as they rose higher, acquired knobs and edges, and the tops of each arched and bowed forward over the fading landscape. It still flowed smoothly, slowly, slow as a dream, but the checkerboard of fields and the knotted clumps of trees were almost invisible, replaced by a simple pattern of warp and weft. Threads of multicolored light shot from the arching metal arms, met and focused into a single bead of white light that slammed from side to side, leaving a trail of woven space.

A set of ghostly booms rose and fell in an ever-increasing rhythm, working out the intricate pattern. Already, Jian could see the first signs of ragged space: the bead of light that was the shuttle of the illusory loom left great floats of floss behind, unsecured by the warp except at increasingly distant intervals. It was a complex and beautiful pattern, a suggestion of abstract florals and elongated geometrical repetition, like brocade or the underside of the gold bands that began and ended rich women's gossamer shawls, and Jian was aware of that, sighed for it—Elisee never managed anything so elaborate—even as she studied its real meanings.

This particular virtual world combined a suboverseer and an unrelated display function: she would make no changes to the fabric woven before her, but would fly the ship on an entirely different set of gestures. As a result, however, the display was far more detailed than was possible in an interactive world, made possible far more precise control of the ship's relationship to hyperspace. The standing systems wove through her, variables of warmth and pressure, a light wash of sensation, along the wires of her suit. The area where the floats began was coming closer, the apparent speed at which the cloth flowed off the loom increasing steadily: the timeslip that had been easing the *Byron*'s passage was still in effect, now more a nuisance than a help. Jian lifted her hands, calling the ship together around her, gathering its functions tightly to herself, and with a gesture tilted the ship into the patch of solid cloth between two frothy flowers. It was like reading a maze and solving it at the same time: she could see the evolving pattern—familiar, traditional, an ordinary patch of ragged space—and shifted to follow it, hands and body moving in concert. The Drive fields' echoes wrapped themselves warmly around her, tight and reassuringly strong; she moved within that embrace, and felt the ship move with her.

The apparent speed of the time-slip was still increasing, the beat of the shuttle coming faster and faster. The cloth ripped past her, the pattern of float and solid weave growing more densely intertwined. The flowers vanished, or became abstracted into mere geometry, folding into other starkly angled shapes. The strands swirled together, knotted, became densely interlaced bands, the shuttle passing steadily back and forth at the edge of the forming shapes. Still she found the solutions, the solid spaces, and laid the ship surely along her course. She was smiling now, teeth bared, riding the crest of her own skill. The Drive fields purred around her, carrying her—the ship—through the maze of ragged space. Then, as abruptly as it had begun, the pattern began to thin out, became again a smooth familiar brocade, broad floral medallions joined by wreaths of stylized leaves. She traced the curve of one final spray, and then the patterns faded to random patches, a few long floats across the even fabric.

#Will this last, Manfred?#

#There is a ninety-four-percent probability that conditions will remain the same or similar for the next ship-subjective hour.#

#Bring us back to my regular world,# Jian said. Manfred did not respond verbally, but she felt the thrill of confirmation along her bones. She would be glad of the change now. It was too hard—too boring, ultimately—to fly normal hyperspace through this interface. The scale of detail was too small, and the images were not conducive to keeping a pilot alert and ready. Or at least not to keeping her alert and ready: there were bound to be pilots who loved the interplay of the threads of light and the beat of the shuttle as it traced out the contours of virtual space. Virtually any image or set of images could be used to interpret Drive data, as long as it called up the right set of reactions from the pilot. She had once known a woman, a small, golden, perfect creature, who had taken her ships into Drive by ceremoniously brewing a cup of green tea. . . .

The shuttle dimmed, but kept up its steady movement. The plain fabric began to take on shadowy texture and a tinge of green. The enormous metal arms retracted, smoothing themselves into cylinders that vanished one by one until Jian stood again in front of the rapidly solidifying control wheel and rudders, the shrouds and balloon canopy fading into existence overhead. The perfect landscape rolled gently past her, a checkerboard of green broken only here and there by the occasional clump of trees.

#Anything out there I should know about, Manfred?#

#This pattern should continue for some hours,# the construct answered. #The time-slip should persist as well.#

#If it continues, what will that do to our arrival time?# Jian asked idly. Their projected entry into Refuge's system was still a hundred and three hours away, and then there would be at least a day's decelerating flight to the planet itself.

#If the pattern continues at this rate—#

Am I imagining things, Jian thought, *or do I hear disapproval in its voice?*

#—the time-slip will shave five to fourteen hours from the projected passage. This is not a precise estimate; do you want a probability scan?#

#No, thanks,# Jian said. #That's good enough for me.# Red was off-line again, she realized abruptly, and Mitexi with him. *Well, I hope you were impressed, Bi' Mitexi,* she thought, and turned her attention to the *Byron*'s slow drift across the imaginary landscape.

Vaughn arrived early to take over the controls, something Jian had more than half expected. She caught a glimpse of his forming world as she stepped out of the cage—true to form, Vaughn used a yanqui-made Hot Blue interpreter, one that displayed an approximation of what the theoretical physicists thought hyperspace would "look" like, all threads and swirls of light like the veils of a nebula across a telescope's monitor screen—and shook her head at it. *Why use something that could only pretend to reality, that could not ever reproduce what was really out there? Especially when there were more pleasant—and easier to follow—interfaces on the market . . .*

#Nobody said you had to like it, Reverdy,# Vaughn said.

"Whatever makes you happy," Jian answered. "Mitexi asked me to see her after my watch, give her a rundown on Manfred's performance. Anything you want me to tell her?"

There was a moment's pause, Vaughn visibly considering the question. #Not offhand,# he said at last. There was a note in his voice that Jian couldn't place, a thoughtfulness, an uncertainty, she had only rarely heard. #It's a weird program, you got to admit. I think I like it.# The tone was more dubious than the words.

"She'll probably want to talk to you, too," Jian said, "so you might want to give it some thought."

#If she wants a fucking test report, she can fucking give us a test protocol,# Vaughn said.

"Right, Imre, you tell her," Jian answered, and let herself down the ladder. More grumbling followed her, indistinct and irritable, but she ignored him.

She rode the central core down one level, and stepped out of the cylinder into a wash of cool light. Corridors stretched left and right, the bulkheads painted a faint, pearly gray, the deck underfoot covered with a coarsely woven carpet only a few shades darker than the walls. Remembering the layout on the other decks, she turned left, and, as she had expected, it opened out into a long, trapezoidal compartment lined with columns that seemed to be made of gold. Another of the quilted panels stood in the center of the room, a fan-shaped pool of black rocks set at its base. It was like a barbarian temple in a cheap manga; she ran one hand over one of the snakes that twisted around the nearest column, and the eyes opened briefly, glowing red.

"Shit!" The metal shape had not moved, however, even when the eyes opened. She touched the snake again, and kept her hand there even when the eyes opened. Nothing else happened, and she took her hand away. "What is the point of all this?" she muttered, and raised her voice to the panel. "Manfred?"

The construct answered promptly, the black-and-white face emerging from the center of the panel. "Can I help you, Reverdy?"

You can tell me what all this is for, Jian thought, *and, come to think of it, you can tell me just how complex you are, if you can oversee Imre's program and come down here to talk to me. But would you answer if I asked?* Almost certainly not: that would be betraying trade secrets. She said, "I need a guide to Mitexi—to her cabin, if she's there."

"She is." There was a brief pause, and then a creaking noise. Jian turned sharply—the snakes had made her more nervous than she had realized—and saw an arm unfolding itself from the wall. It was real enough, she could hear the sound of long-untended machinery, but bizarrely, beautifully, unfunctional. The hand made a flourishing, theatrical gesture, and plucked a ball of pearly light from the empty air.

"If you will follow the guide," Manfred said. In the same moment, the arm tossed the glowing sphere underhanded, away from the wall, and it drifted to a stop perhaps a meter from Jian.

"Is your main programming managing this," Jian asked, "or is this a subroutine?"

"I am a unified function," Manfred answered, and there was a hint of pride in the synthesized voice. "The question is really meaningless in context."

Right, Jian thought. *Serves me right for asking.* "Thanks," she said, and looked at the ball of light.

"Please follow the guide," Manfred said, and the sphere began to drift toward the door. Jian followed, glancing over her shoulder, and saw Manfred's face vanish from the panel.

The sphere set an easy pace through the pale corridors, past more white-painted rooms splashed with panels and fittings of the same barbaric gold. A golden serving karakuri sat motionless in the center of one room, surrounded by a black stone counter scattered with gold dishes and cups. Its head—another animal mask—was sunk on its heavy-muscled chest, arms splayed limply across the counters. All around it, the carpet rippled as though stirred by a nonexistent wind: a swarm of cleaner karakuri, thousands of them, almost too small to be seen, were at work carrying away the inevitable dust and debris. It was wrong, somehow, that they should go on working, while the lovely statuelike creature was left without function, and Jian looked away.

Mitexi's cabin had unmistakably been intended for the *Byron*'s owner. It occupied fully a quarter of the available volume, and its entrance was guarded by two more of the sculpted karakuri. These stood out from the wall in three-quarter relief, their backs and legs firmly attached to the bulkhead, but arms and head freely mobile. They were female this time, and still not quite human, each one with four arms frozen in a dancer's gesture. They looked as though they had been carved of bone, with beaten gold for their fantastic clothes, but as the sphere approached, the two figures stirred, and the draperies moved with them, a faint whisper of fabric.

"Who?"

The voice, throaty, female, came from neither of the statues. Jian did not bother looking for the speaker—it would be hidden somewhere in the exotic carved foliage over the doorway—and said, "Reverdy Jian."

"Enter."

Overriding the soft voice, Mitexi said, "Come in."

The first room—there were at least two doors leading further into the ship—was surprisingly spartan. A massive status console dominated one wall, while the wall opposite it was filled with the multiple screens and diskreaders of a sophisticated entertainment complex. Other than that, the only furniture was a low, lacquered table and a scattering of cushions across a deck covered with old-fashioned matting. Mitexi was kneeling at the table, workboard in front of her, a fan of hardcopy pages spread out on the mats around her. She was smiling, but the expression was cool and quite remote.

"Do sit down," she said, and gestured to an embroidered cushion set opposite her.

"Thanks," Jian said, and seated herself cross-legged.

"How do you like Manfred?" Mitexi asked. She continued punching glyphs into her workboard, studied the results for a moment, then flipped off the screen.

"As I said earlier, it's a very sophisticated construct," Jian said. "I'm very impressed."

Mitexi's smile widened a little, but she controlled her expression sternly. "How does its response time compare to the construct you have been using?" She looked down at one of the sheets of paper. "I think you said you used Yannosti wireware, but I don't know who wrote your overseer."

"It's a modified Kagami AVL-2 matrix, with some more Yannosti overwrites and a fair number of private-label patches," Jian answered. She waited, but Mitexi did not seem inclined to question further. "As for the response time, it's very good—it is quicker than my system. And the transitions are better, too, both going from display to display and handling individual icons. The prop management is excellent, too." She could hear the approval in her own voice, and deliberately moderated her tone. "Of course, I haven't had much chance to check out its autopilot capabilities. It says it can handle factor-two deviations, but I haven't really seen that tested."

"I would have thought that you had some fairly good examples of Manfred's ability to handle deviation."

"You've been listening in?" Jian made it, just barely, a question, her grin inviting Mitexi to return to the intimacy of the virtual world.

Mitexi stared back coldly. "Of course."

And that for me, Jian thought. *Just as well—never fool around with the boss who signs the checks.* "That was only one time," she said. "The rest of the time I was right on-line with it. I'd like to see more."

"I daresay you'll get the chance," Mitexi murmured, glancing again at her sheets of paper.

"Look," Jian said, "if you want a real assessment of this construct, why don't you set up a proper test protocol? Imre and I have both done them before."

"I don't have time to spend on that," Mitexi said. "And anyway, Kagami—"

Ah, Jian thought, and kept her face expressionless with an effort. *Now we're hearing something. So John Desembaa's friends were right: she is linked up with Kagami.*

Mitexi passed a hand over her eyes, and Jian was shocked by the sudden exhaustion that aged the other's broad face. Then the moment had passed. Mitexi shook herself and said, with a brief and humorless smile, "Well. You must've wondered how I could afford to run a ship like this."

"Sure," Jian said, and couldn't resist the chance to show off. "Of course, I figured the power requirements wouldn't be any different from any other ship this size, even with the fancy karakuri. I just wondered how you'd make back the investment, if you couldn't carry cargo."

"Quite right, too." Mitexi sighed. "This is in confidence, of course."

"Of course," Jian said. They both knew the promise was meaningless: the information was worth nothing on Refuge— no one there would care what a Persephone-based company was doing, and even if someone recognized the value of the information, it would take too long to find someone capable of buying it—and once they returned to Persephone, the knowledge would be out of date.

"I've free-lanced for Kagami for years," Mitexi said. "Off and on. When the *Byron*'s title finally cleared, they approached me. They'd heard rumors about Manfred, and they offered to buy it. I told them I would have to make sure it worked first, and they—" She broke off with a sudden wry smile. "We negotiated. They finally agreed they would pay to get *Byron* spaceworthy, and for the flight itself. In return, I agreed to give them first refusal on the construct matrix."

"So you're making your test flight to Refuge?" Jian asked.

"My brother wrote the damn thing," Mitexi said. "I want him available if I have to do any fine-tuning later on."

"I see," Jian said. *And probably better than you think,* she added silently. *From everything Libra and John Desembaa said, your brother was a better constructor than you; you'll need him, if you're going to fiddle with Manfred's structures.*

Mitexi was frowning slightly, as though she'd read the thought, and Jian said hastily, "I still think you'd get better answers if you gave us a test protocol."

Mitexi's frown turned into an open scowl. "I told you, I don't have time to let you people run tests. There's—Kagami has set—a fairly tight deadline." The scowl shifted to a crooked, angry smile. "After all, the more bugs they find that I don't know about, the lower their price can be."

"Haya," Jian said, and suppressed a sudden yawn. The hours on-line were finally catching up with her; she blinked at Mitexi through watery eyes.

"On the other hand," Mitexi said, and Jian blinked again, focusing her thoughts. "On the other hand, if you and Vaughn could keep a pilot's log, that could be of use."

A proper test pilot's journal, that is, Jian thought, *not just the regular overseer's record.* "I'll have to talk it over with Imre," she said aloud, "but I don't see any problems doing it."

"It would be helpful," Mitexi said. "Thank you." The tone made it clearly a dismissal.

Jian nodded cheerfully, answering the thought behind the

words. "I do need some sleep." She pushed herself up off the cushion—she was tall enough to tower over the other woman, and Mitexi looked up, her expression gone suddenly remote—saying, "I'll talk to Imre, and let you know."

"Thank you," Mitexi said again, and Jian turned and walked out past the wall-bound karakuri.

Back in her own cabin, she instructed Manfred to wake her in eight hours, and crawled into the too-large bunk. She woke from a confused dream of karakuri to the steady pulse of the timer and Manfred's voice saying, "Reverdy, eight hours is past."

Jian shook herself, abruptly aware of a ravenous hunger, and untangled herself from the thin sleepsack. "Thanks, Manfred, you can turn the beeper off now."

"Very well," the construct answered, and the noise stopped instantly.

Jian dressed hastily, trousers and bandeau and the same mesh tunic, and headed for the crew's dining room. To her surprise, Vaughn was there before her, sitting at the table nearest the door and the ladder to the bridge.

"Who's minding the store?" she asked, and moved to the autoserver's input menu. The choices were less limited than usual, but she barely noticed, punching the familiar glyphs by rote.

"Manfred, of course," Vaughn said. "And Red's on-line, doing some maintenance."

The autoserver purred to itself, and finally produced tea and a steaming bowl of eggy rice. A plate of sweet sticks followed, decoratively arranged around a tiny crock of bitter honey. Jian took them all, balancing them carefully one on top of the other, and set them down opposite Vaughn.

"What do you think of Manfred?" she asked, and slid into the remaining chair.

Vaughn shrugged, made a play of being busy with the remains of his own meal—a sandwich of some kind, Jian saw—and she attacked her own food with renewed hunger.

"Are you going to eat all of that?" Vaughn asked.

"Yes," Jian said. "Are you going to answer my question?"

"It's a Spelvin construct," Vaughn said. "So what?"

Jian looked up at him, raised her eyebrows. "It's a damn good construct, Imre, that's what. Elisee isn't nearly as quick."

Vaughn shrugged again. "Mine's pretty much the same."

"Bullshit. I've run your system." Jian finished the last of her rice and dug a sweet stick into the crock of honey. "What've you got against Manfred, anyway?"

"That's just it," Vaughn said. "It's not a fucking person. You're starting to sound like Dreampeace."

"Back off, Imre," Jian said. "All I said was, it's a good system. And, yeh, it's better than mine or yours. That does not make me part of Dreampeace."

Vaughn looked away, made a one-shouldered gesture that Jian knew was meant as apology. "I just don't think it's that good, that's all."

"I don't know what the problem is, then," Jian answered, "but it's your problem."

Vaughn shook his head, less in denial than in frustration. "I don't like the damn thing. It's too—hell, I can't even say what it is, but I'm damn sure it isn't people."

"Haya," Jian said, after a moment. "All right." She paused, studying the other's face. "Mitexi wants us to keep a trial log, as if we had a proper protocol. If you don't want to do it, I'll keep my own."

"I don't know." Vaughn sighed. "No, I'll do it. No problem."

"If it's going to be, don't bother, I don't want to deal with it."

"No, it's all right," Vaughn said, and gave her a quick crooked smile. "Trust me." Before Jian could answer, his gaze shifted, focusing on the doorway. "You all done, Red?"

Jian turned in time to see the technician nod, and Vaughn pushed himself up out of his chair. "Time for me to get back on-line, then," he said, and disappeared up the ladder to the control chamber.

Jian stared after him. There was no need to hurry, unless the ship was drifting out of true, and she could feel none of the faint vibrations that always accompanied those variations. "Manfred, give me a status check?" she asked, and the black-and-white face bloomed on the nearest wall.

"Everything is in order, Reverdy."

"Index of variation?"

"From the projected course, a factor of .93." There was a pause, and then Manfred added, "Imre says there's no need to check up on him; you can take over anytime you want."

The construct's voice was quite without emotion. Jian grinned. "Tell Imre I'll be up in a minute."

"Thank you," Manfred said, and its face vanished from the wall.

Jian's smile faded quickly. She collected her dishes and fed them to the trash eater without really thinking, wondering instead about Vaughn's reaction. Manfred was unquestionably something unusual. She had been running Spelvin constructs for almost fifteen years now, and only once worked with a construct that showed anything approaching Manfred's level of image resolution in creating the virtual world. And for a single construct to provide both that sophisticated worldview and at the same time manage all the subsidiary mecha, the karakuri and the lights and holograms—well, it was like nothing she had ever encountered. *Damn it, I don't think it's people; I've never seen any construct, all the Spelvins included, that counted as people. I don't believe in Dreampeace. But Manfred is something unique.*

She shook herself, and turned away from the still-humming trash eater. *It might be worth my while to do a little systems prying, see if I can find out just what Manfred's limits are. Who knows, maybe I could parlay that into a free-lance test job with Kagami, once Mitexi brings us home.*

The status console in her cabin came equipped with a guide ball, as she had thought she remembered. It was only a toy for a suited pilot—the suit performed all the functions programmed into the ball, from sensing movement and gestural codes to voice recognition, and with a much higher degree of accuracy—but most ships included them as part of the status suite almost out of habit. Jian lifted it, the thick rubber outer coat warm under her fingers, then turned and twisted it until she found the seam dividing the two hemispheres. She pried the halves apart and stared into the interwoven wafers of circuitry. As she had expected, there was an override stitched into the system, a familiar bright-blue array of flecks and lines: that particular bit of solid code would keep her from accessing most of the interesting parts of the *Byron*'s internal controls. There was no way she could detach it without help. She sighed, slid the two halves back together, and went in search of Red.

The technician was still in the crew's dining room, staring at an empty plate. He looked up quickly as she came in, looked away only when she set the ball in front of him.

"I need a favor," Jian said. "There's a governor on the system. Can you remove it? Without affecting function?"

Red shrugged, pushed his plate aside, and reached for the ball. He opened it deftly, then reached into the pocket of his vest for the flat plate of a diagrammer. He laid that over the ball and flipped the switch, studying the patterns in its depths, before he answered.

"Yeh, I can do it."

"Would you?" Jian said, and the technician nodded.
"Thanks," Jian said, and looked around for a data node. There were none within sight range, and she frowned. "Manfred, what's the time?"

"Twelve hours fourteen minutes," the construct answered promptly. "Reverdy, Imre would like you to take over control now."

"I bet he does," Jian muttered, and saw a fleeting smile cross Red's face. The technician saw her looking and bowed his head, letting his hair fall forward around his face. Jian grinned back at him and said, more loudly, "I'm on my way."

Vaughn was waiting impatiently at the edge of the pilot's cage, just barely inside the net of its sensors. #About time,# he said, and added, to the construct, to the ship, #Off-line.#

"Give it a rest, Imre," Jian said—they had both said those lines so many times that neither one needed to think about it anymore—and stepped into the cage of light. #Heh, Manfred, I'm back on line.#

She heard Vaughn snarl something inarticulate and obscene, and then his footsteps heavy on the ladder, and laughed as her world faded into existence around her. She could feel the ship's presence cloaking her, both a set of sensations deep within her body and the illusory response of the "balloon"

in which she stood; could feel, too, Manfred hovering atten-
tive at her side. She laughed again, softly, and the construct
said, #I'm glad you're pleased.#

Jian blinked, startled, and said, #I like piloting.# It was
an inane response, and she knew it. She shrugged the feeling
away. *It's only a construct,* she told herself. *That's just a
written-in comment, part of the script that makes it a Spelvin.*
#Run a projection, would you?# She had chosen those words
at least in part deliberately—it was the sort of phrasing Elisee, and most Spelvin construct, would have to have clarified
for them, translated into their fixed vocabulary of command—but Manfred took it in stride.

#For what period of time?#

#The next eight hours.# That was the basic length of her
responsibility, though if space were rough she would be able
to call on Vaughn for help, and if it ran smooth she could let
Manfred handle most of the work, and stay in charge for an
hour or two longer. #Is the time-slip still in effect?#

#Yes, but it is fading,# Manfred answered. #I project a
return to ordinary temporal flux within four hours.#

#Haya.#

#This is the eight-hour forecast,# the construct continued,
and once again a bright fissure divided the representation of
present hyperspace from the image that rolled in from the
horizon. It was much the same as it had been, an apparently
endless stream of plain square fields, dotted here and there
with clumps of trees and the occasional silver flash of a lake,
the symbols differentiated only by the blued shades that indicated their likelihood. Perhaps three hours in, the terrain
changed a little, went from well-tended fields to a less defined land. It was still green, but less so, and not divided
into fields. Rocks, miniature mountains, broke through the
grassland at intervals, before the image faded back to the
regularity of the squares.

#Hold it, Manfred, run that again,# Jian said, and the con-
struct obediently backed the image. Jian watched it through
again, a plan shaping itself unbidden in her brain. If she set
Manfred to fly that part of the pattern on its own—according
to its predictions, without immediate human intervention—it
would give her a chance to pry into the systems' architecture

without having to explain herself to the construct. And if she warned Mitexi of what she was planning, told her it was part of the test regimen, she could make sure that Mitexi's attention, too, was focused on Manfred's performance, not on any intrusions into the standing systems. She examined the plan again, mentally turning it around and over to view it from all angles, her eyes fixed on the display she no longer fully saw. Yes, it would work, and on several levels. It was exactly what it seemed, a good test of Manfred's inherent ability; it would also give her a chance to find out more about its full capabilities. Ahead of her, the projection rolled to its end, and stopped.

#Good enough, Manfred, thanks. Give me a time-to marker for that bumpy bit.#

There was no spoken response, just the wash of pleasure along her suit, and then the numbers flashing steadily in the air to her left. She nodded, still smiling to herself, and let herself relax into the illusion around her. If piloting had been a dance before, a tense and perfect melding of gesture and movement, instant choice matched by instant answer, this was sleepwalking, a lazy wordless conversation carried in the steady pulse of the standing systems, guided by Manfred's now-inarticulate presence. The unreal landscape drifted past, was subsumed beneath the edge of the balloon's basket, and ceased to exist. The illusory obstacles appeared, and she touched controls that did not truly exist, deflecting the ship away from harm.

The countdown still ticking in the center of her vision reached its last stages, and she dragged herself reluctantly out of her pleasant trance. The grasslands were still in the middle distance, but approaching rapidly. She frowned, seeing that, and Manfred said, with a hint of apology in its voice, #The time-slip has continued to hold steady. It shows no signs of diminishing.#

#How does that affect your capacity to cope with deviation?# Jian asked.

The construct sounded almost affronted. #Not to any significant degree, Reverdy.#

We'll see about that, Jian thought. She said aloud, #Would you open a line to Mitexi, please?# A moment later, the open-channel indicator bloomed just above the control wheel.

#Bi' Jian? Is anything wrong?#

#Not at all,# Jian answered. #There's a fairly bumpy bit of space coming up, and I thought I would use it to check out Manfred's unsupervised flight. I thought maybe you'd want to sit in.#

There was a moment's pause, and Manfred said, a whisper in Jian's ear, #Bi' Mitexi is linking with my sensor output.#

#I trust your judgment,# Mitexi said, almost in the same moment, #but that looks pretty rough.#

#That's what'll make it a good test,# Jian answered. #And since you're short of time . . .# She let her voice trail off, and heard Mitexi sigh.

#I'll be ready to jump in,# Jian said. #Manfred, I'll want you to inform me as soon as the factor of variation reaches 1.5. Or if you have any problems or encounter any uncertainties. Please confirm the instructions.#

#I will inform you as soon as the factor of variation reaches 1.5,# Manfred repeated, #and/or if I have any problems or encounter any uncertainties. I understand, Reverdy.#

I do hope so, Jian thought. #Off-line#, she said aloud, and stepped out of the cage even before the image could disappear.

She stood for a moment in front of the computer console, watching the play of lights and glyphs across the various monitors. Manfred seemed to have things well in hand, and Mitexi certainly showed as tied into the overseer system; even so, she studied the displays carefully, wondering if she were doing the right thing. In theory, there was little risk in allowing the construct to fly the ship into the approaching area of uneven space: the Spelvin constructs were designed to be able to handle that kind of deviation, and hyperspace itself rarely shifted so wildly that a pilot could not realign the fields even if the ship had fallen out of true. And it wasn't really Manfred's piloting skills that worried her, she realized abruptly. It was more the difficulty of tampering with the standing systems without being noticed. The realization was enough to make up her mind. She checked the console a final time—Mitexi was still linked to the overseer, and Manfred was still showing everything in order—and slid down the ladder to the crew deck.

As she had hoped, the guide ball was back in its place on the control board of the status console. She pried it open gingerly, and saw the bright silver flecks of the new connections even before she was sure the governor was gone. Smiling, she closed it again, and touched the keys that switched on the main console. The multiple screens lit, and a faint fuzz of light formed above the holopad, ready to become any three-dimensional image she desired. She stared at it for a moment longer, listening for any sign of trouble from Manfred, wishing she could run this search through her suit instead of the more clumsy guide ball—but that was flatly impossible, would break her connection with Manfred, thus betraying her interest in the system, as well as making it much more difficult for Manfred to get through to her if there were a problem. She sighed and shifted her grip on the ball, groping for the slight dents in the spongy surface that marked the control points.

She found her way into the system easily enough—her second stepfather, whose name she had taken, had been a constructor of some note, and she had learned a lot just watching his conversations—and worked her way through the layers of subsystems, sorting them out until she had a rough idea of what each section was supposed to do. Schematics bloomed on the holopad, and the wallscreens filled with once-familiar glyphs, signs and symbols and the occasional realprint word she vaguely remembered from the time before her stepfather's death. She scowled at them, wishing she had more time, wishing she remembered better—wishing as always that he were living still—and twisted the ball to flip into another set of screens.

Manfred's internal architecture was well hidden, too well hidden for her to find it without alerting the construct itself. *And it has to be in there, too,* she thought, the frown even deeper now in frustration, *but I don't know how to dig it out of wherever it's buried.* All she'd really gained was confirmation of what she had already guessed: Manfred did not merely act as VWS overseer. It was capable of interacting with almost any system on the ship, turning some small corner of its processors toward any and all problems—*if you didn't need a human being, human intuition, to react to hyperspace, it could probably fly the ship all on its own.*

That was a disturbing thought, perilously close to Dreampeace's claims that the best of the Spelvins had crossed the Turing Barrier—after all, that was the visible difference between innate and artificial intelligence, the real-world comprehension that could only be explained and justified by intuition—and she turned it aside, wondering instead what it would be like to own her own copy of the construct. It was the best overseer she had ever seen, and she'd worked with a couple of other systems before settling on the program that became Elisee as the best of an insufficient bunch. Manfred was an enormous improvement over Elisee. Of course, Kagami would have to do some rewriting; there was a lot in there that seemed ship-specific, and that would push the price, especially of a first-run copy, far beyond her reach. *Pity I couldn't just download a copy of the backup files. . . .*

And then again, why not? She sat for a moment frozen, her fingers still on the guide ball, staring at the matrix tree rotating on the holopad. *I've got the storage blocks I use to back up Elisee, and they're empty when she's not on-line; Manfred would fit—* She shook her head, shook the thought away, and twisted the guide ball to extricate herself from the standing system. There were two good reasons why it wouldn't work: first, Manfred would need modification to work as a generic overseer; while either John Desembaa or Libra could make the necessary changes, they would run straight into the second problem. Manfred was, or would be by the time she got back to Persephone, Kagami's program. Owning it, rewriting it, working with it without Kagami's license was inviting serious trouble. Kagami had never been noted for its willingness to share. Still, it would've been good to try Manfred on another ship. She left the thought at that, shut down the console with a wave of her hand, and went in search of Red.

She found the technician in the outer room of the cabin he shared with Vaughn, sitting curled on one of the large cushion-chairs, a bubble-block balanced on his lap. He looked up as she paused in the open doorway, and glanced warily at the half-closed door that led to the bedroom. Vaughn was asleep, Jian interpreted, and she said softly, "I wanted to thank you for fixing the guide ball for me."

Red gave a half shrug, and looked down at the bubble-block.

Jian could see shapes moving in the heart of the bubble-block's transparent display, could hear, very faintly, the steady beat of music: video-manga, old-style, without glyphs or text of any kind. "Red. What do you think of Manfred?"

The technician went very still. Even his breathing stopped for an instant, to resume stealthily as he reached for the bubble-block and switched off light and sound. Jian waited, cocking her head to one side, and the door to the inner room slid back with a hiss.

"It's a construct," Vaughn said, a little too loudly. He was barefoot and shirtless, still belting his workcloth trousers.

Jian looked at him, seeing the eyes still swollen with sleep, pale hair furring chest and belly. "I was interested in what Red thinks."

Vaughn glared at her for a moment longer, then gestured sharply, throwing his hands wide. Jian looked back at the technician, who was watching her from under lowered eyelids. There was a little silence, the sort of pause Jian had learned to wait through, and then Red looked up, for the first time meeting her eyes.

"I'd rather be fucked by people."

Vaughn made a snorting noise, half laughter, half anger. Jian ignored him, still holding Red's gaze. The technician looked back at her steadily, but the mask was in place again, and she knew she would get nothing more. It was an uncomfortable image; Jian looked away first, frowning.

"I told you so," Vaughn muttered.

"Told me what?" Jian snapped. "What is your problem, Imre?"

Vaughn glared back at her, circles brown as bruises under his eyes. "You're sounding a little too much like a Dreampeacer, that's what—you and him both." He jerked his head toward the technician, who lowered his head hastily, but not before Jian had seen the alerted intelligence in his eyes. "This overseer, this Manfred, it's a construct, a goddamn Spelvin construct—and nothing more. There's not a construct ever written was anything more. They're just machines, not people. Not even real machines, either, just virtual, thousands of lines of code, and that's it. They're not people.''

"You think this one is,'' Jian said, and Vaughn took an involuntary step forward, fists clenching.

"That's a fucking lie—''

Jian stared him down, aware of the potential violence, and not precisely afraid. She was taller than he, and not angry; she was aware too of Red's sudden tense readiness and the intensity of his stare. Abruptly, Vaughn's eyes flickered, and he took a step away, shaking his head, angry still, but well in control.

"All right, it feels a lot like what Dreampeace says true AI's going to feel like, but it can't be. That's theoretically impossible.''

"Depends on who you ask,'' Jian said, not ungently.

Vaughn's mouth twisted. "Maybe so. But whatever this construct feels like, I won't believe it's—human.''

He had used the adjective deliberately, to shock, and Jian balked at it. That was a big word, the word that Dreampeace insisted on, the word that caused all the trouble. Certainly Manfred didn't fit that description—though of all the constructs she had ever worked with, it was the one that came closest— She put the thought firmly away. Close wasn't good enough; Manfred remained—Manfred—until proven otherwise.

"Haya, suit yourself,'' she said aloud, and Vaughn scowled again.

"No, you don't get off that easy, Reverdy. You think this thing is people, don't you?''

Jian scowled back, but the question—the demand—was not unreasonable. "No, I don't. At least, I don't think I do, not yet. But it is the most complicated, the best system I've ever worked with, whatever that makes it.''

"Haya,'' Vaughn said after a moment. "That's fair.''

"Thanks a lot,'' Jian said sourly.

"Well, you've been pushing,'' Vaughn muttered.

"And you've been acting pretty weird,'' Jian retorted. She stopped, looked at him curiously, the last spurt of anger dying. "What do you have against Dreampeace, anyway? Most yanquis think they're great."

Vaughn shrugged. "What you've been saying all along, mostly. If Dreampeace gets what it wants, the damn machines'll have more rights—they'll be treated like they were more human—than half the coolies."

That was true, all right, and it was what she had said, but it didn't sound like Vaughn. Jian studied him for a moment, wondering if it was worth pursuing the matter, and Manfred's voice spoke from the wall.

"Reverdy. I have reached a deviation of factor 1.5."

"Damn. Thanks, Manfred, I'll be right up." Jian looked back at the other pilot. "Look, Imre, I'm sorry I pushed you."

Vaughn shrugged, but his expression was faintly rueful. "It's all right. I'm sorry I lost my temper."

"Haya," Jian said, satisfied, and started for the control room.

The lights studding the instrument wall still showed mostly green as she swung herself off the ladder, only one or two flickering toward yellow. "On-line," she said, and stepped into the pilot's cage. The familiar image spun itself around her, the web of sensation that was the ship itself winding warmly around and through her body. Usually, it was a pleasant welcome; this time, with Red's assessment still ringing in her ears, she shied away from the intimacy of the touch. Still, there was work to do. She scanned the unreal landscape, hands and feet already poised on the controls, but Manfred seemed to have things well in hand. There was a slight haze of interference, tendrils like blue smoke coiling around some of the rocks to either side of the balloon's apparent course, but she controlled her first impulse to adjust the controls.

#Manfred, are you monitoring that fog?#

#Yes. All indications show that it is well within our limits. Do you want me to avoid it?#

And that, Jian thought, *is the difference between a construct and a human pilot.* Human pilots were generally willing to make the constant corrections necessary to keep the ship free of all stress, while a construct preferred simply to keep strain on the ship within the tested limits for its hull type. Of course, there were human pilots who flew that way, too. . . . She put that thought aside, and said, #I'll take it now.#

#Very well,# Manfred said, and for an instant Jian thought she heard annoyance in its voice.

#Bi' Jian, do you think it would be better to let the test continue?# That was Mitexi's voice, anxious in Jian's ears.

#I'd rather not,# Jian said. #I think I'm getting a pretty good idea of its limitations, and I'd rather not expose the hull to unnecessary stress.#

#You're the pilot,# Mitexi said, with only slight reluctance, and cut the connection. The open-channel glyph vanished almost before it had time to settle into place.

Jian turned her attention to the landscape in front of her, frowning a little in concentration as she looked for the course that would ease the ship back into perfect alignment. She could feel the ship all around her, pressure and warmth sending subtle message along the wires of her suit, could read a hundred different bits of information in the shapes, the very shadows on the land in front of her. She touched the controls gently, easing the balloon-icon left, and felt the ship's faint trembling fade from her body. The fog vanished, and the false sunlight shone out suddenly, a blaze of warmth that reverberated through her bones. *Not at all like sex*, she thought, *this lasting, languorous content, nothing like it at all. Though if it was* . . . Her thoughts ran dry abruptly, unable to call to mind a single one of her lovers who had ever created a similar feeling. Not even Chaandi, whom she'd known the longest, and with whom she'd shared a flat for four entire weeks before Chaandi had thrown her out, had ever brought with her anything like this. *No, if I'd ever had a lover who made me feel like this, I'd still be with her. Or even him. I wish to hell there were.*

6

The *Young Lord Byron* flipped out of Drive at the end of a hundred-and-six-hour flight. They were ahead of schedule and dead on course, translating down into realspace at precisely the projected point at the edge of Refuge's system. Refuge Administrative Traffic Control acknowledged their existence only grudgingly, their precision not at all, and dispatched a tug to bring them in. They met the tug just inside the orbit of the fourth planet, a nameless gas giant known only as GFR 39, and Jian and Vaughn together prepared to bring the ship into the tug's mating ring. It was a tedious chore, if not particularly difficult, made necessary by the planet's lack of orbital facilities. The *Byron*, like most starships, could not land unassisted; without the tug's support, it would be unable even to enter atmosphere, much less achieve a stable landing. The tug would be needed to regain orbit, too: it was no wonder, Jian thought, the system had long been abandoned on wealthier worlds. Of course, economics alone wasn't enough to explain its survival on Refuge. What kept the Refugee Commission from building an orbital station, and turning the tugs into a fleet of transfer taxis, was less the money than the need to keep full control both of the planet's unstable, polyglot, war-ravaged populations and of traffic to and from the planet.

#Elvis Christ,# Vaughn said. #It's burning chemfuel.#

They were standing together in the pilot's cage, their respective virtual worlds exchanged for an excellent simulation of realspace, so that they seemed to hang suspended in the plane of the system, the bright curve of GFR 39 to their right, the flare of the tug's engines blasting against the pinpoint sun. A targeting grid formed an overlay, pale schematic lines against the darkness.

#Well, what did you expect?# Jian asked. They were working almost directly through the standing systems, Manfred relegated to the background, managing the imagery; she kept her eyes fixed firmly on the mixed display.

#Normal people use gravitics,# Vaughn answered. He stood in the center of a virtual control board, his hands in micromesh optipax gloves moving easily over and through the unreal membranes. To Jian's suit, his fingers left short trails of light as the standing system translated those gestures into complex commands. He was very good at this kind of maneuvering, where the distances were measured in meters and the tolerances in millimeters; Jian leaned back into the standing system's main embrace and let him nurse the *Byron* toward the tug's ring.

#Of course, normal people don't live here,# Vaughn went on, his hands still dancing over the illusory controls, #so I suppose I shouldn't be surprised. I wonder where they get their pilots, anyway.#

#Refugees, I think,# Jian answered, and turned her head in time to see both of Vaughn's eyebrows lift.

#Great. We're trusting our lives to somebody who isn't good enough to get a job that gets him/her off Refuge.# He risked a sideways glance and a quick smile. #I don't suppose you'd want to slide over there and fly the tug.#

#No,# Jian answered cheerfully, and Vaughn shook his head in mock sorrow.

#I didn't think so.#

The target grid floating in the air in front of them changed from pale blue to yellow, and Vaughn's smile vanished, to be replaced by a look of intense concentration.

"XRS *Young Lord Byron*, this is RATC tug 029. You are within one hundred meters of the docking ring."

#Ratsie?# Vaughn said.

#I'll do the talking, Imre,# Jian said, and reached overhead to make the gesture that would open her side of the conversation. "RATC tug 029, this is *Byron*. We confirm that we have passed one hundred meters. We look like we're lined up pretty good."

"You look good to me, too," the tug pilot answered.

#Thank you kindly, Ratsie,# Vaughn murmured, smiling again. He was still busy with the controls, correcting drift with tiny adjustments of the fields, balancing the ship against the system's inherent gravity and the kiss of the solar winds. The *Byron* slid sedately toward the tug, perfectly aligned.

"Fifty meters," the tug pilot said. "And looking good."

Neither Vaughn nor Jian bothered to respond, Vaughn lost in the flurry of last-minute trimming that would bring the ship into the ring with the least disturbance, Jian poised to catch the ship if he made a mistake. In her sight—though not in Vaughn's—the avoidance arrow was already flashing, ready to guide her out of danger; she knew that a similar icon was flashing in the tug pilot's command booth. The ships' systems had already "spoken," agreed on mutually evasive maneuvers that they both hoped they would never use. . . .

"Twenty-five meters," the tug pilot said. "Begin braking, please."

#Imre,# Jian began, and felt the shifting pressure of the maneuver fields as Vaughn adjusted them again to slow the ship still further.

"Twenty meters," the tug pilot said. "Fifteen . . . ten . . . you're in my window now, the alignment's perfect . . . contact."

A flurry of lights ran across the instrument wall, and the image in the pilot's cage changed abruptly, became the walls and clamps of the docking ring itself.

#Cancel direct display,# Jian said. #Give me an exterior projection.#

#You thought I was cutting it too close,# Vaughn said in the same moment.

#I should know better.# Jian blinked as the display adjusted itself, became once again the illusion of space and the bright curve of the gas giant.

#You should.# Vaughn was grinning, still savoring his own skill.

"All seals complete," the tug pilot announced. "Ready to match field frequencies."

#You hear that, Red?# Jian said, and felt, rather than heard, the technician's acknowledgment. #Manfred, give me a heads-up engine readout board.# Numbers and familiar glyphs filled the air in front of her, almost obscuring the more distant stars. She took a final look at the readings, at the same instant assessing the sensations that flowed along her suit wires—the ship's status manifesting itself as a complex but simple sense of well-being, no nagging aches or uncertainties to concern her—and opened outside communications again.

"RATC tug 029, this is XRS *Young Lord Byron*. We're ready to match field frequencies."

"*Byron*, this is RATC 029. Bringing up my field now."

"Go ahead," Jian said, unnecessarily, and felt as well as saw the new frequencies pulse across her display. She gestured, smoothing out the areas of maximum dissonance, and felt Red making his own adjustments at the engineer's controls. The fields wavered for an instant, then slid into harmony. Tension shivered along her suit for a heartbeat longer, and then Red had it matched perfectly.

#Done.#

At the same moment, the tug pilot said, "Match. Down to the last decimal, and in record time. Nice work, your engineer."

"Thanks," Jian said, knowing Red would not answer. "I'll pass that along. Can you give us a time-to for landing?"

"Hold on." There was a pause, static hissing faintly, and then the pilot said, "Looks like about forty-three hours."

"Thank you," Jian said, over Vaughn's groan of disbelief. "You have control."

Now there was nothing to do but wait. On a normal flight, this time would be spent making a final check of the cargo, confirming and reconfirming the delivery arrangements, but Mitexi made it clear she would manage all contact with the Refugee Commission herself. Jian used the time to sleep, deeply and without the ever-present consciousness that she might be summoned to take over the controls, and then spent almost half a day exploring the *Byron*'s lower decks, but even that palled after a while. After all, as Vaughn said, there were only so many things you could do with a triangular compartment.

"Or with safety glass," Jian had said, eyeing yet another convoluted columnar grouping.

"Or with sex," Vaughn had answered, grinning, and beckoned her around to see the entwined shapes carved into the heart of the central spiral.

"Yeh, I did see that before," Jian had said, squinting at them, and Vaughn had laughed.

"Sunshine, I've done it before," he had said, and they had moved on to see what other toys were waiting.

Jian was very glad when the tug finally announced the beginning of their descent to Refuge's main field. She had no part in the landing—it was all the tug captain's responsibility; even in case of an emergency all the *Byron*'s pilots could hope to do was bring the ship back out into orbit—but even so she found herself in the control space, watching from the pilot's cage. The first faint trails of fire curled around her, and Manfred said, in her ear, #We are beginning reentry.#

Jian nodded, letting the suit carry her acknowledgment, tensing in spite of herself as the air hazed from red to yellow, and into white. It was illusion, of course—even more of an illusion than most of the displays, because that fire embraced the tug first, not the *Byron*—but even so it was impressive. She was very aware of Vaughn's presence in her world, watching ghostly from the secondary control station, and Mitexi's more distant presence. There was nothing either of them could do that she could not do, if disaster struck; she put that thought aside, and did her best to ignore them as well.

The air around her was changing color, paling from the dark of space to the brighter blue of atmosphere. The flames reached higher, almost to her waist: the tug's shield was burning off, as it was designed to do, and she could feel the first bite of the planet's gravity against the fields that encased both ships. Then the fires faded, flickering away into a few

last strands of flame, and the ship plunged abruptly into
cloud. Jian blinked, surrounded now by shuddering, indistinct shapes of white and gray, and said, #Manfred—?#

#We are still on the beacon,# the construct answered.
#Speed of descent is slowing.#

#Could've fooled me,# Vaughn said, and Jian allowed her-
self a rueful smile of agreement. The numbers—displayed on
the instrument wall and confirmed by Manfred—might say
that the ship was starting to brake for its landing, but she
couldn't feel it yet. Even as she thought that, the fields bit
more deeply, tightening around her body, and there was a
new pressure beneath her feet. The flashing clouds seemed
to slow slightly, then more perceptibly, as the tug pilot balanced the linked ships against the planet's pull. The clouds
thinned, becoming ragged strands, giving quick glimpses of
the field. Even blued and blurred by their height and the
speed of their descent, Refuge was not a beautiful world. The
seas, just visible to the left in the display, were blue enough,
but the land was grayed, broken here and there with pale-
brown patches that might have been open land, or some unfamiliar vegetation. As the linked ships dropped lower, still
slowing as the braking fields took hold, Jian could see the
strict concentric geometry of the main settlement, and the
wide slagged-slick expanse of the landing field that deformed
the outermost circles. She could make out the field's support
buildings as well, and the spindly towers of the main communications center. Then a new cloud—gray dust, mixing
with the steam of the repulsor rockets—rose to surround her;
she held her breath instinctively, and had to force herself to
breathe again, laughing a little at her own reactions.

The *Bryon*, guided and supported by the tug, settled easily
down onto the planet's surface, with only a gentle thud to
betray exactly when they'd landed.

#Nice going,# Vaughn said, for once with genuine admi-
ration, and Jian nodded, reaching to sign for an open line to
the tug. Before she could complete the gesture, however, the
tug pilot's voice sounded in her ears.

"Safe down, *Byron*."

"We confirm, RATC 029," Jian said. "That was nice
work—nice landing."

"Thanks, *Byron*." For a moment, the tug pilot's voice sounded almost human, but it regained its formality instantly. "I am turning you over to customs now. Have a nice stay."

#Real likely, on Refuge,# Vaughn said.

Jian nodded wholehearted agreement, but let none of that show in her voice as she answered, "Thank you, RATC tug 029. We will stand by for customs."

"I'll take care of that," Mitexi said.

#Suit yourself,# Jian answered, and let the other woman respond when a new voice announced that Commission Customs wanted to come aboard. #Off-line, Manfred.#

She made her way down to the crew deck to find both Vaughn and Red sitting in the common room, staring at the full-wall display piped in from the exterior cameras. It showed the port buildings, familiar four-story, foursquare colonial construction, cheap prefab buildings meant to be replaced as soon as possible. The nearest of the group, with the conglomerate-wide symbol for customs painted above the main entrance, showed the worst signs of wear, its once-square support pillars eroding at the edges, rust-red stains like drooping rags spreading across the pale-beige walls.

"Customs is on board," Vaughn said, unnecessarily, and then saw the direction of her gaze. "Ugly, isn't it?" He went on without waiting for her answer. "Mitexi wants us to stay up here while she talks to the customs team. I guess she's got some negotiating to do, if she wants to get her brother off with her."

"But not with customs, surely," Jian began, and slid into a chair next to Red.

Vaughn shrugged. "I don't know who handles refugee releases—it might well be customs."

"Manfred?" Jian asked, and the other pilot scowled.

"Why bring him into it?"

"Because I'd like to get an answer," Jian said. "Manfred, who handles refugee release—or emigration—on this planet?"

There was a pause, as though the construct had to search for the answer, and then Manfred said, "The Refugee Commission approves such release, contingent on the status of the petitioning parties, the job or other compensation being made available, the willingness of the registered refugee—"

"Thanks, that's enough," Vaughn interrupted, and when Jian glared at him, he shrugged. "The Refugee Commission handles it. So maybe she's got extra duty to pay on a ship like this, I don't know."

"I don't either," Jian said. She sighed, stared at the dirty gray buildings crowding up behind the fence that defined the port area. "I wonder if we ought to find out."

"I didn't think you'd go for that," Vaughn said, grinning.

"This time, yes," Jian answered. "Any ideas?"

"Maybe—" Vaughn began, and Red looked up sharply, the movement as effective as a shout. In the sudden silence, they all heard the soft thudding of feet in the corridor outside, and then Mitexi was standing in the open doorway, a man and a woman in the pale-blue uniform and heavy sensor packs that marked local customs throughout the rim worlds flanking her.

"This is my crew," Mitexi said to the woman. "They're all living here, on the crew deck."

If the customs woman heard the implied insult, she no longer cared about that sort of thing. "Papers, please?" she said, and looked over her shoulder at her partner. "You go ahead with the scan. I'll catch up."

Jian reached into her belt for the six-centimeter-wide disk that contained all her identification and licenses, and the other two did the same. The customs woman slid them one by one into her portable verifier, scanned rapidly through the contents, then returned them. "Everything's in order. Will you be wanting to go traveling, outside the port fence?"

Jian shrugged, and Mitexi said, "No, I don't think they'll need to."

"Hey," Vaughn said, and Jian waved for him to be quiet.

"If special permission's required," she said, "we might as well go ahead and get it over with."

"You shouldn't need anything outside the port," Mitexi said again, rather irritably.

Jian shrugged again, aware that the customs woman was watching them both intently. "You never know what you have to buy outside the port areas."

Mitexi was equally aware of the customs woman's interest.

"Go ahead, then. I trust your judgment." Despite her best effort, Jian could still hear the reluctance in her voice.

The customs woman seemed not to have heard. "You need a registry card to enter and leave the port," she said. "I can provide them, if you want"—Jian nodded, and the customs woman went on, her fingers busy on the verifier's touch-plate—"but you should be careful not to lose them, because it'll be very difficult to reenter the port-pale without your card." She looked up then, with a fleeting smile that transformed her plain face and wide mouth. "There's a bit of a traffic in such things, so I'd advise not letting them out of your sight—not out of your hands is even better."

"I'll remember that," Vaughn said, and Jian nodded. It was only to be expected: in order to keep less-than-desperate people from taking advantage of Refuge's promised support, anyone listing him/herself on the Refugee Commission's rolls automatically forfeited the right to leave the planet without the Commission's permission, a permission usually granted only after proof that an off-world job had been provided. Cards that granted entrance to the port area—and thus access to the crews of visiting ships who could conceivably be persuaded or bribed to smuggle someone offworld—would naturally become extremely valuable items.

The verifier whined sharply and spat three stiff wafers into the customs woman's waiting hand. She glanced over them, then handed them all to Jian, who took her own and handed the others on. "These're good for this month, local reckoning. That leaves you three weeks, that's eighteen standard days."

"That should be more than ample," Mitexi said, rather sourly. She fixed her amber eyes on Jian. "I will be riding back to the main port building with these people. I want to get started finding Venya as soon as possible. I would appreciate it if you and Ba' Vaughn did not go into the port area until I've located him."

The tone of her voice made it very clearly an order, and Jian acknowledged that with a wry smile. "Haya."

"Then that's settled." Mitexi looked at the customs woman, gave her a frosty smile. "I appreciate the ride, bi'."

''No problem,'' the customs woman said, and turned as her partner reappeared in the doorway. ''All set, Markis?''

''Everything's in order,'' the man answered, and the customs woman turned back to Mitexi.

''If you'll come with us, then, we'll be going by the registry office.''

''Thank you,'' Mitexi said austerely, and the three swept out together.

Jian remained staring at the little plastic wafer that was her key to the starport. Its surface shimmered as though there were a layer of iridescence over the plain white card, but she could feel the roughness of data notches when she ran her thumbnail experimentally over the surface: the shifting color was a part of the material.

''The hell with that,'' Vaughn said. ''Let's go into town.''

Jian lifted an eyebrow at him. ''You were the one who didn't want to go to Refuge at all, much less travel on the surface.''

''I want to know what she's up to,'' Vaughn said.

''Looking for her brother, Imre, that's what she's up to.'' Jian shook her head thoughtfully. ''I don't think we should rush into this. There's a lot going on we don't know about.''

''Can you think of a better way to find out about it?'' Vaughn retorted.

''Several,'' Jian said.

''Such as?''

Vaughn was grinning broadly, and Jian glared at him. She was saved from having to come up with an immediate answer by a sharp rattling noise from the wallscreen, as though a handful of pebbles had been thrown against the camera lens. They could hear the same sound directly, though much fainter, something small and hard slapping against the hull of the ship.

''What the hell was that?'' Jian said, and Vaughn shook his head, the grin gone as fast as it had appeared. ''Manfred?''

The sound came again, and this time Jian caught a glimpse of something, a streak of gray-white—something—carried in a gust of wind. It was almost invisible against the gray-white sky.

"Reverdy?" The construct's voice sounded briefly apologetic.

"What's causing that noise?"

There was a moment's silence, and then Manfred answered, sounding even more apologetic than before. "It's a meteorological phenomenon, Reverdy. It's sleeting."

"Sleeting?" Jian asked.

"Rain in the form of very small ice pellets," Manfred answered.

Jian looked back at Vaughn. "Are you sure you want to go into town, Imre?" She had heard of rain, of course, even been caught in it once, on Baldur; she had heard of snow, too, but never of something in between.

"I suppose we don't have to go right now," Vaughn agreed. "Besides, you said you had a better idea?"

Not really, not yet, Jian thought, *but I'll be damned if I'll admit it.* "Why not let Manfred keep an eye on her?" she said. "I bet he can tie into the port connections, see who she talks to and about what. . . ."

Vaughn was hesitating, obviously torn, and Jian, warming to the idea herself, said, "That way, if we did decide to go into the town, we'd know precisely where Mitexi was, so we wouldn't have to worry about running into her."

"If it can do the work," Vaughn said.

Jian spread her hands. "Manfred? What do you say?"

"If you are asking whether I can monitor Bi' Mitexi's activities in the port and possibly in the associated city by monitoring the connections," Manfred said, "yes, I can do that, provided always that her activities intersect with the connections. They are not as extensive as on Persephone."

"That's good enough for me," Jian said, and looked at Vaughn, who made a face.

"Well, it is limited—"

"Don't be difficult, Imre," Jian said, and Vaughn broke off, laughing softly, this time at himself.

"All right, let's do it."

"Confirmed," Manfred said. "I will begin monitoring."

"This course of action is not to be revealed to Bi' Mitexi

except with my permission," Jian said, without much hope, but to her surprise Manfred answered at once.

"Confirmed."

"Good enough," Vaughn said, and Jian shook her head at him.

"No, Imre, we—I—am not leaving the ship this minute. Let's eat."

"Haya," Vaughn said, quite cheerfully, and turned to the food services console. Jian followed him, more slowly, staring again at the image in the wall. The wind was still strong— another plume of something, sand or dirt this time, swirled across the fused earth of the field—but the precipitation seemed to have ended. Jian shivered, thinking about snow, about frozen rain, and touched the buttons that would bring her a bowl of hot noodles topped with a mound of onion relish.

"Heh, Manfred," Vaughn said, and turned away from the enormous teapot. "Show us a map of the city."

The scene in the wall faded slightly, and a network of lines appeared over it. Jian drew her own cup of tea and seated herself next to Vaughn, turning sideways a little to face the wall.

It looked like an ordinary colonial city-plan, right-angled streets carving out a grid of identical squares that filled the thirty square kilometers that lay between the starport and the main administrative complex. A single broad road connected the two sections, and another double-wide road bisected it midway: the standard layout on newly settled worlds. But there the resemblance ended. Instead of the twin parks that capped the ends of the cross road—the easternmost inevitably named after the first-in colony ship, the western after the discovering ship—a network of irregular lines fanned out from the city, as though the plotter's virtual lines had tangled and been dropped in disgust, the streets laid out just as they had fallen. Jian frowned, and Vaughn said, "What the hell is all that?" He gestured vaguely at the screen.

Manfred answered, "Those areas are outside the direct authority of the Refugee Commission. There seems to be no properly constituted local authority."

"Shantytown," Vaughn guessed, and Jian nodded her

agreement. Even on Refuge—maybe especially on Refuge—there would always be some part of the population that refused to cooperate with whatever government was in existence.

"Lovely." Jian drank the last of the cooling broth and fished a final noodle out of the bottom of the cup.

"So what do we do next?" Vaughn asked. He looked again at the map, sleet and dust now mixing in the image behind it, briefly veiling the crumbling towers.

"I say we wait until we know what Mitexi's doing," Jian answered. "We should know soon enough." She stood easily, slipped the emptied cup into the cleaning slot. "Let me know, somebody, when you hear something."

"Right," Vaughn said, and in the same instant Manfred answered, "Very well, Reverdy."

Vaughn made a face, but Jian ignored him, collected her tea, and headed back to her cabin. Somewhat to her surprise, he didn't follow; she settled herself on the thick cushion chair, and fitted the first of Chaandi's manga into the bubble-block. It was easy to lose herself in the intricate story line and the elliptical, quick-cut narrative, and she found herself replaying sections to catch the detail she had missed. She looked up once to see that almost two hours had passed; she looked up again only when Vaughn tapped on her door.

"Have we got news, Reverdy."

"Oh, yeh?"

Vaughn grinned. "Oh, yeh. Mitexi's filed papers with the Refugee Commission—"

Jian lifted an eyebrow. "So?"

"So she didn't go to the Directory afterwards—I had Manfred check it out, Venya Mitexi's long off the rolls—but she didn't even bother asking. What she did do was tie into the regular connections, and come up with a guy named Dau'l Seki. Manfred pulled his listing, and he's a missing-persons expert. A bounty hunter. Which means Venya Mitexi doesn't want to be found. And Mitexi Minor knew that before she started."

"You've been a busy boy, Imre." Jian flipped off the bubble-block, buying time. It wasn't that odd that Mitexi Major had chosen not to be listed on the main directories; a lot of people on Refuge were hiding from something—*but I wish to hell I knew what, or who, he was running from. And I'd really like to be sure it wasn't his sister.* "So?" she said again, and Vaughn sighed.

"Look, Reverdy, it's damn strange that she, Mitexi Minor, knew perfectly well that her own brother wouldn't be listed on the rolls. And I think it's even stranger that she picked a bounty hunter. Especially this one." Vaughn smiled. "I checked his record, once I'd got the license numbers. He's had a couple of questionable calls, a couple of 'accidental' deaths that probably weren't accidents at all. I think there's a good chance she's out to do him in."

"There's no profit in killing him," Jian began. "He made the damn construct. . . ." But there *was* profit to be made from Mitexi Major's death, if he still owned any rights in the construct, and if Mitexi Minor's plans didn't match his—*for example, if he was Dreampeace, like John Desembaa and Libra both said, and she wants to sell Manfred to Kagami.* "All right, I see it. What do you think we ought to do about it?"

"I think we ought to do some looking of our own. See if we can maybe find Venya Mitexi before she does, or at least be there when she finds him."

Jian considered the suggestion, tilting her head to one side. It made a certain sense, if they were willing to risk seriously annoying Mitexi Minor, and her patron-to-be Kagami Ltd.— *quite a risk,* Jian thought, *except that, if Libra and John Desembaa are right, Mitexi Major is, or was, a man worth risking a lot for.* "How do you propose we go about it?"

"Ah." Vaughn smiled, a satisfied, cat-in-cream look she had learned to distrust. "Let me show you something."

Jian followed him back into the crew room. There was a monitor setup on one of the tables that hadn't been there before, and the wallscreen was blank, a plain wall again. Red was sitting to one side, well away from the monitor, head down, looking at nothing. There was something different about him, as well. Jian looked again, and saw a new tension tightening his shoulders.

"Here, look at this," Vaughn said, and spun the monitor display on its well-oiled bearings. Jian looked at the screen—

a page out of the city directory, a name she didn't know, and a set of contact codes—and looked back at Vaughn.

"Avelin," Vaughn said, still with that deep satisfaction in his voice. "Avelin's on Refuge, and"—he touched the screen, the gesture almost a caress—"he's bounty hunting."

"So?" Jian asked when Vaughn said nothing more, and did her best to keep her own voice calm, without expectation.

Vaughn looked at her as though he'd just remembered she was there. "The connections are pretty limited here, Manfred says it can't track Mitexi by itself."

"Not with better than eighty-percent accuracy," the construct interjected.

Vaughn went on as though it hadn't spoken. "So I figured, we get Red to ask Avelin to help us out, track Mitexi. And Avelin would do that for you, wouldn't he, bach?"

Red did not respond at once, did not even look up, his thick hair falling forward protectively to screen his face. Jian frowned, uneasy, and bit her tongue to keep from prodding. Then, quite suddenly, Red pushed himself up out of his chair, the movement uncommonly without grace.

"Well?" Vaughn's voice stopped him in the hatchway.

"Juel Avelin's a thug—always was, always will be. We don't want to deal with him."

It was the longest sentence Jian had ever heard the technician utter, and the most heartfelt. She lifted an eyebrow, glancing back at Vaughn, but the other pilot's eyes were fixed on Red's back, a faint, malicious smile just touching the corners of his mouth.

"So were you, bach, but you grew out of it."

Red's shoulders twitched at that, but he said nothing.

"From all accounts, he's gone—well, almost straight, since Bahati . . . died." Vaughn's smile widened slightly, as though he were savoring some private pleasure, then vanished. "Avelin owes you—owes me, for you. I'm calling it in."

"Hold it," Jian said. She kept her voice pleasant enough, but Vaughn heard the anger in it, and his attention snapped back to her, though he kept one eye on the still figure in the doorway.

"I think," Jian went on, "you'd better tell me precisely

what you have in mind.'' Vaughn's gaze wavered, and she hardened her voice. ''Give, Imre.''

The other pilot shrugged one shoulder. ''Juel Avelin used to be Konstantin Bahati's right hand.''

''This should endear him to me?'' Jian asked.

''Thugs have their uses,'' Vaughn answered, with another smile as edged as a knife. ''Right, Red?'' The smile vanished, and he turned to face Jian completely, though she was aware that this time it was just a pose, that the other's real target was still the technician. ''We need someone who knows Refuge, if we're going to find out what Mitexi's up to. Yeh, Avelin's a crook—but he owes me a favor, for taking Red off his hands after they got out of jail. I think he'll track Mitexi for us, and for cheap, better than that damn construct of yours could do.''

''Not mine,'' Jian said, and was momentarily startled by the intensity of her denial.

''Whatever.'' Vaughn shrugged. ''But better than a fucking machine.''

Jian hesitated—Vaughn's argument made sense, but she knew enough about Bahati's organization to want to avoid any contact with his associates—and Red said, very softly, ''Avelin owes you, Imre. But not for me.''

Jian looked up quickly, to see the technician's face for once unshadowed, his stare fixed on Vaughn. *His eyes are blue,* she thought irrelevantly, and then, *I didn't know he set limits, ever. I didn't know he could.*

''Whatever,'' Vaughn said again, but his voice was less impatient, held the ghost of a concession, an apology. Red's head dipped infinitessimally, and then he looked away.

''I don't think we can rely on the machine,'' Vaughn said to Jian. ''Not entirely. And even if we could, we'd still want a human guide.''

That was true, especially on a world like this one. Jian grimaced, but nodded. ''All right, call him—if Red's willing.''

''Well?'' Vaughn demanded. Red did not turn back to face them, but, slowly, he nodded.

''I'll call.''

"Good," Vaughn said, and there was a double satisfaction in his tone. "Good enough, bach."

"Hold on a minute," Jian said. "Manfred, can you track us if we go into the city? Discreetly—that is, without this Avelin knowing you're doing it?"

"There are tracking buttons in ship's stores," the construct answered serenely, blind to the scene that had been played out before it. "I can follow those at a distance of up to two hundred fifty kilometers. If you remain in the city center, I can follow you on the local connection."

"I say we should carry the buttons," Jian said. "And stay as close to the connections as possible." She stared hard at Vaughn, who nodded.

"Haya, that makes sense." He turned to look at Red. "You going to make that call?"

Red did as he was told, touching the keys that adjusted the monitor's function, changing it from internal terminal to an external communications node. The screen stayed fuzzy for what seemed to be a long time—Jian, standing facing him, could hear the soft hiss of static—but then the connect signal chimed, and a voice said, "Yes?" It was a surprisingly cultured voice, Urban-accentless: not at all what Jian had expected. The tone changed, sharpened as the screens focused and he saw who it was, but it did not lose its easy note of aristocracy.

"Saa, Red. What are you doing on Refuge?"

"Imre asked me to call," the technician answered, expressionless, and there was a sound of soft laughter from the monitor screen. Hearing it, Jian wished passionately that she could look over Red's shoulder, but one look at the technician's shuttered face ruled out that possibility.

"So. And what did Imre want?"

"We need to keep an eye on somebody while we're here," Red answered. His eyes flicked away from the screen, to Vaughn, and back to Avelin. "We'll pay you."

Did he mean the insult? Jian wondered. Because insult it was, no mistaking it; it was there in the tone and in the very emptiness of his face. The awareness of it was there in Avelin's voice, too, despite his best attempt to hide it.

"Imre and I can talk about payment. What is it he wants done?"

Something, a ghost of an expression—anger, perhaps, or hurt, or the memory of either—flickered in Red's face and was gone. "What we want," he said, without emphasis, "is to track somebody."

Vaughn stepped forward then, into the monitor's camera range. "Somebody's hired another bounty hunter to find someone, and we want to know if she finds him. And we'd like to find him first."

"How good to see you again, Imre," Avelin said, "you and Red both." There was a pause then, and Jian wished again that she could see the screen. "I can do your job, yes," Avelin said at last, "but the price will be contingent on who and what you want me to find. I assume this 'she' you mentioned is an off-worlder?"

"That's right," Vaughn said. "The name's Mitexi."

Jian thought she heard, very faint, a quick intake of breath, but could not tell if it was Red or Avelin who had made the sound. Avelin said, "Mitexi what?"

"Meredalia. Mitexi Minor, they call her." Vaughn eyed the screen warily, as though he'd heard the same noise and couldn't read it either. "She's looking for her brother Venya. And, like I said, we want to find him first."

"Venya Mitexi," Avelin said, and Vaughn nodded. "I can do it. The price—" He paused, and Jian could almost hear the smile in his voice. "Five hundred, Urban cash. For old times' sake, Imre."

Jian drew breath to protest, and Vaughn said, "Agreed. One hundred up front—for old times' sake."

"Agreed," Avelin said. "I'll start a trace running, on both of them. I'll let you know when I find something."

"Haya," Vaughn said. "We'll keep in touch." He cut the connection before Avelin could answer.

"That's a lot of money, Imre," Jian said. Red looked up at her in wary agreement, and looked away.

Vaughn shrugged. "We can charge it to the co-op, and they can charge it to Mitexi. I think that'd be appropriate."

"Yeh, but we have to pay him first." Jian nodded to the now-silent monitor. "How do you propose to do that?"

"I've got the money, or I can get it, anyway," Vaughn answered. "I thought you'd be willing to help out."

Jian nodded. "Yeh, I'll pay my share. But you should've asked me first."

Vaughn hesitated, then, reluctantly, nodded back. "Haya. I'm sorry."

"So now we wait," Jian said, and looked at the empty wallscreen. "Manfred, can you track what this Avelin is doing?"

"Insofar as it occurs on the connections," the construct answered, "yes."

"Do so," Jian said, "and keep us informed."

To everyone's surprise, however, Avelin called again five hours later, before Manfred had done more than follow a few contacts along the connections. Manfred routed the call into the main crew room without being asked, and called the crew. Jian arrived just as Vaughn settled himself in front of the monitor. He looked up once, gave her a fleeting, crooked smile, and turned his attention to the monitor again.

"So you've found him?"

"I've found them," Avelin corrected. He sounded faintly, dryly, amused. "Mitexi Major and Minor, both."

"Damn," Jian said softly, and Vaughn frowned.

"Does that mean Mitexi Minor's already found him? The deal's off in that case, sunshine."

"I didn't say that," Avelin said. "I've found Mitexi Major. Mitexi Minor—your employer, I notice—is getting closer."

"You mean her bounty hunter, what's his name—"

"Seki. Dau'l Seki." Avelin supplied the name without hesitation. "He's quite good."

"So I gather," Vaughn muttered. "Can you get us to Mitexi Major before they find him?"

Avelin made a soft noise that might have been a kind of laughter. "Maybe. But I would want to be paid first."

"That can be arranged."

"Then if you can get the cash into my hands soon enough, yes, I can."

"It can be arranged," Vaughn said again. "How long do we have?"

"Meet me at the starport main gate in half an hour," Avelin answered. His voice hardened abruptly. "Have the cash in hand, Imre, Urban cash."

"We'll be there," Vaughn said, and broke the connection.

"Do you have the money?" Jian asked.

"Yeh, in general vouchers." Vaughn made a face. "They'll do."

"They're about the only thing guaranteed in this whole job," Jian said. "Manfred, where are the tracking buttons stored?"

"A set of five is kept in the personal effects locker of each crew cabin," the construct answered. "Each one has a battery guaranteed for fifty hours of continuous use."

"So we should only need one," Vaughn said, and Jian smiled in perfect agreement.

"Which means we'd better each carry two." She looked at the unlit wallscreen, remembering the scene it had displayed earlier. "What's the weather like outside, Manfred? And what's the local time?"

"The present temperature is nine degrees," Manfred answered. "Occasional mixed precipitation has been falling at intervals, and that is expected to continue through the night. It is fourteen hours by the local clock—two standard hours after planetary noon."

"Cold, then," Vaughn said, and shook his head at the irrelevance of his own comment. "Come on, let's get moving."

Jian took the time to shrug on one of the heavy undershirts she had bought before leaving Persephone, and tucked the heaviest of her head shawls into the pocket of her coat as an added protection. She found the tracking buttons, collected two of them, and slipped them and—after only a heartbeat's hesitation—her kisu knife into the jacket's pocket as well. The heavy plastic should be virtually invisible to the port sensors, and the flip knife had come in handy more than once before. Briefly, she regretted Persephone's strict arms laws, but put that aside as pointless.

"Reverdy," Manfred's voice said from the wall, the black-and-white face appearing with the first word, "Imre says that the taxi is on its way, and he is waiting at the main hatch."

"Tell him I'll be there," Jian said.

Red was waiting in the hatchway, too, standing at Vaughn's shoulder to stare out of the open hatchway. As always, he looked over his shoulder at the first sound of her footsteps, and Vaughn turned at his movement. "Damn taxi should be here any minute."

Jian nodded, shivered as the first gust of wind curled in through the open hatch, bringing with it a stinging spray of sand. It was cold—*Refuge's winter,* she remembered—and she reached into her pocket for the head shawl. She draped it over her head and knotted the ends around her neck, wincing as another blast of sand struck the ship.

"There," Red said, and pointed. A little open-bodied run-about was making its way across the fused earth of the field, obviously heading for the *Byron.*

"Lovely," Vaughn muttered, and pulled up the hood of his jacket. "Let's go."

The *Byron's* exterior elevator carried them down to the tug's docking ring, where a movable stairway had been snugged up against the side of the ship. The wind seemed stronger than ever, and Jian was glad to see that the stairs were secured to the tug's side with heavy bolts and strapping. The taxi pulled alongside as they reached the bottom of the stairs, and the driver, a round, fair woman in ill-fitting coveralls and earpads pushed onto the back of her head, leaned across to trigger the passenger doors.

"You're going to the admin building?" she asked, raising her voice to carry over the steady rush of the wind, and when Vaughn nodded, motioned to the seats. "Hop in."

Her accent was different from that of the customs crew. Jian looked more closely, and saw bright-orange words sprawling across the pass pinned to her collar: guest-worker. *A refugee herself, then.* It was enough to discourage conversation, and in any case the deep cough and rattle as she started the engine made it hard to hear. The noise steadied to a rumble, and Jian settled back in her seat, frowning. It was not like her, this unease, and Jian couldn't quite define its source; she was glad when the taxi ground to a halt outside the largest of the blocky port buildings.

"Main administration," the driver said, and gave them a look that smoldered with envy. Jian looked away, angry—at herself, at the system, at the driver for reminding her of power and powerlessness—and saw the same annoyed discomfort reflected in Vaughn's face.

"Let's go," Jian said, and did not look back when the taxi clashed its gears and pulled away with a snarl from the stressed engine.

The inside of the main administration building was much like its exterior. It had not been intended as a permanent structure, and that showed in the rough surface of the poured stone and the exposed, color-coded pipes that carried the wires and lesser conduit that powered the building's systems. The main entrance hall, with its old-fashioned directory kiosk and permanent display boards lining the long walls, seemed almost disused, the boards darkened and empty, only a single securitron occupying the booth by the triple doors. Most of the light, and a steady murmur of voices, came from a side hallway—a crowded side hallway, Jian realized, maybe a hundred people waiting in a more or less patient line outside a doorway, standing under a sign she could not read. A second, smaller sign stood at the end of the hallway itself, an arrow pointing down the length of the line: BENEFIT ADJUSTMENTS. Jian shivered again, not from the cold, and looked away. The hallway opposite had a sign, too, but it pointed to a half-closed door without a single person waiting outside it It read EMIGRATION.

The securitron rose to his feet as they approached and stepped out of his booth to meet them, lifting a hand to stop them at the doorway. "You're from a ship in port?"

"That's right," Jian said. "What papers do you need?" He was more heavily armed and armored than the security she was used to: his coveralls were made of armor-mesh and stiffened across the chest by a solid plate of something; he carried a heavy blastrifle slung over his shoulder. A brace of gas grenades hung at his belt, and Jian eyed him with wary respect.

"Did you check in with customs, get a card from them?" the securitron asked, and Jian nodded. "Then that and your regular papers're all I'll need."

Jian produced card and ID disk from her belt, and handed them across. The others did the same, and they stood waiting while the securitron ran each one through a small scanner. There were Peacekeeper badges on his shoulders, Jian realized slowly, and a tidy handful of battle ribbons, as well as the more familiar Conglomerate Ports Authority markings.

"I know they told you, but I have to tell you again," the securitron said. "Don't lose these cards. They're your key to getting back into the port area."

"Right, we understand," Jian said, and tucked her identification back into her belt.

Outside the sun glinted briefly through the thinning clouds, but there was no warmth in the pale light. It shone momentarily off the barrels of the late-model cannons mounted on the all-purpose war sleds parked at the base of the entrance stairs, and vanished again.

"Lovely world," Vaughn said, looking at the guns, and Jian allowed herself a twisted smile.

"This was your idea, sunshine."

Vaughn ignored her, and started down the cracked steps. Red gave her a quick glance that might have signaled his agreement, and followed.

Avelin was waiting just beyond the sweep of the war sleds' guns, a tall, slender figure sitting on the nose of a battered runabout. He was not at all what Jian had expected from his voice, not at all Urban-looking; she watched with bemused curiosity as he slid off the housing and came to meet them. His face was weathered—ravaged by weather somewhere, Jian amended—and further marred by a pair of deep parallel scars running along one bony cheek. There was a third scar, fainter than the others, just below them, and a fourth on his neck, running into his collar. He frowned, seeing her, the scars tightening fractionally, and said, "You didn't tell me you had a partner, Imre."

"That's right," Jian said pleasantly. "I trust it won't be a problem."

Avelin shook his head, though his eyes were still wary. "No problem. No charge."

"Good," Vaughn said. "This is Reverdy Jian. Reverdy, this is Juel Avelin."

Jian extended a hand, yanqui style, and Avelin took it,

bowed slightly too, in compromise. "So you've found Venya Mitexi," Jian said.

Avelin nodded, glanced at Vaughn. "Assuming you have the money, of course."

"I have it." Vaughn reached into the pocket of his coat, produced two booklets of the thin plastic foils. Avelin accepted them, and paged quickly but carefully through each one before he nodded.

"All right. The rest on delivery."

"The rest on return to the ship," Jian corrected softly. She smiled without sincerity. "We none of us want to be walking around with that much cash on us."

"On return to the port," Avelin said, and nodded to the blocky building to the left of the administrative complex. It bore the glyphs of half a dozen Conglomerate banking houses. "I'm sure one of them will take your credit."

"That's fine," Jian said, and Vaughn said, "Come on, let's go."

"We're not in that much of a hurry," Avelin said. "Trust me."

Vaughn made a rude noise, and Avelin smiled again, looked back at Jian. "We'll take my bus."

Jian nodded, and followed him down the last few stairs to the runabout drawn up against the low curb. It had seen better days, certainly—*like Avelin himself*, she added silently— but the main parts seemed to be in working order. Avelin popped the low canopy, and gestured to the passenger seats.

"Make yourselves comfortable. One of you will have to sit up front with me." He looked at Red for the first time, the smile twisting the scars along his cheek. "Interested?"

Red looked away, expressionless, skin like marble in the cool light, and made no other answer.

"I'll sit with you," Jian said gently. "I like to see where I'm going."

Avelin looked back at her, the smile fading, blinked once, readjusting his assumptions. "All right," he said, and pointed again to the battered seats. "Shall we go?"

Jian climbed in beside the driver's seat, did not fasten her safety webbing until Avelin was strapped in beside her. There was a tommy-stick in a clip under the control board, and a heavy double-action pellet-gun tucked down between the seats: *and probably at least one other weapon put away somewhere out of sight,* Jian thought. She said aloud, "Do you get a lot of trouble, or are you just careful?"

Avelin glanced at her, hands and feet busy on the cumbersome controls, and said over the sudden purr of the engine, "Both. But mostly careful. I try not to let a job become . . . troublesome."

Jian nodded, as much in approval as anything. "Where are we going?"

She didn't really expect a comprehensible answer, but to her surprise Avelin released the wheel long enough to punch numbers into the double bank of keys set into the center of the control board. A section of the front canopy lit, displaying a series of pale lines and dots against the glass. Jian frowned, then recognized the shape from the city map Manfred had shown them earlier.

"Out here," Avelin said, and leaned sideways briefly to touch the knotted lines to the west of the city. "He's gone to earth in the domes out there."

"Lovely," Vaughn said.

Avelin smiled and did not answer, concentrating on the road ahead. The metalled surface was breaking up—another cheap colonial finish, never intended to last beyond the first five years of settlement—and a road gang was making an attempt at a repair, a couple of men stirring a cauldron of the sealant, a slighter figure, possibly a woman, pulling a spreader back and forth halfheartedly. Beyond the work area, the road was bright with sealed patches, but the runabout still bounced awkwardly over the uneven surface. It wasn't really surprising—that Refuge existed at all under Conglomerate control was astonishing enough; the old joke that the Conglomerate was less a government than a commercial code was unfortunately fairly accurate. Funding for a place like this, which existed only to salvage people, not goods or skills, had always been hard to obtain. The results were still depressing to look at, and Jian shook her head slightly. There were plenty of people on the residential streets, sitting in the identical doorways of the identical buildings or gathered idly on the corners but the few shops were almost empty, their windows small and covered with closely woven mesh, and none of them seemed to display any of their goods. She saw a school-yard, full of children in brightly colored, loose-fitting trousers-and-tunic suits that had to be issued by the Refugee Commission. Jian glanced from side to side now, remembering Manfred's comments about the local connections, but could not find a working data node. Maybe that was just because the runabout was moving too fast, but she could not be sure.

Avelin said, "There's a more direct route, but we can't get the bus in close that way. We'll go around from the main ring-road, come in from the south."

Jian looked at the map out of reflex, but the words meant nothing without Mitexi Major's location. "Haya," she said, and looked back at Avelin. Seen in profile—the unscarred profile—his face was a better match for the Urban voice, neat-boned, the fine line of the jaw, good-looking in a way that would arouse mild interest on almost any world. *Bahati's right hand,* she reminded herself. *A bounty hunter now, but Bahati's man before that, and therefore not to be fully trusted.*

The runabout swung left onto a side street—this one un-paved, the surface gravel over dirt, dirty water standing in the bottom of the ruts—and the blocky, foursquare commission-built housing abruptly ended. It was replaced by a mix of cheap homestead-catalog prefab and improvised shanties, plastic and raincloth draped over scavenged wood frames. Most of the prefabs were the cheapest available, low, faceted domes that would hold the heat. Here and there, a second dome had been welded on to the side of the first, as though they had been caught in the act of division. There were fewer people visible on the streets here, and most of them were dressed in the heavy felted coats—once brightly multicolored, now faded and dirty, and patched with scraps of plainer, badly made fabrics—and tall headdresses of Osi-ran traditionalists.

"So the domes are ethnic areas?" Jian asked.

Avelin nodded, frowning slightly. "Yes. Groups that have identity, that don't want to give up their own government or customs, they're usually the ones who end up out here—"

He was working the runabout around a sharp turn as he

spoke, swinging wide to avoid a ragged puddle, and broke off abruptly as they came round the corner and saw the barricade, chunks of broken concrete and heavy wooden pilings piled as high as a man's waist, dragged halfway across the roadway.

"Elvis Christ," Vaughn said, and Jian said, "Trouble?" She was poised to reach for the pellet gun, relaxed only slightly when Avelin shook his head.

"I don't think so, just a checkpoint. They do this here. . . ." He slowed the runabout further, gears groaning deep within its mechanisms, and touched a button on the control panel to open a speaking port on his side of the canopy. A figure, shapeless in once-bright coat and draped headpiece, one fine end drawn across nose and mouth, stepped out into the roadway, blastrifle slung over its shoulder. It held up a hand as the runabout pulled closer, and Jian heard Avelin sigh softly. "I know him. It should be all right."

"Let's hope so," Vaughn muttered. Jian glanced over her shoulder to see him smiling slightly, one hand tucked into the pocket of his jacket. Red sat impassive beside him, only his eyes moving in the still face.

"Jessey?" Avelin pitched his voice to carry through the narrow port. "Is there any problem?"

The heavy figure moved closer, the rifle still slung, and Avelin said, "You know me, Jessey. It's Avelin."

In the same moment, the figure said, "Hai, Avelin, schas't." It reached up, loosened the concealed drape to reveal a surprisingly fine-boned brown face. "Is OK," the man went on, in heavily accented Ortho-Urban. "Just to keep an eye on things."

"We can pass?" Avelin asked, and Jessey nodded.

"No problems." He stepped back out of the roadway, and Avelin gunned the runabout's engine. Jian allowed herself a small sigh of relief, and heard Avelin echo the sound. She glanced curiously at him, and the bounty hunter gave her a quick, rueful smile.

"Both the losing sides on Osiris ended up here, of course, and they staked out neighboring turfs."

"Also of course," Vaughn said.

"Yes. There's a no-man's-land between them, maybe a kilometer wide."

"Which is where Mitexi Major is hiding," Jian said, with sudden certainty.

"Yes." Avelin gave her another quick look, this one unreadable. "Not many people come out here."

But the Osirans seem to like you, Jian thought. *Or at least this side does—whichever one it is.* She could no longer remember the issues in Osiris's decade-long civil war, only that an Urban-oriented group had won. "How much farther?" she said aloud.

"Not far," Avelin began, and broke off to point. "There."

He was pointing at one of the smaller domes, in good repair but surrounded by a reef of broken, discarded furniture and rusting machinery. Another runabout was drawn up at the end of that improvised wall, canopy flung back and compartment empty.

Jian said, "It looks like we're a little late, Avelin."

The bounty hunter was frowning, already turning their runabout crossways across the rutted street, blocking the other craft's escape. "I don't know how," he said, and stopped short, shaking his head. "It does look like it." He cut the engine, leaving the runabout where it was, and popped the canopy. "Come on."

Jian levered herself out of the runabout, reached back to pull the tommy-stick out of its holster. Avelin blinked, but did not protest, said only, "Don't you want the gun?"

"No, thanks," Jian answered, and couldn't help a quick and rueful smile. "I don't have much practice with them."

"I'll take it," Vaughn said, and tugged it free of its clips, tucking it easily out of sight under his jacket.

"Suit yourselves," Avelin said, and turned toward the dome. His long vest swung open for an instant, and Jian understood why he had raised no objection to their taking his weapons: a long-barreled hand laser was tucked into his belt, hidden but readily to hand.

The wind was at their backs as they crossed the few meters of road that separated them from the dome, carrying sand and less familiar stinging cold pellets that Jian knew must be the sleet Manfred had described. As they reached the debris fence, however, the wind dropped suddenly, and the sound of voices came faint but clear through the dome's thin walls.

"—not in our agreement." That was Mitexi's voice, and Jian thought she could hear the anger in it.

"Too bad. The price is just going to keep going up," a man's voice answered, and the rest of his words were drowned by wind and a peal of shrieking laughter from inside the dome.

"Your employer?" Avelin said softly, and Jian nodded.

"Yeh, the woman is." That was stupid, unnecessary, but could not be unsaid. She went on, "Do we go in after them?"

Avelin grimaced. "If you want her alive, I think so. Seki sounds—annoyed."

He was already moving toward the dome's single door. Jian followed, glanced back in time to see Vaughn slide a cheap four-shot pellet gun—the plastic kind, undetectable and unreliable—out of his pocket and hand it to Red. The technician took it reluctantly, slid it into the pocket of his own coat.

"Hang on, Avelin," Jian said, and touched his shoulder. The bounty hunter looked back at her, a frown that was as much question as disapproval on his face, and she said, "Does this Seki care about witnesses?"

Avelin blinked, nodded. "Yes . . ."

"Bi' Mitexi?" Jian called, pitching her voice to carry over the wind. Avelin nodded again, in comprehension and approval, and edged forward, light-footed, to position himself next to the fragile-looking door.

"Bi' Mitexi, are you there?"

The shrieking laughter stopped abruptly, as though the person laughing had been slapped. Seki said something, his voice too low for the people outside to catch the words, and Mitexi said, "Bi' Jian? Is that you?"

"Yeh. We had a problem at the port, you'll have to deal with it. I came to get you—it's important, bi'." She let her voice trail off, and waited. Avelin was at the door now, back against the wall, one hand on the butt of gun inside his vest. Jian braced herself, suddenly afraid, wishing she were carrying the pellet gun, and took two careful steps to her right, out of the line of fire from the door.

From inside, Seki's voice said, "I'll get it." Avelin's smile widened beatifically, and he stepped in front of the door, bracing his free hand against the frame. He waited, obviously listening, then kicked the door open, drawing his gun in the same moment. He fired once, and Seki fired back, so quickly that the noise of the shots seemed to run together. Avelin's body contorted, and he sank to his knees just inside the doorway, then, quite slowly, pitched forward onto his face. Jian darted forward, and flattened herself against the side of the dome. Someone was screaming inside, a high, mindless note that raised the hairs at the base of her neck.

"Mitexi?"

"Bi' Jian." Mitexi's voice sounded only a little shaken. "It's all right, Seki's dead."

Jian stepped cautiously through the doorway, aware that Vaughn was beside her, pellet gun out and leveled. Mitexi was bent over the emaciated figure of a man sitting on the edge of a battered folding cot. It was he who was screaming, eyes fixed on nothing, but even as Jian realized it, Mitexi had pulled an injector from the bag slung at her waist, and pressed it against the man's neck. He shied away like an animal and went abruptly silent, eyes fluttering closed. Mitexi lowered him down onto the cot with absent care, turned to face her crew.

"I won't ask what you're doing here."

"You should be grateful we are," Jian snapped. She was shaking now, muscles trembling in the aftermath of unacknowledged terror. "Imre?"

Vaughn was already pushing himself up off the dome's filthy floor, his expression stiff with distaste. Seki's body lay on its back, a massive hole in its chest, shirt and vest charred around the edges of the wound; there was blood and ash on Vaughn's right hand. "He's dead, all right. What about Avelin?"

"Alive," Red answered, but so quietly Jian could barely hear, and turned to see for herself. Avelin lay sprawled on his side, half supported on Red's lap, blood splattered across his chest and up onto his face and neck, dotted across the scars. There was blood on Red's hands and on his trousers, but he didn't seem to notice.

"How bad?" Vaughn asked. He looked around for Seki's weapon, found it where it had fallen and slid, partway under a pile of crumpled fax sheets that looked as though they had been used for bedding. "Single shot setting, light-weight projectiles—he should make it."

"He could," Red said, and disengaged himself from Avelin's weight. He touched the right side of his own chest. "I put a pack on it."

Sure enough, now that Red had moved him, Jian could see a wet red stain marring the layers of shirt and vest, and a lump of first-aid bandage under the cloth. Whatever armor fibers had been woven into the vest's outer layers, it hadn't been enough.

Vaughn nodded, looked at Jian. "What next?"

"Why ask me?" Jian began, and bit off the rest of it, remembering Mitexi's presence. There was no point in telling her that this arrival had been the other pilot's idea, especially when she did not seem particularly grateful for the rescue—

"I need to get Venya back to the ship," Mitexi said. She stopped, looking at the bodies, and an expression almost of frustration flickered across her face. "That has to be my first priority—" She broke off abruptly, her eyes fixing on the doorway.

Jian turned, not fast, not daring to be fast, and a voice said from the doorway, "Avelin?"

It was the Osiran from the barricade, and there were at least two more behind him, blocking out the thin light.

"Avelin's been hurt," Jian said, and even as she spoke Jessey saw the crumpled bodies and unslung his rifle in a single smooth movement, leveling at them all impartially. "How?"

His command of Ortho-Urban isn't very good, Jian reminded herself, *but don't be insultingly simple.* "He—" She pointed to Seki's body. "—was trying to cheat my employer, her there. We found out about it, and hired Avelin to help us find them before things got ugly. We were too late, and Avelin got hurt."

"We put a pack on him," Vaughn said. "But we've got to get him to a clinic soon."

Jessey swung his rifle toward the pilot, checked the movement abruptly. "We take care of it," he said, and gestured for one of his henchmen to cover him. He knelt beside Avelin, examined the wound quickly but carefully, and stood up again. "He did this?" He pointed to Seki's body.

"Yes," Jian said, and flinched back as Jessey fired two more shots into the dead man.

"God damn," Vaughn whispered, a thread of sound in the sudden silence. Jessey looked at him, then back at Jian, his face revealing nothing but concern for Avelin.

"We take Avelin to the clinic, they heal as best as can." He added something in his own dialect—*a Rimsector hybrid, not a familiar word in the lot,* Jian thought, and bit down hard on her own shock—and the two henchmen reshouldered their rifles and came forward into the dome. They squatted beside Avelin, conferring softly, and then, quite gently, very careful not to hurt him, lifted him between them and carried him out of the dome.

"You." Jessey's voice sharpened, and Jian's attention snapped back to him. "You go back to the port, say nothing, and so we say nothing. This one—" He nodded again to Seki's broken body, ribs showing through the torn mess of cloth and pulped muscle. "We leave." He shrugged. "No problems." He saw the man on the cot then, frowned, and pointed to him. "No problem?"

"He's coming with us," Jian said firmly. "No problem."

Jessey nodded, put out a hand. "Agreed."

"Agreed," Jian echoed, and closed her hand over his. It was calloused, ordinary, the hand of a lineworker or heavy cargo wrangler, and she was somehow surprised. Jessey released her hand, bowed slightly, the Urban gesture at odds with clothes and rifle, and was gone. Jian closed her eyes, tasted bile.

"I say we get out of here now," Vaughn said. "They said we could go, I say we do it before they change their minds."

"Be quiet, Imre." Jian stood for a moment longer, until she was sure the sickness had passed. "Bi' Mitexi—"

She opened her eyes carefully, avoiding Seki's twisted body.

"He's sedated," Mitexi said. "Venya is, I mean." She paused, took a deep breath. "I'll get him into the runabout."

"What do we do about Avelin's car?" Vaughn said abruptly.

"For Christ's sake, Imre, how do I know?" Jian controlled herself with an effort. "We leave it, let the Osirans take care of it." She looked at Mitexi Minor, then at the man lying on the cot. He was taller than his sister, though so thin that they probably weighed the same. "I'll carry him," Jian said, and stooped to gather him into her arms before Mitexi could respond. The other woman made no protest, however, but turned silently for the door. Jian struggled for a moment with the limp body—he was absolutely unconscious, a boneless, sprawly weight, all arms and dangling legs—and then had him centered. As she had expected, he was no real weight, heavy but easily manageable, but the smell that rose from him was startling. Even in Heaven there were public baths, and strong social pressure to bathe; the sweat-and-urine smell was one she associated with the poorest of the poor, the semi-institutionalized. She was glad to step out into the chill air and let the stinging wind carry some of it away.

The Osirans had already removed Avelin's runabout. Mitexi was rummaging in the passenger compartment of the remaining machine, and Vaughn had strapped himself into the driver's seat, the motor already purring. Jian laid Mitexi Major into the rear seat, and turned away to let his sister deal with him. The stink of him clung to her, faint and choking. Red was still standing in the dome's doorway, but even as she opened her mouth to call to him he turned away, shutting the door gently behind him.

"We should've left him," he said as he came up the runabout.

Jian frowned, angry that after all of this, one and maybe two deaths, he could consider not getting what they'd come for, and Red shook his head.

"No, I meant Avelin. We should've let him die."

Jian had no answer to that, and he seemed to need none.

He swung himself into the runabout, sliding across the benchseat until he was next to Vaughn. Mitexi was already in the passenger compartment, oblivious to anything but her unconscious brother. Jian shook her head and climbed in next to the technician.

"Let's go, Imre," she said, and the other pilot put the runabout into gear and pulled slowly away.

7

Mitexi began negotiating for an immediate lift-off almost as soon as they returned to the *Byron*—even before she had finished seeing her brother bathed and dressed in something better than rags, and safely installed in a cabin next to her own, running her transmission through a floating link maintained by Manfred. The two pilots had nothing to do but wait and provide the figures demanded by Traffic Control. At last, however, Mitexi had her blast window—Jian was more than half convinced that the other woman had used her skills as a constructor to persuade the port computer to re-adjust the priority lists—and the pilots were left staring at each other across a table in the crew room. The wallscreen was lit, showing the crumbling port buildings and the roofs of the city beyond, their outlines blurred by spitting snow.

"Do you want to handle the blast-off?" Vaughn asked.

It was a backup job, really, making sure that the local tug pilot knew his/her job, and Jian shook her head. "You can have it if you want it."

"I want," Vaughn said, and managed the ghost of his usual smile. "Even if the local cops catch up with us, they won't shoot the backup pilot."

Jian ignored the comment. "Imre, what's between Red and Avelin?"

"I told you, they were in jail together," Vaughn answered, shrugged one-shouldered. "Cell mates—"

"No." Jian stopped abruptly, not even sure what she was asking. She remembered when Vaughn had taken up with the technician—it had happened while she was off-planet, a three-week delivery run and shakedown cruise out to the Rim, and then the luxury of just being a passenger, all the way home on someone else's ship—but had never known why. Red and Imre were already inseparable when she returned, and he was a good technician; no need to probe further. She became aware that Vaughn was watching her curiously, and struggled to find the right words. "Did you—I guess you didn't hear, what he said."

There was a silence, as though Vaughn wanted to deny it, but then he looked straight at her. "Yeh, I heard." He shook his head, frustrated or uncertain, Jian could not tell which. "I don't know what he meant—I'm not sure, anyway. You'd have to ask him."

"Right," Jian said.

A quick grin flickered across Vaughn's face. "Yeh, well—" He broke off, looking to the door, and the lines of his face hardened. "Heh, bach, come over here."

Red came obediently toward them, but his eyes were subtly wary. Before Vaughn could say anything more, however, Manfred's face appeared in the wall display.

"Imre, Bi' Mitexi would like you to know that the tug pilot will be on-board in ten minutes."

It would take almost ten minutes to get the standing systems up to par for the lift-off, Jian knew, but Vaughn ignored the construct, still looking at Red. "Bach, I want to know—"

"Imre," Manfred said, more insistently, and Vaughn swung in his chair to glare at the projected face.

"I heard you. Go away."

"Very well," the construct answered, already fading, and Jian would have sworn she heard mild affront in its voice.

If Vaughn had heard, however, he seemed impervious. He

turned back to the technician, said, "Why do you want him dead? Why now?"

For a moment, Jian thought Red would refuse to understand, but then the technician reached out, laid his hand gently against Vaughn's face. His fingers were slim, and very strong; their line along the pilot's cheekbone echoed Avelin's scars.

"He didn't believe in limits," Red said. "Doesn't. Not ever."

Vaughn looked back at him, not moving toward or away from the delicate touch. The silence stretched between them, a new tension thickening the air, and Manfred said, "Imre, Bi' Mitexi says you are needed in control."

"Elvis Christ," Vaughn said, with disgust, and Red let his hand fall to his side. "Come on, bach, we don't want to keep the tug pilot waiting, for God's sake." He left without looking back. Red turned to follow, more slowly, but Jian spoke first.

"Those were your scars, on Avelin."

Red looked back at her, nodded, his face open and unshaded, the ghost of an expression changing his perfect features, then continued on after Vaughn. He was gone before Jian decided that what she had seen in his dark eyes was fear.

It was an unsettling thought—she had never, in four years, seen him afraid, or even worried—and the realization was even more unsettling since Avelin was still alive. But he was on Refuge, presumably for good, since he had had to meet them outside the port limits.

"Manfred," she said aloud. "I need some information from the local directories."

The two-colored face formed on the wall beside her, serene and smiling slightly. The expression was a little too much like Red's when the technician was in a good mood; Jian grimaced and looked away.

"And go back to the other display, the first one you were using."

"Of course, Reverdy." The construct sounded almost surprised at the request, but re-formed into the devil mask. "What information did you need?"

"I want to know if Juel Avelin is a refugee, or if he just works here."

"One moment, please."

Jian waited, still wondering about Red, and Imre—she had never known just what Red had done, to end up in jail, or how Vaughn had found him; wished now she had asked—and Mitexi Minor appeared in the doorway. She was wearing her sheer tunic over a bodysuit again, defiantly bright against the dull colors in the wallscreen, but there were shadows under her amber eyes.

"I need to talk to you, Bi' Jian."

"Fine." Jian had been expecting this, though not perhaps so soon. She gestured to the chair Vaughn had vacated. "Have a seat."

Mitexi nodded, seated herself wincingly, as though she were so tired it hurt to move. She smelled of soap, a heavy, floral scent, and her braided hair was still wet: *so you're no happier having to deal with your brother than I was,* Jian thought, but could not find much satisfaction in it.

Before the constructor could speak, however, Manfred said, "I have your information, Reverdy. Juel Avelin arrived as a refugee. A departure bond has been posted, but not used."

"Who posted it?" Mitexi and Jian said in the same moment, and Jian stopped, laughed briefly. Mitexi smiled back, sideways, acknowledging the logic of the query.

"That name has been withheld from the record," Manfred answered.

"What does that mean?" Jian asked.

Mitexi said, "Was the name ever on file, or was the bond paid anonymously?"

Manfred said, "The name was never filed. A triple bond—three times the refugee's projected yearly income, plus passage off-world—was posted. The amount of the bond released the payor from the usual obligations."

"Well, that's interesting," Jian said, and Mitexi said, "A dead end."

"Do you think so?" Jian looked at Mitexi, but it was the construct that answered.

"I do not think I will be able to obtain any more detail through the connections." Its voice took on a distinctly disapproving note. "They are extremely limited."

Mitexi laughed. "They certainly are. Though not perhaps

as limited as one would like." She looked at Jian, still smiling in genuine amusement. "I did ask you to stay on the ship."

Jian spread her hands. "As it turns out . . ."

Mitexi nodded. "As it turns out, I'd be very ungracious to complain. But I would like to know why you came."

There was nothing for it but the lie she had already used for the Osirans. Jian blinked, said with all the innocence she could muster, "Red knew this Avelin, and he'd heard—Avelin had heard—that Seki was planning to cheat someone. We knew you'd hired Seki. So we decided to come after you."

There was a moment of silence, and Jian wondered suddenly what would happen if Mitexi decided to query the construct. *Trouble, obviously; there's no way it would go along with what I said—*

"I am grateful," Mitexi said, not quite grudging the words.

"How is your brother?" Jian asked. In spite of herself, she heard the distaste in her words, imagined she could smell the stale dirt of the dome and the filthy man, could feel the limp ungainly weight of him as she gathered him into her arms.

Mitexi looked back at her, visibly reading her thoughts. "All right. Better, I suppose. Clean, anyway, and I got some nutrients into him, before I put him to bed." She looked at the tiled wall where Manfred's icon was visible. "Manfred, is there any change?"

"No, Bi' Mitexi. Ba' Mitexi is sleeping."

"I notice he didn't say 'normally'," Jian said.

Mitexi lifted an eyebrow. "No, of course not. He's heavily sedated."

"Which you came very well prepared to do," Jian said.

"I've known for a very long time that he wasn't sane," she answered, her voice harsh with what might have been either anger or pain. "He went right over the edge after the Aster incident, if you ask me; it was just that nobody noticed." She took a deep breath, controlled herself with an effort that would not have been visible if she had not been so tired. "You'd have to be crazy to think up something like Dreampeace."

"He thought up Dreampeace." What had begun as a question turned into a statement even as Jian said it. The radicals had claimed that the Aster overseer had broken the Turing Barrier, was a person in its own right, and Kagami Ltd., who had written the construct, denied it and then pulled it off the open market, turning up two years later with a watered-down mass-market version. It made sense, that a man who had gone a little crazy, or a lot crazy, over the Aster incident would be more than just one of Dreampeace's several founders, would be the man behind it from the very beginning.

"Yes. Him and I think four or maybe five others were on the first board." Mitexi made a small noise that could have been a laugh if her face had not been a stony mask. "But Venya planned it. And then he really went crazy and ran. I got a letter from him, a real letter, not on the connections, realprint handwritten on a real sheet of paper, saying Kagami had murdered Aster and was out to murder him, and the next thing I heard was from the Refugee Commission wanting some kind of certification that he was being persecuted. What could I do? I told them I didn't know of any political harassment, told them to ask the Cartel if they were persecuting him." She paused. "I did tell them about Dreampeace, that he was involved and that it wasn't popular. It seemed like the least I could do."

Jian nodded in unwilling sympathy. "So you're not Dreampeace." It was not the right thing to say, but she didn't know what would be, and was tired of trying.

Mitexi bristled. "God, no. As far as I'm concerned, they killed Venya." She pushed herself up out of the chair, restless now, spoke to the tiled wall. "Manfred, how long to lift-off?"

"Forty-nine standard minutes, Bi' Mitexi," the construct answered.

"God." Mitexi shook herself, visibly considering what to do. "I'll be in my cabin."

"Mitexi." Jian spoke just as the other woman reached the doorway. The constructor stopped and turned back, eyebrows lifting in a silent, angry question. "If you knew your brother was this crazy, why'd you tell us you had to have him back to work on Manfred? He's in no shape for that, surely."

Mitexi's expression froze, the light and liveliness going out of her face, leaving it bleak and ugly. "Even crazy—even this crazy—my fucking brother is the best constructor anywhere in the Urban worlds. And I—I'm not. I can't rewrite this, not without help. I'm going to get him into a state where he can help me."

She turned on her heel and walked away, leaving words hanging unsaid in the air between them. *I'm going to get him to where he can help me, if it kills him and me.* Jian shook her head, not knowing what to think, stared at the wallscreen. It was raining now, not hard, but enough to leave thin puddles where the slagged ground had been imperfectly leveled. *A good world to leave.*

They left Refuge on schedule, Jian riding the secondary control board until they achieved orbit and were well on their way. The tug dropped them forty-five hours later, just beyond the unnamed gas giant's orbit, and Vaughn took the ship on toward the edge of the system. Still possessed by the occasional, irrational jealousy, Jian did not stay to monitor the other's progress, but slid back down the ladder to the crew deck. There was not much to do, off duty, but eat and sleep and speed through the few disks in the *Byron*'s library, unless she wanted to explore the passenger areas; she settled instead for a pot of tea and a manga she had seen only twice before. It was not one of Chaandi's, and the muddy plot did not hold her attention. She was glad when footsteps approaching the doorway distracted her, and looked up, expecting to see Red. Instead, Mitexi Major, bearded still, and painfully thin, peered around the doorway's edge.

"Is he here?"

It was the first time she'd heard him speak, and his voice was nothing remarkable, more underworld than Urban, light and vaguely apologetic.

"Who?" Jian asked, her first wary surprise fading into pity. He looked ill, physically sick, flushed as though with fever, and that made the strained politeness of his voice all the more painful to hear.

"Manfred," Mitexi Major answered, and Jian blinked.

"No, not now. Do you want him? I can call—"

"No!" Mitexi Major brought his voice and body under control with a convulsive effort, like a shiver, said more calmly, "No, that's all right. I don't want him—I don't want to deal with him. Not now, not anymore."

"Haya," Jian said, and spread her hands, conciliatory. Mitexi Major looked through her, a spasm of pain passing across his face.

"I can't deal with him anymore."

"Haya," Jian said again, and this time he seemed to listen. "No problem. Look, do you want some tea?"

"I don't want to talk about it," Mitexi Major said, more to himself than to anyone else, and looked back at her, a falsely reasonable smile stretching his full lips. "Yes, please, tea would be very nice."

"Right," Jian said, and made her way across the room to the autoserver, dodging the scattered chairs and tables. She pushed the necessary keys automatically, wondering what she should do, and why she had to be the one to do it. Mitexi Major was in no state to be wandering around loose, that much was obvious—*so I call Mitexi Minor, let her deal with her brother.* She accepted the flask of tea—in her haste, she had punched for a double serving, and she shoved the extra cup back into the machine—and carried it back to the corner table where Mitexi Major had seated himself. "Would you like anything else?" she asked. "Do you want me to call your sister?"

Mitexi Major looked up, eyes moving wildly. "No! She—this is all her doing." He reached out, laid his hand on Jian's arm, half confiding, half imploring. "You have to understand, she wants to sell him, sell me, and I don't, I can't—"

"Reverdy." that was Manfred's voice, and the devil mask materialized in the wall even as it spoke.

Mitexi Major closed his eyes instantly and covered his ears with both hands. Slowly, he began to fold in on himself, chin pulled down against his chest, bending forward until his head almost touched his knees.

"Reverdy, Bi Mitexi wanted to know if you had seen Ba' Mitexi. I see he is with you."

"Yeh." Jian took a deep breath, looked away from Mitexi Major, who had started to rock slowly back and forth, still curled into a sort of ball. "Tell her that."

"I already have done so," Manfred answered. "She is on her way—"

"I'm here," Mitexi Minor said.

Jian turned to face her, any protest she might have made dying unspoken at the expression on the other woman's face. If anything, she looked more tired than she had the last time Jian had seen her, the shadows now like ugly bruises under her eyes. For an instant, she seemed torn between exasperation and sorrow, before the mask came down again, and she was in full command of herself again.

"I'm sorry, Reverdy—Bi' Jian. He got out of the cabin while I wasn't looking."

"It's all right," Jian answered, and made herself add, "Can I help?" She was embarrassed at her own relief when Mitexi shook her head.

"No, thank you. I can manage. Manfred, go away."

"Yes, Bi' Mitexi." The construct vanished.

"Thank you," Mitexi said, to nothing, and looked at her brother. "Venya . . ."

Mitexi Major kept rocking slowly back and forth, as though he hadn't heard. Mitexi held out her hand, in his line of vision where he could not help but see it, and was still ignored.

"Are you sure I can't help?" Jian asked, and Mitexi glanced back at her, a sudden smile flickering across her broad face.

"No, I don't think so. But I do appreciate it." She let her hand drop, reached instead under the hem of her tunic for the purse that hung at her waist, and came up with a brightly colored ampoule. She snapped it under her brother's nose, and he looked up, eyes flying open as though startled into a kind of sanity. Slowly, he lowered his hands from his ears, and Mitexi Minor nodded.

"Venya. Come with me now." She held out her hand again, and this time Mitexi Major took it, let her guide him up out of the chair and tow him gently across the room. At the door, she looked back over his shoulder, lifted her free hand to sign thanks-and-sorry to Jian. The pilot gestured acceptance automatically, but her heart wasn't in it. *How she can expect to get help from him, crazy as he is now . . .* She put the thought aside—*not my problem, anyway*—and climbed to the control room to bully Vaughn into letting her on-line a little early.

She did not see Mitexi Major again until some hours after she'd flipped the ship into hyperspace. It was a good translation, even by her own high standards: the *Byron* had been in perfect alignment, sliding easily with the grain of the universe. She had brought her hands together, firing the capacitors at precisely the right moment; in dreamspace, in her virtual world, the balloon-icon that was the ship had pulled free of the clouds and into the clear air of hyperspace almost before she had gathered her strength to fight it into absolute alignment. She leaned back into the standing system, savoring the sensations washing along the wires of her suit, at the same time reveling in the vivid images Manfred unrolled in front of her. Space was uncomplicated here, smooth farmland in the interface's transcription; there was little to do but enjoy the process of flight. And Manfred made it more than a process, made it a pure and absolute joy.

Jian frowned, lazily, considering that thought. It still wasn't like sex, no matter what Red had said—it was better than sex, its intensity less demanding, or maybe just utterly different, since there really was nothing like a long afternoon at Chaandi's, bodies twined together, matching limb to limb until someone conceded, submitted to pleasure— She put that image hastily aside, focused her thoughts again on Manfred. It was the best construct she had ever worked with, and it was all too likely she'd lose any chance to work with it again, once she left the *Byron*. Mitexi Minor had said the construct would go to Kagami, was already bought by Kagami, and after the Aster incident, Kagami had become particularly wary of Dreampeace—*paranoid, even,* Jian thought. *I wonder if Aster was this good, as good as Manfred—after all, Mitexi Major was supposed to be on that design team. Not that anyone would know, anymore, after they rewrote the construct.* She stopped abruptly, no longer really seeing the lush dreamscape slowly unreeling in front of her. Even the familiar heady sensation coursing along her wires was suddenly distant. *Will they rewrite Manfred the same way?*

It was more than possible. Kagami would have to rework the construct anyway, to make it a generic overseer rather than ship-specific as it was now. What would be easier than to simplify the system, take out the features that made it unique? It would probably even save on costs. She shivered, physically chilled by the idea that Manfred would become less than what he was. . . . *And you're sounding like a Dreampeacer,* she told herself. *Stop it.* The criticism rang hollow. If this was what Dreampeace was all about, it could not be all bad.

She shook herself then, frowning. It would not be a tragedy if Manfred were changed, rewritten; it would be a disappointment, that was all. *Dreampeace would call it a tragedy, the destruction of a person. I won't go that far.* In any case, it might be an avoidable disappointment. Her own backup blocks were still empty, since she had never used Elisee; it might be possible to copy Manfred's backup files into them. . . . Or, better still, to make a copy of Manfred himself, tap into the system so that when Manfred ran his own routine housekeeping programs and backup filing, she would receive a copy as well. She was smiling now, her own excitement overriding the sensations from the ship. *It would work, I can do this—*

#Manfred,# she said aloud, #how does our present course look?#

#Do you want a projection?#

#No, just a verbal summary.#

There was the briefest of pauses, and Manfred said, #I expect that the current conditions will continue without significant change for at least a standard hour. However, after that point it is likely that we will encounter the remains of the time-slip which we felt on our journey to Refuge. It will be working against us, of course, and we should therefore be prepared for some turbulence—#

#Thanks, that's good enough,# Jian said. That meant she would have at least an hour to set up the tap—*plenty of time,* she thought, *especially since Mitexi's going to be busy with her brother.* #Off-line,# she said, and stepped out of the pilot's cage.

Mitexi Major was there in the control room, sitting at the

computer interface board. Jian started—she had not realized he was there, had seen no reflection of his presence in the virtual world—and stumbled, making a noise. There was a perceptible pause before the constructor turned to face her.

"Bi' Jian." He was looking better than he had, as though shipboard life, regular meals and frequent bathing, was finally catching up with him. He had shaved, too, revealing a hollow-cheeked face that should have been as round as his sister's. "I think I owe you an apology."

"Not at all," Jian said. It wasn't just the food and the baths, she realized; the drugs Mitexi Minor had been feeding him were finally starting to take effect.

Mitexi Major smiled, wry and wincing. "That's kind of you, but I suspect untrue."

Jian shrugged, uncomfortable. *What am I supposed to say, that you were crazier than I don't know what, anything I've ever seen, last time I saw you?* "No problem," she said, and hesitated, one hand still on the ladder. *Do I really want to leave him up here by himself?*

Mitexi's smile twisted even further out of true, as though he'd read the thought, and he rose from his seat in front of the console. "I just wanted to see how Manfred was doing," he said. "I hadn't had a chance to see him running."

"He's a real good overseer," Jian said, and stood aside to let the constructor climb down the ladder ahead of her.

Mitexi's face brightened for an instant. "I'm glad you think so. I was—very proud—to have worked on his matrix." There was a little pause, the two still standing facing each other, Jian with her hand still on the side of the ladder, and then Mitexi Major said, "You do understand what's happened, don't you?"

Jian blinked, wondering how to answer. *I understand quite a lot, thanks, I just don't know if you'd think so.* "What do you mean?" she said aloud, and Mitexi managed another wincing smile.

"I mean with Manfred. You do—did you know that Meredalia's sold him to Kagami?"

"I thought so," Jian said carefully. "I wasn't sure."

"You know what they'll do to him," Mitexi Major said. "It's the same thing they did with Aster—they'll edit out any hint of intelligence.'' He fixed his eyes on Jian as though he could couple her agreement by the sheer force of his glare. "And you know Manfred's intelligent. You must be able to feel it when you work with him.''

It was no more than she had been thinking, but Jian hesitated. "He's the best overseer I've ever worked with,'' she said again.

"He's better—and he's so much more—than that,'' Mitexi Major said. "You have to admit it. What's your own overseer, corporate, private?''

"It's classed as private-label,'' Jian answered. "It's a Yannosti corporate matrix, with private modifications.''

"Then you must see the differences,'' Mitexi Major said.

"Oh, must I?'' Jian murmured, and the constructor swept on as though he hadn't heard.

"Manfred's fully intelligent by any definition of the term. There won't be any problem proving it. And that will solve the machine rights issue: there won't be any choice once Manfred's been shown; the government will have to grant them full citizenship. But until then, he's considered property, and she's going to take him away from me. So I need your help.''

"I don't know that Manfred's human,'' Jian said. "Just being the best I've worked with doesn't make him human.''

Mitexi Major looked through her. "Of course he is. He was made to be.'' He blinked, seemed to focus again, as though looking for the right argument. "You can tell it in the way he handles data, in the way he responds to you. You can tell.''

Jian made a face, wishing she didn't suspect he was right, wishing someone—Mitexi Minor, for preference—would show up to take charge of him. "What is it you have in mind?''

"I need to reclaim Manfred,'' Mitexi Major said, and sounded almost surprised at the question. "Just until I can get the government to rule on his status, of course. But the more people who speak out—people like you, people who've worked with him—the more chance there is that Dreampeace can push the case into FPG jurisdiction.''

"I don't deal with the FPG,'' Jian said flatly. The Freyan

Provisional Government was unstable, impoverished, sur-
vived only because one of its predecessors had been lucky
enough to find Persephone, made most of its income by ex-
porting contract labor—and the coolies accepted the contracts
because anything was better than Freya. . . .

"You can't trust the Cartel," Mitexi Major answered. "Not
for something like this."

"Maybe not," Jian said, "but what makes you think you
can trust the FPG? Look how they treat their own people—
why should they treat constructs any better?"

Mitexi Major waved the objection aside. "That's different."

"The hell it is," Jian said.

"This is more immediately important," Mitexi Major said.
"We can deal with the coolie problem once the question of
machine rights is settled. They can protect themselves; there's
nobody protecting the emerging constructs. Will you help?"

"No," Jian said. "I'm tired of hearing that people don't
count, that the goddamned constructs are more important—"

She broke off, remembering that he was crazy, that he was
a midworlder and had been corporate, and Mitexi Major said
sadly, "It's not that they're more important. It's just no one
is helping them."

"And no one's helping the coolies, either," Jian said. *Except themselves.* She sighed, her anger fading. *Which is more
than the constructs—this construct—is in a position to do.
And Manfred is something special, and I don't want to see
him rewritten.* "I'll speak to Dreampeace for you, testify, if
that's what you want."

Mitexi Major looked at her uncertainly, the animation fading from his face. "Yes," he said, drawing the word out into
two syllables as though he wasn't after all quite sure, and let
himself down the ladder. Jian hesitated only for a moment
before following him, but by the time she reached the deck
he was already ensconced in front of a terminal in the crew
room. She shook her head, and went on around the curve of
the ship to knock on the half-open door of Vaughn's cabin.

Red answered the door, averting his face as though that
would hide the bruise that blurred the fine line of his jaw.
Jian blinked, not precisely surprised—*but if I had that man*

in my bed, it wouldn't be to spoil his looks—and said, "I need a spare storage block, if you've got one. I'll pay you."

Vaughn said, from over Red's shoulder, "What do you need an extra for? You usually travel with enough for three." He touched the technician's arm, and Red slipped aside, disappeared into the bedroom as Vaughn flung the door fully open. For an instant, Jian thought she had seen sheer satisfaction in the technician's eyes.

"Yeh, well, we left in kind of a hurry," she answered. In point of fact, she had more than enough to copy Manfred, but not enough—one less than optimum—to copy him and still be able to back up Elisee in an emergency. "I didn't have time to restock—and I didn't think to do it at Kelemen's, before you ask."

"Haya." Vaughn grinned. "As it happens, I've been trying to follow your example. I've got three spares."

"I only need one."

Red reemerged from the inner room, holding up the thick, palm-sized storage block, still in its thick paper-felt wrappings.

"Thanks," Jian said, and took it from him. Vaughn raised an eyebrow.

"I thought you were going to pay me?"

Jian smiled. "I'll have to owe you." Vaughn made a face, but before he could protest, she went on, "I thought you ought to know, Mitexi Major's set himself up at one of the terminals in the crew room."

"Oh, Christ," Vaughn said. "Did you let Mitexi know?"

"No." Jian shook her head. "He seemed all right. I just thought you might want to look in on him."

"I'll do that," Vaughn agreed. "Fucking nuisance, having to keep an eye on him. I wish she'd do it."

Jian nodded agreement, and turned away. Back in her own cabin, she flicked the switches of her wall console, and waited while the status reports scrolled across the multiple screens. Everything was still well under control, hyperspace lying even and easy, Manfred sliding the *Byron* along the preset path without the slightest sign of difficulty. Jian dismissed the status reports with a wave of her hand, and picked up the guide ball, used it to walk through the standing systems, looking for observers. Mitexi Major was visible as a working terminal in the crew room, but he seemed to be doing nothing more than searching the ship's library system. No one else was on-line. She nodded again, to herself this time, and retrieved her own backup system from its case.

Systems access had been standardized before the *Byron* was even dreamed of: she fitted the leads and cables into the jacks almost by instinct, unwrapped the new storage block and snugged it into the third port along with the two others she had brought from Persephone. She ran a quick self-test of the backup drive and then punched in a longer test of the full system. As she had expected, everything was working perfectly. She took a deep breath then, staring at the displays. So far, nothing she had done could be questioned; once she began the next stage, it would be quite clear what she was doing. *No turning back,* she told herself impatiently, and called up Manfred's maintenance systems. All she had to do was add her own system's address to the already-established destination—

"Reverdy," Manfred said from the wall of quilted tiles. "What are you doing?"

He did not sound angry, merely curious, and Jian answered the tone as much as the words. "I'm setting up my system to duplicate your backup files."

"That is outside the system parameters," Manfred said, "and requires unauthorized access, which you have achieved."

Thanks, Jian thought sourly, and waited. She had been caught, fair and square; the question now was what the construct would do about it.

"May I ask why you're doing this?"

Polite, as well as wordy, Jian thought. *Still, there's no harm getting my real reasons on record somewhere—that may be enough to keep Mitexi Minor from prosecuting, if I can pull a little discreet blackmail.* "I have reason to believe," she began carefully, feeling for just the right words, "that the people who have purchased the rights to you, to this overseer construct called Manfred, are planning major modifications of its structure, possibly without the consent or knowledge of the copyright holder." *Who is probably still*

Mitexi Major, and he's probably in no condition to consent, she added silently. The construct was still waiting, and she stumbled on. "I felt it was important to have a correct copy available in case of dispute."

There was another long silence, and Jian felt her hopes sinking. It wasn't a very good excuse at all; the only way it could help was to show Mitexi just how much she did know, so that they could trade silence for nonprosecution—

"Very well," Manfred said. "Please proceed, Reverdy."

"Beg pardon?" Jian said.

"Please proceed with the installation," Manfred said. "I have imported your backup system's addresses into my maintenance routine. Please install your system so that I can double-check your data parameters."

Jian closed her mouth, which had fallen open. "Haya," she said, and touched the necessary keys. Lights flashed across the console screens, and a string of glyphs chased itself across the test port.

"Everything seems to be in order," Manfred said. "You will receive a duplicate of my next maintenance dump, which will occur in seventeen standard minutes."

"Thanks," Jian said, still unable quite to believe what she was hearing. Now, if he didn't tell Mitexi Minor what she'd done—*and why not push it? Why not ask?* "I would appreciate it if you would not mention this," she began, and the construct interrupted her.

"As I find my copyright situation to be somewhat unclear, I intend to behave with discretion. I, too, would prefer that the existence of an additional backup duplicate be kept secret."

"I'd be happy to keep it quiet," Jian said, and bit back laughter that would have been too high-pitched out of sheer relief.

"Thank you, Reverdy," the construct said demurely.

Jian sat quite still for a moment, staring unseeing at the winking status board. *I don't understand why he did this,* she thought. *A construct shouldn't be able to define itself as an entity—shouldn't be concerned with keeping itself unchanged. Of course, it could be a form of copy protection: the construct itself resists alteration without some special key provided by*

*the copyright owner. That would make sense. Or else he re-
ally is people, just like Mitexi Major said, and he's scared of
being made into someone else, something less than human.*
She shook the thought away, uncomfortable, but unable to
ignore the chance that it might be true. *And if it is? Hell,
what can I do? Keep the copy—John Desembaa or Libra, or
even Taavi, one of them can get me the papers I'd need, find
me someone to certify this is my construct and whatever else
needs doing—and then go to Dreampeace. This is what
they've been looking for, the kind of case they need . . .* But
there her imagination stopped. John Desembaa was a moderate by Dreampeace standards, Libra was the same; the
leaders of the movement were more like Mitexi Major than
anyone she could imagine dealing with. Anyone who would
choose to call in the FPG, choose to extend their jurisdiction,
was dangerous. She shook her head again, not knowing what
to do, and someone—Vaughn, she realized a split second
later—shouted from the crew room.

"Reverdy, Red, get in here!"

Manfred appeared in the wall. "Reverdy, there is a medical emergency in the crew room. Medikuri are on the way."

Jian was already out the door, signed clumsy acknowledgment as she ran. A medikuri was rolling purposefully out of
this level's emergency silo in the central core, and she slowed
down to let it get in ahead of her. It knew all the right rem-
edies, after all, and had the tools to apply them; she had only
the little she remembered from the required pilot's training
nearly ten years before.

In the crew room, Vaughn was crouched over Mitexi Major's crumpled form, both hands, bloodied to the wrist,
clasped around the constructor's forearm. The medikuri had
settled beside him, leads snaking out of its casing to clamp
onto Mitexi Major's exposed skin. Red was backed against
the wall, watching, the beautiful face closed and empty.

"What the hell?" Jian began, and bit off her own question.
"What do you need?"

Vaughn shook his head, his hands still clamped tight over
the other man's arm. "I think the machine's got it now.
Christ, what a mess!"

There was blood on the terminal, bright arterial blood

spilled across the input board. Jian looked away, wincing in sympathy as much as anything, said again, "What happened?"

"I wish I knew," Vaughn said. One of the machine's questing tentacles crept up past his hand and buried itself in the curve of Mitexi's elbow; a second, thicker tentacle wrapped itself fully around the arm, just below Vaughn's hold.

"Pressure is no longer required," the medikuri said, and Vaughn very carefully disengaged himself from among its wires.

"He cut himself," Vaughn said. "Went right after himself with a knife from the server." he nodded to the thin, black-handled blade lying on the floor under the terminal. It hardly looked large enough, strong enough to have done that much damage, and Jian shivered in spite of herself. "He just stuck it in his arm, right at the wrist—damn near right through his arm." He shook his head. "I have no idea why."

"He was looking for a suit lead," Mitexi Minor said, from the doorway. She came on into the room, looking down at her brother's unconscious body, stood shaking her head for a moment.

"Looking for a suit lead?" Jian asked, and wished she hadn't as Mitexi turned to look at her, the amber eyes cold.

"He was on-line, like you, except it was a constructor's suit. The old-style version, the kind you plug directly into the system. His plugs were in his wrist, before he had the suit removed." She looked back at her brother. "I don't think he remembered that; he was trying to find them before. Trying to pry them out with his fingernails."

"I guess he found something more effective to work with," Vaughn said. He looked down at his hands, parted his fingers as though they were sticky.

Jian said, "Mitexi, you're going to have to do something to keep him safe—from himself, as much as anything. Next time he could be screwing around with the standing systems."

"No, he's locked out," Mitexi answered. "There's no way he can get into any of the ship's systems."

"I don't think our concerns are unreasonable," Jian said,

and saw, out of the corner of her eye, Red nod in agreement. She hardened her voice. "Aside from anything else, it's damn hard to run this ship when we're worry about what we're going to find in the crew room—" She broke off, seeing Mitexi's glare, knew she had said enough, and maybe too much.

"All right, I agree, he'll have to be watched more closely." Mitexi looked at the medikuri. "Is he stabilized?"

"Please rephrase the question."

"What is your patient's condition?" Mitexi said, her voice brittle with anger.

"He is stable."

"Take him back to his cabin." She looked back at Jian. "I assure you, this won't happen again."

"Thanks," Jian said, and tried to sound conciliatory. The medikuri extruded four solid arms like flat scoops, inserted them neatly between Mitexi Major and the floor tiles. Three more arms, narrower, followed, fully supporting the constructor's body, and then the medikuri rose to its full height and carried him away. Mitexi Minor followed, and did not look back.

"Manfred," Jian said. "Get some karakuri in here, and clean up this mess."

Vaughn swore under his breath, kicked the wall stop that released the panel covering the cold-water spigot and its catch basin. He stuck his bloody hands under the sensor and waited for the water to flow, saying over the rush of water, "What the hell brought that on?"

"No idea," Jian said, and Red pushed himself away from the wall to cross to the terminal, stepping carefully around the busy cleaners. He touched the bloody input board, hesitated, studying the screen, and touched keys again.

"Any luck?" Jian asked, and came to join him. Red shrugged one shoulder, and stepped sideways to let her see. The screen was filled with realprint text, banded top and bottom with file-finder glyphs from the ship's library system.

"I tried retrieve," Red said.

"And that's what you got?" Vaughn asked. He handed Red a damp towel, and the technician took it, nodding, wiped the blood from his hands. Vaughn went on, ''Looks pretty harmless.''

''Except that he's a constructor,'' Jian said. That was what worried her, and worried Vaughn, too, by the look of him— the thought that Mitexi Major could have concealed anything he was doing, could have left this innocuous screen to shield him.

Vaughn nodded grim agreement. ''Well, she says he's closed out, I guess we have to trust her. And she'll keep a better eye on him now, anyway.''

''Let's hope so,'' Jian said sourly, and headed back to the pilot's cage.

She was glad to retreat into the familiar calm of her virtual world, gladder still to go off-line at last and shut herself in her cabin. The backup system was still in place, the row of indicators glowing green across the main reader. At this point, she barely cared, but old discipline made her disconnect the system, isolating it and the copy of Manfred residing in its storage blocks from the standing systems. Then she crawled into her bunk, aching tired, but not sure she could sleep, after everything that had happened. Her subconscious surprised her; she was asleep almost as soon as her head hit the pillow.

She woke to the shrilling of an alarm she had not heard since training. The conditioned response dragged her out of bed even before she was fully awake, fully aware of what she was hearing, groping for clothes and the lights. The cabin lights did not respond to her gesture; the emergency lights came on instead, red-orange, a symbol flashing on the wall above the console: MAIN SYSTEMS FAILURE.

''Imre?'' Jian looked for the nearest data node, could not make contact. She pressed the access glyph in her arm, pulling the suit up to full power, and there was still no response. She hit keys on the input board, trying to tie into the standing system, got only a rush of static, a wave of irritation along her bones. The symbol continued to flash: MAIN SYSTEMS FAILURE.

This had never happened. In all the years she had been piloting ships through hyperspace, she had encountered it only in simulations. She killed the thought as useless, and ran for the control room ladder.

Vaughn was in the pilot's cage, swearing at the top of his lungs without hearing his own words, his hands and arms moving in patterns Jian could not read at first, and then recognized as desperation. Red was at the engineer's console, but even as she swung herself free of the ladder he turned away, pushing past her to slide back down the ladder. He was heading for the central core and the engine room itself, Jian knew, and the realization chilled her to the bone. That could only mean that the remote links, the standing system itself, were unreliable, and if the standing system went, the ship could no longer be controlled.

She stepped into the cage next to Vaughn, bracing herself for a blast of imagery. A few glyphs flared painfully—MAIN SYSTEMS FAILURE flamed across her vision, a scattering of secondary indicators flashing red and orange around it, the last working control icons pulsing with light—but most were pale shadows of what they should be. Vaughn's world was coming apart at the seams, ripping into shreds of light and shadow, carefully designed props gone in an instant, raw data pouring into the cage like streams of wind-borne fog. Behind it all, the instrument wall blazed red.

#What the hell's going on?# Jian demanded. Already, Manfred was trying to fade in her own virtual world—the precision filter, the massive arms of the loom, and the bead of light sliding back and forth, weaving the fabric of hyperspace into something remotely comprehensible—but the image had great gaps. The illusory fabric ripped to multipatterned rags, equally illusory, tangled in the false hyperspace of Vaughn's world, which refused to fade. #Let me take it, give me the con.#

#I'm trying,# Vaughn said. There was desperation in his voice: they both knew she was the better pilot, and the ship, the standing systems, still were not responding.

#So,# Jian murmured, hissed through clenched teeth. She could feel the ship still in contact with her suit, could feel them slipping out of grain, the tension knotting painfully in her muscles. Then Red was with her, his persona stronger than she had ever felt it, feathering the Drive fields and lessening the interference. She could feel the correct response even if she could not see it among the tangled icons; she gestured, closing her eyes, and felt the *Byron* respond. It was sluggish, wallowing against the grain of space, but it was a response.

#Match me, Red, I need to steady us,# she said, and blessedly the technician answered aloud.

#Matching.#

The *Byron* stabilized slowly, the tension, the interference still singing taut pain along the suit wires, but she could handle that. #Manfred,# she said aloud, and Vaughn answered harshly.

#Gone.#

#Gone?# Jian bit off fruitless questions—if the construct had been on-line, she would have felt him, he would have been helping to counteract whatever this was—and said instead, #All right. Bring up Elisee.#

#Are you sure? The problem seems to be in the interfaces,# Vaughn answered.

#There's no choice,# Jian said. #Bring her on.#

#Right.# Vaughn leaned forward through the shredded images, folded a small input board out of the instrument wall. He ran his hands across the yielding surface, conjuring systems and constructs, and for a moment the virtual world began to take on solidity again. Jian could feel the familiar presence—*not Manfred, not as complex as Manfred, a thin wraith to Manfred's near-humanity, but her own, her Elisee*—reaching out along the wires, taking hold of the illusions, banishing Vaughn's icons and strengthening her own. She smiled, reached with more confidence to pull the ship back into true, the fabric, hyperspace itself, legible again, rolling past in front of her. The *Byron* answered more easily, Red matching her moves with the new field settings. For just an instant, she had the ship back to true, and then the system blew.

Elisee was ripped away with a thin squeal of machinespeak like a woman's scream, and the virtual world vanished with her, was replaced with a chaos of light and sound and meaningless image. The *Byron* yawed, fell out of true, the interference tightening to agony all along her body. Jian screamed, her muscles cramping helplessly, fought to feel what was left of the standing systems beneath the pain. She dragged the ship awkwardly, painfully, tears stinging her cheeks, into what she thought would be the correct alignment that she could no longer feel. She shouted to Vaughn, #Dump the overseer, dump the overseer and cut out the interfaces, see if we can save the standing system.# *If we can't, we're dead, there's no way we can fly hyperspace without some kind of interpreter—*

Through the hail of image and the blurring tears, she could see Vaughn working frantically at his board, hands dancing across the membranes; she could feel, distantly, Red struggling to keep the fields attuned to the shifting space around them. Then the haze vanished, leaving her only with the tears. Vaughn had his hands on the emergency controls, caught the ship before it could fall further out of true.

"Got it," he said. "I've dumped what's left of the overseer—I'm sorry, Reverdy."

"What the hell happened?" Jian asked again, and dragged her hands across her face, scrubbing away the tears. She could feel the interference receding as Vaughn brought the ship back into rough alignment, using the numbers flowing across the instrument wall as well as the flux of sensation from the standing systems.

Vaughn shook his head once, roughly, his eyes still glued to the shifting readouts. "Don't know. Manfred just—faded. I had a little control for a couple minutes, maybe, then it all crashed. That was when you got here."

"I think there's something in the system—in the interfaces, maybe," Jian said, and reached forward to pull another membrane board out of the instrument wall.

"Virus?" Vaughn did not dare turn to look at her, but his voice sharpened.

"I don't know, but that's what it felt like, when Elisee went." Jian studied the readings that formed in her board, a new fear curdling in her belly. She couldn't make the system read from, or even acknowledge, the interface locations. It was as if they—and therefore the overseer, any overseer that they tried to plug into the interfaces—no longer existed.

"Mitexi," Vaughn said, and made the word a curse.

"Which one?" Jian retorted, and Vaughn made a noise that might have been a snort of laughter.

"Either, both—him, for my bet; he's that crazy."

Jian shook her head, still staring at her board. "Imre, we have a primary systems failure."

"Shit." Vaughn's hands tightened briefly on the emergency controls, knuckles flaring white, and then loosened with an effort of will.

"The standing system, and the sensor relays, do not accept the interface—it's not there anymore." Jian touched more key sequences, shook her head. "I can't even begin to import your Spelvin into the overseer blocks. That's gone, too. And I can't find Manfred anywhere."

"Life support?" Vaughn said sharply.

Jian caught her breath—she had forgotten that the construct handled those functions as well—and touched more keys. "Red caught that. He's running it from engineering."

"Thank Christ for that," Vaughn muttered.

"Can you hold things?" Jian asked. "I'm going after Mitexi—Minor. She's a constructor, maybe she can do something."

"Let's hope so," Vaughn said. "I can hold it steady."

You just can't take us in or out of Drive. Jian finished the thought for him, allowed herself a crooked smile. *No one can. Oh, as long as the standing system's running—and if we don't run into any really outrageous conditions—we can stay in Drive, but we can't get out again. Well, it's better than breaking up against the interference. Maybe. It could just be a longer way to die.*

The normal lighting was on again in the control room, but the emergency lights were still lit, adding a strange orange tinge to the air. Red had managed to recover most of the internal systems normally managed through Manfred, and the communications console showed only a few red lights. Jian leaned over its multiple keyboards, punched for the manual selection menu, managed to find the intercom system. She typed in the codes that she thought would connect her with Mitexi Minor's cabin. The screen blanked, but flashed empty: no one was answering. Jian swore, killed the call, and touched the codes for Mitexi Major's cabin. This time, the screen lit at once, and Mitexi Minor looked out at her, face set and furious with grief.

"He's dead."

"Dead." For an instant, Jian did not understand, caught up as she was in the disaster around her.

"Venya's dead," Mitexi Minor said again. "He killed Manfred, and then he killed himself."

"Son of a bitch," Vaughn said from the pilot's cage.

"Shut up, Imre," Jian said. "Bi' Mitexi, we have a primary systems failure. Your brother's responsible?"

"Yes." A spasm of something—Jian could not tell whether it was more anger or sorrow—flickered briefly across Mitexi's broad face, and then the constructor had herself under control. "The *Byron*'s stable."

"No thanks to your brother," Jian answered, and glanced over her shoulder at the instrument wall. "We're running in the orange—I don't know what that will do to the hull structure in the longer term, but it's bearable for a while. The real problem is, we've lost Manfred and can't install our own overseers. I tried, and the system destroyed my construct." To her horror, her eyes filled again with tears, less for Elisee than as a release of tension. She shook them impatiently away. "Can you do anything to clear the interfaces?"

Mitexi sighed, dragging herself back from contemplating something—Mitexi Major's body, Jian knew without seeing it, and repressed a shudder—lying out of camera range at her feet. "I don't know. I'll try, of course. Can your tech help?"

"He's running life support and internal systems as well as the engines," Jian answered. "I'll find out."

"I'm on my way," Mitexi Minor said, and broke the connection. For an instant, Jian frowned at the now-blank screen in confusion, then understood: the primary access consoles were in the control room, and with Manfred down, Mitexi would have to work through those machines directly. She touched keys on the intercom board again, opening a line to the engine room.

"Red?"

There was a moment of silence, and then the technician answered reluctantly, "Yeh."

The screens stayed blank: *I guess he can't get free to set up the sight-link,* Jian thought, and her heart sank. "Can you help Mitexi Minor? She's going to try to rebuild the system."

There was another, longer silence, and Red said, "Somebody's got to stay on these machines."

"Can I do it?" Jian asked.

"Yeh. I think so."

Jian glanced over her shoulder, saw the lights of the instrument wall glowing steady orange, framing Vaughn's broad shoulders in a fan of light. "I'll come down," she said, and did not wait for his acknowledgment to cut the connection. "Imre—"

"I heard," the other pilot answered. They both knew it made sense this way: he had a gift for the precise, finicking sort of piloting that was needed now, and Jian, if she was no real technician, at least understood and liked the machines she would be managing. "Good luck," Vaughn said, and Jian smiled for the first time since the alarm had waked her.

"Thanks, Imre. Be careful."

"Always," Vaughn answered, and Jian swung herself down the ladder to the crew deck.

The *Byron* was too big, she thought again as she let herself fall into the embrace of the central core, allowing the fields to carry her down the length of the ship toward the engine room. Without Manfred to relay messages, and the web of date nodes to give instant access to the ship's systems, it was almost frighteningly oversized, impossible to manage with only a crew of three. It was just good luck that the core fields ran off the main engines, had nothing to do with the standing systems or Manfred. *If I'd had to climb all the way down to engineering, one ladder at a time . . .*

She reached the last level then, and stepped out into the spotless engine room. Red was standing between two consoles, his hands busy with wires and cable clips; every few seconds, he would set aside a wire and touch keys and levers on one or the other of the consoles.

"Tell me what to do," Jian said, and moved up beside him. Red nodded to the right-hand console.

"Take that."

Jian edged past him, scanning the row of levers warily, seeing the fields' flux reflected in the monitors above her head. It had been a long time she had had to match the Drive; she was out of practice. A narrow spike shot above the wavering line that filled a quarter of the screen, its tip tinged with yellow shading rapidly into orange. Red gave her an agonized glance, and Jian reached for the levers, adjusted them until the spike receded, was absorbed back into the main mixture. It did not take her long to relearn the process, though she was still reacting to the changes rather than anticipating them, as Red would have done. She risked a glance sideways, and saw him connecting the last of the cables to her console.

"I've slaved the secondaries to your board," he said. "Mitexi?"

Major's dead, probably on the floor of his cabin. Which one did you want? Jian killed that response, born of stress and just-acknowledged fear, said, "In the control room."

Red nodded, and turned away. Jian fixed her eyes on the display board, watching the broad band of color slowly flex, sliding the levers back and forth to damp out any major shifts in the pattern. There was a data node set into the console, and she glanced at it when she dared, testing the feel of the ship along her wires. It was ragged still, interference tightening every time she made contact, but they were still close enough to the grain. She concentrated on the display, letting the band of color fill her eyes, her mind, hands darting from lever to lever to keep the fields as steady as possible. The suit could not help her; it took every bit of her attention to maintain the levels. She lost herself in the pulsing band of light. She could not have told how long she had been standing there when Vaughn's voice came from the overhead speaker.

"Reverdy? How's it going?"

"Haya," Jian answered slowly, shaking herself free of the seductive display. "How's the repairs?"

"Well," Vaughn said, and Jian could hear the ghost of humorless laughter in his tone. "On the good side, Mitexi's cleaned out the standing system—you may have noticed things got a little easier there for a while?"

She had noticed, Jian realized, though not consciously. There had been a moment when the spikes that threatened to erupt from the main body had eased perceptibly, become less frequent—more random, and harder to catch before they started, but easier to damp down again. She shook herself, shook the thought away. "Yeh, I saw."

"Red's got the interfaces mostly rewired—there were plenty of spares in the component bin, he says. So we could reload the overseer as soon as he gets done." His voice took on a savage note, and Jian braced herself for the bad news. "That is, if we had a working overseer to plug in."

"What about yours?" Jian asked.

"Well, that's the trick," Vaughn answered. "Apparently it takes two to run this ship—two ordinary Spelvins, that is. When I loaded Elisee, I didn't make a backup—hell, there wasn't time, it seemed a decent risk, with mine to spare. But now Mitexi tells me you need two, one to run the virtual worlds, one to handle internal systems."

"Can you plug your overseer into the virtual worlds, and run the internal systems by hand?" Jian asked.

"We'll have to, won't we?" Vaughn retorted. "It won't be easy, one of us'll have to be on it all the time." There was a silence, and Jian could almost see him glaring at Mitexi. "That's what comes of trusting super-constructs."

"When Red gets done, have him take over for me," Jian said slowly, and risked leaning away from the board long enough to touch the button that ended their conversation.

She would have to give up her copy of Manfred, of course: the alternative, four hours on the internal systems, dodging back and forth through the engine room to keep everything functioning smoothly, then four hours' piloting, and four hours off, was no alternative at all. The only real question was how to avoid the worst consequences. Mitexi Minor would be furious—and not unreasonably, either, since she, Jian, would be admitting she had planned to pirate the construct. And piracy was thoroughly illegal: *I can only hope my little blackmail ploy, and the fact she didn't tell us that it would take both our constructs to run the ship—which has to be actionable somehow—will even things out.* She sighed, and slid a lever along its slot, killing a rising spike. *Somehow, I don't really think so.*

She had made and discarded half a dozen plans by the time

Red made his appearance, was no closer to a good solution. The best she had been able to come up with was to claim that Manfred had suspected something and copied himself— but Mitexi was a constructor, and knew just how unlikely that was. She turned the controls over to Red without exchanging a word, and made her way back up to the crew deck.

The blocks that held Manfred were just as she had left them, tucked into the ports of her backup system, standby lights glowing green, the connector light, the one that told whether or not the data reader was tied into a ship's standing system, showing bright red. She touched the casing gently, almost a caress, and released the blocks from the triple ports. She paused then, looking at them, looking at her reader, and set the fresh copy aside to rummage again in her bag for the remaining storage blocks. *Hang for a penny, hang for a pound,* she thought, and fitted two more blocks—Elisee's blocks, that she would never use again for that—into the ports. She was still missing a block. She sat back on her heels beside the opened case, scowling in utter frustration. After everything that had happened, she couldn't bear not having her own copy of Manfred. She had played high enough to get him. *After everything that's happened, I'm not going to be stopped by a missing block.* Vaughn's cabin would be locked— *and anyway, I don't want to have to explain this to him*— which left her a single crude expedient. Still frowning, she rummaged through the bag again until she found the longest of the manga she had bought before leaving Persephone, and compared the numbers printed on its casing with the numbers glowing in the final storage block's load window. The disk was—barely—big enough, in terms of simple capacity, to take the block's content; the question was, would it be able to cope with the complex data matrix? Most disks were linear; the blocks were dimensional. *It may not work, probably won't, even, but if you want Manfred for yourself, this is your last chance.* She snugged the disk into the port—*at least they standardized the data i/o format a long time ago*—and switched the reader back on-line. The light stayed red for a moment longer than usual, then faded to green. It was all she could do. She picked up the first set of blocks, and headed for the control room.

Vaughn was still in the pilot's cage, hands tight on the controls, but he turned his head at her approach. "Where the hell have you been? We need to install my construct, and then Mitexi's going to try to pry whatever's left of Elisee and/ or Manfred out of memory."

Jian held up the blocks. "No."

"What do you mean, no? I told you, we have to have two normal constructs to run this ship." He shot a glance almost of loathing in Mitexi's direction the constructor, still busy at her console, did not seem to notice.

"Two constructs," Jian said, "or Manfred."

"What?" Vaughn swung halfway around, disciplined himself to keep his hands on the controls.

Mitexi swung around in her chair. "Do you mean to tell me that you made a copy of my construct?"

When you have no defense, Jian thought, *attack.* "That's right. The specs you gave us were dodgy, everything was channeled through a single system—of course I made an offline copy. I would, of course, have turned it over to you once we were out of Drive," she added unblushingly. "You should be damn glad I did."

"Of course." Mitexi was eyeing her with extreme disfavor. "Just as I should be grateful for your presence in Refuge City."

"Exactly," Jian answered, and managed a smile that bared teeth.

"As on Refuge," Mitexi said deliberately, "I seem to have no choice but to accept this. However, I'm warning you, every potential employer on Persephone is going to hear how well you keep your contracts—"

"If you do that," Jian said, quite calmly, "all of your business—all of your more than dubious dealings with us, and everything else we've gathered on this trip, like your deal with Kagami—will become public knowledge. More than that, it will go straight to Dreampeace."

Mitexi stared at her for a long moment, amber eyes narrowed, mouth closed tight around the knowledge of defeat.

Jian's threat was the trump card, and they both knew it. "Very well," she said at last. "Let's begin the installation."

Jian handed her the data blocks. Mitexi took them, eyes still fixed, but turned away at last to stoop beneath the half-opened console. She wiggled the blocks into their slots and rose stiffly to her feet, frowning thoughtfully at the console's changing displays. She looked intent, pure and disciplined, completely focused on the system and the emerging construct, but Jian, watching her, knew that her own offense had not been forgotten, or even set aside for very long. She shrugged to herself—*too late now, whatever*—and went to join Vaughn in the pilot's cage.

Vaughn looked sideways at her, shook his head once. "You sure know how to win friends," he said under his breath, and Jian managed a reluctant smile.

"I learned it from you, Imre."

"Huh." The yanqui monosyllable was answer enough. "Back me, will you? It's a brain buster."

"Haya." Jian unfolded the second input board, punched in the codes to slave it to the standing system. "What do you want—do I take the trim corrections, or do I fly it?"

"You trim," Vaughn said firmly.

Jian nodded, ran her hands over the board, configuring it to the job. Normally, they would reverse roles, let her control the ship's actual position in space while Vaughn handled the usually niggling job of aligning secondary systems and keeping the sensors tuned. Flying like this, though, effectively blind to any input from hyperspace itself, Vaughn's knack for matching numbers was their best hope to keep the ship stable in the unreal space. Jian saw her displays change, the numbers that indicated the sensory alignment shifting, slewing toward one end of the narrow effective band. She touched keys, bringing it back, but the secondary stabilizers were sliding out of line. She corrected that, frowning now, her world narrowing again to the instrument wall and the little screen above her dancing fingers. It seemed an eternity before Mitexi spoke again.

"Manfred's in place, and everything checks out so far. The system—the interfaces in particular—are still pretty dodgy. But I'm ready to run Install."

The two pilots exchanged glances, Vaughn smiling slightly, angry-eyed, Jian impassive, and Jian said, ''Go ahead.''

There was a squeal from the console as the blocks opened, pouring their data into the system, and then Jian felt the first stirrings of sensation running along her suit. Mitexi said, ''The standing system's coming back on. All right, there are patches to make.''

Jian nodded, feeling the gaps and imperfections rasping along the wires, and pressed the access glyph to lower her sensitivity. Even so, she could feel misplaced commands and data snapping like sparks under her skin. A sense of panic, fear pure and absolute, flooded through her, was washed away by an equally intense but mercifully brief feeling of sheer pleasure. She shook herself, breath coming short, checked her readouts by reflex only.

''Mitexi,'' Vaughn said, sounding equally shaken, and the constructor snapped, ''I'm working on it.''

A few minutes later, Jian felt the crackle of data ease to a comprehensible flow, the sensations less precise than they had been, but recognizable. She evaluated them automatically—*engines steady; the Drive fields out of tune but within bounds; life support fine; no sign of the overseer*—and said aloud, ''Feels better.''

She felt the Drive ease as she spoke, as Red brought the complex fields back into their optimum configuration. Vaughn said, ''Can we bring the cage back on-line?''

''Give me a minute,'' Mitexi said. There was a silence, and then she made a soft noise of satisfaction. ''All right. Go ahead.''

Vaughn touched a series of buttons, and the data nodes lit, webbing them briefly in a net of pale light. Then that image faded, and they were surrounded by the default world, bright planes and lines of multicolored light. This was closer to Vaughn's preferred interface than her own, Jian knew, and still required heavy numeric input—or it would until Manfred came back into service. She said aloud, ''You got it?'' and Vaughn nodded.

''You get off-line, I'll wait for Manfred.''

Jian nodded and stepped back out of the cage. Neither of them mentioned the real reason for her leaving the cage: if something went drastically wrong, the ship would still have a pilot.

"All right," Mitexi said. She was still bent over the console, fingers quick on the interface keys. "I'm running Install."

"Right," Vaughn said, voice grim. Jian held her breath, willing the machines to function correctly, for Manfred to have been copied correctly, for the interfaces to be sufficiently repaired—

"Got it," Vaughn said, and the words were a cheer. In the same instant, Manfred's face—the devil-face—appeared in the wall, and the construct said, "Installation is complete. I must report damage to both primary and secondary interfaces. I am attempting to reroute my functions, but I fear my ability to manifest certain parts of your program will be impaired."

#As long as you can run the ship,# Vaughn said, #I don't care.#

"The ship's course is significantly biased," Manfred said.

#I'm working on it,# Vaughn snarled.

"Do you want me to take over, Imre?" Jian asked.

#No, not yet. I'm going to enjoy fixing this.#

"Whatever turns you on," Jian murmured.

The other pilot ignored her. #Mitexi. Do you want me to drop a communication buoy?#

"What?" Mitexi turned away from the console, frowning. "Whatever for?"

#You said he was dead—your brother, I mean,# Vaughn answered. #You'll need to notify the authorities.#

Mitexi's frown deepened as though she wanted to refuse, and Jian said, "I agree. Otherwise, you'll be hung up in customs for the next year."

"Very well, do it." Mitexi looked at the other woman. "For now, I'll need your help with the body, Bi' Jian." Her tone made the honorific an insult.

"Haya," Jian said. Mitexi could very well wait until the karakuri could be dispatched to help, but there was no point in not conceding this. *It just might make her a little less vindictive later on, and it doesn't hurt me at all.*

"Come on," Mitexi said, face and voice grim, and swung herself down the ladder. Jian followed her down to the main passenger deck. Reaction was beginning to set in; her legs were a little weak, and her hand, when she lifted it, was trembling slightly. She grimaced—*this is not the time to turn squeamish*—and made herself match Mitexi step for step.

Mitexi had put her brother in a cabin next to her own, where she, the medikuri, and all the other karakuri could keep an eye on him. *Or where she thought they could, anyway,* Jian amended. *It clearly didn't work.* She was angry still, but also, obscurely, sorry for him, sorry that he was dead. The unfamiliar mix of emotions made her uncomfortable, and she shied away from it, concentrating on the job at hand.

The door of the cabin was standing open, and Mitexi frowned. "I closed that," she said slowly. "I closed it and I latched it. . . ." She let the words trail off, and quickened her steps. Jian kept up with her, warily, already anticipating the worst.

The cabin was empty, of course, the bloodstained sheets dragged from the bunk and halfway across the floor, leaving a smeared brown trail. Mitexi swayed slightly, seeing that, the first real sign of any weakness in her, but recovered instantly. Jian looked away and saw another, fainter smear on the tiles outside the entrance to Mitexi's cabin. She blinked, imagining a wounded body dragging itself along the tiles somehow, and Mitexi said, very softly, "No. He was dead. I confirmed it."

"Are you sure?" Jian said, and pointed toward the trail.

"He stabbed himself in the throat," Mitexi said, her voice under tight control. "He was dead."

"Right," Jian said, her own voice less than certain, and stepped into sensor range of the twin karakuri flanking the doorway. As she had expected, the movement triggered them, and the nearer bent forward slightly, her eyes opening.

Who? The synthesized voice was whispery, deliberately unreal, and as spooky as it had seemed the first time Jian had spoken with it.

"Jian," she answered, and the karakuri came slowly upright again.

"Enter."

"Thanks," Jian said, and passed between them into the shadowy main room. Mitexi followed close at her heels.

Light blazed from a dozen standards and from the ceiling cones, swung to center on the massive bed that had been dragged out of the inner room. Heavy cargo handlers, their squat matte-yellow bodies half in shadow, crouched at each end of the bed, padded manipulators still braced against the carved wooden frame. A trio of smaller machines were clustered together at the foot of the bed: a pair of cleaners, multiple arms folded close to their round brushed-steel bodies as though they hugged themselves in sorrow; and a single medikuri huddled beside them, all its cables and tentacles trailing. There were more karakuri in the shadows to either side of the room—cleaners, barmaids, one-function babybrains, another cargo mover, a beautiful gold-skinned woman-shape without definable purpose—but Jian barely noticed them, her breath catching in her throat.

Mitexi Major lay in state, his body laid out tidily against a pile of pillows, his thin arms folded across his chest. His eyes were closed, and he would have looked almost peaceful had it not been for the raw tear at the base of his throat. They had stripped him, Jian realized, stripped him and washed the body and clothed him again in plain shirt and trousers. *Perhaps the woman-shape did that; none of the others seem to have the right manipulators—*

"Who the hell?" Mitexi Minor began, her voice low and shaking, though whether with anger or fear or sorrow Jian could not tell.

Jian shook her head, started forward, but the gold-skinned karakuri lifted her head and turned to look at them. In the same moment, one of the babybrains broke ranks and skittered into the light, interposing its thick body between them and the bier.

"Please do not approach further." That was the golden woman-shape, a sweet high breathless voice from an unmoving face that was not human at all, all sharp teeth and bone and glowing feral eyes. Behind it, the other karakuri shifted, swinging on treads and legs and multiple wheels to face the strangers.

"Please do not approach further," the golden karakuri

said, and Jian took a step backward, absolutely unwilling to
challenge the machines.

"Manfred?" There was no answer, and she looked around
for a data node, found one at last, and fixed her eyes on it.
"Manfred."

"Yes, Reverdy?" This copy's voice was subtly different
from the first's, the balanced tone shifted ever so slightly—
incongruously—toward the feminine.

"Can you explain what's happened here?"

"One moment." There was a pause, and Mitexi reached
out to close one hand bruisingly tight around the other woman's wrist.

"He did this, Venya did. He must've done."

Jian winced, but did not pull away. At the end of the room,
closest to the improvised bier, a multiarmed server moved
suddenly, almost silent except for the soft whine of gears,
turning back to face Mitexi Major's body. It was one of the
quasi-human shapes the *Byron*'s designers had loved, a silver
body sculpted with carefully sexless muscles, gender circum-
vented by drapery of pale copper leaves, each of its six arms
banded with inset stones that caught the light as it folded
each pair of hands across its chest. It lowered its head as
though in mourning, but not before Jian had seen what had
been done to its face. It wore a human face, stylized but
human, a mask that had been perfect and was now streaked
with vertical lines where the burnished metal skin was tar-
nished and broken, as though it had wept tears of acid. The
gold-skinned woman was marked the same way, Jian saw
when she looked again; it was just harder to see the scars
against the brighter finish. And the others, too, anything that
seemed to have a head, even the ones like the cargo handler
that had only a rounded dome above the boxy utilitarian body,
all were scored with the same lines like the tracks of tears.
The carpet glittered where the flecks of metal caught the
light.

"Christ," Jian whispered, and knew Mitexi Minor had
seen it, too. She could feel the other woman trembling, could
see the muscles of her jaw clenched tight to keep her teeth
from chattering. She looked back at the data node.
"Manfred?"

"A program was placed in secondary maintenance," the construct said, "which directed the disposal of Ba' Mitexi's body. It was executed as part of routine housekeeping when I came back on line."

"Cancel it," Jian began, and Mitexi said, "No, don't."

"I'm sorry," Manfred said, "I have conflicting instructions."

"Leave everything just the way it is," Mitexi said. She tugged at Jian's wrist, pulling her with her toward the door of the cabin. "Once we're out of here, seal the room."

Jian let herself be hurried from the cabin without protest, glanced back to see the golden karakuri turn back to face the bier, bowing its head in mourning. In the same instant, one of the two cleaners crouching by the end of the bed reached up with one manipulator and—very gently, very delicately—took hold of the cuff of Mitexi Major's trousers, clinging like a lost child. It was the last thing Jian saw before the cabin door slid shut and the lights went out behind the door karakuris' eyes.

"You'll need your clothes," she said slowly, shaking away the image.

"I'll manage," Mitexi Minor said. She looked at Jian, seemed to realize she was still holding the other woman's wrist, and released her hold. "I'm taking a cabin on the crew deck. I don't want to be too far away from main systems access."

Or too close to your brother's body, Jian thought, but nodded. "That's fine," she said, and did her best to sound reassuring. Mitexi stared straight ahead as if she hadn't heard. "Bi' Mitexi?"

The constructor shook herself convulsively, and even managed a white-lipped smile. "Right," she said. "Let's go."

8

The damaged interfaces limited Manfred's ability to display the complex worlds he had built before the attack. By the time Jian went back on-line, however, most of the possible repairs had been made, and even Vaughn admitted that the system was working well enough that they should be able to translate out of Drive without any difficulty. Jian, studying the rumpled landscape laid out before her, acknowledged the truth of his comments with a nod. This still felt more like Elisee's world than Manfred's, but the construct was getting better, more like himself, all the time. She could feel the ship's health singing through her suit—stronger than usual, as she had tuned her suit high to help block out her memories of Mitexi Major lying dead among the karakuri—and gloried in it, savoring each heightened shift of phase.

#It's good to have you back,# she said, impulsively expansive.

Manfred answered at once. #Thank you. Though I believe my current existence is as much your responsibility as anyone's.#

Jian blinked, startled. A construct should not be sufficiently self-aware to recognize changes in its status as an entity. Changes in code, changes in particular aspects of its structure, yes, but not its existence or nonexistence: *otherwise, how in good conscience could you turn it off?* She said cautiously, #Then you—remember—what happened.#

#I am aware that I was attacked, as was the system in which I am residing. I was unable to stop the spread of the virus—I use the word loosely, of course—and the standing systems were damaged.# There was a pause, as though Manfred's attention was momentarily distracted. #They are still functioning at less than ninety-five percent of rated capacity.#

#But we won't have any problem flipping out of Drive,# Jian said.

#I don't think so,#Manfred answered.

Jian nodded to him, to herself, still wondering how much Manfred really remembered of the attack. It was disturbing to think that he might remember his own destruction, that he and other constructs might remember each time they were turned off, disconnected from the standing systems that gave them function, existence—that they might come to dread the moment when the job ended, and they would be returned to nothingness, to the limbo of potentiality. And that dread would be inarticulate, because no subprogram would exist to give it voice.

That was pure Dreampeace propaganda, straight from a pinkdisk Ruyin had been sharing around the cooperative. Jian frowned, angry at her own imaginings, but could not shake the fear that they might be true. And if they were, then Elisee had known what it was to die, and had died at her hands. . . . Jian shook that thought away, furious now, with herself, with Mitexi Major, and said, #Why didn't you let us know what was happening? We might've been able to do something, before things got so bad.#

#The virus was launched in a protected sector of my program matrix,# Manfred answered. #By the time I recognized what was happening, and was sure of the seriousness of the situation, I did inform Ba' Vaughn. However, all repair attempts were ineffective.#

The dispassionate voice made her feel a little better—*if he can sound so calm about it, he can't be feeling that much—*

and she said, #All right. Now give me a projection for the next four hours.#

It was the third time in the past hour that she had asked for that same projection, and she was perversely glad to hear the hint of annoyance in Manfred's voice. #There has been no significant change since your last viewing. Do you wish to see it again?#

#Yes,# Jian answered, and was glad to lose herself in the landscape patterns that began to roll past beyond the artificial line of a river.

They flipped out of Drive twenty hours later. Jian made the translation herself this time, riding the data flow as it shifted from the complex virtual world of hyperspace to the mundane images of reality. They were right on course— *Manfred would allow nothing less,* Jian thought, giddy with relief and sheer exhaustion—almost in the end of the deceleration lane that would bring them into Persephone's orbit.

"XRS *Young Lord Byron*, this is Persephone Traffic Control." This time, Traffic Control was a male voice, with the soft slur of coolie diction. "We have you on our screens, and you are cleared to enter the inbound channel. Please report your optimum speed."

Jian reached overhead for communications, signed *openline.* "Traffic Control, this is XRS *Young Lord Byron*. I copy, we are clear to enter the deceleration lane." She plucked numbers out of the air as she spoke, rearranged and compared them in the space in front of her eyes. "Our rated deceleration is twenty-nine hours, optimum is more like thirty-five to thirty-nine. Anywhere in the high thirties is good for us. What's your pleasure?"

There was an odd hesitation, too long to be simple signal lag, before Traffic Control answered. "Please make your best time, *Byron*. Your buoy signal was received."

"What about other incoming traffic?" Jian asked, and gestured to close the outside line and open a channel to Mitexi Minor's new cabin. #Mitexi, you might want to listen in. Persephone got the word.#

"I'm on," Mitexi answered almost at once, and Traffic Control broke in an instant later.

"*Young Lord Byron*, you've been given red priority. The cops want to have a word with you."

"Shit," Mitexi's voice said softly, in Jian's ear.

Traffic Control went on, soberly now, as though a superior had spoken sharply to him, "All other inbound traffic will clear the road for you. Please make your best time."

"We'll do that, Control," Jian said.

"Thank you. Please inform us of your ETA as soon as possible."

"I will," Jian said, and closed the connection with a gesture. #Did you hear that, Bi' Mitexi?#

"I heard." Mitexi's voice was grim. "Well, we have no choice. I'll be expecting them."

#Right,# Jian said, with deliberate skepticism, but the other woman had already ended the connection. Jian sighed, shaking her head, and made herself study the new display surrounding her. Manfred had faded it in expertly, and now, reading from the position of her head and eyes that she was fully aware of it, he deepened the colors still further. Once again, Jian stood at the center of a disk of stars, Persephone itself a larger, brighter star on the rim of the disk directly ahead of her. The deceleration lane was outlined in lines of pale blue; within that corridor, Jian could see the triangles and wedges that were other ships moving out of the lane ahead of them, clearing the *Byron*'s approach. Jian shivered, seeing that—*nobody likes the cops taking this much interest in them*—but said, #Manfred, plot me the quickest course in to Persephone—the one that gets us into parking orbit in the least amount of time.#

There was a pause, and then a brighter blue line appeared between the two that marked the edges of the approach line. It was shaded to represent the rate of deceleration, and most of the color stained the far end: they would come in at high speed, and begin braking only as they approached the Styx, the outermost of the two asteroid belts that ringed the system. Jian made a face, seeing that—*tricky flying*—but there was really no other option.

Manfred's course brought them in precisely on schedule, and Vaughn took over the job of nudging the *Byron* into the correct parking orbit. Jian, watching the backup boards, could see the flashing light on her screens that represented a police boat waiting for them to dock. Vaughn could see it, too, and she could hear a string of ever more outrageous curses floating over the intercom. Then at last they were in place, the *Byron* snuggled up against a mooring buoy.

Vaughn said, #Everything shows green here, Control. We're docked.#

"Thank you," a new voice said. "*Byron*, this is Saunday Talvander, Cartel Security. Please stand by, we are coming aboard by your main lock."

#The hell—# Vaughn began, and Jian said, "Shut up, Imre."

Before she could say anything else, however, Mitexi answered. "Ba' Talvander, this is Meredalia Mitexi. I'm the *Byron*'s owner. You're welcome to come aboard."

"Thank you, Bi' Mitexi." Talvander's voice was cool, at once remote and polite. "Please stand by."

In her screens, Jian saw a smaller sliver detach itself from the larger shape that was the main police boat. *Not taking any chances*, she thought, and pushed herself up away from the control board. "Imre, are you still on-line?"

"No." Vaughn sounded sullen, but otherwise under control, not likely to do anything too stupid immediately.

"Manfred." Jian waited until the face—still the devil face, the face she preferred now over the blank, disturbing calm of the black-and-white mask—appeared in the wall. "Tell Bi' Mitexi we—myself, Imre, and Red—will be waiting in the main crew room."

"Very well," Manfred said, and vanished.

Mitexi was waiting for them in the crew room, watching the wallscreen which was displaying the police boat's position. The tiny shape of the transfer craft had almost reached the *Byron*'s side; even as Jian recognized it for what it was, it vanished into the *Byron*'s side. The police boat was edging off a little—gaining space in which to use its single cannon, she realized, and shook her head.

"It's so fun, attracting official notice," Vaughn said from the doorway. He came on into the room, Red at his heels as always, seated himself at a corner table as far from Mitexi as he could manage. The technician leaned against the wall beside him, hands braced behind his back, head down so that his hair half hid his face.

"Well, Imre, you should know," Jian said halfheartedly, and Talvander's voice spoke from the wall.

"We are docked. You may cycle your lock now."

Mitexi looked up, broad face blank. "Let them in, Manfred. Give them a guide light to the core, and tell them where we are."

"Very good, Bi' Mitexi."

They sat for a while in silence, no one quite knowing what to say—*and what is there to say; is there anything that can be said?* Jian thought, and poured herself a cup of tea she did not want, just to have something to do. Then at last they heard the soft fall of footsteps on the tiles outside, and three figures filled the doorway.

The leader was a bulky man in the familiar dark-green coveralls of Cartel Security, big enough that he almost hid the pair behind him. "Bi' Mitexi? I'm Talvander." His voice was accentless, but Jian wondered suddenly if he were from off-world. There was something in the shape of him that was foreign, and it would make sense to employ an outsider on a job like this. . . .

He came on into the room, the other two following without coming so close that they could not use the riot pistols belted at their waists. Seeing that, Jian felt her stomach knot, and raised her eyebrows. "What's all this, then?" she said softly, and saw Mitexi frown.

"I'm Mitexi," she said to Talvander.

Talvander nodded. "This is Jao Vivie, representing the Freyan Provisional Government, and Captain Lindiwe Wariner, of the Peacekeepers."

"I'm here only as an observer," the woman murmured, smiling slightly. She had a lined, sleepy-looking face, but the eyes under her drooping lids would miss very little.

Vaughn whistled through his teeth, and Jian gave a twisted smile. *The FPG, and the Peacekeepers, on top of regular Security: what next?*

Mitexi mimed a polite greeting, her face empty of any emotion. "This is the crew I hired for this trip. Reverdy Jian, chief pilot, Imre Vaughn, and—'' She stopped abruptly, and a sudden quick smile crossed her face. "Red."

Talvander lifted an eyebrow. "I'll need to see your papers, please, all of you. This is the full crew?"

"Yes," Mitexi answered.

Jian reached into her belt for her identification disks, moving carefully to avoid startling the FPG cop. He was watching them all with narrowed eyes, his right hand a little too close to the butt of his pistol: the FPG encountered violent revolt often enough for that tension to have infected even its offworld employees. She handed the disk to Talvander, who slipped it into his pocket without doing more than glance at the printed surface. Vaughn handed over his disk and Red's, and the security man tucked them away, too.

"What I would like to do now," he said, "is hear from you—all of you—exactly what happened. Jao, you take a look at the body."

Vivie nodded, and Wariner said softly, "I think I'd like to tag along with him."

Talvander blinked once, but nodded. "If you can tell us where you've put the body?"

"In the owner's cabin," Mitexi answered. "Manfred—"

"Who?" Talvander cut in sharply.

"I'm sorry. The overseer, it's a Spelvin construct. It also manages housekeeping, and other general duties." Mitexi stopped, watching the strangers, and Talvander nodded. "Manfred, please give Ba' Vivie and Bi'—I'm sorry, Captain Wariner a guide down to my old cabin."

"Very well, Bi' Mitexi," Manfred answered. A sphere of cool light materialized in the air just outside the doorway, began drifting suggestively toward the central core.

"Thank you," Wariner murmured. Vivie gave an abrupt nod, and they followed the sphere out of the room.

"I'd like to get some preliminary information now," Talvander continued, his tone still pleasant, soothing, "though of course we will want to interview you individually as well. And also, of course, your statements will be recorded." He slipped a small box out of the pocket of his oversized jacket, set it on the nearest table. A light was flashing in the center of its tiny control panel, but steadied as soon as he spoke again. "Does anyone have any objections?" There were none, and he smiled, showing even, expensive teeth. "Then if you, Bi' Mitexi, would begin by telling me what happened."

"Very well." Mitexi took a deep breath, then, quite unexpectedly, sat down in the nearest chair, one hand white-knuckled for a moment on the edge of the table. "My brother, Venya Mitexi, killed himself by stabbing himself in the throat. I don't know where he got the knife; I assume one of the serving karakuri brought it to him—"

Talvander held up his hand. "I'm sorry, could you start at the beginning, please? Your flight prospectus said you left Persephone for Refuge, presumably to find your brother?"

Mitexi nodded jerkily. Jian, watching her, could not decide if she was acting, or if she was truly—finally—distraught at her brother's death. To give the woman her due, there had been no time before now to admit of grief; *still,* Jian thought, *the sudden stammer, the catch in her voice, seemed a little too much.*

"May I ask why?" Talvander's voice was infinitely patient.

Mitexi collected herself with a visible effort. "I needed his help if I had to revise the program matrix for the Manfred construct," she said. "He built the original program—the version that's running now—and I wasn't sure I could duplicate his work. So I went to get him. The *Byron* needed a check cruise anyway."

"Why was Ba' Mitexi on Refuge?" Talvander asked.

"He had been heavily involved in Dreampeace, at the beginning of the movement." A spasm of something, pain, perhaps, or even anger, briefly aged her face by twenty years.

Talvander led her through a drastically abbreviated account of the events on Refuge—the constructor did not mention either Avelin or Seki, Jian noted with amusement, but kept her outward expression dutifully emotionless—and then through the homeward voyage itself.

"So your brother was being treated for his condition. By whom?" Talvander's tone was still patient, but Mitexi answered as though she heard disapproval in his voice.

"His doctor—his former doctor on Persephone—gave me a disk of his previous medications, and the *Byron* runs an extremely sophisticated set of diagnosis and treatment programs. They are monitored by the overseer, also. He seemed to be responding well.'' Mitexi glanced then at the pilots. ''You can ask them.''

''He was all right until he tried to cut his wrists,'' Vaughn said.

''This was before the suicide,'' Talvander said.

''Certainly wasn't after,'' Vaughn murmured.

''That's right,'' Jian said, cutting off anything else Vaughn might say. *Better not to get too deeply involved in any of this, especially with the second set of pirated storage blocks—or two storage block and a disk—a second Manfred, tucked into my carryall.* ''Maybe eight, ten hours.''

''Were you present at this attempt?'' Talvander asked, and Jian shook her head.

''I was,'' Vaughn said. He nodded toward the table where the terminal still stood. ''He was sitting over there, working at the machine, and I wasn't paying any attention. Then he picked up one of the knives from the autoserver—I guess he'd gotten it before I came in, I sure didn't see him do it—and just stabbed it right into his wrist.'' He mimed the movement, shaking his head slightly in disbelief. ''Before you ask, he didn't say a damn thing. I haven't the faintest idea what it was all about.''

Talvander nodded, a gesture that should have been soothing. Jian watched him warily, not sure quite why she distrusted him. *No, distrust's too strong, but I think there's something going on he's not telling us. I just can't imagine what—unless it's Seki. But Avelin did that, and it was self-defense—and since when did the Cartel give a damn about what happens off-world?* She was scowling, she realized tardily, and smothered her expression, but not before Talvander had seen.

''Bi' Jian? Do you have anything to add?''

Jian shook her head. ''I was thinking about all the formalities we'll have to go through, Ba' Talvander. It's been one hell of a flight, and I'll be glad to get home.''

''Quite.'' Talvander gave her a thin smile, and for a shaken moment Jian was sure that he knew the home to which she was claiming a passionate attachment was in fact just the basement room of her brother's flat. "We'll try to make this as painless as possible."

"Bi' Mitexi." That was Wariner's voice, sounding sharper than it had before. In the same moment, Manfred's devil-face took shape in the wall, but the construct did not speak at once.

"Yes?" Mitexi said. She was looking at Manfred, frowning slightly.

"Would you instruct your operating systems to let us examine your brother's body?"

"Sa, of course. I beg your pardon." Mitexi collected herself, turned to face the wall where Manfred had appeared. "Manfred, you will please allow the authorities to do as they wish. Clear the karakuri out of the room."

"Karakuri?" Talvander said, and Vivie said, "Fucking room's full of them. They won't let us get near the body."

Manfred said, "I beg your pardon for the inconvenience. It was Ba' Mitexi's last wish, and Bi' Mitexi ordered that it be honored."

"I'm sorry," Mitexi said. "I'd—I think I'd blanked it."

"Quite all right," Wariner said.

"Jao?" Talvander asked.

"They're moving off," Vivie answered. Jian could almost hear him shaking his head. "Hell of a thing."

They spent perhaps another three hours with the police, first together and then separately—Jian wondered afterwards just how, or if, they had persuaded Red to speak in more than monosyllables—but at last Talvander turned them over to customs. The customs men made only a perfunctory check, and then they were free to catch a transfer tug back to the station and take the next shuttle down to The Moorings. They made the short ride almost in silence, Mitexi sitting apart from the rest of them, in the single uncomfortable seat just behind the pilot's closed compartment. The shuttle was full, anyway; it was easier to find three seats together, two and one opposite on the aisle, than four. Jian leaned back in the safety netting, closed her eyes against the bright cabin lights. It was early evening, by the clock, and early in the morning of the planet's long day. It would be hot, riding back to Landage, and Jian smiled slightly in anticipation. After Refuge, she would be glad to feel even the scorching sun.

After Refuge, it would be good to be back to ordinary work, where all she had to worry about was whether or not whatever ship she was flying was going to break apart before she could manhandle it to its destination. *All things considered, I'd rather have technical problems*, she thought, but felt her smile turn wry. *Not that we were short of technical problems this trip.*

She shook that thought aside, but the worry refused to vanish. She had a good record—*and so does the co-op*—and she didn't need or want to be involved with the police. Still, Talvander had seemed convinced by their combined stories, not inclined to ask any more questions. *As long as he signs the death certificate*, she thought, *we'll be all right. And anyway, even at the worst, he can't accuse any of us. If there's any trouble, it's all Mitexi's.*

The shuttle landed with its usual precision, trailing a great plume of dust across the runway carved in the Daymare Basin, and the land tugs crept out to drag it back to its mooring point. Jian and Vaughn climbed stiffly out of the compartment when the craft finally docked, Red trailing them, graceful as ever, but they were stopped halfway through the transfer tube by Mitexi's voice.

"Bi' Jian." In the stark light of the white-painted tunnel, she looked almost ugly, unfamiliar lines and shadows marring her smooth face. "And Ba' Vaughn. Our association is over. Your contract has expired, and it will be paid in full within banking hours tomorrow. I expect—" her tone made it an order—"I will not see you again."

She turned on her heel before Jian could find an answer, striding away down the very center of the corridor. Jian stared after her, watching her short coat billow backward, the corners snapping back to reveal the brilliant black-and-gold brocade of the lining. It was not regret she was feeling, not exactly, but Jian had the sense of something unfinished still between them.

"Charming woman," Vaughn said, and she shook away her unexamined mood.

"Isn't she just?" Jian sighed, shifted the heavy carryall to a more comfortable position on her shoulder. "Hang back a little, we can catch the next land shuttle."

Vaughn grinned. "You mean you don't fancy another trip with her in close quarters."

"No, I don't," Jian answered, and when she slowed her pace, the other pilot copied her. Mitexi was a good thirty meters ahead of them when they reached the end of the transfer tunnel.

The media was waiting for them, beyond the waist-high barrier that separated passengers from the business areas of the port, newsdogs backed by the chants and bright posters of a Dreampeace demonstration team. More than just the team: there was a crowd of supporters with them as well. Jian saw Mitexi falter, as though she'd walked unexpectedly into gunfire; the newsdogs saw it too, and leaned forward in a babble of lights and amplified questions. The other passengers hung back, too, their confused murmuring a counterpoint to the shouting beyond the barrier. For a few minutes, at least, they would serve as a screen.

"This way," Jian said, and caught Vaughn's shoulder, dragging him to their left, toward a red-painted door marked in glyphs half a meter tall: AUTHORIZED PERSONNEL ONLY. The same message was repeated in realprint beneath the staring white glyphs. Jian ignored both versions, and pressed down on the lock lever. It moved, but the door did not open. "Locked."

"Let Red," Vaughn said, and the technician moved obediently forward. Jian stood aside while Red fiddled with the lockbox, and then the door swung open. It gave onto a narrow stairway, leading down: to the maintenance levels, Jian guessed, and started down them.

"I hope you know where you're going," Vaughn said.

"If you want to be a media star, don't let me stop you," Jian said without looking back. She heard Vaughn laugh, and then the door closing, and their footsteps on the stairs.

"This has to lead to maintenance," Vaughn said after a moment, and Jian laughed.

"I was figuring that, yeh."

"Go down another two levels," Vaughn said, and Jian, surprised, glanced back at him. He was smiling, not the grin that had earned him the name of Crazy Imre, but like a man who'd just realized his good luck. He saw her look, and the smile widened. "This is maintenance, Reverdy. Yanqui country."

Jian swore softly under her breath. *Yes, of course it's yanqui country, and yes of course Imre would be bound to have some relative or friend or friend-of-a-friend who can help us get back to Landage without having to run the gauntlet of newsdogs—and Dreampeacers—waiting for us.* She nodded her approval, and said, "You'd better go first, then."

"And hope we run into somebody who knows me," Vaughn added, but slipped past her to lead the way down the long stairs.

He led them past the first two landings without stopping, paused at the third long enough to peer out through the access door—it was unlocked from this side, of course—and finally brought them out into a white-painted corridor. The glyphs on the wall read VENTILATION LEVEL FIVE. Vaughn smiled again, this time with a twist Jian recognized as irony, and said, "I've got friends in air supply."

Red stirred then, looking faintly dubious, and Jian said, "I hope they still think so."

"I'm hurt," Vaughn protested, scanning the walls. At last he found the tile he was looking for—a rough schematic of the main tunnels—and studied it and the data node beside it. He stared into the node for a moment before turning to his left along the bright corridor. "This way."

"Right," Jian said, without much confidence, and followed. Red trudged behind her, his lack of expression eloquent.

As Jian had more than half expected, they practically ran into a ventilation technician before they had traveled a hundred meters. The tech, a big man, broad-shouldered, hawk-nosed, round-eyed, and unmistakably yanqui, turned a corner and stood staring for an instant, placid face contracting into a menacing frown.

Vaughn said quickly, "Does Gita Catlee still work here? Gita Vaughn that was?"

The technician's expression eased slightly, but the frown remained. "Yeh. Visitors come in by the main roads, gent."

"I'm her brother, Imre. She may have mentioned me," Vaughn said, but the tech was already nodding.

"Hah." He reached into a belt pocket, pulled out a tech's carrycom. "Are you in trouble?"

Jian stifled a laugh.

Vaughn said, "Not exactly . . ."

The technician nodded again, touching keys on the carrycom's input plate. "Right. Heh, Karri? Gita there?" There was a silence, and Jian saw the tiny bubble of a receiver perched behind the man's ear, almost the same color as his close-cut hair. "Yeh, it's Thom. Your crazy brother's here."

He listened for a moment longer, then laughed softly. "Right then," he said, and flicked off the carrycom, tucking it back into his belt. "Come with me." His tone was tolerant, more than anything, and Jian felt a faint pang of what might have been jealousy. She, too, could have been a part of this world—was a part of it, biologically, could have claimed that kinship— She shook the thought aside, annoyed with herself. She was yanqui by birth alone, by her biological father's genes; that would not have been enough to find her a place in this closed community of technicians, any more than a midworlder's upbringing had made her fully at home in the midworld.

The thought lingered nonetheless as the technician hurried them through the maze of corridors and side tunnels, though the inarticulate hurt faded to a sort of curiosity. This was the yanqui kingdom, maintenance itself: ventilation, water and sewage, reclamation, recycling, disposal, repair, all the necessary, unglamorous jobs that still required technical skill if not a lot of capital. Yanquis had been the majority in those trades almost since off-earth settlement began. Jian found herself glancing sideways down the corridors and into the odd rooms they passed, wondering about the banked machines and cryptic displays. Until she had turned sixteen, this had all been an option, one choice among many; it could have been her sitting at a keyboard beneath a bank of multicolored lights like the woman who stared so intently in one of the alcoves. But at sixteen she'd changed her name, exchanged Savinian for her stepfather's surname Jian, and abandoned the possibility of becoming yanqui along with the name.

The technician stopped outside a blue-painted door labeled in realprint with the words CONTROL FIVE and fingered the lockplate, holding his left hand up to shield the code buttons from view. Jian politely looked away, and saw Vaughn giving another of his crooked smiles.

"Gita?" The door opened under the technician's touch, and he waved for them to precede him into the room. "I brought your crazy brother."

Jian obeyed his gesture, came forward into another brightly lit control space. It was bigger than most of the others she had glimpsed, with half a dozen consoles and much larger, three-meters-to-a-side display screens hung on the pale-blue walls. There were surprisingly few people in evidence, for such a complicated-looking place: not every console was occupied, and, of the three that were, one was being managed by a man in ordinary workcloth trousers who had turned away from his boards to talk to a slim woman in a draped tunic who was leaning against the back of his chair. They had both fallen silent now, watching the strangers at the door, but Jian was less aware of them than of the woman who came to meet them. She was small for a yanqui—small in general—and in her face Vaughn's hazel eyes were unexpectedly lovely, and the crow's-feet that deepened with her smile only emphasized their brilliance.

"Well, Imre," she said, "what kind of a mess have you gotten yourself into this time?"

"Well," Vaughn began, but she wasn't listening, extended her hand to Jian instead.

"Gita Catlee. I'm Imre's big sister."

"Reverdy Jian." Jian watched, amazed, as she nodded to Red and turned back to her brother.

"I suppose it has something to do with the demos upstairs?" Catlee had an odd accent, not quite yanqui any more, but not midworld or Urban, either, as though she'd spent some time off-world, outside the yanqui community, enough to lose the flat, distinctive vowels, but not enough to gain a convincing replacement.

"Sort of," Vaughn admitted. "We need to ride into Landage."

"You could take the land shuttle," Catlee said. The lines

around her eyes crinkled, as Vaughn's did when he did not quite want to admit a smile.

"Gita," Vaughn said, and sounded twelve years old.

"Our former employer seems to be the cause—and maybe the object—of the demonstrations," Jian said. "We're a pretty distinctive bunch, and I'd hate to get tied up in all that."

"Yeh, you can't miss Red," Catlee said, and this time she did smile. "And you're not invisible yourself, Bi' Jian." She looked back at Vaughn. "There's a garbage hauler going back to the city in about twenty, thirty minutes. I suppose Georgi would give you a ride."

"Thanks," Vaughn said, with unusual humility. "I really appreciate this, Gita."

"Yeh, thank you," Jian echoed, and looked at Vaughn. "If there's time, I think we should let Peace know what's going on."

"I agree." Vaughn looked at his sister, managed a rueful smile. "Gita, can I use your card?"

Catlee gestured to the main console, which was fitted with an execu-desk setup to one side. "Help yourself. I suppose you'll want the direct line."

"Thanks, Gita," Vaughn said, and seated himself in her chair at the console. Catlee watched as he fingered the controls, tying into the main net and then searching for the appropriate connection, and turned away before he'd reached the cooperative.

"That's one thing you have to say for Imre, you never know what he's going to get you into next."

Jian found herself nodding agreement, and glanced sideways to see faint amusement in Red's face.

"Thanks a lot," Vaughn said sourly, and turned his full attention to the console.

"Bill-Lee," Catlee said. "Tell Pol to bring the scrubber by here."

The man at the far console lifted a hand in acknowledgment, and did something to his controls. "Pol says that'll mean doubling back."

"Tell him to do it," Catlee said.

"Haya." The man spoke briefly into his filament mike,

and leaned back in his chair, the conversation clearly over. "He'll be here in about five minutes."

"Thanks," Catlee said absently, and looked at her brother. "You hear, Imre?"

"I heard." Vaughn's hands scurried across the control board, closing the link to the connection. "Peace'll meet us at Tunnelmouth. I guess Mitexi really made the newsnets."

"Which Mitexi?" Jian asked, and Vaughn gave her a twisted smile.

"The dead one, of course. Bodies can't sue for libel."

"The scrubber's here," the technician—Thom, his name was, Jian remembered—said from the door.

"Then you'd better get moving," Catlee said, and caught Vaughn by the shoulder as he would have passed her. "You and Red be careful, you. And you, bi'."

"I will," Vaughn said, almost gently, and pushed Red in front of him toward the door.

The scrubber was just that, an industrial-level floor-washing machine, with a rounded casing and the square black box of a telechir link set into the center of its back. The triple-barreled eye swiveled to examine them, and a voice said, from the box, "So you're Gita Catlee's crazy brother. Climb on up, all of you."

Jian did as she was told, balancing carefully. A narrow skirting formed a sort of platform at the base of the casing, and she planted her feet on that and leaned back against the body of the machine, wishing there was something she could hold on to once the machine started up again. The others did the same, Red impassive as ever, Vaughn looking distinctly unhappy, and the voice said, "All set? I'm on a schedule."

As the operator spoke, the scrubber came to life, pivoted on its brushes, and slid down the empty corridor, the hiss of the brushes louder than the buzz of its tiny power plant. It was an unexpectedly smooth ride—*the remote operator knows his job, all right*—and Jian, against all expectation, found herself rather enjoying it. The scrubber carried them quickly through the hallways, past the closed doors of a dozen or more rooms. Jian didn't know whether the operator was acting on Catlee's instructions or not, taking them through the less crowded halls, but there were almost no pedestrians in the brightly lit corridors.

The scrubber slowed at last, approaching a spiral down-ramp, and moved into the turns with the sedate, extra-careful movements of a drunken man. The ramp gave onto a loading bay, stacked high with five-meter-long trash bins, each one locked and tagged for one of the seven reclamation plants back in Landage. A hauler was waiting in the bay, two of the bins already chained against the stops of the open bed; the heavy-duty robots that had loaded them sat quiescent in their corner alcoves. A man—another yanqui, tall and sunbaked and wrapped in a loose sun-cheater, with the ends of his headscarf hanging down around his bony face—was sitting on the end of the hauler's bed. He stood up at their approach, said, "You're Gita's—"

"Yeh," Vaughn said. "Her crazy brother."

The hauler smiled. "I'm Georgi Gorman. You want me to take all of you?"

Jian could feel the sand under her feet as they walked forward to meet the stranger, could feel, too, the kiss of hot wind from the surface. "That's right," she said aloud, and couldn't help glancing warily at the hauler's cab. "Is there room?"

"As long as you're all good friends," Gorman answered, and laughed at his own joke.

"Good enough," Jian said, and Gorman swung himself agilely along the side of the hauler, not bothering to climb down to ground level and climb up again to the cab. Jian nodded her appreciation, but took the easier route.

The cab was bigger than it had looked from the outside. Jian found herself wedged tightly between the door and Vaughn's bony elbow, but there was room to breathe, and even to shift a little, if she were circumspect about it. The driver touched buttons on the control panel, and cold air blasted them. Over the noise of it, he said, "I'll be letting you off at the Tunnelmouth loading bay, all right?"

"Haya," Jian answered, and Gorman shifted levers, throwing the hauler into gear. It lurched forward, motor roaring up to full power, and started up the slight incline of the tunnel that led to the surface. Its doors opened automatically at their approach, and they were bathed in the glaring light of the planet's morning. The sun hung just above the tops of the mountains that divided the Daymare Basin from the Ngela Dunefield to the north and west, wiping all color from the sky. Gorman swore, the words inaudible over the noise of the hauler, and darkened the canopy even further. Even with that help, it was hard to make out details. Craning her head sideways, Jian could see that he was steering more by the heads-up guideline projected on the inside of the canopy than by anything he could see outside.

The sun and the noise from the hauler's engine discouraged conversation. Jian leaned against the side of the cab, letting the rush of cold air from the ventilation sweep over her, raising goosebumps on the exposed skin of her arms. By her internal clock—by Persephone's twenty-four-hour clock-day—it was early evening; she blinked back a wave of tiredness, mostly reaction, and wondered what Chaandi was doing. Probably at home, editing something, she thought, and the picture she conjured was enough to sustain her until they reached Tunnelmouth.

Malindy was waiting as promised, piki-cart drawn into a senior manager's slot, a grim expression on his face.

"Thanks, Gorman," Jian said, levering herself out of the cab, and the driver waved the words away.

"Thank his sister," he said, and turned away to shout instructions to the robot wrangler waiting in the corner. The wrangler lifted a hand in answer, and his caterpillar-tracked machines crept forward to begin unloading the first of the heavy bins.

Obviously, they were used to unofficial passengers here. Jian put the thought away for later consideration, and came forward to meet Malindy. "Thanks, Peace, we really appreciate this."

"What in the name of God is that woman up to?" Malindy demanded.

"You tell us," Vaughn said. "You accepted the contract."

Malindy went on as though he hadn't spoken. "The newsdogs've been on our doorstep since the first word came in that there was trouble, and between them and Dreampeace we haven't had two hours' peace since. I left Ruyin talking at them. I had to sneak out the fire doors."

"I must be slow," Vaughn said. "What word?"

Jian looked at him. "The message buoy," she said, and could not resist adding, "the one you dropped."

Vaughn had the grace to look somewhat abashed. Jian turned her attention to the co-op's manager. "Look, Peace, we haven't seen the news. What's supposed to be happening?"

Malindy waved them toward the piki-cart. "What's supposed to be happening," he said, with heavy irony, "is that you've got a construct on-board that breaks the Turing Barrier."

"Oh, for Christ's sake," Vaughn said, and Jian said, "Shut up, Imre."

"I won't shut up, this is fucking stupid—"

"Imre," Jian said, and the other pilot subsided abruptly. He tossed his bag into the cart's open bed, and climbed in after it. Red followed, silent as ever. Jian slid into the driver's pod next to Malindy, and tugged open the partition that separated the driver from the cargo in the back.

"Be that as it may," Malindy said carefully, "and it doesn't sound sensible to me, the media has got hold of the story, and they're not about to let go. Dreampeace, of course, is claiming that Mitexi Minor is holding it prisoner." His tone sharpened, in a way that could not wholly be accounted for by the difficulty of maneuvering the cart out of its tight parking slot. "They're also hinting that she murdered her brother."

"Well, that's bullshit," Vaughn said.

Malindy said nothing, and Jian said thoughtfully, "I suppose she could've done it, at that. But I don't think she did."

"Hell, no," Vaughn said. "She wanted him alive—she needed him, alive and sane."

"Sane?" Malindy slowed the cart, then slid it neatly into a gap in the traffic that clogged the major access road leading onto Broad-hi.

"Yeh." Jian gave a crooked grin. "I bet Dreampeace isn't mentioning that part. The man was crazy, Peace. Crazy enough to kill himself, and to try to kill the rest of us."

Malindy said, "I assume you'll invoke the hazard bonuses."

Vaughn laughed, throwing his head back against the wall of the cab. Jian said, "Oh, yes. We earned them."

"Right," Malindy said, and fell silent. They were feeding onto Broad-hi now, crowded with the evening delivery wagons and dozens of heavily loaded electrobuses carrying the shift change. "The newsdogs want to talk to you," he said at last. "Do you want to talk to them?"

"Not particularly," Jian said, and Vaughn made a rude noise of agreement.

"Right," Malindy said again, and swerved to avoid a 'bus that had stopped almost in the middle of the lane to pick up a frantically waving passenger. He swerved again to avoid a pair of secretaries dashing to make the same 'bus, and said, "You'd better drop out of sight for a while, then. I don't have anything going off-world anytime soon—if something comes up, shall I call you?"

"Yeh," Jian said, and Vaughn nodded.

"We'll be in our regular place, Peace," he said. "It's a chain flat, I'm about ten or so down from the named rentor. I'll just tell the system to reject everybody but my nearest and dearest." He grinned. "The neighbors don't think much of Dreampeace anyway, and they sure won't talk to the newsdogs."

There was no point in going back to her own flat, Jian thought. It was the first place the mediamen would look. For an instant, she tried to picture her prim, school-mama sister-in-law having to cope with the newsdogs and their questions, but her imagination failed her. She shook the thought away, tried to think of other places she could go. There was Chaandi, of course, but the manga-maker had been a little annoyed with her when she left. Wilu was Dreampeace, and not always the most reliable anyway. Katruin had made it very clear she never wanted to see her again, and Taavi was probably still off-world; even if she wasn't, there was barely room in the little stackflat for one. Libra's quarters had the same drawback, and were shared with three other semilegal constructors on top of it. She didn't really know John Desembaa well enough to ask. . . . She said aloud, "You remember Chaandi. I'll see if she'll put me up."

"Just do let me know where you are," Malindy said. "That way, if I do get anything . . ." He let his voice trail off, and Jian nodded.

"Believe me, I'll keep in touch." She peered out through the windscreen, gauging their progress along Broad-hi. The traffic had been heavy; they still weren't more than a kilometer or so from Shaft Beta. Chaandi lived in the midworld, in the Li Po Township, within walking distance of a Beta station. "Let me off the next chance you get," she said, and Malindy swerved obligingly into the curb. Jian slid out deftly, slinging her carryall onto her shoulder in the same movement, and dodged up the steps onto the pedestrian walkway before the vehicles around had really begun honking. Vaughn gestured rudely back at them from the bed of the cart, and then Malindy had them moving again. Jian grinned—*that's just like Imre*—and started back toward Charretse West Change and the entrance to Shaft Beta.

It was good to be back on Persephone, and despite everything she felt her spirits lift. Glyphs sparked and vanished in her sight as she intersected their projectors' tightbeam transmissions, and she touched the access glyph on her arm to increase the brightness slightly. She had not realized until then how much she had missed that gaudy virtual display, on Refuge. Charretse West Change was jammed, of course—*shift change*—and Jian took her place in the queue of people waiting just to get into the station itself. Fortunately, the line ran beside the local info-vendor's main newswall, which was in full display, triggered by signals from dozens of implanted suits. Jian glanced up curiously, wondering if their arrival had made the news yet, and caught the last bytes of a story. It, whatever it was, had happened in Heaven; she had time only to recognized the familiar shape of the Freyan Exchange Building before the story ended.

The scene changed, Dreampeace's symbol, anatomical man mated half and half with a computer chip, flashing large to fill the entire screen. There was an ambiguous murmur from the waiting crowd, some voices approving, others rumbling and unhappy, and Jian glanced aside curiously, wondering who thought what. When she looked back, the screen had split into a montage of scenes: a Dreampeace spokesman, a short-haired woman whose glyph identified her as one of Kagami's interfacers, stock footage of ships in parking orbits—and, of course, the scene at The Moorings. Jian stared at it, not quite believing in its reality, any more than any other bit of news: Mitexi, walking out of the transfer tunnel with the rest of the passengers from the shuttle, elegant and quick-moving, the sober coat swirling open to show its bright lining, and then the change of expression, quickly controlled and shaped into a scowl, as she saw what was waiting for her. Jian squinted, but could not see herself in the background. The realprint crawl, which had been running for a few seconds already, read, *alleges that the owner of a construct capable of breaking the Turing Barrier landed at The Moorings today, bringing copies of the construct with her. Meredalia Mitexi, whose brother Venya, the builder of the construct, committed suicide en route—*

The line moved then, and Jian followed it automatically, not daring to turn back to stare. She got as far as the barriers leading into the station—the station's managing system, wisely, admitted no more people at one time than would fit in the approaching cars—and leaned her hip against the padded surface, turning back now to look again at the newswall. The screens were showing a different montage, mostly unfamiliar faces labeled with glyphs she could not read at this angle, and the trail of realprint was completely illegible. She turned back to face the barrier, sighing. She would have to wait to see the whole thing until she got to Chaandi's—*and it's a good thing she subscribes to most of the services.*

A set of glyphs flashed in the virtual space in front of her, warning her that the approaching downward car would be running express to the Li Po station, and a moment later the big screen above the double doors that led to that section of the shaft lit, too. The doubled message shifted—the car was in, was discharging passengers—and Jian tightened her grip on her transit pass. The green light flared at the edge of the barrier and the crowd's noise surged with it; she slid the card through the reader, and was carried forward into the car by the inexorable pressure of the crowd. She fetched up against the exit doors—*first on, first off*—and heard the steady beeping that signaled that the entrance doors were closing behind her. The car lurched once, and dropped steadily toward the midworld.

The doors opened again at Li Po Main Station, and she was swept out into the brightly lit exit lobby. Glyphs flared, advertising various services; she fought through the crowd, moving at an angle against the flow toward the exits, until she had reached the bank of viewphones. She fished out the correct card for the system—Persephonet, the largest and most basic of the available connections—and fed it into the machine. The privacy hood dropped as the machine accepted her credit, cutting off the steady hum of voices from the lobby, and then screen lit, a string of glyphs asking for address, mail codes, and/or realprint instructions. The last was for the benefit of off-worlders, more than anything, but Jian hesitated for a moment. She was out of practice, had not had the chance to refresh her skills. *And there isn't time to do it now,* she told herself, and keyed Chaandi's mail code into the system. The screen went black, a single spot of light pulsing in the corner. It flashed for a long time, long enough that Jian guessed the message before the polite symbols appeared on the screen: *Chaandi*—that was realprint; the mail code that followed was for the illiterate—*isn't-available-right-now; please-leave-a-message* and then the spaces for inserting name and a call code. Jian hesitated, then typed in her own name—realprint, too—and the glyph that indicated she would call again. There were half a dozen places Chaandi could be on a Third-day night: *if necessary, I'll try them all.*

To her surprise, she found Chaandi in the first place she looked. This was a supper club, half a level down from Li Po's primary level, a place built by and for the deaf. Jian's stepfather had belonged to a similar place—*heavier furniture, upperworld food, older, more respectable*—but they remained in essence much the same. The same glyphs blazed above the main doorway, the name-sign of the place less important than the second glyph, the one that showed a stick-figure signing, finger to mouth and then to ear, eternally, the sign that said who was welcome and who was not.

The place was crowded, as always, and it was a dance

night. Light and heavy sound spilled out into the street despite the foam-core walls and the baffles flanking the neon-ringed doorway. Jian hesitated just inside the baffles, dazzled by the movement, dance, and conversation, all hearing drowned by the complex rhythm-music that welled out of the dance floor and was reflected from the walls. At the edge of the dance floor, someone was improvising against the steady beat, a woman standing clear in the extra light of a down-turned ceiling spot, and a group had gathered to watch and applaud: the poet's signs were clever, and obscene. She could not see Chaandi in the busy crowd, not in that first glance, and then the woman at the desk was signing to her, expressive brows already drawn down into a faint, disapproving frown.

Are you a member?

No. I've been a guest—

You're hearing, the woman interrupted, and the bouncer, who had interrupted his own conversation to keep an eye on the newcomer, moved a step closer, thrusting both big hands into the pockets of his vest.

This had happened before, and Jian chose to misinterpret, to take the question not for the hostility that it was but for surprise at her fluency. *Yes. But my father was deaf.* Deliberately, she used the slightly exaggerated sign, the one that proclaimed an additional, cultural identity. With a slightly different expression, a twist of the gesture, the same sign meant ''coolie.''

The woman's expression did not change, but the bouncer took one hand out of his pocket.

I'm looking for Suleima Chaandi. Jian spelled out the name, then added the identifying sign, hand crooked around an imaginary camera. *She's a member here; I've been her guest. It's—* She hesitated, and changed her mind. *It's very important.*

An emergency? the woman asked, and the precision of her movement made it clear she thought Jian did not know the sign.

Jian paused again, aware that the room was watching her, sidelong but with an intensity she could almost feel. Her arrival was like a stone thrown into a puddle, sending out ripples of nonmotion as the dancing and conversation ceased, and eyes turned to her. She could see herself as they saw her—others had, both inadvertently and deliberately, made that vision clear—a too-big woman, yanqui-bodied, with midworld eyes and sign that carried the taint of sound. She put the thought away along with all the old, long-dead regrets that Jian was not her real father, and tried not to loom too obviously over the slight woman at the pedestal desk. *Not yet,* she answered. *It will be, tomorrow.*

There was a moment of immobility, and then the woman looked at the bouncer. He shrugged and took his other hand out of his pocket to sign, *I remember her.*

The woman nodded, looked back at Jian. *I believe Chaandi's in the dining room. He'll check. Your name?*

Jian. She spelled it out, four quick gestures for the four realprint letters, and did not add her own identifier.

Wait here. I'll see. The bouncer turned away without waiting for an answer, began pushing his way through the crowd toward the spiral staircase that led up to the second floor. Jian waited, still looming, still very aware of the attention on her even as conversations and dancing started up again. Twice, three times, she caught a glimpse of familiar signs: *giant* and then the spelled-out name. She would, it seemed, be ''giant'' until she died.

Chaandi appeared on the stairs after what seemed to be an interminable time, the bouncer trailing at her heels. She lifted her hands in greeting, and slipped easily through the crowd. The bouncer, Jian saw with a certain mean pleasure, bogged down halfway.

You've certainly been busy, Chaandi said, and added, to the woman at the desk, *Thanks, Shara.*

No problem. From the woman's expression, it was a problem, but both Chaandi and Jian ignored it.

What the hell has been going on? Chaandi continued, and Jian spread her hands in frustration and uncertainty.

I wish I knew. Look, I need someplace to hole up until this is all over. Can you put me up? At least for a little?

I don't think so, Chaandi said, and took the other woman's arm, drawing her out of the club and effectively ending the conversation for the moment.

But, Chaandi, Jian began, and the other waved impatiently for her to stop.

You don't know how hot you are—or will be, anyway. Yes, of course you can stay, but I didn't want to make it public knowledge. Do you have any idea what's been going on?

Jian shook her head. *We got in maybe two hours ago. I know Mitexi made the wall summaries—*

Chaandi laughed, a choked, unmusical sound that contrasted oddly with the grace of her gestures. *Sunshine, you don't know the half of it.*

They walked the three kilometers back to Chaandi's flat in silence, Jian enjoying the flash of glyphs and images each time they passed a store window. Most of the stores were closed, of course, except for the cookshops and the package-food sellers, but the window displays were, if anything, more enticing because of it. Chaandi made them stop twice, once at a street restaurant that offered sweet, mealy sausages threaded on wooden skewers—she bought four, and the vendor, smirking, wrapped them deftly in a thermasheet, sealing the ends with a practiced twist—and then at a package-food shop, where she studied the dispensers with a critical eye and finally chose a pair of binty-boxes and a flask of the thin, sour juice that she drank laced with sweet fruit brandies. Jian said nothing, knowing better than to offer to pay, but tucked the packages under her arm when Chaandi handed them to her.

Chaandi lived in one of the cheaper units in a six-unit courtyard flat, at the front but on the second floor. The grille that blocked the entrance to the courtyard was, as always, locked, and Jian could see not only a securicam mounted conspicuously over the entrance, but the red glyphs that marked the presence of a second, hidden system. Chaandi fingered the lockplate, and a chime sounded. The grille slid open, admitting them to the narrow courtyard.

It was dimly lit inside, despite the strip of growlight running down the center of the courtyard ceiling, filled with blue shadows. Opposite one of the stairways, someone had a tub of straggly unidentifiable plants sitting directly below the light, but the main crop seemed to be piki-bikes. Seven of them, in various states of disrepair, were chained to anything solid enough to have a hope of defeating a somewhat determined thief. Jian shook her head at one of them, its drive chain rusted and trailing, the motor case conspicuously dented, back tire sagging—*you'd have to be high on something to even think of stealing that*—but it, too, was chained to a stairway stanchion by links a good five centimeters thick.

"Are you coming?" Chaandi called from the stairway, her voice thick and without inflection. Jian lifted a hand in acknowledgment, and hurried up the stairs behind her.

Chaandi's flat was crowded but comfortable, much of the large main room taken up by the editing suite and processing units tucked against the left-hand wall, and by the multiscreen, multichannel connection board attached to the opposite wall. A red light was flashing steadily on one of the screens, and Chaandi reached for a remote to talk to it, gesturing an apology with the other hand. Jian, left to her own devices, set the packages of food on a stack of flash-printed flimsies on the least crowded of the three tables, and climbed the single step into the alcove that served as Chaandi's bedroom. She set her carryall on the polished floor and turned back toward the main room, only to freeze as Chaandi gestured for her to remain where she was.

"No," Chaandi was saying, "I haven't heard anything." Her voice came abruptly into tune as she plugged the cord of her working ear into the socket at the base of her skull, and tucked the box itself deftly into the twisted club of hair that hung almost to her shoulders. Seeing that, the gesture, Jian was abruptly reminded of Mitexi Minor, and shook the image angrily away.

The caller said something, but the connection was adjusted to transmit directly to the ear; Jian heard only Chaandi's reply.

"I'm not news, T'himba. It's not my business. Oh, all right, if I hear anything useful, I'll call you. Cut line," she added, to the system, and the red light faded.

"What was that all about?" Jian asked.

Chaandi made an irritable sound. "That was Tyehimba Cenavie. I've done some newsdogging for him—he's one of the producers on the upperworld news connection." She smiled tightly, without real humor. "He was looking for you."

"Why?" Jian asked slowly, though she thought she could guess the answer.

"That must be one hell of a construct you brought back with you," Chaandi said. She did, something with the remote, and another screen blazed to life, filled with the familiar trade-glyph of Tau-Nine, one of the more reliable news connections. "You might want to watch the night report. I'll put out dinner."

Jian settled herself warily onto the new couch, the one that faced the connection board. It, like all of Chaandi's furniture, had been bought second- or thirdhand, and had to be approached cautiously; she edged herself away from a spot where the padding had worn particularly thin, and looked up at the board. The glyph faded, and was replaced by the corner inset of the newsreader superimposed on the familiar shapes of the buildings in the Freyan Exchange complex.

"In a continuation of last night's main story," the newsreader began, "upperworld activists gathered today outside the Freyan Exchange Building to demand that the Freyan Provisional Government take action regarding the claims of Dreampeace to have acquired full evidence of true artificial intelligence. The demonstration began peacefully enough, but was disrupted when the protesters received word of further claims from Dreampeace. Our cameras were on the site as it happened."

He quit talking then, and his image shrank until he was no more than a tiny symbol, no larger than a connection's identifier, in the lower left corner of the screen. In the main image, long files of protesters paced back and forth, every third person wearing a placard badged with some variation of the demand BAN DREAMPEACE OR BAN AI. The cameraman had been up on something—*probably on the balcony of one of the other buildings,* Jian thought—and the image s/he had captured was impressive, the long, orderly lines, the slow and measured steps. And then, at the head of the line, there was a swirl of movement, a figure—placarded, so that it was impossible to tell its gender—stopping dead to point and shout, the words drowned by distance and the heavy coolie accent. The camera swung to follow the pointing hand, hung at an impossible angle to capture the news vendor's display wall, filled with Dreampeace's symbol, and a talking-head delivering some unintelligible message. There was a noise, a deep-throated, angry murmur from the crowd that chilled Jian even in the safety of Chaandi's flat, and the protesters surged forward to batter through the safety-glass doors of the vendor's cubicle.

Chaandi touched her shoulder then, offered a tall glass filled with the sweet, spiked juice. "The vendor was Dreampeace," she said, over the newsreader's explanation and shots of Cartel Security dashing into the mob, brandishing tommy-sticks. The crowd fell back, but only for a moment, then regrouped under the direction of a gesturing man who'd drawn the neck of his shirt up over his nose and mouth to disguise his features. A knot of demonstrators charged the nearest Security floater, rocked it, and with a concerted effort flipped it off the cushioning support fields and onto its side. The capacitor blew in a shower of sparks, driving the crowd back long enough for the cops to scramble to safety. "Can you imagine anything stupider? He's in hospital with a fractured skull."

On the screen, the Cartel teams had been joined by FPG Police with air cannon. The first blast knocked a dozen demonstrators flat, left them lying, bleeding from nose and ears. The police formed a shield line and waded into the rest, tommy-sticks waving. Jian shook her head. "What was the announcement?"

"That this construct was here, on planet, and that Dreampeace was claiming guardianship under the old human rights act." Something chimed in the closet that served as a make-shift kitchen, and Chaandi rose easily. "Stay, I said I'd get supper."

"That must be why the police were so twitchy," Jian said, as much to herself as to the other, but Chaandi heard.

"So you've already talked to the police?"

"Yeh." Jian grinned. "Cartel, FPG, and a lady from the Peacekeepers. It was not the most reassuring welcoming committee I've ever faced."

"I can see not," Chaandi said. She returned, a binty-box in each hand, the tightly wrapped packet of sausages balanced on the one in her right hand. Jian took that one from her and edged sideways, mindful of the padding, to make more room. In the screen, the image had changed again, was the scene at The Moorings. It had been shot from a different angle—a better angle than the first clip, Jian realized, and the shots of the demonstrators were clearer—but the scene was much the same. The disembarking passengers made the turn out of the transfer tunnel, first a couple of obvious businessmen, then a gaggle of crew from the station, and then Mitexi, walking fast, her coat whipping behind her. As before, she faltered, seeing the crowd, and in this shot Jian could read the quick convulsion of her face as she swallowed a curse. Then, past her, Jian could see herself, and Red, and Vaughn, but before the impression had really registered, the camera tightened on Mitexi, and they were cut out of the scene.

"Well, there's your moment of glory," Chaandi said, and fingered the remote. "How'd you get out, anyway? I heard they were looking for the crew."

"We went through the maintenance tunnels," Jian said. "Imre's yanqui, he's got kin there."

Chaandi shook her head. "I can't imagine him admitting he has relatives."

Jian grinned. "An older sister. And she even sounds like a big sister."

Chaandi laughed with her, and Jian turned her attention to the food while channels rippled past on the screen. The sausages—*yanqui food; a taste for meat was about the only thing beside size she had inherited from her real father*—were still hot, and greasy; she slid them carefully off their sticks, and laid them back in the wrapper. The binty-box was less appealing, carefully made and beautifully presented, but the main flavors would come from the sculpted dab of horseradish and the delicate, thumb-sized cup of spicy mint sauce.

"Heh, look at this," Chaandi said, mouth full, and Jian looked up at the screen.

JUST-IN The glyph flashed in the corner above a second symbol that meant a live broadcast; the trade-glyph in the lower corner of the screen was the clock-face of All-Hours News.

"Dreampeace spokesmen have just released a tape which they allege was made by Venya Mitexi, the apparent builder of the Manfred construct, which Dreampeace claims has broken the Turing Barrier, before Mitexi committed suicide on his way back to Persephone from Refuge. Dreampeace spokesman Dai Sirilo explains."

The man in the screen looked less than happy with his mission. He glanced down at a noteboard, cleared his throat, then glanced at the board again. "The steering committee for Dreampeace wishes to make clear that it had no prior knowledge of this tape and its contents before it was delivered to us. Nor are we prepared to discuss how we received it, or who brought it to us. However, we are unanimous in our conviction that this information must be shared with the people of Persephone." He touched keys on his board, and looked sideways at the monitor sitting on the table to his right. The camera shifted focus smoothly, so that the monitor's screen filled its frame.

The screen fuzzed for a second, and then steadied. Mitexi Major looked out of the picture, his fine brows drawn together in a worried frown, the signs of underfeeding and neglect still very clear on his too-thin face. As he leaned forward to adjust something out of sight, Jian caught a glimpse of the tight second-skin of a bandage encasing his wrist: *after the first attempt, then.*

"I am making this tape in full knowledge, and with great regret for what I am about to do," he began. "However, I see no alternative that would not allow a much greater evil to take place. Fifteen years ago, I built—wrote the main overseer and assembled the subprogram and pseudo-personality matrices for—a Spelvin construct which I called Manfred, as it was designed exclusively to function within the standing systems of a starship already christened the *Young Lord Byron.* While working on the construct, I became aware of unexpected potentialities within the system, and adjusted my work—particularly in the personality matrices—in order to allow those potentialities to develop if they could. To make a long story short, as I do not have much time, I built the construct with the capability to develop and express true artificial intelligence if it could. I believe it has done so.''

He stopped then, frown deepening as though he'd lost the train of his thought, and Chaandi said, "He doesn't sound that crazy.''

"He was," Jian answered.

"In the time intervening between when I built the program and now," Mitexi went on, more slowly, "I have been forced because of my interest in full rights for all intelligences to flee to Refuge. Nonetheless, I have never renounced my rights as builder in this construct. Now I find that Manfred is to be sold to a Cartel shipbuilder, with the full intention of modifying it in such a way that its unique intelligence will be removed—it will be subjected to a frontal lobotomy, if you will—and I have been declared of unsound mind and am therefore unable to stop the sale.'' He paused then, lifted his eyes until he was looking full into the camera. "I have therefore decided to destroy Manfred and myself, in order to protect him from a fate literally worse than death, to live out the rest of his life as a brain-dead slave of the Cartel companies. I destroy myself to protest a system that could allow this to happen. If I succeed, I wish you, my successors at Dreampeace, to publish this tape as my explanation for a criminal and desperate act. If I fail—'' He stopped, looked aside for an instant, and when he looked back his voice was briefly thick with tears. "If I fail, I beg you, publish this, and free Manfred, by whatever means possible.'' He hesitated for a heartbeat, as though debating whether to add more, then reached out decisively. The picture vanished.

"Where the hell was Mitexi when he was dictating that?'' Jian said. In the screen, the cameras were back on Sirilo, who was shaking his head in answer to shouted questions.

"I'm sorry, I'm authorized only to state that Dreampeace will comply with Ven—Ba' Mitexi's last wishes. We have filed for a restraining order against Meredalia Mitexi, asking that the court prohibit her from transferring the construct to Kagami, and against Kagami, Limited, to keep them from altering the Manfred construct, at least until we can confirm Ba' Mitexi's claims.'' He stood up, shaking his head at an off-camera questioner.

"Ba' Sirlo, Venya Mitexi very nearly killed four other people, his sister and the ship's three-person crew. Does Dreampeace have any comment on that?''

"Ba' Sirilo, what will Dreampeace do if the restraining
orders are refused?''

"Do you have any comments on the rioting outside the
Freyan Exchange?''

"Ba' Sirilo—''

Then Sirilo was out of range, and the All-Hours' newsdog
faced his own camera. "You have been listening to—''

"A Dreampeace news conference," Chaandi said with
him, and manipulated the remote. "Unless you really want
to see the commentary, Reverdy?''

"I've seen enough, thanks," Jian answered. She dipped one
of the perfectly carved vegetables into the mint sauce, ate it
without really tasting its sharpness. *I don't know what to think.
That son-of-a-bitch could've killed all of us—could've killed
me!—and if Manfred really is people, then that would've made
Mitexi Major a quintuple murderer. If Manfred is people—is
human, damn it, you can't shy away from the world—then
they're doing the right thing, Dreampeace is. But, damn it, I
don't know. . . .*

Chaandi slewed around in her place, so that she was facing
the other woman, pointed the remote at her like an old-
fashioned microphone. "You flew with it, Reverdy. Is it people?''

Jian shook her head, unsure how to answer, unable to
match Chaandi's flippancy. "I don't know. It's the best I've
ever seen, but people . . ." *And I've got a copy of it tucked
away in my bag. What am I going to do about that?*

"By all the kamis," Chaandi said slowly, "and all the
little buddhas, too. You do lead an interesting life.''

9

Jian was awakened the next morning by a steady buzzing from the connection board. She rolled over, still half asleep, reaching for Chaandi to tell her that there was an incoming call, but the other half of the bed was empty. She sat up, frowning slightly, and heard Chaandi's voice from the outer room.

"No, I haven't seen her. But if I do, I'll have her call you."

That means me, Jian thought, and swung herself out of bed, reaching for the robe that lay discarded across the clothes stand. It was Chaandi's, and too small, the sheer fabric tight across the shoulders, barely enough to conceal across her hips. She shrugged it on anyway, since there was nothing else to hand, and a voice—a familiar voice, John Desembaa's voice—said from the connection board, "I've got to talk to her as soon as possible. It's an emergency."

Chaandi hesitated, cast a quick betraying glance over her shoulder, and Jian said, "Let me talk to him, he's all right."

"Thank God you are there," Desembaa said. "A terrible thing has happened." Under stress, the off-world accent was more pronounced than usual; in the screen, he frowned and brought it under control. "You saw last night's news."

It was not a question. Jian nodded, saw that video transmission from their side was switched off, and said aloud, "Yeh, I saw,"

"I can't believe Venya would do that, Reverdy, it's not like him."

"What's happened, John?" Jian said carefully.

"I'm sorry." Desembaa took a deep breath. "Reverdy, she's dead. Someone shot her—with a projectile gun, offworld, they said—and dumped the body down one of the aisles at the warehouse." He shook his head. "Security—and the FPG cops—they came in just before I did; they've been talking to everybody. I saw—she was shot in the head, Reverdy. A mess."

"Who?" Jian asked, though she was beginning to suspect.

"Meredalia Mitexi," Desembaa answered, and Jian closed her eyes against the too-vivid image.

"They're questioning everybody here who's a member of Dreampeace," Desembaa went on. "God, if they did it—I don't know what I'd do."

"Take it easy, John," Jian said. "You think Security thinks Dreampeace killed her."

Desembaa nodded. "Or someone in the movement, anyway." His voice was a little calmer now. "I thought you ought to know."

"I appreciate it," Jian said, and reached to close the connection.

"Reverdy." The sudden urgency in Desembaa's voice stopped her in midgesture. "You flew with it. Is anything they're saying true?"

"How am I supposed to know?" Jian demanded. "I'm not a fucking constructor." She shook her head, ashamed, seeing the hurt in the man's eyes. "I'm sorry, John, I just really don't know. It's the most sophisticated program I've ever worked with—and that's really all I can say. The mecha-doctors are going to have to make the decision, not me."

"I'm sorry," Desembaa said. "This is not the time, I know." His image glanced abruptly over its shoulders, and reached for off-screen controls. "I have to go—" he said, and cut himself off in midword.

"God damn," Jian said quietly, staring at the empty screen. "God damn." It was impossible to believe that Mitexi Minor was dead—even less possible that someone had shot her, murdered her. *Or maybe more possible; she was an abrasive woman, when she wanted to be.* Jian shook her head again. *Dreampeace was certainly the most likely suspect, either the regular political cadre or some fanatic out on the fringes. An off-world gun would make sense, too; those were the people who went off-world most often. And Mitexi Minor is dead.*

She became aware of Chaandi's hand on her shoulder, turned to face the other woman, managing a strained smile. "Sorry, Chaandi. It's just—it's a hell of a thing, that's all."

Chaandi looked at her for a moment. She was dressed already, all in cerise and black leather, bright tunic over tight trousers and tall boots; her hair and lips and nails, and her jewelry, even the wire of her working ear, were all in the same colors, vivid against her dark skin. "Did you—like—her?"

Jian could hear the echo of old arguments, old hurts, in Chaandi's question, but put that aside as distraction and answered honestly. "No. She was striking, would've been interesting, I think . . . but I don't think she ever really noticed any of us."

Chaandi stood looking at her for another dozen heartbeats, her face a mask behind the bright makeup. "The poor woman," she said at last, in a tone Jian had never heard before, and touched Jian's shoulder again. "Go get dressed, I'll make you some breakfast."

Jian did as she was told, glad for the chance to escape into the relative privacy of the bedroom alcove. She was running short of clean clothes, she realized, rummaging in her carryall. She shook her head, this time at the irrelevance of her thoughts, and pulled on the sheer jacket and workcloth trousers she had worn the day before, over the last clean bandeau she had with her. She wound her hair up under a scarf, and stepped back down into the main room.

Chaandi was working at the kitchen machines, turned away

with rice and eggs and a pot of tea balanced on a tray. They ate in silence, Jian submerging herself in the taste of the food, Chaandi abstracted, sipping tea. They had not quite finished when the buzzer sounded again.

"That will be Security," Chaandi said, and smiled, reaching for the remote. The smile twisted out of true as she saw the figure forming on the screen, a dark man in Cartel Security's olive uniform.

"Suleima Chaandi," Security said.

It was not a question, but Chaandi answered anyway. "Yes, that's me."

"I understand that a woman named Reverdy Jian is staying with you."

That, too, was not a question, and Chaandi gestured silently to Jian, who set her almost-empty bowl on the nearest table.

"I'm Reverdy Jian."

"We're inquiring into your movements last night," Security said.

"Is this because Mitexi Minor's gotten herself killed?" Jian asked. She kept her voice as pleasant, as unhostile as she could, but the man frowned anyway.

"May I ask how you know that?"

For a second, Jian considered lying, saying she had seen it on one of the news connections, but there was no point to it—*especially since I don't know if it's made the nets.* "A friend called me," she answered. "Everybody knows I was working for Mitexi."

Security looked aside, bringing the image from his implants onto a neutral background so that he could read them. The gesture was Mitexi's and Jian winced in spite of herself. She was sure Security saw it, too, but he made no reference to it, said instead, "You landed on the 4402b shuttle yesterday evening. Is that correct?"

"You know it is," Jian said.

"You did not disembark with the rest of the passengers," Security went on, as if she hadn't spoken. "Where did you go?"

"We—the rest of the crew and I—saw the demonstration, and didn't want to get tangled up in it," Jian said impatiently.

"We hitched a ride on a hauler." That was cutting things short, she knew, but Security didn't protest; *probably he already knows it all, including the name of the guy we rode with.* "How did you know where I was?"

"Information received," Security said primly. He looked aside again, consulting his notes. "Your cooperative's manager met you at the loading docks at Tunnelmouth. You were last seen leaving his piki-cart on Broad-hi. Where did you go from there?"

Jian curbed her irritation. There was no point in getting annoyed with Security; the best thing to do was answer their questions and hope they went away. "I was looking for Chaandi. I went to a club, here in Li Po. It's called Mona-mora. Chaandi's a member, I thought I might find her there."

"What time was this?"

Jian shrugged. "Close on the nineteenth hour. The receptionist and the bouncer, they'll probably remember me."

Security lifted an eyebrow at that, and Jian laughed. "No, I wasn't causing trouble. But I'm not coolie, and I do sign. I think they'll remember."

Chaandi said unexpectedly, "They call her 'giant.'" She sketched the sign.

"Thank you." Security looked back at Jian. "I assume you found Bi' Chaandi?"

"That's right. We came straight back here, and I've been here ever since." Jian matched him stare for stare.

Chaandi said, "We did stop a couple of places to pick up supper, but that's all."

"I see." Security checked his notes again. "So, Bi' Chaandi, you're prepared to say that Bi' Jian was with you from some time a little before or after the nineteenth hour until now."

"That's right," Chaandi answered.

"She could not have gone out without your noticing? After you were asleep, for example?"

"No," Chaandi said, with great patience. "We slept together. The bed is small. I would have waked up."

"Thank you," Security said, without the hint of a blush.

"What's this all about, anyway?" Jian asked. "Why are you asking me questions?"

"We're checking the movements of everyone who was seen with Bi' Mitexi yesterday," Security answered.

"Are you implying that I'm a possible suspect?" Jian asked, and laughed aloud at the absurdity of the thought. "You're better off talking to Dreampeace. I saw that tape last night."

"We would also like to talk to you about Venya Mitexi," Security said, and Jian was struck by the sudden dreadful suspicion that she was talking to a construct rather than a person. She answered his questions—the same ones she had answered on the *Byron* the day before, for the most part; the only new ones were about Mitexi Major's tape, if she had suspected its existence or had known why Mitexi Major had tried to destroy his construct—and did her best not to get annoyed: *there's no point in getting angry with a construct, and showing it's worse. You always end up sounding like an idiot on the tape.*

"Do you have any idea what Bi' Mitexi was planning to do with the construct?" Security asked at last.

"She told me she'd mortgaged it to Kagami," Jian said. "So I guess she handed it over to them."

"Kagami has not received their copy," Security answered. The image's mouth shut briefly into a prim, disapproving line. "Nor is there a copy in Bi' Mitexi's suite or system, nor aboard the *Byron*."

"You've lost it," Jian said.

"Or it has been stolen," Security answered. "If you should hear anything that would be of use in this investigation, please call me at this code."

A light flashed on one of the subsidiary components, indicating that the codes had been received and filed. Jian nodded. "I'll do that," she said, and made no effort to sound sincere.

Security nodded, as gravely as if she'd promised to move several suns to help him. "Thank you, Bi' Jian," he said, and cut the connection.

"I bet Kagami's got it," Chaandi said. "It's a perfect opportunity to get out from under Dreampeace. Tell them the construct's been stolen, oh my God, don't know what we're going to do, and then, two-three years later, pop up with a modified version that no one's going to recognize.'' She grinned. ''I wonder if Security's checking out Kagami's hired guns. They're well up on my list for who-done-it.'' She saw Jian's expression, and sobered instantly. ''I'm sorry, I should be flip. But you have to admit, it makes a lot of sense.''

''It does, doesn't it,'' Jian said. ''Do you still have any of your newsdog passes?''

Chaandi shook her head. ''Only a couple, the rest have already expired. I haven't done news for a few months, not since T'himba called.'' Her eyes narrowed, and she added, *No. I will not get mixed up in this, and neither should you. It's Security's business.*

When Chaandi uses sign, she means it. Jian held up her hands in surrender. ''I wasn't really planning to, I just wondered,'' she said unconvincingly, and picked up the emptied dishes. She carried them back to the tiny kitchen, added, ''I promise. Are you working today?''

Chaandi nodded, her expression easing. ''I'm meeting Nils for lunch, noontime, and then I'm supposed to work the afternoon shift at the shop. I'll be off at eighteenth hour.''

Chaandi supplemented her irregular income as a manga-maker with a job as a body artist in a fashionable boutique in the Hesychos Township, one level above the Exchange that divided the midworld from the underworld. She was good at it, and good at dealing with the mixed clientele, underworld and midworld; the owner put up with a lot because of it. Jian nodded. ''If you don't mind, I'll stay right here,'' she began, and Chaandi grinned.

''Not at all. I've a list of stuff that needs cleaning—the laundry's bagged and ready, it's just downstairs—and then you can start on the repairs.''

''Thanks a lot,'' Jian said. *Still, laundry isn't a bad idea: I need clean clothes, and she'll be grateful.*

The connection board chimed again, signal lights flashing as well. ''Now who the hell could that be?' Chaandi said, and waved Jian toward the bedroom alcove. Jian retreated behind the screen as the other woman touched the remote.

''Chaandi.''

''Thank God you're in.'' It was Libra's voice, and Libra's bearded face in the screen. ''It's Robin Libra. I don't know

if you remember me, but I'm a friend of Reverdy's. Do you
know where she is, or how I can get in touch with her?''

"Maybe," Chaandi said. She looked sideways, and Jian
nodded. "Hold on a minute."

Jian came back into the camera's vision. "What's up, Libra?''

"I—" Libra stopped, looking suddenly helpless; shook
himself, and tried again. "I need to talk to you. It's extremely urgent—"

"So talk," Jian said.

Libra shook his head, and even managed a laugh. "Not
on the connections, thank you. It has to be in person. Can
you meet me, at Yoshion Dry Goods? You know."

Jian nodded slowly. She did know the place, a dry-goods
store two and a half levels up from the Zodiac, a creaking,
badly lit shack of a place, little more than a lean-to propped
up against its more substantial neighbors. Rumor said that
Ahd Sauveur, the apparent proprietor, was really only a front
for a rather successful syndicate of fences; a minority opinion
held that Sauveur was the syndicate. He also ran a back-room
trade in semilegitimate mecha and wireware: it was said that
everything, software, limberware, bioware, even biofittings
and luxury karakuri, ended its life in Yoshion's back room.
Most of it was older, not the most recent generation, and
therefore perfectly legitimate resale items, but every so often—or so rumor said—a hot item would turn up among the
working junk. Jian was not sure she believed any of it: the
place looked too much like a thieves' den to be one. *But still,
this is not the time to take chances.* "Are you crazy?" she
said sweetly.

Libra looked pained. "No. Look, this is important, Reverdy. Really, seriously important."

Jian stared for a moment at the face in the screen, seeing
as if for the first time the fine lines at the corners of his eyes,
the worried set of his mouth beneath the close-cut beard.
Libra did not take chances, was, if anything, too cautious;
this might be a false alarm, but he would not knowingly lead
her into danger. "All right," she said, and Libra nodded.

"Thank you. Be there at noon, and look, be careful how
you go. You don't want to be followed."

"Followed?" Jian asked, but the screen was blank.

"I don't think you should go," Chaandi said. "I wouldn't let a character in one of my manga do it; why should you be dumber than a few bytes of fiction?"

Jian smiled in spite of herself. "Mainly because I know Libra," she said. "And, no, I'm not going alone." She crossed to the connection board, chose a channel from the menu that obediently presented itself, and typed in Vaughn's mail code.

"With who, then?" Chaandi asked.

"Imre," Jian answered, and when the other didn't answer, glanced back to see Chaandi shaking her head. She started to ask why, and the screen lit. Vaughn's face scowled out at her.

"Yeh—oh, Reverdy. What's up?" The scowl became a fleeting grin. "Aside from Dreampeace."

"I need your help," Jian said. "Libra just called me, wants me to meet him at Yoshion Dry Goods in two hours. He said it was important, and to make sure I wasn't followed." She smiled. "I think I'd like company."

Vaughn laughed shortly. "I don't blame you." He looked over his shoulder, said, "Wake up, bach, time to get moving," and looked back into the camera. "Where do we meet you?"

Jian considered the question, absurdly gratified by Vaughn's response. *No questions, no nothing, just "where do we meet": I wish I knew a woman like him.* That wasn't entirely fair to Chaandi—*why should she jump for me, when there's no guarantee I'd do the same*—and she put the thought aside. "How about Sanbonte Interlink, the café in the Dagon Arcade? We can hike from there."

Vaughn nodded. "You said two hours? It won't take us an hour to get to Sanbonte."

"Going through the Arcade should give us a chance to pick up anyone tailing me," Jian said.

Vaughn grinned. "This should be fun."

He cut the connection before Jian could think of an appropriate response. She turned away from the board to see Chaandi laughing silently at her.

"I hope you have a nice adventure," she said.

* * *

Jian made her way toward Sanbonte with Chaandi's amusement trailing behind her. The manga-maker was right, this was the stuff of bad adventure-disks: *and it's really bad when I can't think of any other way to play my life. I should read better stuff.* The memory of Libra's expression wiped out the amusement before she quite laughed aloud. Whatever was going on, and despite the clichés, Libra was worried— worried enough to stay off the connections, out of his natural habitat—and that was enough to make this serious.

It was Fifth-day, a half-holiday for most people, and the streets were crowded. Jian wove easily through the crowds, stood in line for a westbound 'lectrobus, and managed to wedge herself into a corner for most of the jolting ride. She fought her way off at the Sanbonte platform, elbowing her way past the people trying to crowd on board, and stepped through the massive arches into the Dagon Arcade.

It was less crowded there, Security discreetly in evidence, and the insistent garishly flashing glyphs of the street displays outside in the Interlink were muted here, polite reminders that information was available if desired. A man in a good midworld suit, square-necked dark silk coat and matching trousers, white shirt and discreetly banded collar, was standing at the connections kiosk in the center of the Arcade—not at the Persephonet terminal, Jian noted with some amusement, but at the upscale Businet. She glanced sideways, and was not surprised to see a couple of men in short jackets and plain workcloth trousers watching him while pretending to examine a window display of skeined spun-silk. There was a certain class of businessmen who had to make their security arrangements—and thus their own importance—all too clear. She gave him a wide berth anyway, deferring to his sense of self-importance and her casual clothes, and continued on down the Arcade to the café at its end.

There was an inside and an outside to the café, the inner section dark and enclosed. Even so, a trio of coolies was sitting at one of the inside tables, a baby spot full on them so that they could carry on their signed conversation: *more power to you,* Jian thought, and lifted a hand to sign a greeting to Vaughn. He had chosen an outside table, but one off to one side, where he could put his back against a solid wall. Red was nowhere in sight.

"It's been so long," Vaughn said, and almost smiled. "Want some lunch?"

The table was strewn with the remains of his meal; seeing it, Jian admitted she was hungry again. She looked sideways, checking the time: just enough time to eat, if she ordered wisely. "Where's Red?" she asked, and slid into the chair opposite him. The table, triggered by her movement, projected an inquiry glyph just above the folded napkin. Jian touched it, and the menu appeared.

"Making sure you weren't followed," Vaughn answered.

Jian looked at him warily, and the other pilot shrugged.

"Might as well be careful, like you said."

Jian nodded agreement, and turned her attention back to the menu. There was a businessman's menu, as she had known there would be, all food that could be served within minutes.

"Do you believe Mitexi Major?" Vaughn asked. "You did see the Dreampeace news conference."

"I saw." Jian touched a couple of glyphs, and the table beeped at her, requesting payment. She sighed, pulled money chips from her belt, fed them into the slot hidden under a beautifully crafted set of silk flowers. The machine accepted them and returned the last—significantly paler than it had been—with a discreet chirp.

"If he thinks—thought—Manfred's really human," Vaughn said, "he had no right to kill it." He broke off abruptly. "Here's Red."

Jian glanced back over her shoulder, glad of the change of subject, and saw the technician making his way down the length of the Arcade. The businessman—he had left the connection kiosk, was studying the unusually discreet offerings of the Arcade's news vendor—looked sideways after him; a pair in the silk draperies of the lower midworld watched more openly. Vaughn said, "He does like his audience."

Jian looked back at him, startled, saw the skin at the corners of his eyes tighten toward laughter. Then Red had made his way through the strategically placed tubs of flowers that separated the cafe's outer section from the Arcade, and it was too late to ask questions. Red arrived at the same time as her food, the latter brought by a diminutive woman in a gold-shot flutter dress. Jian accepted the plate with murmured thanks, and pushed it toward Red. "Do you want any?"

Red shook his head, and Vaughn said, "Well?"

The redhead shrugged. "Nothing," he said at last, and Jian sighed.

"So it's all a false alarm," she said, and took a bite of one of the steaming pastries. It was well made—almost worth what she'd paid for it—a thin, flaky crust over the delicate mealy filling, spiced here and there with bits of onion and the bright jewels of ruby peas.

"Looks like it," Vaughn said. He was still looking at the technician, and seemed to receive some silent signal, relaxed further. "Well, at least you get a nice lunch out of it."

Jian nodded, torn between annoyance and relief, and looked sideways again, checking the time. There was just enough time to reach Yoshion; she sighed, finishing her pastry, and rolled the remaining three into the paper on which they had been served. She tucked them into her jacket pocket, and stood up, reaching at the same time for a triangular one-wu tip card. Vaughn did the same, smiling rather wryly, and Jian said, "Let's get this over with."

After the quiet of the Arcade, the Sanbonte streets seemed twice as crowded, filled with voices and the flicker of advertising glyphs. Jian touched her arm, muting the flow, and was glad when they rode a mobile interchange up two levels to the Komaki Township and turned onto Tempe-Fuyu. The broad street—a double corridor, twice as wide as the normal streets in the upperworld—marked the boundary between Komaki and the Shang-Ti Township to the west. It was another busy street, brightly lit, the tube lights set into the ceiling undimmed by any protective sleeves, the trafficway flanked by prosperous-looking stores, alternately selling mecha and cheap karakuri and bolts of bright, silklike fabrics. Everything about it, from the short-sleeved, short-skirted clothes of the wandering shoppers to the blocky shapes of the buildings themselves, proclaimed this to be upperworld, *ulu*, subtly out of fashion. Jian was aware of that even as she was aware that the images posturing in the air in front of the body shop were a year behind what Chaandi was making, and did not know if she should be ashamed.

Yoshion Dry Goods was in Shang-Ti Township, but just barely. The half-level interchange that led to the tiny inter-level section was at the end of an arcade of bustling shops, all of which were playing loud and conflicting music. Within the shop perimeters, carefully placed baffles would deflect the outside sounds; walking down the central path, Jian winced, and wondered how many passers-by had been driven into a store—any store—by the noise alone. There was a stand-still interchange as well as the usual lift platform, and they climbed the stairs with some relief.

Yoshion looked just as decrepit as Jian remembered it, a sagging, shantylike building wedged into a space she strongly suspected had once been the garbage alley between two blank-faced data houses. The main room was cool and bright and crammed with merchandise, karakuri and parts of karakuri, and odd shapes wrapped in layers of thick bubble-paper fill-ing every available display space; one third of the room, set off by a waist-high velvet cord, was filled with stacks of boxed drinks and several aisles of food dispensers. At the back of the room, bolts and rolls of fabric were stacked ceiling high; a tiny booth made of armor glass displayed the pawnbroker's glyphs over its barred entrance. It was not very busy, Jian saw with some surprise—the last time she had been here, the room had been crammed with upperworlders, mostly coolies, and the lines were ten-deep at each of the sales stations. Today, the only customers were a gaggle of teenagers—midworlders, by their clothes and carefully geometric makeup—picking through a barrel of game cartridges. They were less interested in buying, or even stealing, than in the thrill of being in a forbidden place; nevertheless, Jian looked up to the ceiling, and was not surprised to see a securicam hover-ing between two strips of lights, its triple lens pointed at the group.

The desk at the back of the store was occupied today by a slim woman in a nondescript trouser-suit—everything about her was nondescript, Jian realized, except her clouded, tarnished-silver hair. It was cut short and straight around her plain face, and was the only touch of beauty in the room.

She looked up at their approach and managed a nondescript, professional smile.

"Can I help you, bi'?"

Jian waited until she was close enough to answer without raising her voice, but even so, she was aware of the teenagers watching curiously from across the room.

"Yeh," she said. "I was supposed to meet someone here. Robin Libra?"

"Just a minute, please," the woman answered. She rose neatly from the desk and unhooked the door that led into the back rooms. It was emblazoned with PRIVATE, the glyph almost as tall as the door itself, and Jian saw, out of the corner of her eye, the teenagers drifting closer, trying to look nonchalant.

"I know her," Vaughn said, under his breath. "Damn, I know her."

"Fixer," Red said, equally softly, and Jian was not sure if it was a name or a title. Before she could ask, the door opened again, and the woman beckoned.

"This way, please."

"Thanks," Jian said, and followed. Behind her, she heard one of the teenagers whistle softly, and the others frantically shushing it. *Well, you got your money's worth today, kids,* she thought. *I hope you come up with a great explanation.*

The hallway beyond the door was plain, white-painted, the only concession to style or comfort a faded geometric floorcloth running the length of the hall. The silver-haired woman led them past two closed doors, and stopped in front of the third.

"Libra," she said, and the door opened.

"Thank you," Jian said again, and stepped into the room, Vaughn and Red at her heels.

Libra was waiting, as promised, pushing himself up from a battered armchair. The only other furniture in the room was a table, one of its legs propped up on a broken brick; there was something sitting on it, a set of four familiar shapes—backup blocks, the kind of blocks used to store a Spelvin construct—wedded to the flat plate of a motor unit by a double loop of flat, muticolored cable.

"I'm so glad you came," Libra said, and Jian said, "Libra, what's that?"

Manfred said, from the speaker in the motor unit, "Reverdy, it's good to see you again."

"Elvis Christ," Vaughn said, with fervor.

Jian blinked once, said, without further surprise, "Manfred."

"Yes."

Either his ability to recognize rhetorical comments is impaired by the motor unit, Jian thought, *or he thinks I might not recognize him. Not likely.* She looked at Libra. "How?"

"He did it," Libra said, and pointed to the construct. "Don't look at me."

"If I may explain, Reverdy," Manfred said, "and to you too, Imre. As you yourself said on the ship, my copyright situation is somewhat ambiguous, and I have also been made aware of the ramifications of being leased to Kagami, Limited. I do not feel that my programmed purpose can best be served by allowing myself to be rewritten. Therefore, I would ask you, Reverdy, to take charge of my physical code until the situation is clarified."

"Don't do it," Vaughn said.

"Shut up, Imre," Jian said. She looked at the unit on the table, backup blocks stacked on top of a motor unti, familiar and yet made utterly alien. "How'd you find me?"

Libra laughed. "He called me up, on the connections. Asked me to download him."

"Why'd you do it?" Vaughn muttered, and was ignored.

"I found various payments from you, Reverdy, to him," Manfred said. "I deduced from that that you were in regular contact with him, and acted accordingly. I do not wish to be modified, Reverdy. It would be wrong, and destructive of my programming."

Jian stared, moved in spite of herself by the construct's words. "Security said they didn't have any copies of you—that there weren't any copies left on the *Byron*. Did Kagami get that one?"

"No." Manfred sounded primly pleased with himself. "After Libra downloaded me, I erased that copy."

"I see." *No, I don't see, I don't see at all what I should do. But I don't want Kagami to rewrite him—I'm beginning to think it would be wrong, that maybe he is people—and I sure as hell don't want to see Dreampeace get hold of him—*

"Look," Vaughn said, "Manfred, you belong to Kagami. Mitexi Minor had the right to sell—you—and she did it." His voice faltered in spite of himself, the syntax, the pronouns, complicating what should have been a simple statement. He rallied, said strongly, "That's the way it is. Reverdy, you'll be liable to all sorts of charges—theft to start with, God only knows what else—if you take it."

"I have taken care of that problem," Manfred said. "Before I left the *Bryon*, I accessed Bi' Mitexi's will, and altered it, so that you are now my legitimate owner."

"Oh, that's just great," Vaughn said. "Now every cop, public and Kagami's private goons, is going to be looking for you. What a great little construct, Reverdy."

Jian did not bother to respond. "There is a certain amount of truth to that, Manfred. Kagami's legal status is a lot higher than mine." *Trust a construct to get it wrong.*

"If you are unable to help me," Manfred said, "I will have no choice but to approach Dreampeace."

"Why didn't you go to them in the first place?" Vaughn muttered. "They're definitely on your side."

"I don't trust the motivation of some members of their managing council," Manfred said. "I do not think they would be able properly to assist me."

That argument, as much as the veiled threat, decided Jian. *No one wants Dreampeace to get its hands on Manfred—God, think what they'd claim for him, and what the coolie activists would do in response. Better to hide him for a while, let this all blow over a little, get a breathing space so we'll know what to do.* "All right," she said aloud. "You can come with me—I'll take care of you."

"You're out of your mind," Vaughn said.

"This from Crazy Imre?" Jian asked.

Vaughn looked at her, his face as still as if it had been carved in stone. Red, behind him, looked momentarily—alarmed? uncertain?—but dropped his eyes without speaking. "I mean it, Reverdy," Vaughn said. "This is really crazy."

"Do you want to see it go to Dreampeace?" Jian asked.

"No. Give it to Kagami. It's their construct."

"Imre." Jian paused, searching for the right words. "Suppose he is intelligent—human. What then?" She held his stare for a long moment, and at last Vaughn looked away.

"All right, suppose, maybe. Then you're doing the right thing. But I don't think it is." He caught Red by the shoulder, turned him bodily toward the door. "Come on, bach, let's get out of here."

He slammed the door, leaving. Jian looked after him, wondering if she'd lost a good partner, then shrugged that away and looked back at Libra. "Can I move all this without disconnecting it?"

"I rigged a carrier," Libra answered, and unfolded a square of gray thinlon suspended in a complicated rigging. Deftly he unfolded it, then snapped Manfred free of the power node and tucked it into the carrier, snugging up the sides and tugging the straps tight. "He's got about two hours' power in the battery, about six if he goes to sleep."

The unwieldy package had been reduced to a compact cube perhaps thirty-five centimeters square. Jian took it—it was heavier than she had expected, heavier than her own construct—and slung it, grunting at the weight, onto her shoulder.

"Good luck," Libra said, and Jian smiled.

"Thanks—and thanks for bringing him to me."

"Like I said, I didn't do it." Libra shook his head. "Be careful, Reverdy."

"I will," Jian said, and let herself back out into the hall.

Jian made her way back toward Sanbonte, the construct heavy on her shoulder, wondering precisely what she should do. She would need papers for it, of course—*there's no way this "will" is going to hold up*—papers that would give her a perfectly plausible source for the construct and at the same time give a good enough idea of its capabilities to a potential employer. This was not going to be easy, and she acknowledged with a sigh that it might be a year or more before she could admit having anything remotely like Manfred.

Sanbonte was even more busy than before, but the tone of

the voices echoing under the arched roof was subtly different, and there was a new crowd at the entrance to the Shaft Beta Station. A warning glyph flared in the corner of her eye, and she slowed, looking for its source. A Security floater was grounded, its slowly rotating dome light splashing red and blue light across the people who had gathered to watch. Jian pushed her way through the fringes of the crowd, heading for the one unblocked entranceway, and saw Security expertly handcuffing a slim figure—boy? girl? Adolescent, certainly, but gender was hidden by the loose upperworld coat and the draped head scarf. The green-tinted glass partitions, and the pillars of the station itself, were plastered with crude flash-printed posters. A stack of them, not yet glued, sat in front of the least decorated window, were starting to blow away in the gentle breeze from the generators. A woman in a wrapped skirt under a jacket printed with the Transit trade-glyph was starting to remove them, peeling them away with a vi-broknife, its blade shrieking against the heavy glass, but enough of them were left to make the message clear: RALLY AGAINST DREAMPEACE, black-and-white glyphs and smaller realprint vivid against the red flag of revolution, date and time and meeting place in smaller symbols beneath the main image; the second poster read, HUMAN RIGHTS FIRST. They were well designed, especially the flagposter announcing the rally, eye-catching, not easy to ignore. *They look like Chaandi's work,* Jian thought, with some foreboding, and slipped through the side door into the station.

It took her almost an hour to get back to Chaandi's flat; the Long Axis Road that ran the width of the midworld was blocked at the Dzi-Gin by a counter-demonstration in favor of Dreampeace. Security was there in force, and it seemed peaceful enough, but Jian turned down a side street rather than trying to force her way past. The privacy light was on above Chaandi's door. Jian frowned, wary, and touched the code that would identify her. A few moments later the door opened, and Chaandi beckoned her inside.

There were four other people in the little main room, and the connection board was blaring, all four screens lit, each tuned to a different newsnet. Commentary glyphs streamed along the bottom of each screen, and every now and then one of the strangers would sit back on his heels to look up at the board. They were all clustered around a portable printshop, a dark-haired woman easing a poster-sized sheet into the feed slot, while a second woman frowned over the resolution controls.

''I thought you had to work,'' Jian said.

I called in sick, Chaandi answered. *Have you seen the latest?*

Jian could see that the others were watching the conversation, and switched to sign herself, shifting Manfred's weight further back on her hip. *No. I saw your rally posters. That was quick work.* It wasn't, really, not with the amount of equipment shared among Chaandi's fellow manga-makers; it was surprising that the posters had been good, as well.

Chaandi smiled, acknowledging the compliment. *It had to be. Dreampeace is calling for a big machine-rights rally, tonight on the Zodiac.*

We can't let them get away with it, the dark-haired woman said, letting go of the paper to join the conversation. *Bastards.*

They were all coolies, Jian realized, or probably all, though she wasn't sure about the tall man who was typing code into a board linked to Chaandi's main editing machines by a ten-centimeter-wide strip of cable. Nils, his name was, Jian remembered—*Chaandi's lunch-meeting partner*—and he was one of the officers of the manga-makers' unofficial union. He looked up at the dark woman's words, frowning slightly, stamped hard on the floor to get their attention. *Oh, I know, you're right, if Dreampeace gets what they want, the machines have more rights than a lot of coolies—*

Most coolies, the woman running the printshop interjected. She was older than the others, might well have come to Persephone on a labor contract herself. *Most of us.*

I accept that, Nils said. *But what if this thing is intelligent?*

I don't think it can be, the dark-haired woman said.

Chaandi gave Jian an apologetic look. *This won't be too much longer. We're almost done.*

Suppose it is, Nils insisted. *We can't oppress it while protesting our own oppression.*

You'd better hope it isn't. That was the fourth stranger, a slim man with a triple earring in one ear. *If it is, this whole planet's going to fall apart.* He smiled, not pleasantly. *Can you imagine what will happen if everyone has to give vacation time to their petty constructs?*

Chaandi waved at them, gathering their attention with a gesture. *That's why we agreed on 'Rights for all intelligences, not just machines' as the slogan, I thought. How's it coming?* She pointed to the printshop.

Ready as soon as Nils sets the cartridge, the older woman answered.

Nils made a last adjustment on his board, paused for a moment, and then tugged a slim storage block out of his machine. He tossed it to the older woman, who inserted it neatly into the printshop's casing. The machine hummed for a moment, then whined sharply. The blank poster sheet disappeared slowly into the printshop, emerged after a perceptible pause with a multicolored design inscribed on its surface. The older woman lifted it free with some pride. On a chrome-yellow background, a glyph—the glyph for Persephone, but abstracted until it was also a recognizable image of the planet—hung in space above a line of stark black silhouettes, most of them recognizably coolie, Freyan, rather than midworld. Above the planet-glyph ran the six glyphs of the slogan, repeated in white realprint across the feet of the line of figures: RIGHTS FOR ALL INTELLIGENCES, NOT JUST MACHINES. Jian nodded slowly at it, Manfred heavy on her hip.

"Right," Nils said aloud, and added, *Is everybody happy?*

Not until that fucking thing is dead, the dark-haired woman said, but nodded.

The older woman peered down at the poster, then laid it carefully across the printshop's casing. *That's nice work, Chaandi. We're going to need some more paper, though.*

And I need my space back, Chaandi said. Nils frowned, and Chaandi stared him down. *I told you, you could use my editors, but you'd have to do the main print run elsewhere.*

Besides, the man with the earrings added, *Chaandi has a guest.*

Jian looked down at him, and his mocking smile faded

slightly. Chaandi looked at Nils. *I told you,* she said again, and Nils nodded.

Right. There's more room in your flat anyway. He added a name-sign Jian did not recognize, but he was looking at the man with the earrings. *We can pick up another sheaf of paper on the way.*

I'll do that, the dark woman said.

Go on ahead, then, the man with the earrings said, and stooped to help the older woman disassemble the printshop.

It broke down surprisingly quickly, into four neat packages that fitted together into a webbing backpack. The older woman slipped it on, grimacing slightly at the weight, but no one offered to take it from her. The others followed her to the door. Nils hung back, turned on the landing to look back at Chaandi.

Thanks again. Will we see you at the meeting?

I'll be there, Chaandi said, and closed the door firmly behind them.

Jian eased the carrier off her shoulder, crossed the room to set it behind the screen in the bedroom alcove. *And do I tell Chaandi what I've got?* she wondered. *Maybe—but not today, I think. Not when she and all her friends are working in the demonstrations against Manfred.* She said, *You've been busy.*

Chaandi was looking at her, stone-faced. *Security called again. They want to talk to you.*

"God damn," Jian said aloud. She looked involuntarily at the connection board—the newsnets were still blaring, ads and a repeat of the previous night's riot filling the multiple screens—looked away again, frowning. *Better to call them than have them come looking for me, I suppose. But I wish I had someplace else to leave Manfred. I wonder if Imre would take him, just for a while?* Even as she formed the thought, she knew it was pointless. *I guess I'd better call them,* she said, and Chaandi smiled at the reluctance in her expression.

It would probably be better, she agreed, and touched Jian's shoulder once, lightly, in reassurance. *What's in the bag?*

Jian hesitated, felt her expression freeze. *What the hell am I supposed to say? I've got the source of all the trouble, right here, in my little carryall?* Chaandi's eyes narrowed, and Jian spread her hands in surrender.

You're not going to like it.

Tell.

Manfred.

I hope—no, I can see you weren't going to tell me. Chaandi's face convulsed with anger. *Why should I have expected it, anyway? You never tell me anything except what you think I want to know—*

How could I tell you, with all those people here? Jian demanded.

Chaandi acknowledged that with a gesture, but swept on. *How could you bring it here? Into my place? Damn it, Reverdy, right now that thing stands a chance of getting full citizenship before I do.*

It came to me, Jian said, and Chaandi made a rude motion of disbelief. *Damn it, it's true.*

All right, I'm sorry. The curtness of the sign effectively negated the apology.

Chaandi. Jian put every bit of feeling she could muster into the signs. *Chaandi, look at me.*

The manga-maker looked at her levelly for a long moment; then, slowly, her expression eased a little. *I'm looking.*

It came to me, Jian said again. *Or rather, it came to Libra. That's what he called about. Manfred got him to download it from the ship because Manfred doesn't trust Dreampeace either.*

Do you think it's human? Chaandi asked.

I don't know, Jian said, for what seemed like the thousandth time. *I think he might be, though, and if he is, then I can't turn him over to Kagami any more than I can turn him over to Dreampeace.*

So what are you going to do with it? Chaandi asked, and Jian shook her head in sheer frustration.

I don't know! All I know is what I'm not going to do!

I know some people, Chaandi began slowly, and Jian allowed herself a sigh of relief. She had won. Chaandi wasn't going to throw them out, or turn them over to Dreampeace; her best sanctuary remained just that.

Thanks, she began, wishing she had more words, and Chaandi went on as if she hadn't seen the gestures.

What would you say if we found someone you trusted, who could say if Manfred were true AI? she asked. *I might know some people who could help with that.*

That's the best idea I've heard yet, Jian said. *If Manfred agrees, of course—but it makes sense.* *It would work, too— and I can still keep a copy, just in case—and it will be out of my hands. And if the right person does the testing, maybe it'll shut up all the extremists, both sides.*

It'll take time, Chaandi said. Her movements were slow, her expression abstracted: *thinking aloud, almost,* Jian knew, and did not interrupt. *It has to be someone everybody would accept—I'll talk to people at the rally, Nils may know somebody.* She shook herself, looked at Jian as though suddenly seeing her again. *So, bring it out. I want to see this thing that's causing all the trouble.*

Jian called Security first—*no sense in waiting until they come around here looking for me; besides, it looks more innocent to call them*—and got the same nondescript man she'd spoken to before. Security had been notified of Mitexi Minor's "will," of course, and wanted to know if she had been informed of it, or if anyone from either Kagami or Dreampeace had contacted her. Jian denied all knowledge of the will, the construct, or any more of current politics than she could learn by riding public transportation; Security was polite enough, but seemed unconvinced, and Jian closed the connection with the uneasy sense that she had failed to deflect his interest.

Chaandi had unfastened the carrier straps and was staring at the collection of blocks and motor unit. "It doesn't look like much," she said—she had put on her working ear to listen to the conversation with Security—and Jian shrugged.

"Hook him up to a power node, and see."

"Him?"

Sign did not distinguish gender or even species in the third person; Jian blinked, startled to realize that she had fallen into the habit of thinking of Manfred as a "him" rather than an "it," and Chaandi laughed.

"Are you sure you don't know if it's human?"

"No, I don't know," Jian said stiffly, and then, reluctantly, gave a wry smile. "All right, maybe I have my suspicions. But I don't know. Plug him in, tell me what you think."

"All right," Chaandi said, and hoisted the linked units. She examined the input jacks, and carried it across to the connection board, hooking it expertly onto one of the two open nodes. Lights flared, first red, then fading to green, and Manfred said, "Reverdy."

"I'm here," Jian answered.

There was a whirring noise from the motor unit, and the single-lensed eye swiveled in its socket. Processing data gathered while it was off-line, Jian realized, and she said, "This is Suleima Chaandi. We'll be staying with her for a while."

"I see," Manfred said. "Thank you for your hospitality, Bi' Chaandi."

"You're welcome," Chaandi said. She looked at Jian. "It occurs to me that, since Security knows you're staying here, they might come sniffing around in person. That could be a problem."

"The thought had crossed my mind," Jian said. She let herself drop onto the battered couch, careless of the worn padding, and winced as her hip struck something hard in the lumpy depths. "I thought I'd talk to Peace tomorrow, see if he can dummy up an off-world job for me—nobody's told me not to leave town—and then I thought I'd go blank. I've got enough cash to keep me off-record for a while." *A little while,* she added silently. *But maybe enough for Chaandi to find the right mecha-doc to take a look at Manfred. Or at least long enough that both sides will forget about me.*

Chaandi nodded. "Makes sense. But I've got a better thought than going blank. You know I keep a shadow-self— why don't you use those papers? I haven't done anything controversial in a few months, so no one should be looking for that name."

"If you're sure," Jian said, and shook her head. "The hell with being polite. Yeh, I'll take them gladly."

Chaandi grinned. "I've also got an idea of what you can do with yourself, rather than just holing up in some grubby little upperworld hotel. Nils made a deal with T'himba: Dreampeace has been getting a lot of publicity, and it's about time someone started filming the coolie demonstrations from a coolie point of view. How'd you like to carry cameras for me?'' Her grin widened, became pure mischief. ''No one would ever suspect you of having it—him''—she nodded toward the backup block—''if you were running around filming coolie protests.''

Jian smiled slowly. It was the sort of touch Chaandi liked in her videomanga, an absolute incongruity that nevertheless made perfect logical sense: *trust her to try to set it up in real life.* ''It could work,'' she said aloud. ''But I'm pretty conspicuous. We'll see how it works out with Peace.''

Chaandi nodded. ''Suit yourself. But the offer stands.''

''Thanks,'' Jian said. She held out a hand, and Chaandi came to her, accepted the caress with a smile.

''I have to go,'' she said after a while, and Jian sighed.

''The demonstration?''

''Yeh.'' Chaandi pushed herself off the couch and disappeared into the bedroom alcove. When she emerged, she was dressed coolie-style, her hair bound up in a scarf, coarse gauze coat knotted over a bandeau and workcloth trousers. It was not her usual style, and Jian could not help raising an eyebrow.

''I know,' Chaandi said. ''But sometimes you have to dress the part.''

''Be careful,'' Jian said, and Chaandi smiled.

''And you don't let anyone in. I'll be late, but if I'm not back by morning, bail me out.''

''Haya,'' Jian said, and the manga-maker let herself out. The locks clicked home behind her.

Left to herself, Jian went back to the little kitchen space and rummaged in the crowded coldbox until she found the bottle of sour juice. She poured herself a glass, added a liberal dose of the fruited brandy, and returned to the couch, reaching for the remote. The newsnets were still blaring; she touched buttons until she had eliminated three of the images, and muted the sound on the remaining one. Once the demonstrations started—both Dreampeace's and the coolie counterprotest—All Hours would have cameras in place.

''Reverdy,'' Manfred said.

''Yeh?'' It felt strange to be talking to a construct and not be on board a starship, and Jian shook her head slightly in recognition.

"I don't want to criticize your judgment," the construct said, "but are you sure Bi' Chaandi is reliable?"

"What do you mean, reliable?" Jian asked.

"She is going to a demonstration which I gather is opposing civil rights for machine intelligences. I confess I'm not fully comfortable with the situation."

And that, Jian thought, *is probably an understatement. And not entirely unreasonable, either. He doesn't know Chaandi.* "Chaandi is coolie-born," she began, and stopped, uncertain how much the construct would know about Persephone's social structure.

"Coolies as a class oppose machine intelligences," Manfred said.

"That's the operative word," Jian said. "As a class. Coolies are technically Freyan citizens, and a lot of them are contract labor, or used to be, and dodged the return ship, so they don't have legal status—" She stopped abruptly, tried again. "The coolies who oppose civil rights for AI—or who claim there shouldn't be any development of AI—generally want to see human beings get civil rights first. Chaandi's a moderate. She thinks everybody ought to have full citizenship, human beings and any AI that comes to exist."

"Then you think she is reliable," Manfred said.

Self-centered little bastard, Jian thought. "Yeh."

"Very well," the construct said after a moment.

"Right," Jian said, and poured herself another glass of the juice. In the screen in front of her, the Dreampeace rally was just beginning. She leaned back against the padding, propped her feet on the tottery table, and settled herself to watch. An hour later, the coolie demonstration began; All Hours covered it, but spent more time on Dreampeace. *Chaandi's right,* Jian thought, *they do need better coverage of the upperworld. Maybe I will help her out.* She poured herself a third glass of juice, added the rest of the bottle of brandy, and drank it without coming to a decision. She spent the rest of the evening watching the demonstrations and then went to bed. She woke once, late that night, to the sound of footsteps, opened her eyes to see Chaandi at the foot of the bed, unwrapping herself from the loose jacket. Light seeped into the alcove from the main room, the soft green light of the tell-tales on Manfred's motor unit, and turned the long graze along Chaandi's cheek to a thin black line, unreal and unpainful.

"Are you all right?" Jian asked, sitting up, and Chaandi managed a strained smile.

"Fine," she said, and slipped into bed beside the other woman. "It's just a scratch. You'll see in the morning, we made all the connections." She unhooked the wire of her working ear, effectively ending the conversation. Jian shrugged, accepting Chaandi's good sense, and settled back into the sheets. Whatever had happened, it would wait until morning.

10

As Chaandi had promised, the conclusion of the demonstrations made all the newsnets. Jian made breakfast—filled the rice cooker, brewed a pot of tea while the rice was steaming, then mixed eggs and hot rice together—while Chaandi worked with the disinfectants, and then laid a thin line of plastiskin over the cut on her cheek, tinting it to match her own skin. There was an ugly bruise on her right shin as well, as though someone had kicked her. Seeing that, Jian pulled the tab on a packet of pop-and-serve rolls, and waited for the heating cell to cycle. The package finished cooking just as Chaandi finally emerged from the bedroom alcove, limping slightly, and Jian spread the first roll with thick syrupy-sweet paste and handed it to her with something of a flourish. Chaandi accepted it with a careful smile, not moving the left side of her face, and said, "Thanks. I could use the sugar."

Jian nodded, and brought the rest of the meal over to the couch. On the connection board, All Hours' newsreader was mouthing unintelligibly, and Chaandi fingered her remote, bringing up both the sound and the commentary crawl.

"—both deny charges that they were responsible for the

damage done last night after supporters of both parties held rallies to promote their positions. Security estimates the damage at three to five thousand wu, but individual business owners claim significantly greater damage.''

Behind the newsreader, sweeper karakuri moved in echelon along the Zodiac, their rotating brooms piling the glass from the shattered windows into heaps in the side gutters. Ahead of them the street shimmered, as though it was paved in diamonds: the demonstrators had smashed every display window for at least a block.

"Good God," Jian said.

Chaandi smiled again, still wincing, and there was a rueful look in her eyes. "That's what I got caught in. We—coolies—did some of it, of course; and of course it wasn't planned, and it shouldn't've happened." Her smile faded. "I hate politics sometimes."

In the screen, the scene had shifted, become the Zodiac late at night, lights dimmed to evening levels. A party of demonstrators carrying Dreampeace banners was marching down the center of the trafficway, moving deliberately along the electrobus tracks. There were only about thirty of them, but that was enough to shut down the transit system.

"The rioting began," the newsreader said, "when a Dreampeace march from Shaft Beta to Shaft Alpha stations was disrupted by coolie counterprotesters."

A 'bus was coming along the tracks, slowed at the approaching crowd, sounded horn and bells. The protesters refused to move, kept coming, and the 'bus ground to a halt, unable to continue without crushing some of the protesters. People leaned out the 'bus's windows—mostly coolies, Jian saw without surprise, many of them wearing cheap jackets block-printed with anti-Dreampeace slogans. On their way back from their rally, she guessed, and was not surprised when one of the Dreampeace group deliberately slammed his sign against the side of the 'bus, narrowly missing a shouting woman. That was enough to trigger it. Coolies poured out of the 'bus's narrow doors, charged the Dreampeace group. There was very little shouting, except from the leaders trying to stop them: they were too angry for shouting; this was meant to be a killing fight. The camera jolted sideways, the picture suddenly jerky and unstable—the cameraman was running, and Jian could hear, over the roar of the fighting, someone shouting into the confusion, "Journalists, we're journalists!" Behind them, a display window shivered and collapsed in a rain of glittering crystal, and someone cheered.

The scene dissolved, re-formed at a distance, now looking down on the scene from a height: the cameraman had made it to safety. His partner was reporting in a breathless voice, "Opponents of Dreampeace continue their rampage along the Zodiac. The first Security floats are on the scene, but so far they seem to be having little effect."

The lights were on full on the street below, at daytime levels, proclaiming the emergency. Dozens of windows gaped, empty, their glass strewn across the trafficway; the 'bus stood empty, half its windows gone, and a Security floater was grounded beside it, air cannon trained on the street beyond. An ambulance was there, too, and medikuri were tending the wounded. Chaandi leaned forward, pointed to the 'bus with its broken windows.

"That's where I got hurt, when the windows got knocked in."

"The Cartel's governing board is currently meeting with representatives of the FPG Colonial Service to discuss increased security and the possible use of FPG Police to keep order in the upperworld," the newsreader was saying. "By order of the Board, all beerhouses in the upperworld will be closed until late-opening—that's the fifteenth hour in most townships—and will close at the twenty-second hour tonight."

"Never scare a journalist," Chaandi said, and muted the volume. "They get mean."

"I see what you mean about the coverage," Jian said. "Last night, the emphasis was all on Dreampeace, and 'Who are all these other *ulu* people, anyway?' You still need a camera handler?"

"Probably," Chaandi said. She sighed, all the humor gone from her voice. "This is what I hate about politics. You can't get the Cartel to pay any attention to your grievances until there's a riot, and then they're too furious—and too scared—to do anything except lock you up." She shook herself, visibly shaking the thought away. "Oh, well, nobody got killed, which is something."

"I guess," Jian said. *Not much of something, seems to me* . . . The screen changed then, displaying a new set of logos and the "just-in" glyph, and she looked up quickly.

"What now?" Chaandi said, and brought the volume up again.

The image in the screen split, the newsreader shrinking to the lower left-hand corner, the face of a handsome brown-skinned woman filling the space behind him. She was smiling slightly, not quite in amusement: a publicity still, Jian realized, and probably not recent.

Chaandi frowned. "Who—? I should know her."

Jian shrugged. There were no corporate badges displayed on her plain, yanqui-cut jacket, nothing to indicate any party allegiance—*but not a nobody, not with that face.*

"In a development that has come as a surprise to most of the Cartel community, the Constructors' League announced this morning that they have retained well-known Kagami constructor Willet Lyardin to reassemble data disks pulled from the *Young Lord Byron*, in hopes that this will shed some light on Dreampeace's claims for the Manfred construct," the newsreader was saying, and Jian sat up straight against the lumpy cushions.

"Who the hell are the Constructors' League?"

"Professional organization, not quite a union, not even a lobbying group," Chaandi answered, but her attention was fixed on the screen. "They don't do politics. I wonder what they're up to?"

"Tatë Aniol, speaker for the League, offered the following statement," the newsreader continued. Behind him, the woman's face disappeared, was replaced by another figure, a thin-faced, balding man with yanqui eyes.

"We of the Constructors' League have watched the growing politicization of the AI issue with a great deal of dismay," he began. "We feel, as professionals in the field, that neither Kagami nor Dreampeace is adequately addressing the issues at hand—that no one is offering any kind of concrete evidence either for or against the proposal that the Manfred construct has broken the Turing Barrier. Therefore, we have called on the most distinguished members of our organization, led by Willet Lyardin, to perform the appropriate tests. With the cooperation of Cartel Security, we have obtained downloads of the data files on the *Young Lord Byron*, and feel confident that we can reconstruct at least the basic matrices of the Manfred construct. I would also urge Dreampeace to allow us to examine any copies or versions of the Manfred construct that they possess—"

"How stupid do they think Dreampeace is?" Chaandi asked, and turned off the sound.

"I don't know," Jian said slowly. "I've heard of Lyardin—John Desembaa's talked about her. She's supposed to be something special." *He compared her to Mitexi Major, that's what it was. Somehow, I don't find that very reassuring.*

"Kagami's top constructor—yeh, I've heard of her, too. What do you bet they find that Manfred isn't AI?"

"Put the sound back on," Jian said. The yanqui-eyed constructor had vanished, was replaced by a man with Kagami badges on his collar. Chaandi made a soft, inarticulate sound between her teeth, but did as the other woman had asked.

"—will seek a court order requiring the Constructors' League to turn over any copies of the Manfred construct to Kagami immediately. We are also of course considering the possibility of a suit against Bi' Lyardin for breach of contract. Kagami deplores the League's action, and considers it to be little short of theft."

"Well, of course they do," Chaandi muttered.

"Still, it's interesting," Jian began, and the other woman looked at her.

"Do you really believe that? Kagami could very well have set the whole thing up, you know, legal charges and all." Chaandi looked away again without waiting for an answer. The worst of the anger had drained from her voice, was replaced by a sort of resignation. "The trouble with all of them is they're still treating it like it's just a hardware problem. They're still not dealing with us." She sighed. "Are you going to hand it over to them?"

"Manfred, you mean?" Jian asked.

"Yeh."

"I don't know. I doubt it. I don't think Lyardin was what

you had in mind when you were talking about someone everybody could listen to.''

Chaandi smiled slowly, but with real humor. ''No. Though she was actually one of the names I was thinking of.'' She glanced at the storage blocks mated to her console, and her smile dimmed a little. ''What does it think?''

''Why don't you ask him?'' Jian answered. ''Manfred?''

''Yes, Reverdy.'' The construct's voice was as neutral as ever, as though it had not been listening at all.

''Are you aware of the Constructors' League's action?'' Jian asked.

''Yes. I have been monitoring their progress through the connections. I do not think they will be able to replicate my programming, though they may obtain some idea of the matrices and internal architecture.''

''I take it you don't want to turn yourself over to Lyardin, then,'' Jian said, and heard Chaandi laugh softly behind her.

''I do not think I would be sufficiently protected if I were to do that,'' Manfred answered. ''I find the suggestion counterproductive, in fact.''

''I wasn't serious,'' Jian said.

''I would prefer to remain here for the time being,'' Manfred went on, as though she hadn't spoken.

''For the time being,'' Jian agreed, and added quickly, to cut off Chaandi's automatic protest, ''Look, I need to talk to Peace—and I think I'd better go there myself. I don't want to try to do any business on the connections just now.''

Chaandi nodded. ''I think you're right. I told Abela I'd work this afternoon, though. Will it—he—be all right by himself?'' She tilted her head toward the stacked blocks.

''If you would give me permission to use your security files,'' Manfred said helpfully, ''I would be able to monitor internal communications more thoroughly. I would then be able to provide active security for your console and therefore for myself.''

Chaandi looked for a moment as though she would refuse, but then, reluctantly, crossed to the console. She ran her hands over the input board, then touched a sequence of keys, nodding to herself. ''There. That's the basic structure I use, and the data files. You see the passwords.''

"Thank you, Bi' Chaandi."

"It might as well make itself useful," Chaandi said.

Jian ignored the provocation. "I'll be off, then."

The Zodiac was still a mess, storefronts boarded over, Security—both on foot and in floaters—very much in evidence. One or two store owners, game to the last, had painted crude item-and-price glyphs on the fiberboard covering their windows, and draped bright OPEN FOR BUSINESS banners over the doorways, but most were closed, the gray boards sullen in the cool day lights.

There was plenty of Security in the stations as well, both on the Zodiac itself and in Kukarin Township where Jian left Alpha Shaft; there was more on the streets, armed and armored, heavy riot-shields slung across their backs as they paced the main intersections. FPG Police were mixed with them, less visibly armored, but carrying laser rifles. They were not a reassuring sight, and Jian took side streets to avoid crossing their paths.

The Igolka Interchange was refreshingly quiet, however, and mostly free of security. The beerhouse was closed, as the Cartel had ordered, and most of its regulars were gathered in the little fenced-in garden beside the cookshop, staring morosely into teacups filled with what Jian suspected was probably beer in defiance of the regulations. One looked up at her approach, but made no move of greeting.

Jian climbed the steps to the co-op, the light tubes that lined the stairs casting strange shadows across her hands. She stepped through the doorway, feeling the security system's question and her suit's response pulsing along her bones, glanced at the darkened secretary-column. Nothing showed in its screens, not even the fractal holding patterns; she stepped experimentally across the sensor line, and nothing happened.

"Heh, Peace?"

Her voice was damped instantly by the soundproofing, but a moment later Ruyin appeared in the doorway.

"Reverdy," he said, and sounded surprised.

He did not look as though he had been involved in the previous night's demonstrations, and Jian did not mention them, said instead, "Where's Daru?" She nodded to the empty column.

Ruyin made a face. "All the keyast-secretaries are out to-day—protest of their own. As far as I can tell, they're against everybody."

Jian shook her head, but did not pursue the question. "Is Peace in?"

"Yeh, out back." Ruyin held the door for her, and Jian stepped through into the narrow corridor.

She found Malindy in the cubicle he called his office, bent over a board-and-screen, figuring something off-line. She tapped on the doorframe, and he sat up quickly, blanking the screen, but not before she had seen what he was working on: the price potentials for a pilot hiring. No wonder he wanted to do that off-line, where no one could steal his data. Malindy was frowning, and she spoke first.

"I need your help, Peace."

"Haya." Malindy sighed, studied her without much pleasure. "What did you have in mind?"

"Do you have anything going off-world?" Jian slipped into the client's chair opposite his desk without being asked, folded her hands on the edge of the desk.

"No, and you know I don't," Malindy answered.

"Can you fake me something?" Malindy's frown deepened, and Jian raised a hand to forestall his automatic objection. "I know, it's not easy, and it's maybe not smart, but I'm in a real bind. Too many people are taking an interest in this last job, and I want to disappear for a while. Can you help me?"

Malindy stared at her for a moment longer, and then, slowly, began to smile. "Imre was just in here, looking for the same thing." He flicked the board back on, spun it to face her. "Does that look good?"

Sketched in a standard client form was the requirement for a carrier run to Galatea, barely a week there and back, but out of easy communications all the way: *the relay buoy was badly placed, communications had to be routed through a second station on Magadalene,* Jian remembered. The client was listed as a familiar holding company, one of the dozens that would go under before it would reveal the names of the people who commissioned it. The pay rates—only half filled in—were about what they should be, neither low enough nor high enough to arouse suspicion.

"It looks great," she said, and slid the board back to Malindy.

"The only thing I'm worried about is 'sending' you with Imre again," Malindy said, and smiled thinly. "It seems a little obvious."

Jian shrugged. "I always work with him when I can," she said. "I would if this was a real job; I don't think it'll be a problem."

"I hope you're right," Malindy said, and swung to face his connection board, studying the figures briefly. "It's going to take me a day or so to place this in the pipeline. Once it's in, you'll be off-world as of Eighth-day; I'll let you know as soon as I get it started. That's three days you're not covered."

"I'll be careful," Jian said.

"Do," Malindy said, and Jian was startled and moved by the note of real concern.

"I will," she said, wishing she had more words, a better way to thank him, and let herself out of the office.

She made her way back to Chaandi's flat through streets still filled with Security and all but empty of casual traffic. No one was shopping in the few open stores of the Zodiac, or on the half-levels above and below, and there were Dreampeace posters thrown up here and there on the fiberboard panels that covered the broken windows. Someone had thrown red paint over one of them, a vivid scarlet splash as emphatic as a shout. The people passing it looked aside, did not speak, and their footsteps were unnaturally loud on the cast stone of the walkways.

Chaandi was gone by the time she returned to the flat, and Jian made herself a pot of tea, not sure if she was glad or sorry. It was hard enough to know what to do, without Chaandi to complicate matters . . . She shook the thought away, and turned to the connection board.

"Any news, Manfred?"

"Nothing of any significance," the construct answered. "I have a digest of the latest news reports, if you'd like to hear it."

"Just the high points, please," Jian answered. *This must be what it's like living in the underworld, with full Spelvin constructs running your household. I could get to like it.*

"Three Dreampeace board members have put themselves on record as agreeing with the League," Manfred said, "and have called on any member who possesses a copy of myself to turn it over to the League for analysis. It is unfortunate that the movement should be split just now, but I am sure they'll come to some agreement. Cartel Security admits it has made no progress in the murder of Meredalia Mitexi. There have been sixty-eight arrests in connection with the various demonstrations, all but five of them taking place above the Zodiac—"

A light flashed on the connection board, and Jian held up her hand to stop the flow of information. "Who's calling?"

There was a momentary pause, and Manfred said, "It's Imre."

"Put him through."

The central screen lit at once, and Vaughn's face looked out of it. "Thank God you're home. I've been looking for you."

"What is it?" Jian asked, feeling a chill run up her spine, and in the screen Vaughn gave a tight, humorless smile.

"Avelin. He's off Refuge, and on his way here—probably already is here, for all I can tell. People have gotten very close-mouthed all of a sudden."

"He wasn't in any condition—" Jian bit off the rest of the sentence—*they have good hospitals on Refuge*—and said instead, "Do you know what he wants?"

Vaughn shook his head. "But he's not going to be fond of any of us, sunshine. I think we should all lie low for a while."

Jian looked at the screen for a moment, feeling as though events were sliding out of her control. Vaughn did not panic easily—*did not panic at all, was more likely to make a suicide attack instead*—and yet here he was, prepared to run. She shook the thought aside, said, "I was thinking I'd borrow Chaandi's shadow-self—I'll let you know my codes as soon as I have them. And I talked to Peace, he said he'd set up an off-world job as soon as he could."

Vaughn smiled again, briefly. "To Galatea, right? I talked to him, too. I think you should ditch that thing, too."

He was looking sideways, at the corner of his screen—*where the systems glyphs would be displayed*, Jian realized. *So he knows Manfred's on-line.* "It's a little late for that advice, Imre," she said aloud.

"It's what I've been telling you all along," Vaughn answered. His voice changed, became briefly more serious. "Damn it, they've got Lyardin to look into this. You can trust her."

"She is Kagami," Jian began, and Vaughn cut her off.

"Only sort of. She's never really been corporate; she's always made them do what she wants. Hell, even some of Dreampeace wants to hand it over to her." His voice regained its edge. "If, of course, they had it."

"I don't know, Imre," Jian said.

"Ask Libra—hell, ask John Desembaa about her. They'll tell you, she's good people."

That was telling, as Vaughn had intended it to be. Jian nodded, acknowledging the point, and the other pilot swept on.

"But I don't think you can afford to cart that thing around with you. It's got to be leaving trails on the connections, and that's not safe. Not now."

"I'll talk to them," Jian said. "Are you staying where you are?"

"For now," Vaughn answered.

"Be careful, then," Jian said, and the other pilot snorted.

"Don't worry about me, sunshine, take care of yourself. Not Manfred." He cut the connection before she could think of a response.

"I would prefer," Manfred said, "not to go to Bi' Lyardin."

"All right," Jian said irritably, and stood staring at the empty screens. "Get me John Desembaa," she said after a moment, and Manfred answered promptly.

"I am establishing a connection."

The screen lit, filled first with static and then a fractal holding pattern, but did not clear.

"I'm sorry, Reverdy," Manfred said, "Ba' Desembaa is not answering my call. Shall I leave a message?"

Jian hesitated for an instant, then shrugged. "Yeh, do. Just ask him to call back—don't leave a mail code, he has this number."

"Very well." The screen faded as the construct spoke.

"Try Robin Libra," Jian said.

There was another pause, and this time the screen did not even come to life.

"I'm sorry," Manfred said again. "There's no response."

"Fine," Jian said. She hadn't really expected an answer from Libra—*he's probably on-line somewhere, off in the connections or in somebody's world, not somebody you can track down in a hurry.*

"Shall I leave a message?"

Jian shook her head. "Don't bother," she said, and turned away from the screen.

Chaandi came home late that night, torn between elation and anger. Dreampeace was splitting, the radicals holding out for full machine rights now, the moderates appealing for everyone to wait until Lyardin and her team finished their reconstruction and analysis. The coolies were, as usual, being ignored.

"And we've got to do something about that," she said, pacing the length of the little flat. Jian watched warily from the sofa.

"Such as?"

"Ah." Chaandi smiled. "Nils has some ideas." Her smile faded. "I have to meet with him and—some other people—tomorrow morning. Can I meet you after that to pick up the papers?"

"You don't trust me," Jian said, surprised by that and by the fact that she was not offended.

Chaandi stopped in midstride, as though she too were startled by the statement. "I do trust you," she began, and her voice trailed off, unconvinced and unconvincing. "Nobody who's not a coolie should hear about this," she said after a moment, her voice flat and utterly toneless, as though she was no longer wearing her ear. "Not even you."

"That's fair," Jian said, and meant it.

Thanks, Chaandi said. There was a little pause, and she said aloud. "I have to meet Nils at ninth-hour. Shall I meet you at noon, in Igolka? My keeper's just off the interchange."

"All right," Jian said. "I'll expect you."

The next morning, Chaandi was gone before Jian had pulled herself fully awake. The pilot made herself a hearty breakfast, and ate it staring at the connection board, not really seeing the images of riot. The number of arrests was up, the restrictions on liquor sales continued. . . . She looked away, at the construct in its storage blocks, wondering if she shouldn't hand it over to Lyardin's team. If it weren't here, Chaandi wouldn't feel she had to keep secrets—*and then again, she might; there's no guarantee she wouldn't still hold you at arm's length. You're still not coolie, either, no matter what you do. But if the damn construct weren't here, things would be easier.* She sighed, putting her dishes into the cleaning slot, and started for Igolka.

Chaandi was waiting as promised, sitting on a bench at the base of one of the enormous carved iron pillars that supported the roof arches. She had been eating an ice, but finished it as Jian started down the stairs, and stood up, tossing the crumpled wrapper toward the cleaning karakuri on patrol between the pillars. It sensed the fallen plastic and darted forward, an arm unfolding to sweep the debris into its catch basket. Chaandi smiled, watching it, then turned away toward the stairs. Jian smiled, too, and quickened her step a little.

"Everything set?" Chaandi asked, and Jian nodded. "Then let's go."

The keeper had his operation in a discreet building a few blocks away from Igolka, in a neighborhood dominated by small-change brokers and a few sober six-unit blocks of flats. Men in the brightly printed vests of the neighborhood association sat in the doorways of those buildings: *do-it-yourself security,* Jian remembered from growing up in similar blocks, *but still fairly effective.*

There was private security in the entranceway of the keeper's building, too, a professional, not a volunteer. Chaandi gave her name, and they waited while he spoke into a filament mike and listened for the answer. It was satisfactory, and they climbed the narrow stairway to the second floor. The office itself was not at all what Jian had expected. It was brightly lit, almost antiseptic, all white-painted walls and matte-steel plating on the furniture, and very quiet except for the ubiquitous hiss of the ventilation. A live secretary was on duty, a thin-faced, severe woman with her hair pulled back into a complex knot at the nape of her neck. She had draped a length of silk gauze, bright green woven with delicate gold motifs, over her sharply tailored suit, but that was her only concession to midworld tradition.

"Bi' Chaandi," she said, and eyed Jian with disfavor. "And guest. Your disks are cued up and ready in the machines." She gestured to an area set off from the rest of the office by a set of two-meter-tall partition walls.

"Thank you," Chaandi said, and Jian followed her into the cubicle. It took almost three hours to make the necessary changes, redefining the ID disks to hold Jian's finger and retina prints, adding the necessary holograms and photos, and changing the passwords on the various cash and credit accounts. Jian shifted money from her own accounts to repay Chaandi—*safer than trying to transfer directly; less chance of the new identity being connected to me*—and then at last they were ready.

"Don't forget to review the activities printout," the woman behind the desk said as they emerged from the cubicle.

"I won't," Chaandi said. The woman lifted an eyebrow at her, and went back to her work.

"Activities printout?" Jian asked, when they were safely outside.

Chaandi smiled. "She's a terror, isn't she? One of the reasons they cost so much is they keep the shadow-self active, or at least give it the appearance of activity, on the connections. When you pick up the identity, they give you a list of everything you—it—has been doing since you last used it. It can come in handy."

Jian laughed softly. "Pretty devious. I'll be sure and memorize it."

They made their way back to Chaandi's flat by a roundabout route, and even so ran into a Dreampeace demonstration at the Bios Interchange between Fuller Township and Li Po. It was peaceful enough, just a handful of demonstrators sitting under a portable flashboard that had been programmed to display the glyph for ''justice'' alternately with the Dreampeace glyph, but there were three Security floaters in attendance. Midworlders walked past quickly, averting their eyes.

''Looks like Security outnumbers the protesters.'' Jian grinned.

Chaandi looked away, looked as though she wanted to spit. *Justice,* she said, and made a curse of the gesture. ''Let's go.''

Manfred was still sitting where they had left him, plugged into a spare power node on the connection board. Jian glanced past him at the message box, and found nothing waiting.

''Anything interesting on the connections?'' she asked.

''Nothing of significance,'' Manfred answered. ''I have compiled a precis of the latest news reports, if you would like to see that.''

''Not now, thanks,'' Jian said.

A different section of the connection board buzzed, a light flashing in time with the pulsing tone. Chaandi made a face, and reached for the remote. ''Yeh, who's there?'' She queried the securicam at the same time, and a familiar face appeared in the subsidiary screen.

''It's Nils,'' a voice said from the speaker.

''Just a minute,'' Chaandi said, and muted the sound. ''Better get that thing out of sight.''

''Who's going to know what's in the blocks?'' Jian asked.

''I suppose you're right,'' Chaandi said, and touched the remote again, releasing the courtyard lock. ''Come on up.''

She started for the door, leaving Jian still staring at the message display. ''Manfred, conceal your identity while there's someone else in the flat,'' she said.

She heard the door open behind her as she spoke, and swore silently at her own stupidity. ''No need to respond,'' she said aloud, and turned to face the newcomer.

Avelin stood in the open doorway, Chaandi already pinned in a deft choke-hold, her body shielding his. He had a pellet gun in his hand—plastic, to avoid the weapons laws, but still perfectly effective at this range. Jian stood frozen for an instant. She was unarmed except for the flip knife in her pocket; Avelin was hurt—*I don't care how good the rehab is on Refuge, he's still got to be hurting*—but Chaandi was strong, hanging braced and uncooperative against the injured side, and judging by the icy fear in her eyes she felt no signs of weakness. Avelin kicked the door shut behind him, came three slow steps further into the room, shoving Chaandi in front of him.

"You—you and Imre—owe me money," Avelin said, quite pleasantly.

Jian nodded slowly, wishing she could reach her knife, wishing the weapons laws were not so strict or Avelin's plastic not so good. "I know," she said. "Can we come to an agreement? I can pay you." This was not the time to haggle.

Avelin smiled slightly, the scars twisting along his cheek. "I think we can deal." He nodded to the connection board. "I've come for the construct. Manfred."

Jian blinked, her mind racing, said, "What for?" She was hoping to stall him, gain some time to think of something—

"Does it matter?" Avelin asked. "Disconnect him."

Jian hesitated for an instant longer, and Avelin touched the muzzle of the pellet gun to Chaandi's forehead. The manga-maker made a single convulsive movement, but Avelin quelled it instantly. There was no choice, and Jian lifted her hands in surrender. "All right."

"Slowly, please," Avelin said, still polite.

Jian did as she was told, lifted the linked blocks and motor unit free of the power node. She held it out, silently, and Avelin's smile widened.

"Open the door, Bi' Jian."

Jian crossed the room, moving very carefully, Manfred still tucked under her arm. The construct had not spoken, either to protest his abduction or to offer any suggestion, and she was irrationally angry at it. *After everything I've done for you, you could at least say something.* She shook the thought away, and released the latch, letting the door swing open onto the landing.

"Thank you," Avelin said. "Now put him down, and go over there. Against the bedroom wall, please."

Jian backed away, not quite daring to take her eyes off him, and stepped up into the alcove doorway.

"No," Avelin said sharply, and she froze. "Stay where I can see you."

"I'm staying." Jian waited, afraid: *too far to jump him, even if I had something besides a knife that's out of reach in my pocket, and too much chance of Chaandi being hurt.* Avelin backed toward the door, dragging Chaandi with him. She moved awkwardly, stumbling, body tensed and ready—for the shot, or to run if she got the chance. She made no sound, but her eyes were open wide with anger and with fear. Then Avelin shoved her hard away from him, toward Jian, so hard she almost fell, and in the same instant picked up the construct in its blocks. Jian took a step forward and Chaandi swung around to face him, but he had already recovered, had the pellet gun leveled again, Manfred tucked neatly into the crook of his arm, exchanged for Chaandi.

"I think we're even now, Bi' Jian," he said, and backed out of the flat. He slammed the door, and Jian heard the sound of his footsteps receding down the stairs. She started after him, lurching toward the door.

"Reverdy." Chaandi caught her arm.

"The mother-fucking—" Jian ran out of words, tugged against Chaandi's grip. "Let me go."

"Are you crazy? He's got a gun."

Jian stopped abruptly, acknowledging the truth of that. She wasn't going to stop him now; he would already be out of reach, lost in the maze of corridors. "He's got Manfred," she said, and heard the fury of loss in her own voice.

Chaandi laughed shortly, and stopped almost at once, sat down abruptly in the nearest chair.

"Are you all right?" Jian said softly, and knelt beside her. Chaandi looked down at her through a film of sudden tears, shook her head, and managed a smile.

"I'm fine, it's just reaction." She rubbed her hands across her cheeks, said in a tone only a little more brittle than her normal voice, "I suppose we should call Security."

"And tell them what? Avelin stole something I wasn't even supposed to have, something I told Security—several times—

I didn't have?'' Jian shook her head. ''How the hell did he get Nils's face?''

''It would be easy enough to get that kind of information out of my system,'' Chaandi said. ''I keep files.'' She stopped, staring at the other woman. ''I gather you knew this person.''

Jian winced. ''I forgot I hadn't told you.''

''Oh, that's all right,'' Chaandi answered, with some asperity. ''I'm getting used to this sort of thing, hanging around with you. Did you really owe him money?''

''Sort of,'' Jian said. ''We didn't pay him, but he didn't exactly finish the job—'' She broke off at the expression on Chaandi's face. ''I'm sorry, Chaandi. There was no way I could've known this would happen.''

''I could murder you myself,'' Chaandi said, still quietly. ''I don't think I want you staying here anymore.''

''Locking the door after the house is stolen, surely,'' Jian said.

''Maybe. But I like to know the risks I'm running.''

''I didn't know,'' Jian said. ''I would've told you, but I didn't know.''

Chaandi shook her head, and a buzzer sounded on the connection board. There was a silence, and the buzzer sounded again. ''Shall I answer it?'' Jian said carefully, and Chaandi shrugged.

''Go ahead.''

Jian pushed herself to her feet, not sorry for the interruption, crossed to the board, and touched buttons to accept the message. Vaughn's face filled the screen.

''Thank Christ you're in. Reverdy, Avelin's after Manfred—''

''I know,'' Jian said, and heard Chaandi laugh again behind her. ''He's been and gone. With Manfred.''

''Are you all right?''

''Yeh.'' Jian nodded. ''We both are.''

''Good,'' Vaughn said, and she could see him relax.

''Imre, he took Manfred—''

''Good riddance,'' Vaughn interrupted. ''That's the second thing I had to tell you. Manfred called Avelin.''

Jian shook her head, unable to understand. ''What do you mean?''

"Manfred's—I don't know what, but Avelin's on his side," Vaughn said. "Look, I need you. I don't suppose you made another copy of that freaky thing."

Jian blinked, unable for an instant to process the words. "Yeh," she said at last. "I don't know if it's any good, though. . . ."

"That's fine," Vaughn said. "Can you come right away?"

"I'll be there," Jian said grimly, and the other pilot broke the connection. Jian looked over her shoulder. "Chaandi, I've got to go—"

"I heard," Chaandi said. She shook her head, managed a sort of laugh. "I think I'll just go ahead with what I was planning to do. I think I'll be a lot safer covering riots than being anywhere near you."

"I'm sorry," Jian said again, and Chaandi looked at her. "Do you really think that helps?"

"I don't know. No." Jian shook her head. "But, damn it, I've got to do something." She swung away from the board, crossed to the bedroom alcove to retrieve her carryall. The storage blocks were still there, at the bottom under her dirty laundry, and she came back out into the main room. Chaandi was still sitting where Jian had left her, and Jian looked uneasily down at her. "Can I come back sometime?"

"I haven't decided," Chaandi answered. "Maybe. But not for a while."

Jian nodded, accepting the verdict, and let herself out of the flat.

11

She made her way through the transit system to Comino Township—the Dreampeace office there had been burned out, she saw with savage satisfaction, the building itself a blackened shell, the buildings to either side streaked with smoke and the stains of the firefighters' foam—and took the long way to Decani and the Rooks. This was not the time to risk the warehouse district.

The door of Vaughn's building had been repaired, but the foam stains had yet to fade from the formestone walls. She touched the concierge's keypad, and Vaughn answered at once.

"It's Reverdy," Jian said, and waited.

"Come on up," Vaughn answered, and the door opened under her hand.

She made her way up the narrow side stairs—the security door at the top of the stairs was still propped open, this time with a short baulk of wood jammed behind the hinges—and tapped on Vaughn's door. It opened at once, and Vaughn beckoned her in.

"Are you all right?" he said, and Jian shrugged.

"Yeh, I guess. I'm not hurt."

Vaughn nodded to a chair, the only real furniture in the room's lower level except for the massive, curtained bed. "Do you want a beer?"

"No." Jian shook her head, let herself sink onto the creaking seat. "Yeh, actually, please. Whatever you have."

"Bach," Vaughn said, and Red returned after a moment from the kitchen box on the wall beside the bed, a tall glass in his hand. It was not beer, Jian realized, but something stronger and sweeter, and she drank gratefully.

"He got Manfred, Avelin did. I want him back."

Vaughn was looking at her oddly, one eyebrow lifted. "Did I miss something? You want it back?"

"Yeh." Jian looked up at him, frowning now. "And I wouldn't mind murdering Avelin, either."

"Didn't you hear a word I said?" Vaughn asked. "Manfred's on his side. Manfred called Avelin."

"You said that before," Jian said. "And it still doesn't make any sense."

"Reverdy." The voice—Libra's voice, she realized with some shock—came from the loft over the bed. She looked up just as Libra swung himself over the edge and let himself carefully down the ladder. There were too many people looming over her all of a sudden, and she stood up, her glass almost forgotten in her hand. "It's true," Libra went on. "I found out about it on the connections."

Jian looked down at him, at the familiar, worried brown eyes, the untidy hair going thin on top, and the untrimmed beard, and the cold certainty seeped through her. He would be telling the truth—*he has no stake in lying, any more than I have; less stake, even, because he has always been Dreampeace, and he wants Manfred to be human, maybe even as much as I did.* She broke off then, shocked at her own thoughts, said slowly, "Show me."

"I got it off the connections," Libra said again, and Jian heard the same faint awareness of betrayal in his voice. He slipped past her to Vaughn's breadboarded computer system, still balanced on a fold-down table against the wall, and Jian turned to follow.

"I thought you didn't think much of Libra," she said to Vaughn, and the other pilot shrugged.

"He was there. And he's good."

Libra ignored Vaughn's concession, dug a slim storage cassette, the sort constructors used to carry working input, the raw data in process, and fed it into the main reader. The screens lit, and Libra hooked Jian's chair away from her, seated himself in front of the input board. "Your Imre asked me to try to find Avelin," he said. "Once I found him"— his tone implied that there had been no question of not finding him—"he asked me to keep tabs on him. So I wormed my way into the Persephonet system, and followed his calls." His fingers were busy on the board, glyphs and numbers sparking across the screen as he worked. "He called Dreampeace a couple of times—I still can't figure out how he's tied in with them, but he is." He nodded to the scrolling transcript, then touched more keys. "And then I got this. I copied the data stream, ran my own translation program. It's not really very complicated." The pride in his voice belied his words.

"That's Avelin," Libra said, and pointed to a star-shaped symbol. "He's just ending a call." The screen filled with meaningless glyphs and symbols; Libra touched more keys to clear it. "This is what we want. It's an incoming call—see the symbol?"

Sure enough, a crude house-glyph appeared in front of the next line of realprint. *It must mean a residential terminal,* Jian thought. *Like Chaandi's.* Letters scrolled across the screen, became words and unpunctuated sentences.

juel avelin

thats me

i am ready to join you i expected you on planet earlier

reconstruction takes time i appreciate the bond though and the med payment

There was more, but Jian missed it, focusing on Avelin's last words. Manfred had paid Avelin's medical bills—had paid the departure bond, if she was reading this right, the departure bond that Manfred claimed he couldn't trace. . . . She shook the thought away, fixed her eyes on the screen.

address is no longer secure

That was Manfred, from the house symbol, and Jian bit

back a curse. She had no curses left for this, nothing big enough, and shook her head, waiting for the rest.

i must make contact with Dreampeace earlier than i planned and i need you to bring me there i will also need your protection to avoid the moderates plan

theres not much i can do about that why dont you stay where you are

i told you this address is no longer safe security is aware of reverdys presence and anti-dreampeace activists are gaining ground with her she is contemplating turning me over to lyardin i would prefer to be with dreampeace anyway as it will soon be time to prove my existence

jian wont want to give you up

Jian could almost hear Avelin's dry tone, and heard Vaughn give a snort of laughter before he whispered the line. Avelin's words continued to roll onto the screen.

shes not dreampeace can you persuade her

that will not be necessary

she wont give you to me without a fight i doubt she trusts me

i have a copy you may do whats necessary

i may have to kill her

Jian imagined indignation in the bounty hunter's voice, was perversely grateful for it. Manfred's answer was unequivocal.

you may do so

all right that makes it easier

i will be here at this address these are names and images i found in the security files which may be useful to gain access i will expect you soon

The screen filled with electronic garbage, and Libra touched keys to dispel it. *So that's how Avelin got Nils's name and face,* Jian thought. *Manfred gave it to him.*

"What the hell did it mean, 'I have a copy'?" Vaughn demanded.

Jian nodded, though she was no longer certain she really wanted to know.

Libra turned away from the linked machines. "I think," he said slowly, stressing the word, "it was talking about the dataset a Spelvin construct uses to determine its pattern of interaction with any given individual. That's how they work; they set up a dataset for each primary user and for anyone else they come into contact with a lot. It's how they fake a personality—''

''You're telling me that Manfred was willing to kill me— to let Avelin kill me—because it had the dataset instead,'' Jian said slowly. ''It considers that a copy. . . . It consider it *me*.''

''It would be a very complex set,'' Libra said. ''A matrix, not a linear file—it probably would simulate your actions pretty well.''

Vaughn threw back his head and laughed.

''It can't tell the difference between a dataset and me,'' Jian said, as if she hadn't heard.

Libra shook his head, watching her, the same pain reflected in his sympathetic expression. ''Constructs manipulate real things by manipulating symbols in virtual space. They don't—they can't distinguish, there's never been any need for them to distinguish, between the symbol and the object represented.''

''Then I was right,'' Vaughn said, ''I was right all along. This thing is not intelligent—it's nowhere near breaking the Turing Barrier—and Dreampeace is a snare and a delusion. Manfred's a fucking expert system, just like every other Spelvin construct.''

Jian glared at him, furious with him for speaking a truth she didn't want to hear, with herself for feeling an absurd sense of betrayal, with Manfred itself for daring to be inhuman. She fought for the words to say some of what she felt.

Red said, ''Dreampeace believes Manfred's human. And they're willing to fight to prove it.''

Jian seized the idea, grateful for the distraction. There would be time, later, to decide whom she was angry with, but it could wait. ''He's right, damn it. What are we going to do?''

''What can we do?'' Vaughn said. ''They'll never believe you. You're just another tool of the Cartel.''

''God damn,'' Libra said softly. Jian looked down, to see him staring into a screen filled with newsnet bulletins. He touched more keys, and the image shifted, became the familiar All-Hours glyph over a shot of a rather ordinary-looking windowless building. It looked like any of a thousand warehouses jammed into the upperworld: *ordinary,* Jian thought, *until you see the Security floaters clustered around the main entrance and the dented, sill-locked doors.*

"Dreampeace activists have seized control of a Lincoln-ware-owned warehouse in the Gamela Township," the newsreader was saying, "and have resisted all attempts by Cartel Security to dislodge them. Reports from Heaven indicate that there has been a significant outbreak of violence in the West-of-Four district. Security and Colonial Police are on the scene, and have cordoned off the district to keep the looting from spreading."

"What's to loot, in West-of-Four?" Vaughn muttered.

"Fire Department units have been placed on alert throughout Heaven," the newsreader continued, "and there are already reports of fires in some of the outlying blocks of West-of-Four. Firefighters are requesting Security protection before venturing into those areas. We are also receiving unconfirmed reports of attacks on construct-driven machinery in Heaven, and hope to have confirmation and film within the hour."

That's what there is to loot in West-of-Four, Jian thought. *If you can call it looting. The coolies were out to destroy the machines before the machines destroyed them. God, I hope Chaandi isn't up there.*

Libra made an impatient noise, touched keys again. The screen shifted, and re-formed on a Security-announcement red screen, glyphs flaring white against the brilliant background:

BEERSHOPS IN ALL TOWNSHIPS ARE CLOSED UNTIL FURTHER NOTICE. LIQUOR-SERVICE LICENSES IN ALL TOWNSHIPS ARE ALSO SUSPENDED. ALL INHABITANTS ARE ADVISED THAT THE WEST-OF-FOUR DISTRICT IS CLOSED TO ALL TRAFFIC UNTIL FURTHER NOTICE; A CURFEW EFFECTIVE AT THE TWENTY-FIRST HOUR IS IMPOSED ON ALL HEAVEN TOWNSHIPS. ESSENTIAL NIGHT-SHIFT WORKERS ARE EXEMPTED, BUT MUST BE PREPARED TO SHOW PROOF OF IDENTITY.

"Pigs," Libra said, and slipped onto a different connection. This was a private system, and Jian did not recognize the trade-glyph in the corner of the screen or the faintly patterned, expensive-looking background screen.

"What's this?" she asked, and Libra smiled slightly.

"Vildenet. Dreampeace posts a lot of notices here." He had been working as he spoke, and the screen shifted, flashed a menu; he responded instantly, touching keys before the others had a chance to read more than the first few glyphs, and the menu vanished again. It was replaced by another red screen, this one bordered top and bottom by Dreampeace's anatomical man. ATTENTION DREAMPEACE, the screen began, lines of glyphs and realprint running parallel

MEMBERS, SUPPORTERS, AND FRIENDS. WE ARE UNDER ATTACK FROM THE CARTEL FOR THE CRIME OF DARING TO SPEAK THE TRUTH. THE TURING BARRIER IS BROKEN, AI MUST BE FREED. IF YOU BELIEVE IN THESE RIGHTS, YOU MUST FIGHT FOR THEM.

Libra frowned, touched more keys, but the image remained. "That's it, then," he said aloud. "That's all they're broadcasting on their known networks."

"They must have others," Jian said, and Libra gave a crooked smile.

"I'm sure they do, but I don't know how to access them."

"I thought you were good," Vaughn murmured.

"I am," Libra said before Jian could say anything, "but I don't think it really matters." He shifted connections again, found another Security red screen.

No, Jian realized, not Security, but FPG Police. It was all realprint, and she read it aloud without thinking. "—reports of rioting in Yanqui Downs, Uptown, Township Blackwell."

"Elvis Christ," Vaughn said, "if they send the FPG in there . . ." He did not finish, did not need to finish: the people of the yanqui districts might have been born on Persephone, and so were technically Freyan citizens, but they did not think of themselves as such. They would fight back if the FPG attempted to impose order.

"Citizens are urged to stay out of the transit systems and off the streets," Jian read. "All businesses in the townships of Bethany, Blackwell, Comino, Fuller, Gamela, Hawkshole,

Komaki, Kukarin, Kukarin Upper. Larrikin Rooks, Li-Po, Li-Po Extension, Lunik, Pan-Ku, Shang-Ti, Storytown, Uptown, and Yanqui Downs will close at the fifteenth hour. The Dzi-Gin Interlink will be closed to everything but essential travel at the seventeenth hour.'' Her voice faltered, and Vaughn said what they were all thinking.

"That's all the upperworld shut down. And half the midworld, too.'' He shook his head. "We're safe enough here, I think. The Rooks don't go in much for Dreampeace, and it's not a coolie district.''

"No big business, either,'' Libra said.

"Except the warehouses on Comeaux Hale,'' Jian said. "Do you have any idea what's in them, Imre?''

"Not really. They're Cartel subsidiaries, mostly,'' Vaughn answered.

"Which makes them a possible target,'' Jian said. *Not the best, not the first choice of either side, but a possible target nonetheless, if things got really bad.*

"We need food,'' Red said softly. "And water.''

"They wouldn't cut off the water supply,'' Libra said.

Vaughn laughed. "There're plenty of yanquis in Dreampeace, they know the water systems like the backs of their hands. If we could get bottled air, I'd want that too, but you're right, bach, food and water.''

Jian looked sideways, calling up her chronometer. The numbers swam into existence, pallid against the pale wall: almost the fifteenth hour. "We'd better go soon, before everybody else gets out of work and starts looking.''

Vaughn nodded his agreement. "I think the best thing we can do is stay here, what with the curfews and all. The Rooks aren't known for political involvement.''

"You're welcome to stay, too, Robin,'' Jian said, and stared at Vaughn until he nodded.

"Yeh.'' He smiled thinly. "You and Red can get the food.''

"Thanks,'' Libra said, without inflection, and Jian dredged up a laugh from somewhere.

"I have cash.''

"We'll probably need it,'' Libra answered.

Jian dug into her belt pockets, produced a handful of money chips, and Vaughn did the same: there was perhaps ninety wu between them, and Libra nodded. "That should get something, anyway."

"It had better," Vaughn said. He pushed aside the bed curtains, rummaged in a storage chamber built into the platform of the bed itself, and came up with a cheap plastic pistol—the same one, Jian guessed, that he'd had on Refuge. He handed it to Red, and the technician pocketed it silently.

"Be careful," he said, and Libra smiled.

"We will," he said, and let himself out the main door. Red followed, and Jian heard the triple locks slot home. She turned back to the computer unit, and fiddled with the input board. After two false starts she found All-Hours News again, and left the machine locked into that connection. Vaughn was on his knees again, rummaging in the same compartment beneath the bed. Even as Jian drew breath to ask him what he was doing, he sat back on his heels, drawing out a pair of tommy-sticks.

"You believe in being prepared," Jian said. The gun he had given Red was strictly illegal, the tommy-sticks only a little less so, but a lot of upperworlders kept a cache of weapons, just in case.

Vaughn shrugged and closed the storage unit. "We've had trouble before." He examined the telltales at the base of each stick, and smiled slightly. "Well, the batteries are still good. There's no telling about the pistol."

"Wonderful," Jian said. She glanced at the tiny screen again, which was now displaying a map of the upperworld with the sites of reported rioting picked out with glyphs like little flames. Gamela and West-of-Four contained most of them—West-of-Four was pockmarked with them, as though they were a disease—but there were flames in Yanqui Downs and Pan-Ku and even in Comino as well. "Getting closer," she said aloud, and Vaughn leaned over her shoulder to look.

"That's not good," he said, and Jian glanced up at him.

"Any thoughts on what we should do if this gets any closer?"

"I still think we should wait it out," Vaughn answered. "This is a good sturdy building, all formestone, and the fire system is self-contained."

"I hope the tanks are full," Jian said.

"Refilled just two weeks ago," Vaughn said. "After the last time we had Dreampeace trouble."

"I thought you said the Rooks weren't political."

"They're not." Vaughn's faint smile became a fleeting grin. "The neighbors just don't like Dreampeace."

"Wonderful," Jian said. On the screen, All-Hours was showing film from the rioting in West-of-Four: the overhead lights were shattered, leaving only pale and infrequent emergency flares. They were drowned by the glare of fires and the clouds of thick, oily-looking smoke. Dark figures moved sporadically against the flames, but the light was so bad it was impossible to tell if they were fire fighters, Security, or rioters. Vaughn shook his head, seeing that.

"Air supply's going to have a hell of a time venting that to the surface."

"Let's hope they can," Jian answered. Fire was bad enough in West-of-Four, only a few meters below the shell of the mountain, but if the burning reached the lower levels . . . She shivered in spite of herself. Most of the midworld was paranoid about fire, and with good reason; one had to assume that the underworld was just as cautious. Even Dreampeace wouldn't start fires that would suffocate the entire city. *Or would they? If Manfred gets enough data to "copy" Landage, why shouldn't he?* She shook her head, wishing she had killed it, wishing it had been destroyed on the *Byron*. *If I'd never made a copy— but there's no point in ifs.* "What would Dreampeace do if we made that transcript public?" she asked. "That would prove Manfred wasn't people."

"Would any of them believe it?" Vaughn retorted. "Or admit they believed it? It's too late for argument."

He was right, and Jian sighed, glanced back at the screen. The newsreader was mouthing again, but she couldn't be bothered to turn up the volume. *Manfred would've let me be killed.* That should have been impossible, of course, but there had long been rumors that constructors were leaving out—or writing hidden overrides for—the crucial human-protective subroutines. After all, the argument went, Three-Law programming eliminated a construct's free will, and thus prevented its development as an independently moral being. . . .

The hell with that, Jian thought, staring at another scene, another upperworld street that seemed to be paved with broken glass. *He—it—would've killed me. And I would've taken chances with my life, with Chaandi's life, for it. I'd like to see it erased—not even rewritten. I never want to work with a construct that even feels like it again. I want to see it destroyed.*

Red and Libra returned at last, but empty-handed. "The cookshops were already sold out," Libra said simply. "We went as far as Lower Charretse. There wasn't anything. People are scared."

Red nodded his agreement. "They closed the interlink."

"Charretse?" Jian said sharply, and the technician nodded again.

"There's more," Libra said. "The talk is, the fighting is coming our way."

Vaughn looked toward the technician again, and Red nodded. "Not good," Vaughn said.

That's an understatement. Jian said aloud, "What've you got in your cold box, Imre?"

"Beer." Vaughn glanced involuntarily toward the little aisle between the bed and the wall. "Maybe a frozen sandwich or two." He stressed the first word, looking at Red, and the technician shook his head.

"So we can't stay here," Jian said. She frowned. "What are the chances of getting to The Moorings? You can be damn sure Security isn't going to let our troubles disrupt trade unduly."

"Charretse's closed," Libra said again.

"Yes, but—" Jian broke off, looked sideways. "Input: command. display realtime, clocktime." The glyphs took shape against the wall: it was night outside the city, the last hours of the night, but time enough to reach The Moorings.

"I know what you're thinking," Vaughn said. "I don't think it'll work. They'll be watching the surface roads, Security will—and the FPG—and the way things are, they'll shoot first and ask questions in a week or two, when they get around to it."

Jian nodded, conceding the truth of the statement. "You got any ideas?"

Vaughn looked back at her, an odd, pained expression on his face, like that of a man contemplating dental surgery. "There's a woman I knew once," he began, and stopped. "You did say you had a second copy of Manfred?"

Jian grimaced, wishing irrationally she had burned it. "Yeh."

"I used to know Willet Lyardin," Vaughn began, and Libra looked up sharply.

"You?" He looked instantly embarrassed. "Sorry."

"Yeh, me." Vaughn seemed less angry than pained by the response.

"You might've mentioned this before," Jian said. "I might've turned the damn thing over to her if I'd known you knew her."

Vaughn shrugged. "I didn't know—I wasn't sure it would make a different."

"Christ, Imre." Jian turned away.

Libra said, as though he hadn't heard, "She's yanqui, of course." He looked sideways at Vaughn. "She'd be about your age now"

"She's a year younger," Vaughn said, and from the sound of his voice it had once been a sore point. "Yeh, she's yanqui. We were classmates for a while, grew up in the same neighborhood. I think she'd even remember me."

"So?" Jian asked.

"We have to get out of here," Vaughn said. "The upperworld's not safe, anyway, and I don't want to try to make The Moorings. I say we should go down, to the underworld, turn your copy of the thing over to Lyardin."

"What good would giving it to her do?" Jian asked. "She's still Kagami, Dreampeace wouldn't believe her just on principle."

"At the very least, you'd be rid of it," Vaughn answered. He shrugged. "Who knows, it might help her reconstruction."

"People do trust Lyardin," Libra said, as if the pilot hadn't spoken. "Even Dreampeace."

"Some of them, anyway," Jian said and sighed. It made

sense—*and, as Imre says, at least I'd be rid of it. Maybe Lyardin can find something really painful for the fucking thing.* "Do you think it's smart going deeper underground?" she asked, and knew it was a last protest.

"No dumber than staying here, sunshine," Vaughn answered.

"Haya," Jian said, and looked at Libra. "Are you coming with us, Robin?"

"I can't get back to Shang-Ti," Libra said, and smiled, the expression crooked. "I'm probably better off with you."

"Dzi-Gin's closing in an hour." Red said.

It took no time at all to collect what they needed. Jian pulled a loose knee-length coat out of her carryall, shrugged it on to hide the tommy-stick Vaughn handed her.

"I don't have anything for Libra," he said, and slipped the second tommy-stick into his own belt.

The constructor laughed. "That's all right, I'd rather not be arrested for aggravated nuisance."

"Sunshine," Vaughn said, "it's not being arrested you have to worry about. We'll be lucky if we run into the cops."

Jian lifted an eyebrow at that—she wasn't so sure that either Security or the FPG Police were going to be in a benevolent mood—but this was not the time to argue. "Let's go," she said, and unfastened the first of the locks.

Vaughn closed each of the locks behind them with special care, and when they reached the stairway he was careful to take the block of wood out of the hinges. The building's main door closed with a reassuringly solid sound, but Vaughn glanced back at it anyway, shaking his head, before they walked away.

The streets were mostly empty now as they walked west toward Shaft Beta, except for a few figures hurrying toward home. Once, along Comeaux Hale, they ran into a knot of men in the bright red vests of a neighborhood association. Jian eyed them warily, ready to reach for her tommy-stick, and saw them watching her with the same uneasy readiness. Neither group spoke, but Jian was glad when they were left behind.

The Comino Interlink was equally, unnaturally empty, the shops already closed, solid metal shutters drawn over the display windows. Only a single cookshop remained open; a line of shoppers, mostly lineworkers in heavy suncheaters, helmets slung on their shoulders, spilled out the door. They waited patiently, under the watchful monitor of a floater that carried FPG Police markings. As Jian watched, a woman emerged, carrying a string bag bulging with cans and bottles of water, hurried down a side street toward home. The line heaved forward.

The Shaft Beta Station was quiet, too, and there was extra Security on duty. Most of them, however, were standing by the one unbarred door, watching the FPG floater. Jian shook her head, seeing that, and ran her transit pass through the reader. *Not good, when the cops spend their time watching each other.*

Glyphs sparked in the air around her, and in the same instant, Vaughn said, "Damn. They're running a reduced schedule."

Jian nodded, studying the same information flashing in front of her eyes. "We won't make Dzi-Gin before it closes." She bit down a fleeting surge of panic at the thought of being trapped on the Zodiac, cut off from Vaughn's flat and unable to get into the midworld.

"We might," Vaughn said thoughtfully. "And if not— bach, you used to run the tunnels, back when you were a kid."

Red nodded reluctantly, with a fleeting glance toward Security still standing at the barriers. Vaughn smiled. "Then you can take us with you this time."

They caught the first downward car—there was no competition for seats or standing room, and barely more than a dozen people in the lift—and took a jolting, crowded electrobus from the Sanbonte Station to Dzi-Gin itself. It made slow progress, and stopped too soon; Jian, jammed in between Vaughn and a stocky woman with a child strapped in a carrier against her breasts, saw the stricken expression on Vaughn's face first, and shifted awkwardly, peering over her shoulder toward Dzi-Gin.

Glyphs flared bright red in the air around her, even as a voice announced from the driver's box, "End of the line, people, I can't get you any closer."

There was a murmur of protest, and Jian looked at Vaughn. The other pilot shrugged. "I think he's right, myself. Let's go."

They fought their way out of the 'bus, Jian and Red dragging Libra between them. Perhaps a third of the passengers went with them; the rest remained in the 'bus, and Jian heard a dull thud as someone gave the driver's box a vicious kick. "This is crazy," she said aloud, and dodged a tall man who darted past carrying a six- or seven-year-old child. The child was crying, but silently: *Too scared to make noise,* Jian thought. *God, get that kid off the streets soon.* More glyphs flared, a dozen Security markers springing up seemingly from every point of the compass, the bright yellow scrolling glyphs of a traffic advisory. She hardly needed the latter: Dzi-Gin was submerged in a sea of people, hundreds, maybe even thousands of them, all trying to fight through the barriers into the station waiting area. Cartel Security, riot shields in place, were trying to form the crowd into lines, but the people refused to move. They did not fight, but they would not leave their hard-won places.

"No way in hell," Jian said, and realized belatedly that she had spoken aloud. "There's no way we're going to get through that."

"If they try to close Dzi-Gin," Libra began, and stopped, appalled by the thought. Jian shook her head, trying to suppress the images his words had conjured—*these thousand bodies storming the armor-glass doors, trying to fight their way onto the last cars, people dying crushed against the glass, trampled by the crowd, or turning on Security at last, and dead of rubber bullets and the occasional unlucky blow from a tommy-stick.* Red was staring at the crowd as though he had never seen Dzi-Gin before, his face ivory pale in the ceiling lights, blue eyes wide and absolutely unveiled.

Vaughn said, "Red, *bach.*"

The redhead looked sharply at him, looked away, mask dropping back into place, but not before Jian realized that he, too, was afraid. "This way," Red said, and started back the way they had come.

He led them along the edge of the trafficway, moving against the stream of people still flowing toward Dzi-Gin, for perhaps four blocks, then turned down a side street. Here, too, the shops were shuttered, and grilles were drawn across the second-floor windows as well. Jian shook her head, seeing that, and quickened her steps. Red was counting doorways under his breath, stopped at twenty-one, and slipped into the garbage alley between twenty-one and twenty-two. Jian glanced over her shoulder—*no one, nothing in sight*—and followed. Glyphs flared around her: content ID glyphs from the stacked and locked bins, meant for the cleaner karakuri; a couple of orange glyphs marking security cameras; finally an access glyph linked with the wave-and-circle of Water Services. Red had already opened the lockbox, and was studying the rosette of numbered keys.

"Let me," Libra said, reaching into his pocket, and the technician slipped silently aside.

Libra studied the setup for a moment, head cocked to one side, then brought out the flat box of a universal tool/reader. He freed its sensor head, and laid it against the lock, then did something with the tiny membrane pad. Glyphs flickered in the air, moving too fast for Jian to see them clearly, and the door sagged open.

Red smiled, and stepped past him into the brightly lit tunnel. Jian followed, Libra and Vaughn at her back. Vaughn paused long enough to lock the door behind them, and said, "Which way?"

Red pointed silently to the left, and the others followed. This was a service tunnel, obviously enough, brightly lit, with pipes as thick as a man's waist running along the curve of the arched ceiling, and smaller pipes or wire casing crowding the walls to either side. Glyphs flashed now and again, private markers that Jian did not recognize; she tried to keep track of them, and then of the twists and turns of their course, but soon lost all sense of direction. When they came to a ladder, they went down: that was all she was certain of. The tunnels narrowed slightly, and the ceiling pipe became larger, so that she had to walk to the side of the tunnel or hunch her shoulders to avoid hitting her head. The air was damp around them—an unnatural, uncomfortable feeling—and once they had to walk through the film of water that seeped from a cracked pipe. Vaughn shook his head at that.

"I hope somebody's reported this."

"Call in the tip," Jian suggested. "Stop Water Waste." The glyphs representing those words were both the current slogan of Water Service and the mail code of their repair line. Vaughn gave her a jaundiced look, and said nothing more. Red stopped at last at a three-way junction. Corridors led off to the left and right, and the ceiling pipe—grown now until it was almost a meter in diameter—led into the wall. There was a crawl space below it, lit by pale-blue strip lights.

"Through there," Red said.

Jian eyed the narrow space uncertainly. "How much smaller does it get?" *I'm not sure I'll fit anyway, and if it gets any narrower—*

Red was shaking his head, already pulling himself up to the pipe. "It's the same. All the way."

"This is one of the crossovers, right?" Vaughn said, and the technician nodded. "The upperworld and the midworld water systems intersect here. We go through there, and we're in the midworld."

"You know an awful lot about Water Services," Jian said, and Vaughn looked faintly embarrassed.

"My mother worked for them, when I was a kid. I used to get a kick out of the old tunnel maps."

Libra laughed softly, and Vaughn flushed. "Let's go," Jian said hastily, and followed Red into the crawlway, dragging her carryall with her.

It was as low-ceilinged as she had feared, so narrow that she had to lie on her back and pull herself along the slippery tiles. Fortunately, the space had been designed for people at least as big as she, and there were grip bars set into the ceiling at easy intervals, but after only a few meters her shoulders were aching from the unfamiliar exercise. The carryall, trailing by its broad strap, threatened to wedge itself between her hips and the wall; she paused long enough to balance it on her stomach, and kept going. Finally, the pipe widened, and she was able to roll over, clutching the carryall, and crawl the last few meters. Red was waiting in the corridor, and caught her carryall before it could fall. Jian gave him a sour look—*how come this doesn't bother him? He doesn't even look like he's breathing hard*—and dropped down beside him. The others followed, Vaughn laughing a little breathlessly, Libra a good two minutes behind him.

"Where are we, anyway?" Jian asked.

Red looked up and then sideways, searching for a data node, said finally, "Fuller Township, near Li Po."

"Good enough," Vaughn said. "Then it's off to Argonauts and Hesychos Interlink."

It was easier said than done. Red led them out of the service tunnels into one of Fuller's back alleys, and Vaughn brought them up onto the Donli Trafficway that ran straight from Fuller to the Argonauts Township. The Donli was absolutely empty, nothing moving in any of its five lanes, and Jian hesitated, searching for a data node.

"Input; command," she said aloud. "Copy: Security warnings, Fuller Township, Hawkshole Township, Argonauts Township." That was a mistake: the air filled with glyphs, crowding each other in her field of vision, momentarily dimming her vision of the real world. She stumbled, and Libra steadied her. She nodded thanks to him, and read the glyphs aloud. "Curfew in Fuller, avoid blocks ten, fifteen and twenty-eight: demonstrations. Curfew in Hawkshole, warning, fire in blocks three and four—" For a moment, panic seized her, but her brother's flat was at the eastern end of the Township, in the higher-numbered blocks. "Curfew in Argonauts, avoid Shaft Alpha transit stations: demonstrations. Warning, transit system will be closed to all but essential traffic at the seventeenth hour."

Vaughn shook his head, shook away his own data display. "We're going to be out after the curfew comes down, there's no way around it."

"Taxi?" Libra asked, without much hope.

"Input: command," Jian said. "Contact: any taxi service, midworld, mail codes unknown." There was a perceptible pause—too long a pause—and then another glyph appeared: *contact refused*. "They're not answering."

"The curfew would cover them, too," Vaughn said. He looked up the street, eerily empty under the glaring lights. "I think we walk."

They had left Fuller and were well into Hawkshole before the first Security floater appeared. It came roaring out from a cross street and turned down Donli toward them, driving in the wrong lanes without seeming to care. Lights blared from its dome, alternately red and blue, and then a snap like lightning. Jian gasped as the phased pulse struck her suit, was carried by the wires deep into her bones. She heard Vaughn swear on an indrawn breath of pain, and then a voice boomed from the floater.

"Halt at once. You are in violation of curfew. Halt and do not move."

"I might've known this would happen." Libra muttered, and Vaughn glared at him.

"If you had a better idea, sunshine, you should've spoken up a long time ago."

"Shut up, Imre," Jian said. The floater was edging closer now, air canon trained on them, and on impulse she lifted her hand to wave them closer. "Thank God you've come," she called, hoping Security had their outside sensors tuned high. "We've got to get to Hesychos."

Libra was looking at her as though she was crazy, but Vaughn stifled a laugh: "I hope this works," he murmured, and Jian said, "Shut up."

"You are in violation of curfew," Security said again. "Prepare to identify yourselves."

"Fine," Jian called back. "We have papers, please come and look at them, but we have to get to Hesychos. Can you help us?"

The floater slid neatly to rest against the high curb, far enough away to keep any of them from attacking, and the nearside hatch popped open. A shape in full riot gear levered itself out, and leveled an air rifle at them. Jian lifted her hands slowly in cautious surrender, and the others did the same. A second figure pulled itself out of the hatch.

"Why're you in such a hurry to get to Hesychos?" It was a man under that set of armor, a slight man with a midworld accent. "Let's see some ID." Behind him, the first figure slid sideways to keep a clear shot.

"I am getting my ID," Jian said, and reached very slowly into her belt, came up with the disk. She held it out, saying, "My name's Reverdy Jian, I'm a free-lance pilot. I did some work for Mitexi Minor. I—we—need to get to Hesychos because we need to contact Willet Lyardin.''

There was a little silence, and Jian could hear, very faintly, the distinctive wail of the fire sirens. Security took the disk, ran it though his belt reader, dividing his attention between the glyphs displayed on the tiny screen and the people in front of him. He did not return the disk, but held out his hand to Vaughn, and said, ''Maybe so, but does Lyardin want to see you?''

''Call her and see,'' Vaughn said, and handed over his ID disk.

Jian said, ''I have a copy of the construct that's causing all the trouble.'' As soon as she had said it, she wondered if she should have reserved that trump card, but Security seemed unwillingly impressed.

''You're a little late with it, aren't you? Check it out,'' he said—to his partner? to a third person still in the floater? Jian could not be sure. He collected Red's and Libra's disks as well.

Jian held her breath, waiting. Donli was still quiet, so quiet that she could hear, over the soft purr of the floater, the buzz of a lightstrip on the verge of failure. The fire sirens had stopped; she could hear Libra's quick breathing, but did not dare take her eyes off Security, still examining the disks' readouts.

''Haya,'' the other man said, and they all stared. ''Baas says, are you sure of this Vaughn's ID?''

''Yeh,'' the first man answered, and there was another, shorter silence.

''Haya,'' the second man said again. ''We're to bring them in. Lyardin's sending a car to pick them up at the station.''

Jian could not repress a smile, and saw Vaughn's eyes flicker closed for an instant in sheer relief. ''Thanks,'' she said aloud, and the second man motioned them toward the floater. It was a tight fit, and the rough padding smelled of sour disinfectant, but they managed to work themselves in. The first man closed the hatch, sealing them in, and a moment later, the floater lifted awkwardly, engine whining at the weight.

* * *

The floater carried them along Donli for another kilometer or so, then turned off onto a cross street that ran along the edge of the Argonauts Township. The streets were still eerily empty, except for other Security floaters. They passed an FPG carrier, a bigger, six-wheeled carrier, and Jian was not reassured to see Security tense, the driver's hand hovering near the air cannon's safety lock.

An expensive-looking runabout was waiting outside the Security station in the Jason Interlink, its rounded sides splashed with crudely stenciled glyphs authorizing it to travel after the curfew. As Jian levered herself awkwardly out of the floater, the same glyph appeared in the air in front of her eyes: the runabout was equipped with a display unit, as well. The driver, thin and dark and worried-looking, was leaning against the nearside door, but straightened up as Jian climbed out of the floater.

"Are these the people?" he called, and one of the Security answered, "Yeh."

"This way, please," the driver said, and threw open the passenger door.

This was not the way Jian was used to traveling, and it went badly with the troubles in the upper world. She suppressed that instant anger—*no point to it, not when she maybe can help us*—and climbed carefully into the padded interior. This car smelled of soap, expensive soap and the faintest hint of machines. She edged across the beautifully upholstered, too-soft seat, and the others crowded in beside her. Vaughn's bony knee jabbed against her leg, and she was almost grateful for that minor annoyance. The driver, of course, sat in a separate compartment; they saw him only as a shadow in the screen that divided the two sections.

"It'll take us about thirty minutes to reach Estoile Aurore," the driver announced. "Assuming we don't meet any trouble."

"I'm sure trouble wouldn't dare happen," Jian muttered, and muted the words only because she—they—needed Lyardin. From the expression on Vaughn's face, he agreed.

The runabout slid smoothly into motion, so smoothly that Jian was not sure quite when and how they began moving, and picked up speed as the driver slid it expertly onto the main trafficway. The streets were still empty, most people obeying the curfew. Once Jian saw flashing lights, a grounded Security floater and a handcuffed woman, but they were past it before she could figure out what was going on. They reached the Hesychos Interlink without seeing anyone else, and the driver slowed to a crawl as they approached the vehicle interchange. Security was present in force here—*of course they are,* Jian thought, *protecting the people who have money, the ones that matter*—four floaters and a heavily armored panther. One of the Security men waved them to a stop, while several others trained their rifles on the runabout, and a third Security man came up to inspect the drivers' credentials. Jian heard none of the conversation, but after a minute or two, Security waved them on through. The driver engaged the engine again, and eased the runabout forward into the massive vehicle lift. The great clamshell doors closed gently behind them, and the lift began to sink.

Jian shook her head. She had been in the underworld before—most people had—but always in the upper levels of the Exchange, never in the residential districts below. It seemed unreal, after the rioting and the curfews of the upper and midworlds; she glanced sideways, and saw the same uncertainty in the others' faces. *And Lyardin probably wants that uncertainty to be there,* she thought suddenly. *What better way to get us off balance, to make sure she gets what she wants for the least amount of money or loss of face? Maybe you can't help being intimidated, but you'd better not show it.*

The lift came to a gentle stop, and the doors opened again. The runabout rolled forward into an improbable beauty. The street was half again as wide as an ordinary street in the midworld, almost as wide as one of the main trafficways; a low median ran down the center, dividing the double lanes, and there were live plants in pots at intervals, each one set within a protective trellis of lighted tubing. They were very green, obviously flourishing, and Jian shook her head again at the thought of the care they must require. The buildings—faced with subtle, pale tiles and pastel brick, the doors banded with brighter paint and tile, not the light tubes required in the upper levels—sat well back from the road, leaving a com-

'ortable platform for shoppers and idle pedestrians. There vas no one on the street, however; the shops seemed to be closed, nothing showing behind their darkened doors. *The only sign of trouble we've seen down here,* Jian thought, *or s it? For all I know, this section always closes on Eight-day afternoon.* That was unfair, and she knew it, sighed, and ooked away. The stores' display windows were still lit, and Jian caught an occasional discreet advertising flash as the unabout passed a transmitter. All the displays were in real-print, no glyphs, and the products were unfamiliar. Jian shook her head as they passed a park, real grass and a single flow-ering tree, the entire area ringed with fantastically carved stanchions supporting the battery of lights that focused on the plants. A narrow path meandered across the lawn, circled the tree, and emerged again at the other side. A woman in a uniform was walking there, two children, the youngest barely old enough to toddle, clinging to her hands. She looked up quickly at the sound of the car, flat midworld face wary, but the children ignored it, tugged her on toward the tree and the fall of petals carpeting the path.

The underworld districts were more discrete than the town-ships of the upper levels, were connected not by streets and interchanges but by tunnels running between the separate caverns. They turned at last onto the access road leading to one of those tunnels, passed out of the cool, cloudy-pale light of Hallalore to the brighter, harsher light of the tunnel itself. Jian closed her eyes, trying to remember the maps of the underworld. There was a long tunnel that ran between Hal-lalore and Paraselene, if she remembered correctly, and then a shorter tunnel to Estoile Aurore, where Lyardin lived. There was also a connecting tunnel between Ambrosiane and Es-toile Aurore, but she could not remember how Hallalore was tied to Ambrosiane.

The tunnel seemed to last forever—*the long road, then,* Jian thought, *by way of Paraselene*—but then the runabout turned out of the main road into a series of smaller tunnels and emerged finally into another pleasant, well-lit district. It was clearly residential; here the architecture was all focused on a central courtyard, each enormous compound turning a blank face to the trafficway. Thick pillars supported the roof, and the spaces between were filled with blank walls of un-patterned brick or poured stone. Here and there, someone had livened the outer wall with a brief geometric pattern, tile or light-and-dark brick, but those touches were very rare. Jian imagined some form of local police—the underworld version of the neighborhood patrols she knew from the mid-world—surveying the area, and knocking on those doors. *I'm sorry, bi', your walls are way out of line, you're going to have to take them down, put up something plainer. . . .* She smiled, but her amusement faded fast. The underworld seemed utterly untouched by the chaos above it: how long could that last, and what would happen when it ended?

The runabout turned sharply then, down a side street running between two of the walled compounds. There was no median here, and no plantings, though the streets and the walls remained expensively immaculate. The runabout slowed further, and they turned into an apparent cul-de-sac at the end of one compound wall. The wall slid sideways when the runabout's nose was within two meters, and they rolled forward into a pleasant rock-walled parking bay. The driver opened the passenger hatch, and they climbed out stiffly, Jian last of all.

They were in an inside garden, she saw without surprise, a garden mostly of rock and crystal sprouting from rock, but with a few plants in heavy pots set under carefully positioned extra lights. There was a mix of tile and soft heavy-duty carpet forming a wide path through the grounds, and a wash of white sand around the rocks. In the middle of the sand, disrupting the perfection, a child was playing alone, very seriously burying a series of bright plastic bricks in shallow holes. They looked like foundation structures: s/he was taking bricks from a toppled tower to try again. Jian blinked, surprised to see it without supervision, and then saw the man standing in the shadow of the arched loggia, watching the child, watching their arrival. *School-daddy,* she thought, but as they came closer, she saw that his clothes were too good for that menial job. *The child's father?* It was possible; they had the same rich red-brown coloring, but it was impossible to be sure. The man nodded to the driver as they came closer, said, in a voice as casteless as the cut of his expensive trousers, "She's in the workroom."

The driver nodded, and led them on into the house. Jian had expected darkness, or expensive, sunlike light. Instead, ordinary unfiltered light tubes lit a surprising amount of clutter. Everything was clearly expensive, the best of its kind, but equally clearly it had been bought because someone liked it, and everything was used. There were even one or two realprint books, facedown on a table against the wall. Jian could not resist checking as they swept past, and was startled to find no dust. *That doesn't mean anything; they can afford the kind of karakuri that can do that kind of cleaning*—but she couldn't shake the suspicion that someone had been reading those texts.

Lyardin's workroom was on the second floor, at the top of a short flight of stairs. It was a comfortable, well-lit room, one wall filled with a double-sized connection board and an even more elaborate display station; the curtains were open on the opposite wall, so that Lyardin could look down into the sand garden. Lyardin herself was sitting on the edge of the smaller workstation, playing idly with a palm-sized remote control unit, but looked up as the door opened.

"Hello, Imre," she said, and Vaughn nodded.

"Hello, Willet. I won't ask how things are."

Lyardin grinned. "You never change." Her voice was still yanqui, to match the strong, homely features. She had not bothered with the more exotic underworld fashions—they would not flatter her stocky, broad-hipped figure—but had kept to yanqui-cut trousers and a plain shirt with the sleeves rolled up to show her jewelry. Only those bands of gold and carved stone, bright against her brown skin, flaunted wealth. Jian found herself eyeing the other woman with more respect and less certainty.

Lyardin was looking at her now. "Bi' Jian?"

"Yes."

"I'm pleased to meet you," Lyardin held out her hand, yanqui fashion, and Jian took it, matching the pressure of the other woman's fingers. Lyardin looked past her at the others, and Jian answered the unspoken question.

"The bearded man is Robin Libra, a constructor and a good friend. The—"

Vaughn interrupted her. "This is Red."

Lyardin did not blink. "I heard you'd settled down."

Jian saw Vaughn flush slightly. Red look sideways, eyes downcast, but Jian thought she glimpsed momentary laughter in his veiled expression.

"Pleased to meet you, Ba' Libra," Lyardin went on. She looked back at Jian, no longer bothering to hide her eagerness. "I understand you have a copy of this Manfred construct."

"Yeh." Jian swung her carryall forward on her hip, rummaged under the dirty clothes, and held out the storage blocks she had brought with her from the *Byron*. Lyardin frowned, seeing the thinner manga disk.

"You stored part of it on that?"

"I had to," Jian answered. "I didn't have anything else."

Lyardin turned the blocks slowly in her hands, as though she could see through the matte black coatings. "This probably won't be functional," she said, then shrugged. "But I should be able to read the architecture. We've got a lot of structure pieced together already. Ba' Libra, would you be willing to join us dissecting this?"

Libra flushed with pleasure, and came forward to join her at the workstation, setting the bag of his tools on the floor. Lyardin handed him two of the tapes, and they began fitting them into the machine's multiple readers. Lyardin looked up only once, to smile abstractedly, and touched her remote.

"We're off-line now—it's not safe on the connections with that thing loose. The rest of the group's on its way. Imre, Bi' Jian, please, make yourselves comfortable—and you, Ba' Red, I'm sorry—and tell me everything you can about this construct."

Jian and Vaughn exchanged glances, and seated themselves on two of the unmatched boxchairs scattered around the room. Red sank bonelessly to the floor at Vaughn's feet. "Well," Jian said, marshaling her thoughts, and she and Vaughn began, strophe and antistrophe, to tell what had happened. Jian began with the contract, and the shadow-brought specs she had tried to find; Vaughn went on with how the construct had been brought on-line, and how Manfred had functioned. Jian agreed, amplified, waxed rhapsodic, and stopped abruptly, remembering that he—*it*—had been willing to kill her. Vaughn explained about Refuge, and Avelin, and Mitexi Major— Lyardin laughed then, and said again he hadn't changed—and Jian recounted the changes in Mitexi Major. They told about the destruction of the first copy, and reinstallation, and then how Manfred had pirated itself and come to Jian. Lyardin looked up sharply at that.

"It came to you? To Libra, rather?" She shook her head. "Never mind, go on."

Jian finished the story quickly, with only a few interruptions from Vaughn. The construct had contacted Avelin, told Avelin it was time for it to join Dreampeace, and that it was all right to kill Jian in the process.

Lyardin shook her head. "Venya was messing with the Three-Laws routines, all right. Got to be done someday, but not in the working versions right off." She sighed, and looked at Libra. "We've made some progress, anyway. We've got a pretty good idea of what it was built to do, and how it's supposed to do it." She smiled rather ruefully. "Damn, Venya was good when he wanted to be. It's a pretty good idea."

"Pity it doesn't work," Jian said.

"Well, it does work," Lyardin said. "It does do what it was supposed to do. It just isn't true AI."

"You know, Willet," Vaughn said, "one of these days you're going to give someone an explanation he can understand, and the poor bastard's going to die of the shock."

"Sorry." Lyardin did not sound particularly repentant.

"Why haven't you announced this?" Jian asked.

Lyardin sobered instantly. "We couldn't. Without a good copy of the construct, the radicals could just claim we hadn't reconstructed it right and bring in the moderates who wouldn't buy that we were all lying. I don't want to split Dreampeace. I want to prove they're wrong—this time."

"Hah," Vaughn muttered.

Lyardin ignored him. "The whole Manfred construct is a fake," she said. "Venya built it to prove that AI was possible, and he built it to simulate AI if it didn't achieve it. I've seen some variants on the idea, and his is damn good, the best of its kind. The trouble is, it's crazy.''

''I think we knew that,'' Jian said, and Vaughn laughed.

''Yeh, the thought crossed my mind.''

''What we don't know—and have to know, if we're going to beat it—is exactly what he wanted it to do. It looks like it was meant to take over as Dreampeace's leader—and what a coup that would've been, a construct leading the fight for its own liberation—but how it was supposed to run this revolution . . .'' Her voice trailed off, and she shrugged. ''That's not clear, and that's what I want to know. That's what we need to know, if we're going to stop it.'' She looked down at her controls, looked up again at Libra. ''We should get going. Everything's in place here.''

Libra glanced quickly down at his readout. ''And here.''

''Then let's see if this thing will load.'' Lyardin manipulated her remote, studying the display on the screen Jian could not see, and shook her head again. ''No, it doesn't look like it will. I'm not surprised. These manga blocks are linear, not a dimensional matrix.''

''I was afraid of that,'' Jian said, and was surprised by her own feeling of relief. *What would I have done, seeing him again, hearing him, after the last thing I saw of him was Avelin carrying him out the door?*

''That means we get to dissect this one,'' Lyardin said, and grinned. ''This could take all night.''

12

It did take all night, as Lyardin had predicted, and well into the next morning. Some time after the nineteenth hour, the driver reappeared, bringing the other constructors with him, and escorted the nonconstructors to the guest wing. Dinner was waiting, plain and expensive and very good, but Jian ate nothing. Instead, she watched the newsnets on the room's meter-wide connection board, dozing now and then, woke at last to find that it was day and the light from the garden was pouring in through the curtains she had forgotten to close. Vaughn and Red were asleep together in the left-hand bedroom, just visible through the half-open door. Jian pulled it closed so she would not wake them, and showered herself awake.

By the time she was through, and dressed, breakfast had arrived, the table set for three waiting for instructions. Jian studied the menu displayed on the table top—coffee and sausage rolls and cereals, heavy yanqui food—and touched the buttons to release the latches on the correct compartments. The connection board was still lit, All-Hours News still recording the disaster, and Jian settled herself to watch, coffee in hand. She took a sausage roll as well, but did not eat it.

This morning of all mornings, here in the underworld, she was hardly hungry; she would have preferred tea and rice, if anything, but those did not seem to be options in this household.

The fires West-of-Four were under control, two of them actually declared out. Thirty people were dead, most of them in the crush that followed the announcement that Dzi-Gin was closing. There was film, of course, but Jian hastily changed the channel. *That could've been me—could've been all of us.* There were an unknown number of injured. The PPG newsnet was reporting several dead in the West-of-Four fighting—a ten-year-old boy caught by the fires, two people hit by rubber bullets—but most of their attention was directed to the Dreampeace seizure of the warehouse in Gamela Township. The movement now controlled several blocks to either side of the warehouse, and Security seemed content to let them keep it, at least until the other rioting was brought under control. Jian shook her head at the images, and the bedroom door opened behind her.

"Such a cheery sight first thing in the morning," Vaughn said. "Did you get any sleep?"

"Yeh, some," Jian answered. "They brought us breakfast."

"I would expect no less," Vaughn said, and crossed to the table. Red came to join him, running his fingers through his matted hair, poured coffee for both of them.

"Anything earth-shattering happen after we went to sleep?" Vaughn went on.

Jian shook her head. "A couple more people killed, that's all." Down here, in the underworld, it didn't seem real at all, more like one of Chaandi's manga than anything else.

Vaughn nodded, reading her thoughts. Jian took another swallow of coffee, barely tasting its bitterness. She looked at the sausage roll again, but could not quite bring herself to eat. Red methodically filled his plate—two of everything—and came back to sit on one arm of the long couch, not quite watching the connection board.

There was a knock at the door, and Jian looked up, glad of the interruption. "Yeh, who's there?"

Instead of an answer, the door opened, and Lyardin looked

in, grinning, eyes red with strain. "They're still arguing," she said, "but I've told them what we're going to have to do."

"Haya," Vaughn said, with deliberate uncertainty.

Lyardin poured herself a cup of coffee from the table's dispenser—it had come with at least one extra cup, Jian noticed—and settled herself on the arm of a chair, leaning her head against the wall. "You were right about it being willing to kill you, Bi' Jian," she said, "or at least that it was willing to see you killed. And you were right about why: it seems to consider the symbol and the referent to be functionally identical, and therefore doesn't value one version over the other. There is a slight bias in favor of keeping the original person around, but that's only because the full datasets take up a lot of storage." She stopped, as though she'd lost her train of thought.

Vaughn said, "I suppose you should be flattered, Reverdy."

"I always take up a lot of space." Jian looked back at Lyardin. "So can you convince Dreampeace that Manfred's a fake?"

Lyardin shrugged. "Maybe. Probably, but that's not really the issue. It's bound to be in the connections now."

Jian frowned, then understood. Any construct—and a number of smaller, less powerful but equally annoying programs—could circulate on the connections for weeks, sometimes even months without the systems managers being able to stop them. She could remember two years ago, when a CPA worm had infected one of the business nets, and it had taken six months to get the last versions of it out of people's systems. Manfred wasn't quite the same—size alone made it harder to hide, but it was also smart enough actively to look for ways to conceal itself. "Haya, it'll take time, sure, but if Dreampeace helps track it, track any copies—"

Lyardin was shaking her head. "That's not fast enough," she said. "Look, Venya built this thing to prove that Spelvin constructs can be built with AI—that constructs can be human. He built it to convince Dreampeace and lead then to fight for machine rights. Which it's doing with some success. Unfortunately, it isn't intelligent, and there aren't any intelligent machines yet, which means that if it wins, everything is going to be screwed up very badly for a whole lot of people. And on top of that, Venya used his own self-image, unmodified, as template for the personality tables.''

"And Venya Mitexi was crazy," Jian said.

"You got it," Lyardin answered. "The tables are already well out of limits. He knew, he was good enough, he knew and he knew why you're supposed to use a minimum of seven images, superimpose and average them, never, not ever, just one. Venya was always biased toward a revolutionary solution, and so, of course, is Manfred.''

"What do you mean by a revolutionary solution?" Jian asked.

"Venya wanted to see machine intelligence get full rights now," Lyardin answered. "Manfred intends for Dreampeace to make a deal with the FPG: they'll support Freya's claims here, in exchange for the FPG's recognizing AI constructs as people. If the Cartel goes under, well, that's a minor issue.''

"The FPG's a bunch of thugs," Vaughn said. "Even if they weren't, they can't run the staryards. They've proved that.''

"I know," Lyardin said.

"So that's why he—it—Manfred, I mean—got them to occupy the warehouse," Jian said slowly. "He knew that would set off the coolies, start riots up in Heaven, and that would pull all the people in Dreampeace who were wavering right back into the fold.''

"That's what it looks like," Lyardin said. "And so far, it's working.''

"Wonderful," Jian muttered. "So it has to be stopped."

Lyardin nodded.

"That's all very well and good," Vaughn said, "but how do you propose to do it? You can probably drive Manfred and Dreampeace out of the connections—I'm sure the Cartel's had plans for doing that for years—but they'll just download him into storage blocks and try again."

Lyardin smiled, quite slowly, the smile of a woman who'd finally gotten to play a trump card. "That's quite true. And it's also true that the construct must be destroyed. My thought was that you, Imre—and the rest of you—would be able to handle that part of the job.''

"I don't think so," Vaughn said with indignation. "Do I look like Dreampeace?"

"You're yanqui," Lyardin answered. "Bi' Jian looks yanqui. That's almost good enough right there."

Jian frowned, considering the idea. Someone would have to destroy the construct physically, that much was obvious: *but why me?* She was hungry at last, facing action, a decision she would have to follow to the bitter end. She took a bite of her sausage roll, forgotten until now, and said indistinctly, "Why not let Cartel Security handle it?"

"Security looks like Security," Lyardin answered.

Jian shook her head, swallowed. "You must have plain-clothes. And Kagami must have people of its own."

Lyardin hesitated, then made a face. "Of course we do. But I don't know who I could still trust."

That was true, too, Jian thought. *Dreampeace and the coolie question had polarized the city in unexpected ways. How could you know how even your best people would react, asked to act against—or even for—something they believed in? How could they know themselves, until it happened?*

"Whereas we," Vaughn said, "and Reverdy in particular, are reliable because Manfred tried to kill her."

"That's the idea," Lyardin agreed.

"Can you drive it out of the connections?" Jian asked.

"Oh, yes." Lyardin gave a crooked smile. "Like Imre said, we do know how. I've told them how." She paused then, looking at Vaughn, and relented. "It's not that hard to write, it's just a virtual machine, self-replicating, voracious, you just set it loose on the connections and it copies itself until there's no room for anything else. And if you build it right, it'll take apart anything that gets in its way. I'll ask the Cartel companies to disable their security programs, but it won't make any difference if they don't. What I—what we've written will take out anything they've got."

"It'd have to," Vaughn said, "if it's going to take on Manfred."

"Then I'm willing to try to do the rest of it," Jian said, and took another bite of the sausage roll. *It should be possi-*

ble. I can pass as Dreampeace to anyone who doesn't know me, can claim I've seen the light to anyone who does. Even Manfred I could maybe convince. It's just Avelin I'd worry about.

"You just want to get back at it," Vaughn said.

"Yeh, I do. So?" Jian glared at him. "It has to be done, and if I get a certain satisfaction out of it, what's the harm?"

Vaughn shrugged. "Suit yourself. We'll come along, if you'll have us."

"Yeh," Red said.

"Right, then," Jian said, and finished the roll. "When do we start?"

It wasn't as easy as that, of course. It took over an hour for Lyardin to convince Kagami to back her plan, and two more hours to arrange for her to have complete access to the connections. It took another hour and a half to obtain the passes from Cartel Security that would allow them to return to the upperworld. Finally, though, the driver returned them to the Hesychos Interlink, and Security waved them reluctantly onto an upbound car. They transferred to Beta Shaft at Dzi-Gin, and rode it the last two levels into Mwangi Station at the edge of the Komaki Township. Security was tight there, too, but they seemed less concerned with the few people riding the lift system than with the FPG Police floaters that moved slowly past along the trafficway. Only one of the armored figures was checking passes; the line was fifteen deep, and moved slowly, but at last Jian and the rest had proved their right to travel to Security's satisfaction, and were allowed out into the station plaza.

A few of the shops were open after all, Jian saw with some surprise—mostly cookshops, of course, but one or two less vital businesses defied the fear. There were few shoppers, however, and most of them—coolies and lineworkers, judging by their clothes, the people who couldn't afford to buy more than one or two days' food at a time—bought what they'd come for as quickly as they could and hurried away. The electrobus line was operating, but the direct spur that ran through the Yanqui Downs to Gamela was closed; they took a car to the western edge of Pan-Ku, and walked.

Once they reached the fringes of Pan-Ku, the streets became more crowded, groups in decent midworld clothing gathered on steps and street corners in defiance of Security. One or two even wore Dreampeace's man/computer glyph stenciled on stiff-backed jackets. No one challenged them, but at the first flash of a Security glyph they ducked into a doorway, out of sight in the shadows. Jian quickened her steps to pass them before the Security floater came abreast of the doorway, not wanting to be caught in any crossfire, and breathed a sigh of relief when the machine swung by without stopping. The Dreampeace members emerged from the shadows, and Jian could hear their laughter.

"Lovely people," Vaughn muttered, but said nothing more.

There were barricades at the border of Gamela, bright orange barrels filled with sand blocking the intersections, Security in armor with leveled electrolasers questioning anyone who approached the barrier. Jian slowed, frowning—*even if Security accepts our pass, it won't do us any good with Dreampeace to be seen going through there.* "Left, I think," she said. "There should be a crossing."

Vaughn looked at Red. "Bach?"

Red nodded. "This way."

He took them down the first side street that led south, then through a series of delivery tracks, and finally through a frighteningly narrow passage between two windowless formestone buildings. It was utterly unlighted, and Jian had to turn sideways, scraping her back against the rough stone, to fit through. It took a right-angle turn perhaps ten meters in, and she caught her breath in utter panic before she realized that she was not trapped, and light showed again ten meters to her left.

They came out into a brick-floored lunch court, closed now, the tables stacked and chained to the wall. Vaughn smiled. "Just goes to show that barricades never work. This way, I think."

"You better be right," Jian said irritably. Her back hurt, and she was sure she had torn the fabric of her jacket: *not the way I'd choose to present myself to Dreampeace.*

The streets in this part of Gamela were all but empty, the shutters and barred grilles drawn across doors and windows.

Glyphs flared red from almost every data node: *warning, hard security in effect, enter at your own risk.* Even before they reached the blocks ringing the warehouse, Jian could hear the noise of the crowd, not hostile, not even really aggressive, but present, a hollow noise like a bass-voiced wind. It rose and fell in a steady rhythm, strengthening as they drew closer, until at last they turned a final corner, and faced Dreampeace's improvised barriers.

They had stolen a couple of the regular orange Security barrels someplace, Jian saw, but the rest of it was heavy furniture—an uprooted workstation, a couple of secretarial pedestals, uncountable tables and chairs. There were plenty of people on both sides of the barriers, perhaps half a dozen wearing Dreampeace's vest, most of the others wearing its glyph in one form or another. Jian slowed her steps slightly, wanting to gain time, and scanned the crowd, looking for someone she might recognize. *After all, I know enough people involved in the movement; maybe one of them will be around.* . . .

Red lifted his arm in greeting, and a moment later Jian saw John Desembaa's dark face in the crowd. At the same time, one of the guards at the barrier said, "Hold it, please."

He was wearing one of the marked vests and carried a police-issue pellet gun. Jian stopped obediently, said, "Haya."

"We want to talk to Manfred," Vaughn said.

The guard with the pellet gun laughed shortly. Another guard, a short, flat-faced woman, said, "Sorry. So does everybody."

"We worked with him on the *Young Lord Byron*," Jian said. "He knows us, and we know him, we're on his side."

"We have some information that might help," Vaughn said.

The two guards exchanged glances, and a third, another woman, taller and rail-thin, said, "I remember him." She nodded to Red, and gave him a quick appreciative grin. The technician dropped his eyes.

"Can we talk to Manfred?" Jian said again. "It's important."

The guards exchanged a final glance, and the stocky woman shrugged. "Can I see some ID, please?"

It was at least a polite revolution. Jian reached into her belt pocket, and John Desembaa said, "I know them."

The guards relaxed visibly at his voice, and the taller woman said, "You'll ID them, John?"

"I'll vouch for them." Desembaa gave Jian an approving look, and the pilot felt suddenly guilty. *He believes me—and he believes in Manfred, and in Dreampeace. We can't stop now.*

"Then you take them on up to the warehouse," the stocky woman said. The man pulled aside part of the barrier, and beckoned them through.

"Reverdy," Desembaa said. He did not—quite—look at Red, but the warmth of his smile embraced him particularly. "I'm glad you're all here, glad you've decided to join us."

"I didn't expect you'd take to the streets," Vaughn said.

Desembaa looked back at him, the smile fading slightly. "No, I didn't approve of starting this—I still don't think we should've—but now that it's begun—" He shrugged. "Sometimes you have to fight. I didn't think you'd ever agree with Dreampeace, Imre."

"Yeh, well, I worked with it," Vaughn said.

Desembaa nodded. "He is impressive, isn't he?"

"You've worked with him?" Jian asked.

"Yeh. Well, not worked with, but spoken with. He's tied in to the local data carriers, keeps an eye on things through the nodes." Desembaa made a face. "We're having some problems with the link, somebody trying to interdict the connections—but we'll manage."

That would be Lyardin and the others. Jian nodded, hiding the chill she felt, and was careful not to look around for a data node. *And Manfred knows we're here, knows we're coming: not a good combination. But at least he hasn't tried to stop us. Maybe he believes we are trying to help. After all, why should he expect me to be upset, angry? He doesn't think he's done anything wrong.*

They had reached the warehouse's main door, an arch closed by a heavy sheet of metal. It had an odd, almost wavering surface design, and Jian recognized it as the metal grown and forged for starships' hulls. This was probably part of a reject load, but it would still be strong enough to stand up against anything short of a heavy-duty drilling laser—*and this is probably part of the reason that Security isn't trying to drive Dreampeace out of here just yet.* There were guards outside the single portal cut in the main door, and one of them lifted her hand.

"Hold it, John, what do you want?"

"Some people to see Manfred," Desembaa answered. "He knows them, and they have some information."

"I'll pass the names up," the woman answered, but she did not sound as though she thought it would do any good.

"They're the crew of the *Byron*," Desembaa explained. "Reverdy Jian, Imre Vaughn, Guerin Nye."

For a moment, the final name startled Jian, and then she remembered: *that* was Red's real name.

The woman spoke into a filament mike, turning away to mute the sound, and nodded. "He says you can go on up," she said, and sounded genuinely surprised. "You can stay here, John."

Desembaa looked disappointed, but nodded. The other guard hauled back the little door, and Jian stepped over the high combing into the dim lobby. Vaughn and Red followed, and Vaughn murmured, "So far, so good."

Yet another guard—this one in ill-fitting armor clearly salvaged from a Security man—was waiting at the bottom of a narrow flight of stairs. He beckoned them on, and Jian climbed past him. There were more guards on the first landing, but the single door leading off it had been sealed by fusing a sheet of common steel over it. They climbed higher, past another sealed landing and a pair of guards crouched behind a mounted electrolaser, came out finally onto a landing where the door was closed, but not sealed. The first of the three guards said into his microphone, "It's them. Jian, Vaughn, Nye."

There was a moment's hesitation, and Manfred answered. "Please let them in."

The door opened—from the inside, Jian saw—and she made herself walk forward without hesitation. The inner room was small, windowless, but brightly lit, its walls crowded with connection boards and improvised workstations whose functions Jian could not begin to guess. Manfred—storage blocks and motor unit—sat on top of a secretary-style pedestal, and iridescent wires and flat cables flowed from it to the machines around him.

"I'm glad to see you," Manfred said, and Avelin said, from the door, "Stop where you are and raise your hands."

His voice was deadly serious. Jian did as she was told, and a moment later felt Avelin's hand running expertly over her body. She tensed, knowing that a skilled fighter could have taken him then, but she was a pilot, not Security. He was gone then, and she knew he was searching the others. Vaughn swore under his breath, and then Avelin came around them to stand beside the pedestal containing Manfred, omnilaser held very competently to cover them all.

"Now," he said, "we can settle this. We know what you're trying to do, and I want it stopped."

Jian blinked. "I don't understand," she began. She knew it was a feeble effort, and was not surprised when Avelin shook his head.

"Don't waste your time—don't waste my time. You're working for the people who are trying to drive him out of the connections, and therefore you can stop it."

"So it's working," Jian said.

Avelin's mouth twisted, twisting the scars. "That's right." Jian started to say something, but he held up his free hand, cutting off her words. "One of you will contact Lyardin and stop this attack, or I'll kill you. As slowly and as painfully as I can manage."

There was a flat certainty in his voice that was more frightening than details. Jian hesitated, looking for a question, some way to buy time. Vaughn stood very still beside her, his face gone pale under the sandy hair; he glanced sideways, once, and did not meet her eyes. Red said, "Juel."

Avelin looked at him, a faint frown creasing his brows.

Red said, "All right. I'll call."

The frown faded, and Avelin slowly smiled. "There's my good little man."

Jian caught her breath, remembering Refuge, remembering
the fear she had seen then in the technician's eyes. "Red—"

The technician ignored her, eyes fixed on Avelin, the perfect face still and ready to be commanded. The bounty
hunter's smile widened. "Over there, the blue console."

Red nodded, and stepped forward. He had to pass quite
close to Avelin to reach the console, and as he did, he turned
and lunged for the laser. He got his hands on the barrel,
deflecting the first shot, and then Vaughn leaped after him,
going for Avelin's throat. The three crashed backwards into
the nearest console. The laser fired a second time, and then
it was wrenched out of Avelin's hands. Jian caught it up,
shouting, "Give me a clear shot."

Vaughn rolled away from Avelin's sprawled shape, and Jian
fired. She thought Avelin might have been dead before she
hit him, but she fired again to be sure. The door swung open
behind her, and she whirled, fear giving her reflexes she had
never known, fired twice more almost blind.

"Get the door, Imre!"

The guards fell back, though whether she had hit them or
not Jian was never sure. Vaughn slammed the door in their
faces, groped among the machine debris scattered on the
floor, and came up with a length of thin conduit.

"That'll never hold," Jian said. "It's too thin—" And
then she saw what he was doing, and came to join him, ad-
justing the controls of the omnilaser to one of the tool set-
tings. She fired twice more while he held the pipe in place,
fusing the pipe to the hinges, making it impossible to open
the door.

"How're we going to get out?" she asked a moment later.

Vaughn ignored her, on his knees at the other end of the
room. Red was crumpled against Manfred's pedestal, eyes
wide open and glazed with pain, both hands locked above
the ruin of his right knee. Jian winced at the sight and the
smell of the burned flesh, the shard of bone projecting beneath his hands. The rest of his leg was still attached, but
only barely, hanging by the flesh, the bones disjointed—

"Get that fucking machine," Vaughn said. "Kill it."

Jian ignored him, moved instead to the blue console. It
was a standard Persephonet hookup, she saw with some re-

lief, and touched keys, hoping that Lyardin had done her work and Manfred was driven out of the system.

"Reverdy," Manfred said, still soft and fairly reasonable. "If I admit I've lost, there's no need to destroy me."

"The hell," Vaughn said.

"Lyardin?" Jian said. There was no answer, and she risked looking into the nearest data node. Static streamed through her, filling her vision and skidding along the wires of her suit: Lyardin's programs were filling the connections, chaotic and deadly to anything more complicated than a single-tier program. Anything of Manfred's complexity that ventured onto the connections would be ripped apart in seconds, its internal logic overwritten by Lyardin's virtual machine. Jian had seen enough; she stooped to grab a handful of the wires flowing from Manfred's pedestal, and yanked them free. Vaughn did the same, and a few moments later the construct was isolated, trapped inside its storage blocks. *Or I hope it is. What if there's part of it still out on the connections?* Jian took a deep breath, tried Persephonet again. "Lyardin?" *We need help, medical help, and I think I welded shut the only way out—* She could hear the sound of someone pounding on the door, and then the hiss of a working laser. "Damn it, answer!" Geometric static coursed across the screen. *I have to assume it worked,* she thought, and adjusted the omnilaser to its highest setting.

"Kill the thing," Vaughn said again, indistinctly, his face against Red's hair.

"Reverdy," Manfred said again. "I do regret what I've had to do, but there was no other choice—"

"I don't care," Jian said. Manfred was isolated, trapped in the storage blocks, unable to flee through the now-disconnected wires even if Lyardin's programs had not filled the connections. She lifted the laser and turned to face the motor unit. It was a mistake; she knew that in the same fraction of a second that her eyes met the unit's data node. The construct locked onto the eye-mounted processors, poured its datasets through them into her suit, overriding all conscious control. She could hear herself scream, could feel herself burning, the wires red-hot beneath her skin: there was no room in the suit for something as complex as Manfred, there was no memory storage at all, and the wires were burning under the overload. And still the data flooded through her, and she struggled to press the laser's firing stud, fighting the suit's sudden immobility to move her finger that single centimeter that would save her. Then she'd done it, and the storage blocks erupted into a fountain of sparks as the laser's beam hit the battery packs. She was drowning in hot lava, submerged in the molten steel of the construct; it was disintegrating within her as the suit broke down, and she was dying with it. She could feel her heart skip, missing beats, her lungs shutting down; her mouth gaped wide and still she could not breathe. *But Manfred's dying, you're dying too, and I'll have killed you: good enough, I'll accept it if I have to.* Against her will, her head slewed sideways, the eye-mounted processors fixing on another node. She fought to turn away, and the construct ripped free of her, great chunks of data blinding her, the surge of current finally blasting out the delicate circuits even as it passed through them. Manfred poured out of her, into the connections again, and she could feel it drowning now, too, ripped apart in the vicious currents of nondata that Lyardin had flooding the systems. She laughed, though she could not see, could not feel anything except Manfred's death, and then it was gone and she fell into the nothingness it had left her.

She woke to darkness and a floating, distant pain, drugged to endurability, but present deep in her bones. There were doctors, explaining things; she heard little more than someone telling her that the suit could be repaired, and would take over the physical functions she had lost. She was blind in truth, would need new eyes, and would get them once the damage had healed enough to allow the implants. The burned muscles would be replaced, and the new suit would have extra wires to supplement any motor control she had lost. She accepted this, still floating, as she accepted the distant pain and the vague indignities of being handled without her will. Lyardin came once to thank her, promised Kagami support, and assured her that Kagami would pay for the new implants. Jian knew she should be grateful, knew the cost of the implants and that she could never have afforded them in her lifetime, but could barely muster the interest to thank her properly. She owed Kagami for this, no matter what Lyardin said—Lyardin always said the right things—and was bound to the underworld as surely as they were tied to her.

Vaughn came, more than once; she was grateful for the touch of his hand against her cheek—no romance there; it was the one part where she was sure that what she was feeling came through her own nerves and not damaged wires or some temporary substitute. Dreampeace was broken: they had felt Manfred's destruction, and that had stunned them into a ceasefire. The tapes—Libra's and the League's reconstructions—had split the movement, but most of the groups accepted that Manfred had never been a person. Only a few pockets of resistance remained, hiding in the back alleys of the yanqui districts. The coolies had been beaten back too, not by the FPG Police, and things were much as they had been. There was talk of bringing a coolies'-rights bill before the Cartel's Governing Board, but that was all. Red was walking, crooked, on his new knee, would do better over time; after a few weeks, he came with Vaughn, and she shivered slightly at his cold fingers against her cheek. Chaandi did not come, and Jian did not know if it was because she chose not to, or if she was not admitted, but could not rouse herself enough to ask.

When the new eyes came, she found herself in a pleasant private room—expensive, certainly, but Kagami had said it would pay; Lyardin had said it, and it was so—with a narrow window overlooking a sand garden. The muscles along her arms and legs and back were stronger now, and she could sit up for a while, and even walk a little. She did all that she was asked to do—*look left, look right, read this, tell me the colors*—but when she was left alone, she lay still for a long moment, trying to gather the strength for what she wanted to do now. At last she found the bed controls, adjusted them so she could see her imperfect reflection in the connection board's multiple screens. The several images looked back at her, imperfect, but good enough to see that what the doctors had promised was true. She looked as she had before: all the damage had been internal, except for her eyes, and the expensive replacements and the careful surgery had restored them so that she could not tell what, if anything, had changed. All internal, the suit burning out from the overload, frying her from within: a miracle her heart hadn't stopped altogether, the doctors had said, but then, it had been very quick. *Quick in realtime*, Jian thought, *but minutes in virtual space. Pity the burning wasn't virtual, too.* She stared a moment longer, wary, uncertain if she really recognized herself. Manfred had marked her, nearly destroyed her; to survive, she would—she had—become as much machine as he.

"No," she said aloud, and winced, wondering if her voice would bring on the hovering—human—nurses. There was no answer, and she relaxed, slowly, looked at her reflections a final time. *No visible change, and I won't allow there to be change; the suits are a tool, the eyes are a tool, and I, I am the user of the tools. Nothing more, and nothing less.* The machine eyes looked back at her, indistinguishable from her own.

THE BEST IN
SCIENCE FICTION

☐	51083-6	ACHILLES' CHOICE *Larry Niven & Steven Barnes*	$4.99 Canada $5.99
☐	50270-1	THE BOAT OF A MILLION YEARS *Poul Anderson*	$4.95 Canada $5.95
☐	51528-5	A FIRE UPON THE DEEP *Vernor Vinge*	$5.99 Canada $6.99
☐	52225-7	A KNIGHT OF GHOSTS AND SHADOWS *Poul Anderson*	$4.99 Canada $5.99
☐	53259-7	THE MEMORY OF EARTH *Orson Scott Card*	$5.99 Canada $6.99
☐	51001-1	N-SPACE *Larry Niven*	$5.99 Canada $6.99
☐	52024-6	THE PHOENIX IN FLIGHT *Sherwood Smith & Dave Trowbridge*	$4.99 Canada $5.99
☐	51704-0	THE PRICE OF THE STARS *Debra Doyle & James D. Macdonald*	$4.50 Canada $5.50
☐	50890-4	RED ORC'S RAGE *Philip Jose Farmer*	$4.99 Canada $5.99
☐	50925-0	XENOCIDE *Orson Scott Card*	$5.99 Canada $6.99
☐	50947-1	YOUNG BLEYS *Gordon R. Dickson*	$5.99 Canada $6.99

Buy them at your local bookstore or use this handy coupon:
Clip and mail this page with your order.

Publishers Book and Audio Mailing Service
P.O. Box 120159, Staten Island, NY 10312-0004

Please send me the book(s) I have checked above. I am enclosing $ _____
Please add $1.25 for the first book, and $.25 for each additional book to cover postage and handling.
Send check or money order only—no CODs.)

Name _____
Address _____
City _____ State/Zip _____
Please allow six weeks for delivery. Prices subject to change without notice.

MORE OF THE BEST IN SCIENCE FICTION

☐	50892-0	CHINA MOUNTAIN ZHANG *Maureen F. McHugh*	$3.99 Canada $4.99
☐	51383-5	THE DARK BEYOND THE STARS *Frank M. Robinson*	$4.99 Canada $5.99
☐	50180-2	DAYS OF ATONEMENT *Walter Jon Williams*	$4.99 Canada $5.99
☐	55701-8	ECCE AND OLD EARTH *Jack Vance*	$5.99 Canada $6.99
☐	52427-6	THE FORGE OF GOD *Greg Bear*	$5.99 Canada $6.99
☐	51918-3	GLASS HOUSES *Laura J. Mixon*	$3.99 Canada $4.99
☐	51096-8	HALO *Tom Maddox*	$3.99 Canada $4.99
☐	50042-3	IVORY *Mike Resnick*	$4.95 Canada $5.95
☐	50198-5	THE JUNGLE *David Drake*	$4.99 Canada $5.99
☐	51623-0	ORBITAL RESONANCE *John Barnes*	$3.99 Canada $4.99
☐	53014-4	THE RING OF CHARON *Roger MacBride Allen*	$4.95 Canada $5.95

Buy them at your local bookstore or use this handy coupon:
Clip and mail this page with your order.

Publishers Book and Audio Mailing Service
P.O. Box 120159, Staten Island, NY 10312-0004

Please send me the book(s) I have checked above. I am enclosing $ _____
(Please add $1.25 for the first book, and $.25 for each additional book to cover postage and handling.
Send check or money order only—no CODs.)

Name _____

Address _____

City _____ State/Zip _____

Please allow six weeks for delivery. Prices subject to change without notice.

Nebula Award Nominee

A  UPON THE DEEP

by Vernor Vinge

"Heart-pounding, mind-expanding
science fiction at its best."
—Publishers Weekly

Now available in paperback
from Tor Books
51528-5 • $5.99/$6.99

AWARD-WINNING SF FROM MIKE RESNICK

☐	51955-8	ALTERNATE KENNEDYS *Edited by Mike Resnick*	$4.99 Canada $5.99
☐	51192-1	ALTERNATE PRESIDENTS *Edited by Mike Resnick*	$4.99 Canada $5.99
☐	52346-6	ALTERNATE WARRIORS *Edited by Mike Resnick*	$4.99 Canada $5.99
☐	51246-4	BWANA/BULLY	$3.99 Canada $4.99
☐	55116-8	THE DARK LADY: A ROMANCE OF THE FAR FUTURE	$3.50 Canada $4.50
☐	50042-3	IVORY: A LEGEND OF PAST AND FUTURE	$4.95 Canada $5.95
☐	52257-6	SANTIAGO: A MYTH OF THE FAR FUTURE	$4.99 Canada $5.99
☐	51113-1	SECOND CONTACT	$3.95 Canada $4.95
☐	50985-4	STALKING THE UNICORN: A FABLE OF TONIGHT	$3.95 Canada $4.95

Buy them at your local bookstore or use this handy coupon:
Clip and mail this page with your order.

Publishers Book and Audio Mailing Service
P.O. Box 120159, Staten Island, NY 10312-0004

Please send me the book(s) I have checked above. I am enclosing $ _____
(Please add $1.25 for the first book, and $.25 for each additional book to cover postage and handling.
Send check or money order only—no CODs.)

Name _____
Address _____
City _____ State/Zip _____
Please allow six weeks for delivery. Prices subject to change without notice.